T0301100

King's Enemy

About the author

Ian Ross was born in England, and studied painting before
turning to writing fiction. After a year in Italy teaching English
and exploring the ruins of empire reawakened his early love for
history, he returned to the UK with a fascination for the period
known as late antiquity.

His six-novel *Twilight of Empire* series, set in the late Roman
world, was published in the UK and worldwide between 2015
and 2019.

More recently, he has turned his attentions to the
medieval period, and in particular the tumultuous era
of mid 13th-century England.

Also by Ian Ross:

The *De Norton* Trilogy:
Battle Song
War Cry

Twilight of Empire series:
War at the Edge of the World
Swords Around the Throne
Battle for Rome
The Mask of Command
Imperial Vengeance
Triumph in Dust

King's Enemy

Ian Ross

**HODDER &
STOUGHTON**

First published in Great Britain in 2024 by Hodder & Stoughton Limited
An Hachette UK company

1

A CIP catalogue record for this title is available from the British Library

Hardback ISBN 978 1 399 70892 0
Trade Paperback ISBN 978 1 399 72763 1
ebook ISBN 978 1 399 70893 7

Typeset in Perpetua Std by Manipal Technologies Limited

Printed and bound in Great Britain by Clays Ltd, Elcograf S.p.A.

Hodder & Stoughton policy is to use papers that are natural, renewable and
recyclable products and made from wood grown in sustainable forests. The logging
and manufacturing processes are expected to conform to the environmental
regulations of the country of origin.

Hodder & Stoughton Limited
Carmelite House
50 Victoria Embankment
London EC4Y 0DZ

www.hodder.co.uk

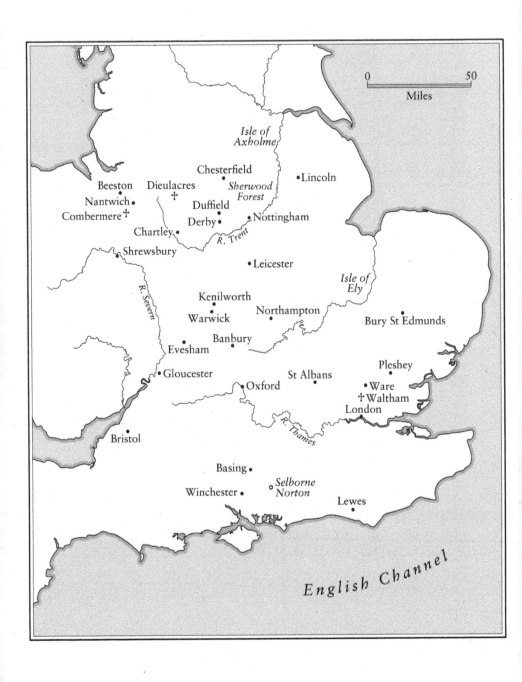

0   50
Miles

Isle of Axholme

Chesterfield
Beeston •   Dieulacres   *Sherwood* •Lincoln
           ✝   *Forest*
Nantwich •
Combermere ✝   Duffield
          Derby• •Nottingham
Chartley•
            R. Trent
•Shrewsbury

        •Leicester

R. Severn   Kenilworth   *Isle of*
         •   *Ely*
    Warwick   Northampton
           Banbury   •Bury St Edmunds
Evesham•
                     Pleshey
  •Gloucester   St Albans •
           •Oxford   •Ware
                    ✝Waltham
                    London
Bristol•
              R. Thames

        Basing•
             ○*Selborne*
Winchester•   *Norton*
                 Lewes
                    •

English Channel

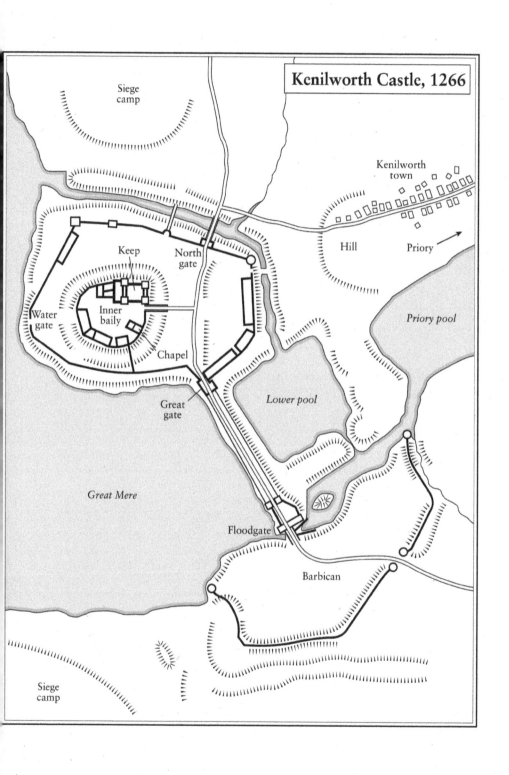

Kenilworth Castle, 1266

Siege camp

Kenilworth town

Hill

Priory

Priory pool

Keep

North gate

Water gate

Inner baily

Chapel

Great gate

Lower pool

Great Mere

Floodgate

Barbican

Siege camp

1265: at the Battle of Evesham, the king's son Edward inflicts a crushing defeat on Simon de Montfort, the rebel Earl of Leicester who has overthrown royal authority and ruled England for more than a year. Lord Simon is slain, and hundreds of his followers are massacred.

With King Henry III restored to full power, he and Lord Edward begin revoking the reforms of de Montfort's government and seizing the lands of those who supported him.

But even as father and son declare peace, their realm seethes with demands for justice and threats of violence. All know that England's fury is about to erupt, and plunge the kingdom once more into bloody conflict.

Part One

Chapter 1
October 1265

The forty-ninth year of King Henry III

Birds of prey screamed around the castle towers. From the wall Adam tracked them against the clouded sky. One of the birds, a hawk, pitched suddenly in its flight, falling in a killing swoop upon a flock of starlings. Adam held his breath as the killer met its prey and snatched it from the air.

'You fancy you could be like them, eh?' a cold voice said from behind him. 'Grow wings and escape from this place?' A bark of scornful laughter followed the words.

Adam said nothing, turning instead to the surrounding landscape. The wind tousled dark curls around his narrow face.

'Well, don't try it!' the speaker continued. He stepped past Adam to lean against the parapet of the wall. 'If you fly from here, I'll come after you! I will catch you in my net, Sir Adam de Norton. You will never escape Gaspard de Rancon!'

Still Adam held his silence. De Rancon was a French mercenary from Poitou. He was also deputy constable of this castle, and Adam's jailor. A sinewy man with long pale hair and a leering smile, he wore a clutter of gold and silver amulets and medallions around his neck.

'It's funny, you know,' he went on, angling his gaze at Adam. 'A messenger came this morning from Lord Edward, asking

after the health of his noble prisoners, Humphrey de Bohun and
Henry de Hastings. No mention of Adam de Norton though.
Not a word! Maybe he has forgotten you? A pity. Without an
order to release you, we are bound to keep you here. Even for
the rest of your life!'

Adam tightened his jaw. He knew that de Rancon was merely
goading him, but a grim mood rose through him all the same.
If ever he felt able, just for a moment, to forget the weight of
his captivity, de Rancon was always ready to remind him of
it. His right hand strayed instinctively to his belt, but he had
no weapon – even his eating knife had been taken from him.
Gaspard de Rancon, however, had a fine sword buckled at his
side; he curled his gloved fingers around the hilt, and his smile
became a mocking grin. 'Accept it, Adam de Norton,' he said.
'Not even God Himself cares anything for you now!'

With a snort of laughter, the jailor turned and stalked away
across the bailey.

Two months, Adam thought as he watched the man depart.
Two months and eleven days, to be exact, since he had been
brought to this place as a prisoner. He kept the count accurately,
obsessively. Two months and twenty-one days since that bloody
morning on the hill above Evesham, when Lord Edward and
his allies had destroyed the army of Simon de Montfort. Even
now, Adam often woke in a sweat of terror, nightmare images
crowding his mind: the slaughter around the high altar of the
abbey, the mutilated remains of Lord Simon borne in triumph
along the street outside the gates. The crowing of the victors,
and the anguish of defeat.

Adam had expected to die that day. His friend and mentor,
Robert de Dunstanville, had been slain on the field of battle,
and not a day passed when Adam did not grieve his loss. Not an
hour that the oath he had sworn to his friend – to carry his dying
word to the woman he loved – did not ache in his soul. How
could he do what he had promised, when he was a prisoner?

And how could he ever make amends to Isabel de St John, the woman he had once promised to marry? If Edward really had forgotten about him, then he could die here and none would ever know.

The Castle of the Rock, men called this place, though Beeston was its true name. It occupied the summit of an isolated crag, which rose from the surrounding plain like the stump of a broken tooth. At the crag's highest point, a stone rampart and a ditch cut into the rock enclosed two sides of the inner bailey; on the other two sides, sheer cliffs dropped to the wooded slopes below. On days of mist or drizzle, the castle seemed to float suspended in the sky.

At first there had been several other prisoners here. Guy de Montfort, the dead earl's youngest son, had been held at Beeston only a few weeks before an order arrived that he was to be transferred to Windsor Castle. None were sad to see him go; the young nobleman's alternating grief and bellowing rage had worn at the nerves of even the jailors. Two other knights captured in the battle had similarly been held at Beeston before being moved to another prison. Their departure had saddened Adam more. Both were older than him, but they occupied a similar status in society, and had treated him as an equal. He could not say the same of the two that remained.

'What did de Rancon say?' a voice demanded, and Adam turned to see Henry de Hastings striding over to join him.

'Little worth repeating,' Adam replied.

'If that prancing Poitevin dog utters another word to me,' de Hastings said between his teeth, 'I'll seize him by the throat and shake him till he snaps!'

Sir Henry had been one of Lord Simon's leading captains; he was thirty, and his hair was thinning prematurely, but his muscular build and the beard he had grown during his captivity gave him a savage look. Since coming to Beeston, he had guarded his formidable anger much more ably than had Guy de Montfort.

But he kept it simmering even so, his rage glowing within him like the heat from an iron brazier.

'Lord Edward has written to enquire after Sir Humphrey,' Adam told him.

'And?' de Hastings said, falling into step beside him as they paced a circuit of the bailey. 'Has his condition improved? Is it . . .' He halted suddenly, planting a firm palm on Adam's chest. 'Is it contagious, what he has?'

Adam shook his head. 'Wounds are not contagious,' he said. 'Nor is the pain in his soul, I think.'

'Shame,' said de Hastings. 'If there was a contagion here, then the king would have to transfer me elsewhere.'

'Inconvenient for you,' Adam said, shrugging off the man's restraining hand.

'Why do you keep visiting him anyway?' de Hastings asked, his brow bunching. 'Surely there's no real fellowship between the two of you?'

Adam had asked himself that same question many times. 'A man should not die alone,' he said.

De Hastings nodded as they walked. Both of them kept their left thumbs hooked in their belts, missing the hilts of the swords that had been taken from them. 'Perhaps I should visit him myself then, one of these days,' de Hastings muttered. 'But by the seven wounds of Christ,' he said, suddenly impassioned, 'surely the king doesn't mean to keep us penned up here until Candlemas next?'

He and Adam paused to watch a huddle of men in the stone-lined passage below the gate arches. Within the huddle, two cockerels squabbled and hacked. Voices echoed, their cries harsh and brutal.

'Winter approaches,' de Hastings said, 'and I have a wife and children living as beggars . . . Easier for you, I daresay. You had so little to lose.'

My lands, my honour, Adam thought grimly, hiding his annoyance. *My faith, my love. My betrothed.*

The gang of soldiers watching the cock-fight gave a roar; one reached in to snatch up his victorious bird, while another grimly removed the bloodied carcass of the loser. Adam and Sir Henry walked on towards the well, where two men heaved at the winch to bring a bucket up from the depths. The mechanism let out a grating wail as it turned.

'Deepest well in England, so I hear,' de Hastings said, rubbing at his balding pate. 'Bored down through solid rock. That's why the water's so cold when they draw it up.'

The men gave the winch a last turn and the brimming oaken bucket emerged into the daylight. 'They say,' de Hastings went on, dropping his voice, 'that there's a tunnel down there. Inside the well shaft. A tunnel that leads *out of the castle . . .*' He raised an eyebrow. 'Apparently old Ranulf of Chester had it dug, when he built the place. A route of escape, should he ever be besieged here.'

Adam looked again at the well. One of the men swung the bucket over and poured an icy torrent into a pail at his feet. The thought of that great shaft, descending through the cold rock into the endless darkness below, brought a shudder of loathing.

De Hastings grinned and slapped Adam on the shoulder. 'Don't worry, I wouldn't try escaping without you,' he said as he turned towards the tower that housed his own quarters. 'I'd be sure to send you down there first!'

Adam had feared, when first he arrived at Beeston, that the prisoners would be kept shackled in dark cells far from the sun. The reality was quite different; noblemen like Henry de Hastings or Guy de Montfort would never be kept in such conditions. Instead they were lodged in the tower chambers, and had the freedom of the inner castle, more or less. The bailey with its wooden kitchen hut and pigsty, its pigeon loft and well, allowed few distractions. Only the low parapet along the cliff edge granted a wider view, over the vast plain that stretched towards the distant sea, the hills to the east and the snow-capped mountains of Wales far to the west. A prospect of freedom that drew Adam inexorably, and filled him with bitter sorrow.

From the bailey he climbed the creaking wooden stairway to the covered landing, where a low door gave access to the upper chamber of the eastern tower. Another guard waited here, slumped on a stool with a blanket pulled around him. He merely grunted as Adam approached, then lifted the locking bar and shoved open the heavy iron-studded door. As Adam crossed the threshold the smell met him instantly.

Humphrey de Bohun, eldest son and heir of the Earl of Hereford, lay on the bed with the covers thrown back. Bolsters propped his body up on one side, and in the dimness of the shuttered room Adam could not make out whether the man was conscious or not. The air was sour with the reek of burnt tallow, sweat-sodden linens, vinegar and medicinal salve, and beneath it all the foulness of suppurating flesh.

Adam edged open the shutter, and beams of grey light shone through the wooden bars of the window, falling across the bed and the injured man lying upon it. Sir Humphrey sucked air through his teeth in a gasp.

'De Norton, that's you?'

'It is,' Adam told him.

The injured man's shoulder twitched, and he exhaled heavily. 'I thought you were a devil, come to . . . torment me. I see them, you know. They come through the window and dance around the bed . . . asking me questions I cannot answer!'

'Dreams,' Adam told him. 'Bad dreams, born of fever.'

'No, no,' Sir Humphrey said, as another gasp racked his body. 'It is my sins . . . My sins that have cursed me.'

'You want me to call the physician? He could change your dressings at least . . .'

De Bohun's features tightened into a snarl. He shook his head. As he stretched out his right hand to point, Adam noticed how wasted his body had become. He had been a big man once, but now the bones showed through his fevered flesh.

'Wine,' he said. '*Give* . . .' Then, when Adam hesitated. 'I beg you!'

The physician used the wine only to clean the wound in de Bohun's back, and had forbidden his patient to drink it. But Adam took the flask from the table beside the door, slopped wine into a wooden cup and carried it to the bed. Sir Humphrey heaved himself up, gripping Adam's shoulder as he twisted his head to drink. He sucked the wine down as if he had drunk nothing for days. Then he slumped back onto the bed again. 'Thank you,' he said. 'Thank you . . . my friend. My last friend!' His face looked terrible as he grinned.

Humphrey de Bohun had not always been Adam's friend. In fact, Adam had never considered him a friend at all. Sir Humphrey was the son of his first master, the half-brother of his second, and the husband of a woman Adam had loved hopelessly and for far too long. But still Adam had carried him from the field at Evesham, and defended him as he lay wounded. Somehow the two of them had come through that slaughter, and lived. Seeing the man now, so reduced by suffering, hanging at the very brink of death, it was impossible to feel anything but pity for him.

Adam lifted the sticky linen sheet and looked at the dressings on the wound. An arrow or a spear, nobody could be sure which, had struck de Bohun on his right side, just above the hip, as he tried to rally his fleeing troops. So he had claimed, anyway; Henry de Hastings was convinced that Sir Humphrey had been fleeing himself at the time. It was a bad wound, but at first it had appeared to be healing well. Two weeks after arriving at Beeston, de Bohun had been on his feet and walking unaided.

Only at the beginning of October had the pains begun, the swelling of the flesh around the scar, the dark fever that set in with deadly speed. Something was trapped inside the wound, the physician had declared. A fragment of the weapon, or a scrap of broken iron mail. He had insisted on opening the scar to provoke suppuration; the body would expel the foreign object naturally, so he had claimed. But de Bohun had fallen deeper into fever, his flesh putrefying as the wound became uglier and more inflamed. A curse from God, so Humphrey himself believed; divine punishment for rebelling against his father, who had fought for the king.

Adam dropped the sheet back, and a moment later the door from the stairs banged open and the shapes of two men blocked the light from outside. '*Wine?*' a voice boomed from the archway. 'You have been giving him *wine*, against my clear and direct orders?'

'He wanted it,' Adam said as the physician and his attendant entered the chamber. 'For the pain.'

'And you would give him death too, if he asked for that, I suppose?' the physician said. 'No matter, we shall have to bleed him again by and by, before the wine heats his blood and brings on a violent flux of the humours. But first let us examine the progress of the wound.'

Master Bernard of Grantham was not the sort of physician who deigned to touch wounds, blood or mangled flesh. He had a barber-surgeon to do that for him, while he stood by the window with his mouth tucked into the fur-lined collar of his tunic, taking shallow breaths of fresh air. Beneath the dressing, the wound was covered by a poultice made of pigeon dung ground with linseed oil and fenugreek. The smell was exotic, and disgusting. As the surgeon washed the injured area with wine from the flask, Master Bernard stepped closer, leaning to peer and examine.

'Good, good, a laudable pus,' he declared. 'Soon enough the flesh will purge itself of diseased and poisonous matter, and the putrefied humours will once more return to their proper alignment.'

'He's getting worse, not better,' Adam said, with a prickle of anger. 'His wound is rotting, anyone can see it! You should stitch it closed, at least.'

'You think to correct my prognosis, young man?' Master Bernard asked, drawing himself upright. 'You would seek to correct Galen too, I suppose? You would correct the Aphorisms of Hippocrates?'

'I know what I can see,' Adam replied. He stood up from the bed, and they faced each other with the injured man lying between them.

'Knights,' the physician said, with an outraged sniff, 'should confine themselves to tourneys and battlefields. Yes, and to showing loyalty and good service to their king! Instead of following that excommunicate and traitor Simon de Montfort. Remember the words of Isaiah – *woe to you who justify an impious man!*'

'You know nothing, leech.'

'Ha! You descend to mere abuse. Well, we should expect little more from one so treasonous. But I shall instruct that you be kept from here in future.'

The surgeon was already preparing his knife and brass bowl, to drain blood from Sir Humphrey's arm. De Bohun himself had lapsed back into unconsciousness, or was feigning it. 'We had better hope,' the physician said as Adam turned to leave, 'that our patient recovers something of his vital spirits by tomorrow at least.'

'Why?' Adam asked, pausing at the doorway.

'Because tomorrow,' the physician said, 'his good wife, the Lady Joane, will be visiting him, and no doubt praying to see some improvement.' For the first time, he sounded less than entirely pleased with himself. 'I understand a message has been sent also to the patient's father, the Earl of Hereford . . .' He cleared his throat. 'Who is at Westminster with the king, we believe.'

Adam stood a moment, digesting the news. The surgeon was tying a leather strap around Sir Humphrey's forearm, but the patient appeared entirely unaware of what was happening.

Adam's gaze shifted to the array of polished steel and bronze blades laid on the mattress, and the bright honed lancet. With only one such weapon, he thought, he might stand a chance of escaping this place.

*

From the ramparts the next morning he stared down at the road that crossed the plain far below, watching as she drew nearer.

'She won't be coming up here much longer, I reck'n,' the guard standing beside Adam at the rampart said. ''Cept to view the corpse, by and by.' He crossed himself quickly, then spat over the wall, as if to rid his mouth of the mention of death. 'Not much call for widows in this place.'

Adam hid his anguish at the thought. Squinting into the low sun, he tracked the small mounted party as they turned off the high road and approached the gates of the lower bailey. Joane de Bohun, Sir Humphrey's wife, was lodged at Nantwich, two hours' ride to the south-east. This would be her third visit to Beeston Castle. She was accompanied by two maids and her personal chaplain, with four armed men escorting them. From this vantage they appeared as black flecks moving in the bright distance. But Adam could not draw his eyes away from them. He followed their progress through the gates and up the slope of the bailey to the rock-cut ditch and the wooden bridge. He heard the clatter of hooves on the bridge planking, then the creak as the inner gates swung open. Still he waited.

By the time he turned from the rampart, Joane and her party had dismounted inside the gateway. Henry de Hastings had already gone to join her. Adam could see him talking and gesturing, demanding any fresh news that Joane might have brought from the outside world. He saw Joane's apologetic shrug.

He was halfway down the stairs when Gaspard de Rancon stepped out to block his way. 'Prisoners need permission to converse with visitors,' the jailor said, his smile flickering.

Adam took another step downwards, and de Rancon gripped the hilt of his sword. Behind him, Adam could see Joane and her party crossing the bailey towards the tower where Humphrey lay dying. She glanced once in his direction, then walked on. De Hastings had remained at the gateway, questioning the men of Joane's escort.

'Then I am requesting permission now,' Adam said through his teeth. 'And if you do not grant it I shall summon the constable and ask it of him.'

'Oh?' de Rancon said. 'And you think he will be angry with me, hmm, for denying the rights of a knight to chatter with visiting ladies? I tell you now, he will not care. Nobody cares about you, de Norton. You may as well die, like your friend de Bohun.'

For one ungovernable moment Adam was about to drive a punch into the smirking Frenchman's face. He mastered himself – he would only be giving de Rancon an excuse to beat him more savagely in return, or get his guards to do it. The thought that the man was trying to provoke Adam to such a humiliating display in Joane's presence was worse still. With an effort, he drew a long breath and let his blood slow. Then he turned to climb the steps once more.

Joane and her companions had entered the eastern tower now. Adam strolled a few paces along the rampart walkway to the door of his own tower lodgings. The guard watched him carefully, picking at his teeth with a peeled twig. Forcing himself to remain nonchalant, Adam leaned on the coping of an embrasure and stared into the sunlight. He tracked the flight of a bird across the sky, the movement of cloud shadows across the plain. Then, when he could wait no longer, he glanced back over his shoulder. As he had hoped, Gaspard de Rancon was nowhere in sight.

Back down the steps, Adam strode quickly across the mud around the well and took a position near the gateway, where the men waited with the horses. Across the bailey he could see Joane and her companions leaving de Bohun's tower. She noticed him as they approached. Her Flemish maid saw him too and made a gesture of warding against evil.

'Wait with the horses, Petronilla,' Joane told the maid. 'You too, father.'

The chaplain bowed his head, and with an anxious glance at Adam paced on after Petronilla.

'How was he?' Adam asked as he joined Joane.

'Dying, obviously,' she replied. 'Tell me, what is St Eloi's Sickness? The physician believes that Humphrey might have contracted it.'

Adam could only shake his head. 'And you?' he asked, dropping his voice. 'How have you been?'

Joane smiled, but Adam could see the tension in her features, the darkness smudged beneath her eyes. 'L'Estrange treats me like his prisoner,' she said. 'Although to one in your position that must seem an offensive exaggeration.'

'Not at all,' Adam said. But his mood had darkened at the name. Sir Hamo L'Estrange had dealt the mortal blow to Robert de Dunstanville on the battlefield of Evesham. For his courageous and loyal service to the king, he had been rewarded with the post of Sheriff of Shropshire and Stafford-shire, and granted Chartley Castle as his residence. L'Estrange had escorted Joane north, and now acted as her custodian.

'Here, I brought this,' Joane said. Reaching beneath her mantle, she produced a parcel wrapped in waxed linen. 'Cin-namon cake,' she explained. 'The baker at Nantwich made it.'

'For your husband? He eats little, I'm afraid . . .'

'No, for you,' Joane said. 'You look gaunt, Adam. Gaunt and pale.'

Adam was surprised for a moment. He knew his hair had grown long and his beard needed trimming, but had been unaware of any other changes in his appearance. 'Thank you,' he said, taking the package. Their hands met briefly, with the slightest touch.

They had barely spoken during Joane's previous visits. But Adam knew that she had attended the great parliament held at Winchester the month before. Many other wives and widows of men captured or killed at Evesham had been there too: united in their grief, they had gathered to hear the king's judgement. And the judgement had been harsh. Treason not only erased their husbands' rights of property and inheritance, the king's marshal had declared, but their own rights too. All dowry lands and estates were to be seized by the royal officials. Those who had fought for Simon de Montfort were to have nothing, and their families too would be rendered destitute.

'I'm sorry I bring no better news,' Joane said as they walked. 'And now I hear that Humphrey's father is on his way north to see him. That cannot please you, I'm sure.'

Adam merely shrugged. He had been a squire for many years in the household of the Earl of Hereford, and knew him well. He had captured the earl in battle at Lewes the year before, and then sold the ransom to his son, Sir Humphrey. Most of that ransom, he had long since accepted, would never be paid.

A shout came from the gatehouse. Gaspard de Rancon was striding towards them, his hand raised. 'Enough!' he shouted. 'Away, you have no permission!'

'Sir Adam was merely asking after the health of my husband,' Joane said, in a frosty tone of unmistakable authority. 'I would expect more civility from you, in the circumstances.'

'My lady,' de Rancon said, and bowed to her with ill grace. But he kept a fierce eye on Adam as the two of them parted and Joane joined her companions at the gate. One of de Rancon's more brutish-looking guards tore the package from Adam's hands and ripped it open. He looked disappointed that it contained only cinnamon cake, no concealed weapons or tools, no stash of gold or silver.

The horses were stamping and jostling in the flagstone passageway beneath the gate arches. Petronilla and the chaplain were already mounted, and one of the accompanying soldiers stepped up to help Joane into the saddle. She looked back over her shoulder as the party moved off through the gates into the sunlight. The slightest glance, but Adam caught it. And Gaspard de Rancon saw it too.

'Very nice,' he hissed to Adam as the gates closed. Nodding, chuckling, he swaggered away.

*

It was late the following evening, the rain tapping against the window shutters, when Adam heard the cries from outside his tower. Flinging back the shutter, he stared out into the wet gloom. A procession was crossing the inner bailey; Adam made out the priest in his surplice and vestments, the servers going before him carrying the cross and the holy vessels. He heard the mournful clanging of the handbell, and saw the figures gathered in the dimness sinking to their knees as the sanctified host passed before them.

He pulled on his shoes, threw a mantle around his shoulders, then hammered at the door until the guard outside unbarred it. By the time he had crossed the bailey the priest and his party had disappeared into Humphrey de Bohun's tower chamber. The crowd that had followed them from the gates still lingered on the stairway, and Adam pushed his way between them. Gaspard de Rancon was there, but for once he made no mocking comment. He stood aside, and Adam passed him and entered the tower.

The chamber was crowded, bodies packed close around the dying man in the sickly glow of the rushlights. The priest stood at the foot of the bed. '. . . and do you fully believe that Christ died for you,' he was saying, 'and that you may never be saved but by Christ's passion, and do you thank God with all your heart?'

'Yes, yes,' de Bohun managed to say, his face waxen and his mouth stretched, as he thumped at his breast with the heel of his hand. All around the bed, gazing down at him, were unshaven men at arms, kitchen servants and priest's clerks. The air was thick with the smell of sweat and wet wool and breath, mingling with the sourness of smoke and the thin high reek of death.

'And you know that any sins you have not confessed will be revealed at the Last Judgement, before the high throne of God?' the priest demanded.

De Bohun drew a long breath, then groaned as he exhaled. He blinked, and for a heartbeat his face appeared to gain focus. '*My father*,' he said. 'To him I must confess . . . *He* must grant me forgiveness!'

'Only God can forgive!' the priest cried. He turned sharply to Adam. 'Pray for him – pray for his mortal soul!'

Adam's knees buckled and he dropped to kneel. Many of the others in the chamber were kneeling too, as the priest granted his absolution and applied the sacraments, then sprinkled holy water over the dying man.

'Excommunicate dog!' somebody muttered. 'This is a travesty!' Others snarled at the speaker to keep silent.

Adam, eyes closed and head bowed, felt the tears rush to his eyes. He had not thought that de Bohun's death would move him in this way, but now the moment was here he could not hold back his tears. This man had been a burden to him, a bane and a threat, but he had been a connection too; a living link to his fallen half-brother Robert de Dunstanville, and to his wife Joane. Without de Bohun, Adam was entirely on his own in the world. All was sundered. All was lost.

He was still weeping when he heard the sudden clang of the passing bell. Three deep tolls, brutally loud in the narrowness of the chamber. Then the priest intoned the commendatory prayer. '*Proficiscere, anima christiana, de hoc mundo, in nomine Dei Patris omnipotentis . . .*'

And when he opened his eyes, Adam saw only a wasted corpse upon the bed. Humphrey de Bohun was no more.

Chapter 2

'*Requiem aeternam dona eis, Domine . . . Et lux perpetua luceat eis . . .*'

The voices of the choir rose to fill the arched ceiling of the abbey chapel. Rain was falling outside, as it had been falling for three days now. Adam could hear the water dripping from the eaves, the stamp of the horses in the yard outside, the clink of bridles. He was exhausted. He had spent the previous night in silent vigil, keeping watch over the coffin. Now he wanted only to be gone from this place. Even the return to the confines of Beeston would be a relief. He had given an oath to Gaspard de Rancon that he would not try to slip away during the funeral or the journey to and from the abbey. The six armed guards who accompanied him, and waited outside in the rain, were a further insurance against escape.

Most of those filling the chapel were paupers, dressed in rags of black and grey, drawn by the promise of free food and clothing at the funeral. They kept up a constant sniffling and groaning as the priest sang out his prayers. Aside from Adam, Joane was the only friend or family member of the dead man. She was kneeling a short distance away, and Adam could see only her back, swathed in ashen widow's weeds. They had not had a chance to exchange a word since he arrived the evening before.

On the far side of the chancel arch, the dead man lay in his coffin before the altar, the bier draped with a black cloth and three wax tapers burning over him. As a Cistercian house, Combermere Abbey did not permit outsiders to enter the precincts, and certainly not women. But here in the gate-house chapel, the border between the sacred space of the abbey and the profane outside world, the final mass for the soul of Sir Humphrey de Bohun could be conducted freely. Sir Humphrey had agreed to burial at Combermere weeks beforehand, after receiving a letter from the abbot himself, Adam had since learned. The monks were always happy to be granted charge of the bodies of great noblemen, and all the masses for which their relatives would pay. The Cistercians, it seemed, were happy to ignore the lingering rumours of excommunication as well.

Voices came from outside, loud and demanding. A horse whinnied, and other men spoke in reply. The priest went on with his droning chant, oblivious to the disturbance, but others in the congregation twisted to look back at the doorway.

The door banged open, and a file of men entered, each of them touching their brow with holy water. They shuffled forward, mantles dripping on the tiled floor, and one by one sank to kneel. A single glance told Adam who they were. Humphrey de Bohun the Elder, Earl of Hereford, had arrived at last for his son's funeral. The two youths with him, Adam assumed, would be Sir Humphrey's sons from his first marriage. Heirs to their grandfather's estates now. A pair of household knights accompanied them; it would have been a hard journey, all the way from Westminster on wet roads in a sinking season, beneath lowering skies.

'*Requiescat in pace*,' the priest declared, raising the crucifix over the bier and coffin.

'*Amen*,' the congregation replied in one voice. Monks in black and white habits closed around the coffin and lifted it between

them. They would carry it from the chapel and down the cobbled lane into the sacred precinct, where Humphrey de Bohun
would be laid to rest beneath the flagstones of the abbey church,
until the Day of Doom when all the dead would rise from their
graves to greet the return of Christ.

As the paupers filed out into the yard to seize the bread
and ale provided for them, Joane rose to her feet and went to
speak with Earl Humphrey. Adam watched her. He saw Joane
bow her head before her former father-in-law. He saw the jut of
Earl Humphrey's jaw, the twist of his lip as he spoke. The earl had
always been a stern and forceful man. Now he was approaching
sixty, and had surrendered none of his steel. His grandsons, one
a downy-moustached lad in his teens and the other a boy, stood
watching with open mouths and narrowed eyes.

Joane took a step back, gave another curt bow, and then
moved for the door. The earl's gaze was coldly wrathful as he
swept the chapel interior. His eyes fell upon Adam, and his
mouth tightened into a sneer. He gestured, summoning Adam
to him.

'My lord,' Adam said stiffly, as he paced across the tiled floor.
He met Earl Humphrey's eye and held it, determined that he
should not appear unnerved.

'You were with my son as he lay dying, I hear,' the earl said.

Both your sons, Adam thought.

'I thank you for that, it was a Christian kindness,' de Bohun
went on. 'He was a rebel and a traitor to his king, and I cannot forgive him that, but I would not have wanted him to die
unmourned.'

'Sir Humphrey was not a traitor, lord,' Adam forced himself
to say.

The earl's jaw tightened, his eyes blazing. 'Any man who holds
his king and the heir to the throne *as a prisoner* is a traitor! And
I would have said that to my son, if they were the last mortal
words I spoke to him.'

'He asked for your forgiveness, lord, before the end.'

'Did he?' Earl Humphrey snorted a laugh, but just for a heartbeat his expression softened, and he appeared almost human, almost a grieving father. Then his gaze hardened. 'Well, I've paid the abbot for three times thirty masses for him, and the dedication of a chantry chapel, so I think I've shown sufficient care for his immortal soul. Now God alone can judge him. But he gave you something, didn't he, in his last hours? Something for me.' He leaned closer. 'Give it to me now,' he ordered. 'And I shall do what I can to aid you.'

'Your son gave me nothing,' Adam replied, perplexed.

For a moment Earl Humphrey glared at him, as if he suspected a lie. Then he blinked and looked away. 'Well then,' he said, 'you've made your bed and must lie in it – and if it be sackcloth and ashes, or red-hot coals, then so be it.'

A stiff parting nod, and the earl turned on his heel and stalked from the chapel. The two boys followed him. In Adam's mind flickered the passing memory of the battlefield of Lewes, where the earl had lain pinned beneath his fallen charger, and Adam had demanded his surrender. So long ago that seemed now. A different life altogether, and a better one.

Joane was lingering just inside the chapel door as her maid fastened her hooded mantle and the last of the paupers shuffled past into the rain. Adam joined her, and was struck by the ferocity of her expression. Her face was hollowed with rage.

'What did you say to him?' Adam asked.

'*Nothing*,' she spat. For a few moments she struggled to speak, and when she did, her words were tight with disgust. 'The king has granted all of my husband's properties to Earl Humphrey,' she said, 'even those I brought to the marriage as my dowry, and the dower lands that are my widow's right. But I refused to plead for what is mine. There are beggars enough in this place, and I won't be another.'

Adam nodded. 'What will you do now?' he asked her. He was painfully aware that this might be the last time he spoke to Joane, but could find nothing else to say. Sorrow was flooding through him.

'I'll remain here for thirty days more,' Joane told him, weariness damping the fire of her rage. 'The abbot will provide lodgings close by, and I'll visit the chapel and pray for Humphrey's soul.' She was speaking stiffly, each word distinct. 'Then I'll have to go back to Chartley Castle, and the custody of Hamo L'Estrange.'

She turned to him, as if to bid farewell, and Adam's heart clenched in his chest.

'If I can return here again, I'll break my journey at Nantwich,' she said, quickly and quietly. 'I'll send word. There's a hospice in the town of St Nicholas – can you find it?'

'Yes, but . . .' Adam's mind fogged. Joane blinked, and glanced downwards. He followed her eye, and saw the small object that she had dropped in the shadowed corner just inside the doorway.

'May God keep you,' Joane said, then drew up her hood and walked out into the rain. Adam waited while Petronilla brought the horse over and helped Joane onto the saddle. Only when he was sure that he was unobserved did he stoop and snatch up the object from the door. It was about the size of his fist, and wrapped in a dark rag. He felt the weight of metal, the shifting of coins. A leather purse, but it held something else besides money, something hard and as long as his palm. Through the leather he felt the hilt of a clasp knife.

*

At Beeston the seasons quickly turned. The trees covering the slopes below the castle flared into autumn red and gold, and then dropped into bare winter brown, and the winds that blew in from the Irish Sea howled around the towers and rattled the shutters. Adam made a point of asking the guards at the gates and on the ramparts about the distance to the Welsh frontier, and what the best roads might be. They just laughed and told him nothing, but he knew they reported everything he said to de Rancon.

Henry de Hastings departed soon after Martinmas. 'I've been handed over to Thomas de Clare,' he told Adam, as he waited on horseback before the castle gates. He cast a last grimace around the inner bailey. 'Hopefully he has a more comfortable prison than this place, by Christ! De Bohun's death must have sparked some mercy in the king's heart, at last. God knows, that'd be the only use that coward ever was to anyone.'

Adam stood beside de Hastings's horse, a cloak pulled tight around him. 'Sir Humphrey was no coward,' he said. He surprised himself; once again he had felt the need to defend de Bohun's memory.

De Hastings glanced at him, his smile wryly twisted. 'Maybe not. Although, according to our friendly jailor,' he said, 'you made a cuckold of him. I must say, I'm impressed if you did. I'd heard rumours, of course, but not believed them . . .'

Adam felt the blood flaring in his face, and a feeling between rage and shame burned in him and then died abruptly. He said nothing more, but his mood curdled.

'Anyway, best of luck!' de Hastings said as the gates opened before his escort. Then, without another glance at Adam, he shook his reins and rode onward into the wintry daylight.

That evening Adam lay on his straw pallet, counting off the days. Three months, he realised, his captivity at Beeston had lasted. Still no word from Joane. He had almost given up hope of hearing from her. How would she communicate with him anyway? Perhaps, he came to realise, he would have to find his own way of escaping the castle. Without somebody to help him on the outside, he would surely be recaptured very swiftly. But he had considered it often enough, even so.

His tower chamber had a solid wooden door, studded with iron and firmly barred. A sentry sat outside, at the head of the stairs, though the man often dozed through the silent hours of darkness. That difficulty at least Adam thought he could overcome. Getting out of the inner castle ward would be a far greater challenge. The gates were sealed with a double portcullis, and both the gate passage and the rampart walkways were patrolled by sentries. A clasp knife was no weapon to use against a man in a gambeson and iron helmet, with a shield and falchion. Even if he somehow got over the wall undetected, Adam would have to cross the rock moat beyond; if he succeeded at that task, he would only find himself in the castle's outer bailey with yet another wall between him and freedom. No, he thought, if he wanted to escape he would have to take a harder and more hazardous path.

Another month, and the weather grew colder and bleaker. Christmas came and went, unmarked by festivity. Gaspard de Rancon did not have much use, it seemed, for religious solemnities. Adam kept to his chamber, and remembered the year before, when he had first met Isabel de St John, his betrothed, in the hunting park at Basing. He recalled every moment of those days that followed, at the Christmas court of her father, Lord William. He recalled Isabel herself, lost to him for so many months. As the short winter days slid past, and the hope of any word from Joane faded, Adam dwelt increasingly in memories of the past, and of Isabel, and after a time the torment of loss became a balm instead. As thoughts of the one woman receded, so thoughts of the other took their place. Darkness giving way to light. But which was which?

Then, as the sixth month of his captivity began, the message came.

Gaspard de Rancon seldom allowed pedlars or other wayfarers to enter the castle, still less penetrate the inner ward. To one in particular, however, he always granted access. Adam saw the man on the Morrow of St Hilary, waiting inside the gatehouse arch while de Rancon and his men gathered to survey his wares.

They were shiny things, golden chains and brooches. The only things that de Rancon loved. As Adam watched from a distance, the jailor held up a pendant, then draped it around his neck with the rest of the glittering clutter he wore. Coins changed hands.

Adam would not have been drawn to the pedlar normally, but he caught the man glancing in his direction once or twice. Idly he strolled closer, until he stood just outside the ring of customers. The preening de Rancon was distracted by his new purchase, and none of the other guards paid Adam any attention. As the pedlar lifted his packs back onto the saddle of his shabby horse, he turned in Adam's direction.

'Something for you, sir?' he asked with a smile.

'Ignore him, he's got nothing!' one of the guards called.

The pedlar smiled again, and seemed to wink. 'On St Agnes, your friend says.' He had spoken almost without moving his lips.

Adam stared back at him, startled. Swiftly he made the calculation. Seven days until the Feast of St Agnes. Time enough to prepare. It was all he could do not to thank the man.

But already the pedlar had turned his back, and moments later he was gone.

The following days passed slowly. Nervous tension charged Adam's every waking moment, and he tried to cover it with a show of lassitude. He stood idly near the well, watching the men hauling buckets up from the depths. He watched the guards at the gates and on the rampart walks, studying their movements, and how long each of them spent at his post. He honed the clasp knife Joane had given him, grinding the blade against the hardest stone in his tower chamber, until it was keen enough to mark his skin at the slightest pressure.

The clouds were low on the Eve of St Agnes, and by night-fall the rain was setting in. All the better, Adam thought. He knew he could delay no longer. After curfew, with the door of his chamber securely barred and the tapers doused, he dressed himself in his thickest clothes and waited until he guessed that midnight had passed. The purse of coin that Joane had given him was secured at his belt, and the clasp knife laid on the stone window seat. From outside, the sound of the rain was a constant hiss and spatter.

The single window of the chamber looked out into the bailey. It was just large enough for Adam to fit his head and shoulders through, but two heavy wooden bars were set into the mortar at lintel and sill. For the last month Adam had been scraping and gouging at the mortar with the tip of his knife, digging until only a crust of masonry secured each one. Now, slowly and carefully, he swung back the shutters and gripped the first bar. A firm tug, and the wood came free with only the slightest crunch. The second bar was harder to pull loose, only yielding after Adam set his foot against the wall and heaved at it. A crack, a few chunks of gritty mortar tumbling to the sill, and the bar came free.

Adam stood tensed and listening. No sound from outside the tower door. Only the rushing of the rain from the open window.

No time for thought, or for delay. Clambering up into the embrasure, Adam swung his feet through the gap and pushed himself forward. Clumsily he struggled through the window, twisting his body until his legs hung below him. For the first time fear gripped him. The drop was twelve feet or a little more; seen from outside, in daylight, it looked possible to jump safely. Now, braced on his grazed elbows, the rain soaking the arch of his back, he felt less certain. Teeth clenched, muscles burning, he lowered himself until he hung suspended, his fingers hooked over the sill of the window.

A long breath, a surge through his body, and he kicked himself away from the wall and released his grip. For a moment he was falling, twisting in the air, concentrating on keeping his knees bent so he might drop and roll safely.

He fell much harder than he had expected, the ground rushing up and clouting him, knocking him sprawling. He felt the gritty wet mud beneath his palms, and for a few rapid heartbeats he lay still, face down, waiting for his blood to slow and the pain of a twisted ankle or a broken leg to bloom through him.

There was no pain. No sound from the stairs, no shout from the rampart walkway. Forcing a silent prayer through tightened lips, Adam dragged himself to his knees and then ran, stooping, around the corner of the tower and along the wall to the well. Crouching again in the deep shadow beside the coping, he peered into the darkness, his senses primed. Footsteps sounded on the soaked ground. Adam kept his head low, unblinking as the rain streamed down his face. A figure passed in the middle distance, crossing the bailey to the latrines. The man walked heavily, head down, a spear across his shoulders. Adam waited. Water dripped from the winch mechanism above the well and dropped silently into the depths below.

At last, the spearman stamped wearily back across the bailey to one of the towers. Adam heard the creak of a door, then the slam as the man went back inside the lower chamber. Exhaling, he wiped his face with his palm. Then he set to work.

The heavy oaken bucket was standing on the well coping. Adam lifted it, poured the collected rainwater from it and set it on the ground. He drew up the rope that trailed down into the well's mouth and coiled it roughly at his feet. Then he began to turn the winch, unspooling the rope from the windlass and coiling it with the rest. The mechanism was stiff, the wood swollen in the dampness, but the spattering of the rain covered the steady creak as the drum turned. It took much longer than Adam had anticipated to unroll the whole length of the wet black rope. Twice he paused, his heart drumming against his breastbone, but the night remained still and empty.

The deepest well in England, so Henry de Hastings had said. Adam could only hope that was true. A final turn of the handle, and he saw the tail of the rope firmly secured to the windlass drum. Leaning, not daring to consider the shaft that dropped into the aching depths below him, not daring to consider the

tunnel that de Hastings had told him about, that false promise
of freedom, he sawed at the rough fibres with his clasp knife.
Again it took some time to cut the rope free. Breathing hard,
his body flowing with heat beneath his damp woollen clothing,
Adam stuck the knife back in his belt and drew the rope into
a single coil, heaving it across his shoulder. It was heavy, an
unwieldy burden, and as he set off the end was already trailing behind him. *This is madness*, a voice said in his head. *This is
doomed to fail.*

He was praying as he walked, a rapid near-wordless exhor-
tation to the Blessed Mary, to hide him from the eyes of his
enemies. To Holy Saint Agnes, whose vigil he so abused, for forgiveness. To Christ and all the preserving saints, for just enough
luck to carry him through what lay ahead.

Steering a slanting course across the bailey, using the cover
of the kitchen huts and the animal pens where he could, Adam
reached the far wall that edged the cliffs. The rain felt wetter
here, driven aslant by a gusting wind, but he was glad of it. The
men on the rampart walks would be keeping their heads down
on a night like this.

The wall along the clifftop was no more than waist high, the
few merlons that jutted here and there intended only as a shelter
against the wind from the Irish Sea. Adam picked his way along it
until he reached the section that he had identified; the cliffs fell a
hundred feet or more to the wooded slope beneath, but in places
the tops of the trees rose slightly higher, and he suspected the
slope rose with them. All he could see now was a gulf of blackness beyond the stones of the wall, seething with rain.

Quickly, his hands numb but the grazes on his skin smarting,
Adam looped the heavy rope twice around the nearest merlon
and fastened it with the bucket hook. He was remembering
the time – not six months ago, but it felt like years – when he
had escaped from Bridgnorth Castle by scaling down the wall.
The drop then had been little more than twenty feet, but it had

seemed daunting enough. *Do not think about it*, he told himself. *Do not consider the risk.*

With the rope firmly secured he gathered the great coil in his arms and hurled it out across the coping of the wall. It fell into darkness, and he heard it rattling and tapping against the rock of the cliff as it unravelled. He could only trust that it hung straight, and had not snagged on some outcrop or thorny bush. *Do not think . . .*

He was tying rags around his hands, knotting them clumsily to protect his palms, when he heard the damp thud of a footstep on the muddy ground behind him. Stepping away from the wall he turned quickly, drawing the knife from his belt and unclasping it.

'So you think this is a good time to fly away from here, eh?' Gaspard de Rancon said. He was approaching out of the rain with his sword drawn, his long hair hanging wet around his face. 'You think I haven't been watching you all this time?'

Adam edged a step further from the wall, holding the knife out before him. The blade was no longer than his thumb, a puny weapon compared to de Rancon's sword. Fear was coiled inside him, slick and greasy, and he fought to master his nerves.

'One shout and I summon my guards,' the mercenary said, smiling as he circled to Adam's left. 'But maybe I take this opportunity with you, eh? Perhaps you might be injured while you try to escape. Perhaps you might die?'

They were both edging closer, the tip of de Rancon's blade only an arm's length from Adam's neck. Rainwater streamed along the steel.

'Or maybe,' de Rancon said, 'I just cut you a little on the face? So the fine smooth-limbed ladies no longer find you such a pleasant sight?'

'I don't want to kill you,' Adam managed to say, but the words came out as a tight gasp.

De Rancon barked a laugh. 'Kill me? With that little knife?' He appeared genuinely amused. 'You could not even touch me!'

Adam let him arm drop, easing forward a step. Then he flung the knife with all his strength at de Rancon's head. The jailor let out a cry, slashing with his sword to knock the weapon away from him. As his blade swung wide Adam dropped his head and charged, ramming into him and flinging his arms around his hips. The top of his skull caught de Rancon in the gut, just beneath the arch of his ribs, and drove the air from him in a deep grunt. With the momentum of his charge Adam lifted the man and hurled him sideways, toppling him against the wall. The jailor's body collided with the parapet just as Adam released his grip. Winded, de Rancon let out only a breathless cry, his fingers scrabbling for grip on the rain-slick stones, but the momentum carried him over the wall before he could grasp it.

A dull crack of flesh striking stone, then a heartbeat later the muffled crash of the body falling through the bare trees far below. Then there was no sound but the rain.

Adam knelt as he fought to catch his breath and slow his speeding heart. Now that the moment had passed, fear charged through him, and nausea came in its wake. He had killed men before, in the heat of battle, but what he had just done was murder. No matter that de Rancon had wanted to maim him, even kill him . . . Then, just as suddenly, the feeling was gone. Adam lifted his head, and discovered that he felt no remorse at all.

He eased himself up and leaned against the merlon. At any moment he expected to hear the cries from the bailey behind him, the flare of lanterns and the footsteps of the spearmen as they closed in around him.

Silence instead. Silence, and the slow pattering of water.

De Rancon's sword lay where it had fallen. A fine blade, but there would be no way to carry it safely on his descent. Picking up the weapon, Adam tossed it out over the wall and it vanished into the night. No sign of his knife, and no time to search for it. While the nervous fury still gripped him, Adam threw his leg across the parapet and lowered himself down on the far side.

Sloping rock beneath the soles of his shoes. The cliff edge swelled outwards from the base of the wall. Grasping the rope and pulling it taut, he began walking backwards down the slope. Water streamed around him. He was feeling his way, near blind in the darkness and all too aware of the great emptiness at his back. Ten scrabbling steps, feeling for footholds all the way, and he reached the brink. The precipice fell away sheer beneath him.

Lowering himself onto his elbows, hands gripping the rope tight, Adam swung his legs below him until his toe caught a ledge in the rock. Slowly, taking tight shallow breaths, he eased himself further downwards.

The cliff was not, as it had appeared from above, a single straight drop. Instead there were angled spurs and crevices all the way down, like the stones of a vast wall built by giants. Keeping the rope taut above him, Adam found that he could feel his way from ledge to ledge with his toes. At one point he reached a shelf of rock broad enough to squat for a moment and relax his arms. Water cascaded down the cliff above him in rills and streams.

Risking a glance behind him, Adam saw that he was still above the tops of the tallest trees. He could see them clearly, their tracery of bare branches packed tightly below him. For a moment his heart quailed. *I cannot go on . . .*

But the thought of remaining all night trapped on a wet ledge was more horrifying still, and Adam pushed himself into motion. Scrabbling his feet below him he felt for another toehold, then pulled the rope to take his weight and began to descend.

Suddenly there was a void beneath him, and horror filled his chest. The rope was hanging loose in the air, and Adam could see that the cliff hollowed too deeply for him to reach a toehold. For a few breathless moments he clung on, staring over the bunched muscle of his shoulder and wildly hoping that he might see some alternative way of getting down.

There was none, unless he scaled back up the cliff again and shifted over to one side or the other; even then it was too dark to make out a better route. Sagging against the cliff, Adam felt his eyes fill with tears of exhausted despair. The rain streamed down his face and washed it clean. His palms were burning now, the rags he had wrapped around his hands dragged aside, and he could feel the stinging ache of ripped skin.

A deep breath through gritted teeth. Another, tipping back his head to let the cold rain bathe his burning face. Then he kicked away from the cliff and clung tight to the rope, letting himself slide a few feet until he was holding his full weight suspended. He tried to catch the hanging rope and grip it between his ankles, but the effort just made him spin dizzyingly. Fighting down panic he began to ease the rope through his bloodied palms, dropping downwards in juddering descents. Pain racked his arms, his muscles flaming.

Just when he could barely hold on any longer he saw the loom of the rock again, directly beneath him, and his toe found a ledge. A precarious balance, but he almost cried out in relief. Another glance behind him: he was below the treetops now, level with the upper branches. Something caught his eye, a pale object floating oddly in the streaming darkness. It took Adam a few moments to realise that he was looking at Gaspard de Rancon, the jailor's hair catching the scant light as his broken body hung suspended in the crook of a tree.

He would have crossed himself if he could. Instead he muttered a quick prayer and then fed the rope through his palms, letting himself drop a little further until his other foot found a toehold.

Adam paused for a moment, breathing rapidly as he braced himself for the next descent. It was then that he noticed that the rope in his hands felt different, light and airy, waving slightly beneath him. He glanced downwards, and the shock of terror almost broke his grip. Ten feet or so beneath him, the frayed end of the rope was hanging in space. It was too short, or he had tied too much of the length around the merlon at the top. For a few long heartbeats he could not breathe, could not think, lost to the stark terror of imminent death.

He could not hang on much longer, he knew that. He lacked the strength to haul himself back up. He could see nothing, even the trees now lost in shadow and rainy darkness.

Eyes tight shut, chest burning, he willed a last pious thought, a last prayer. Nothing came to him but the screaming that filled his mind.

Then he released his grip on the rope, and fell.

Chapter 3

Blackness pressed upon him, wet and cold as death. He felt it slithering on his skin as he moved. Dirt covered his face, but when he lifted a hand and scrubbed it from his eyes he saw the faint light of the moon through the mesh of bare branches above him. Raindrops fell slow and thick through the trees.

He ought to be dead, he knew that. Dead, or grievously injured. But when he moved again, flexing his limbs, he felt only the burn of grazes and the throb of bruised flesh. No bones broken. No gashed limbs. He had fallen onto sloping ground, he realised, and a thick drift of dead leaves matted over dry bracken had cushioned the impact. But he had tumbled and slid, the slippery mulch of leaves massing around him, until his shoulder struck the bole of a tree. Gazing upwards, he thought of de Rancon's corpse suspended high overhead, and a shudder went through him so fierce he almost cried out.

Crawling sideways, he managed to sit upright. The trees grew thickly here, cutting all but the faintest light. As he leaned backwards, Adam could make out the loom of the cliff rising over him, vast and implacable.

The shivering in his body was becoming constant now, his teeth rattling, and he clenched his jaw. Cold was soaking through him, and as the immediate terror of his fall left him, the aching in his limbs and the tremor of his heart grew. He had to get up, he had to move – before long the men in the castle would discover the broken window bars of his chamber, and it would take only a little time more for them to find the rope tied around the merlon and realise how he had made his escape. All of it, he told himself, all of this risk would have been for nothing if he could not evade capture.

Up; up now. Using the nearest tree for a support he dragged himself to his feet, braced against the slope of the hillside. He needed to get clear of the woods before he could determine which direction he should follow. He began edging downhill, tentative at first, reaching out from one trunk to the next to steady himself. His clothes were soaked and heavy, filthy with dirt and leaf mould, his hands and face blackened and his body shivering, but he forced himself onward. Soon he was forging his way through dense thickets, crushing the bracken underfoot as he shoved branches away from him.

Then he was out, staggering through long grass and dropping to his knees. The castle was behind him, high on its black crag against the sky, and Adam could make out a flat empty landscape spreading away from him under the rain. He mastered himself, fighting down the shuddering of his body and breathing slowly and deeply. He was somewhere to the west of the castle mount, he supposed; the road he wanted lay on the far side, to the east. But the flanks of the crag were thickly wooded on all sides, and navigating his way around them would take him far too close to the main gateway of the lower bailey.

Instead he struck north across the open country, scrambling across rutted ditches and low hedges. Thick wet mud underfoot, and his shoes were soon soaked and squelching. After an hour, Adam met a road or droving track that crossed his path. Chester lay somewhere to his left. Nantwich, then, should be in the other direction. He turned to his right, pushing himself to a jog along the verge of the track. Head down, rainwater dripping from his hair and clinging in his beard, he stumbled onward through the night.

*

First light summoned a colourless world, a landscape smeared beneath an ashen sky. Strip fields edged the track, bare in winter dun, and on the far horizon Adam could make out dark streaks of smoke rising from a town or village. The thought of hearth-fires made him shiver in his wet clothing. The thought of fresh bread, warm from the oven, tightened the knot in his belly.

Through the hours of darkness he had met nobody else on the road, but now he passed hooded men with hoes and mattocks over their shoulders, going out to the fields to begin the day's work. They kept their distance, and when Adam called to one of them and asked if the town of Nantwich lay ahead, he got only a brusque and silent nod in reply. Night had numbed his body, but daylight awoke the pains of his scratched and bruised limbs. He felt battered, as if he had fought his way through a melee, and taken a bad fall from his horse, and been kicked and trampled by the beast too.

A few times during the night he had rested, and managed to wash the grime from his face with water from a ditch. But still he was dirty and unkempt, alone on the road. He had no beggar's sack and bowl, no pilgrim's staff and scrip. He looked exactly like what he was: a renegade and a fugitive. He looked like a murderer, and few of those he passed would return his glance. Every few paces he peered back over his shoulder, certain that the grey of morning would show him the tracking dogs and the riders galloping after him.

Ahead lay a river and a bridge, with the town on the far side. A lane branched to the left, snaking across the open fields towards a large building with a wall around it and an arched gateway. Adam paused at the turning, waiting until a man passed him leading a packhorse hung with panniers.

'Is that the Hospice of St Nicholas?' Adam asked. His voice was hoarse and cracked, and although he was speaking in English, the language of the common people, his question still sounded like a demand.

'That? Naw, that there's the leper house,' the packman said, his nose twitching in distaste, as if the contagion might sicken the air. His accent was thick and nasal, and Adam found him hard to understand. 'If it's the spital you want, you'll find it on the far side of the ville. You'll know it by the great gaggle of begging folk in the road!'

At the bridge, the tollkeeper cast a wary glance at Adam and then waved him across. An old castle stood on the far bank of the river, and the town of Nantwich clustered around its flanks in a tangle of timber and thatch. The fortification was little more than a rotting palisade and a wooden tower on a mound that looked like it was about to slide into the water. Overgrown ditches sur-rounded the bailey. Adam wondered if that was the place where Joane had been lodged during her stay in the town, and hoped that Hamo L'Estrange had found her better quarters.

Across the bridge he entered the town marketplace. It was still early, the bleary winter sun not yet above the rooftops and the church bell ringing for matins, but already there were more people thronging the muddy lanes and open spaces than Adam had seen for months. He sensed their eyes on him, their sus-picious glances and muttered words. Once or twice he heard somebody spit in his wake, and his hand twitched to his belt before he remembered that he had no sword, no weapon at all. If they set upon him now he would have only his grazed fists to defend himself.

Pulling his mud-spattered cloak tight around his body, Adam walked quickly through the marketplace and along the lane beyond, following the curve of the castle ditch. On the far side, past the church, he found a wider road leading eastward away from the town. *On the far side of the ville,* the packman had told him, but Adam could not be sure if he had come the right way. His heart sinking, he stalked on along the road, and as he passed the last of the houses he saw the huddled figures along the verges ahead, and the clutch of low stone buildings almost obscured by a copse of trees. His spirits woke, and he lengthened his stride.

'Worthy lord,' one of the beggars called as he approached, throwing himself down to kneel in the road's dirt. 'Worthy lord, for God's love of heaven!'

He was rattling a pebble in his empty bowl. But even as Adam passed him the rest of the congregation had flown from their perches at the roadside to kneel and beseech.

'Some goodwill, my gentle master?' one young woman cried, stretching thin bruised arms from her dirty mantle. Adam saw the pleading look in her eyes and his hand strayed to the pouch of coin stashed inside his tunic, but he hardened his heart. He was little more than a beggar himself.

'Is this the Hospice of St Nicholas?' he asked another of the kneeling men.

'It is, good master. And for your mother's blessing, a half-penny?'

Adam could only nod his thanks. Another figure had dropped into step beside him now, a man with a round fur hat on his head and a sack slung over his shoulders. 'God's peace to you, Sir Knight!' the man said, reaching into his sack and producing a small bundle tied with twine. 'Look here, sir – the knucklebone of St Andrew! Certified by document – what better luck could one gain?'

'Why did you call me knight?' Adam asked, breaking his step.

The man looked back at him with a cracked smile, one eye meeting his own while the other wandered off towards the road's verge. 'Because you look like one, sir, and walk like one!' the relic-pedlar said. 'For all you have no spurs or belted sword, it's plain to see . . . A mere three pennies and St Andrew's bone is yours, messire!'

Adam walked onward, steering a path between the kneeling beggars towards the gatehouse of the hospice, but the pedlar dogged his steps. 'Or this,' the man said, drawing another little bundle from his sack, 'the baby tooth of Little St Hugh, who was foully slain by the Jews of Lincoln! Proof against all bodily aches and agues . . . Or perhaps Sir Knight would value this more? A scrap of the hairshirt worn by the martyr Simon de Montfort, cut from his body as he lay mauled upon the field of Evesham, and still marked with his blessed blood . . .'

At the name Adam had paused. Now he turned on his heel and caught the man by the bunched folds of his mantle. 'What's that you said?' he demanded. 'A martyr, you called him?'

'Why yes, sir!' the pedlar replied, swallowing down his yelp of surprise. His one good eye was bright with the promise of a sale. 'So they say, at any rate . . . More than one miracle is counted to his name already, so the Franciscans tell me. Soon it will be Saint Simon, indeed, once His Holiness the Pope has ruled on it . . . Just as we have St Thomas Becket!'

Adam frowned. Was it not the Pope that had passed a sentence of excommunication on de Montfort? He had followed Lord Simon gladly once, and been knighted by the man himself. But he had seen him slain too, his body mutilated, and plenty of good men had died at his side. The thought that de Montfort might be a holy figure now, a saint indeed, troubled his soul.

'You there!' another voice cried. Adam glanced towards the hospice gateway and saw the warden, a muscular man with an iron-grey beard, brandishing his fist. 'Get away from here! You'll not hawk your rubbish and birdbones at my gate!'

Stooping, the warden snatched up a clod of dirt from the road and hurled it at them both. 'This is a house for the honest poor and needy!' he snarled.

Adam released his grip on the pedlar's mantle and turned towards the gateway. A last bleating offer followed behind him. 'A penny for it then . . .?'

The warden was standing in the open gateway, arms folded across his cassocked chest. 'You're a friend of that shite-hawker?' the man demanded as Adam approached. 'You'll find no custom here.'

'I'm not,' Adam said, and tried to appear suitably deferential. He recalled the pedlar's words. *You look like one, sir, and walk like one* . . . He was still speaking in English, but he knew that his accent would proclaim his status easily enough. 'I'm . . . a wayfarer, that's all. A pilgrim. I was robbed on the road, past Chester . . .'

'Aye, well,' the warden said, regarding Adam with a squint above his beard. 'You may be an honest man, but we don't take in strangers till after compline. Come back then and maybe we'll find you a bed.'

'Please, goodman,' Adam said, forcing the words out. He knew how desperate he sounded, and how untrustworthy he must seem. 'At least let me shelter in your gatehouse, and hear mass . . . I can offer a donation, if that would be acceptable?'

For an uncomfortably long time the muscular warden said nothing, jutting his beard. Behind him Adam could sense the gaggle of beggars drifting closer. He heard one of them placing a bet on whether the stranger would be admitted.

'Maybe two pennies, for the poor, you understand,' the warden said. 'And if you give me your *paternoster* you can sit under the gatehouse till noon, let's say. After that the master decides.'

'I thank you,' Adam said, and pressed his palm to his chest. He rattled his way through the Lord's Prayer, crossing himself thrice, then the warden nodded and stepped aside. 'You may as well be one of Red Reynard's men, come to rob us all and slit our throats,' he said, 'but I'd not keep a Christian from hearing mass.'

Between the gatehouse arches there was a flagstoned passage, with a masonry bench on either side. Adam sat on one of the benches, peeling off his wet shoes and outer tunic and laying them to dry. A couple of hospice inmates came and sat on the facing bench, peering at him curiously, but neither said a word. A lay brother brought him a mug and a basin of water and he drank deeply and then washed his face and hands.

Let them take me now, he said to himself. *I can run no more, and have nowhere else to hide.* And without another thought in his head he slumped back into the corner and fell asleep.

*

Pale sunlight on his face as he opened his eyes. The bell chiming for mass had woken him, and Adam realised that he must have slept for over an hour. Bleary, still light-headed, he joined the shuffling throng from the hospice as they entered the chapel and gathered in the nave. With them he knelt, stood, prayed, and witnessed the Elevation of the Host. He still felt like he was sleeping, and at any moment he would wake and find himself back in his tower chamber at Beeston, with the leering face of Gaspard de Rancon before him.

The jailor's death still weighed upon him. As the congregation left the chapel Adam stopped one of the priests and asked if he might hear his confession. *Later*, the priest said, *after compline.*

In a corner of the yard, between the bakehouse and the infirmary, Adam sat on a bench and tried to make himself inconspicuous. One of the brothers brought him a half-loaf of gritty bread and a mug of ale to break his fast, and a wandering barber staying at the hospice gave him a shave and trimmed his hair, in return for a silver penny. He was just brushing the cut hair from his shoulders when he heard the stamp and snort of horses from the road outside the gateway. He froze, his heart suddenly banging in his chest. *They're here.*

'Friends of yours, sir?' the barber asked, in a hopeful tone. Adam gave no reply. He heard the clink of bridle fittings, the creak of harness, and the low deferential voice of the gate warden. How many riders could there be? Already he was glancing around the yard for any other way out of the hospice.

'You there,' the warden said, emerging from the gatehouse. 'You're wanted.' He gestured curtly.

Hope flickered in Adam's mind. Surely the guards from Beeston would not summon him in that way. They would come and do it themselves, and relish the chance of dragging him out of the yard. Hardly daring to consider what awaited him, he pulled on his damp tunic and walked to the arch of the gateway.

Outside, Joane de Bohun sat sideways on the saddle of her jennet, coldly beautiful in her widow's grey and black. A rouncey and a laden packhorse waited on the road. 'There you are,' she said as she noticed Adam, in a brisk tone that suggested she had seen him only recently. 'Come on then,' she commanded, gesturing to the saddled rouncey. 'We must be away from here.'

Breathless with relief, not even chancing to look at her, Adam slipped his foot into the stirrup and swung up into the saddle. Behind him he heard the warden talking to Joane. 'Four hours'll get you to Newcastle-under-Lyme, my lady. Just keep going steady and follow the broadest track – there's few travelling in this season, mind . . .'

'I'll be safe enough,' Joane told him. 'Especially now I have my groom to accompany me.'

They set off without a backward glance, up the salter's way that led eastward from Nantwich. Adam had the packhorse on a leading rein, while Joane rode ahead of him. They let the horses walk at first, then as they crossed a rise and the town fell away behind them they smartened their pace. Turning in the saddle, Joane swung her leg across the horse to ride more comfortably astride.

'You had no difficulties escaping your prison then?' she asked.

Adam was unable to detect any humour in her question. Even now, shaved and trimmed, there was no disguising his filthy and unkempt appearance, the bruises that mottled his skin or the scratches that scarred his face. 'None to speak of,' he told her.

'How long until they come after you?'

'Not long. Although I may have led them to think I would make for Chester or the Welsh border instead.'

'Well done,' Joane said, inclining her head. Adam could tell she was impressed, but was guarding any greater praise.

'You had no doubt I would be here, then?' he asked.

'I chose to put my faith in you,' she said, reining back her horse until he drew level with her. 'As you did in me, I see.'

'Then at least we have faith in each other, my lady.'

Joane smiled, amused by his sober attitude. She reached out and took his hand. 'Thank you,' she said. 'I would not have made this journey without you.'

Then she leaned from the saddle and embraced him, their horses closing the distance between them. Adam felt the warm pressure of her body against him, of her lips as she kissed his cheek. But the embrace was quite chaste, as if they were no more than friends, or cousins. After a moment she pulled away and composed herself.

They rode on in determined silence for a while longer. Joane's mention of a journey suggested she had plans of her own, but Adam had little idea what his part in them might be. Instinctively his fingers went to his throat and he touched the medallion he wore there, a gift from Joane many years before. St Christopher. *Protector of travellers.*

'We're not bound for Newcastle-under-Lyme, I'm thinking,' he said at last.

'We're not,' Joane replied. 'Though it helps that anyone asking after us might be sent in that direction. Our way branches off, an hour or so ahead of us.'

'Then we had best make all the time we can,' Adam told her. Joane snatched a glance at him, and he saw the flash of her smile. Then she nudged with her heels, and her slim jennet stretched forward into a trot. Adam kicked at the flanks of his rouncey, pulling on the leading rein of the packhorse.

As he felt the motion of his mount beneath him, the stream of the cold breeze in his face, he knew for the first time that he was truly free.

Chapter 4

'What happened to your maid, and the chaplain?'
It was around noon, and Adam was standing in the lee
of a clump of thornbushes, changing into the clean clothes that
Joane had brought on the packhorse. The feel of clean dry wool
against his skin was a delicious caress.

She was waiting with the tethered horses on the far side of
the bushes. 'I had to part with them back at Combermere,' she
called back. 'The road I'm taking is a hard one, and I've led poor
Petronilla and Father Hubert into enough danger this last year.
I left them coin enough to keep themselves, and instructions on
where I might be found a few months from now, should they
want to seek me out again.'

'Did you tell them where you're going?'

'I did not. To be honest, I did not even tell them I was leaving.
May the Blessed Virgin forgive me, and protect them both!'

Adam heard the lightness of her tone, and wondered how
genuine her guilt might be. He finished dressing, then went to
join her.

'So I am your groom now?' he asked. He was certainly dressed
as one, in a short tunic, hose and hooded cowl, a linen coif and a
thick mantle. He had hoped that she might have thought to bring
him a weapon too, but he remained unarmed.

'For the time being,' Joane told him. She took another pack of clothing and went behind the thornbushes, leaving Adam with the horses. 'Sadly you cannot also be my dressing-maid. Clothing oneself is not the easiest task.'

From where Adam was standing, Joane was obscured by the thicket of bushes. He heard the rip of fabric, her stifled curse. There was a footprint in the mud nearby, the print of Joane's shoe. He took two paces sideways, until he was standing where she had stood. When he glanced over his shoulder he was surprised to notice a gap in the swirl of thorny scrub just behind him. Through it he could see Joane, just as she would have been able to see him. She bent forward, pulling her black gown off over her head, then straightened. He saw the paleness of her back above her shift, the nape of her neck, and the flash of her dark copper hair as it spilled from its bindings. For a heartbeat his gaze lingered, and he remembered keenly the hours they had spent as lovers, so many months ago. Then he looked away.

'So where does our journey take us?' he called to her.

'To find my cousin, Margaret de Ferrers,' Joane replied. He heard her catch her breath as she struggled into a new gown. 'I need support in recovering my lands and estates. Of all my more powerful relations, Lady Margaret is the one most likely to help me.'

Adam had long been amazed and baffled by Joane's family connections. On her mother's side her ancestry went back to King John and Llewellyn the Great, but her father's de Quincy heritage seemed to link her to half the great magnate families of the realm. He remembered the name of Ferrers in particular. 'Isn't she the mother of the Earl of Derby?' he said.

'Of Robert de Ferrers, my first cousin, yes,' Joane replied. 'She still holds the title of dowager countess. And her daughter Elizabeth, who you met at Monmouth last summer, is the earl's sister. A widow now, since Baron William Marshal died at Evesham. I last saw her at the parliament at Winchester . . .'

But Adam was remembering what he had heard of Earl Robert de Ferrers. The *Devil of Derby*, his friend Hugh of Oystermouth had called the man. De Ferrers had waged his own private war against Lord Edward in the north, seizing his castles and manors, and then refused to hand them over to de Montfort. Lord Simon had summoned him to London back at the beginning of the previous year and had him imprisoned.

'Has Earl Robert been released then?' he asked.

'That I don't know,' Joane said, appearing from behind the thorn thicket dressed in her new clothes. She no longer looked like a wealthy widow. Now she looked like a merchant's wife, or the wife of a town burgess, dressed in simple travelling clothes of bluet and broadcloth. She was just fastening her white woollen headscarf as she spoke. 'When last I heard of him he was still being held at the Tower, or at Windsor Castle,' she said. 'But his whereabouts are unimportant. His mother is the one I need to find. We'll go to Derby and enquire after Lady Margaret there – she may be at Tutbury, or Duffield, or one of the other Ferrers manors.'

Adam helped her back into the saddle of her jennet. Her words were so direct, her scheme so considered and certain, that he found himself plunged into a dark mood. She had aided his escape, he told himself as he mounted his rouncey, and now he was bound to aid her. But as her servant, he realised now, her *groom* in reality as well as pretence. Nothing in her intentions to reclaim her lands and dignity involved him. Nor should it, he supposed. But the truth left him cold inside.

So intent had Adam been on his escape that he had no idea how he might proceed now. Even freeing himself from the confines of Beeston had seemed an impossible hope. He had imagined, perhaps, that he might make his way back to his lands in Hampshire, find Isabel de St John and somehow revive the hopes he had once held of marriage and a future life with her. But these were idle dreams; far more than mere distance lay between them now. Adam was a rebel and a traitor, an enemy of the king. By escaping from Beeston he had placed himself outside all mercy and all law. He was a fugitive, to be hunted and captured, or slain with impunity. All England was his adversary.

Joane too, he supposed, was a fugitive, from the king's guardians if not from his law. Fortune appeared to be driving their paths together. Isabel, Adam told himself, was the woman he truly desired. But every time he glanced at Joane, the image of his betrothed seem to ebb in his mind, like the memory of a dream.

'Very well,' he told her as she jogged her pony forward. 'I'll escort you as far as Derby, or to find your cousin if she's elsewhere. And then . . .' He paused. And then what? He did not know. No idea how he might scrabble back any of the honour that had been stolen from him, the lands that had been stripped from him, the promises of future happiness so cruelly denied.

But Joane merely nodded back to him, as if such matters were as unimportant as the fate of Earl Robert de Ferrers, and a moment later Adam gave the rein of the packhorse a sharp tug and rode on after her.

*

They were following the saltway that snaked steadily eastward towards the high country, passing through woods and over heathland desolate under the winter skies. Here and there they passed villages and hamlets, but did not slow or halt. By mid-afternoon, with the light already beginning to fade, they were riding up steep and stony tracks, following the narrowing valley of a river into the hills. Rain had come on again, thinning into a grey mist that cloaked the ridges above them.

'This is not the straightest road to Derby, I would say,' Adam commented, after they had ridden a long way in silence.

'It's not,' Joane said. 'But the straight way would have taken us close to Chartley Castle, and Hamo L'Estrange. His men escorted me back to Combermere – by now they'll have noticed that I'm missing and be out on the roads searching for me. We don't want to be caught between them and L'Estrange himself. He promised Earl Humphrey that he will keep me in his close care – what they fear I might do, I cannot say.'

'Exactly what you are doing, I suppose,' Adam replied.

He heard Joane's laugh, and wondered what else she might have neglected to tell him. Already it was growing so dim and misty that the track they were following had faded into the grey landscape.

'There's an abbey up ahead of us,' she said. 'A Cistercian house called Dieulacres. They told me of it at Combermere, and how to reach it. With God's blessing we might find shelter there tonight.'

'Would the Cistercians give lodging to a woman?' Adam asked. He knew that the order was the strictest in keeping all females from their precincts; back at Combermere, Joane had not been permitted to pass beyond the gatehouse chapel.

'They will have to,' Joane said, a little more briskly than Adam liked. 'I shall represent myself as a traveller in need.'

The early winter dusk seemed to be coming down quickly now, darkness falling from the air with the thin mist and gathering in the valley ahead of them. Aside from a few sheep on the barren slopes, there was no sign of life or habitation. The hooves of their horses ringing on the stony track were the only sounds in the muffling stillness of evening.

'When you were at Winchester, or any time after that,' Adam asked, just to stir the quiet into motion, 'did you hear any news of William de St John of Basing? Or of his daughter, Isabel?'

He could just make out the pale patch of Joane's headscarf moving as she looked back at him. 'I did not,' she said, her tone empty. 'But I suspect that his family will have profited from the king's peace.'

Adam suspected the same. The St Johns of Basing had shifted their allegiance to Lord Edward's side unexpectedly, and stirred a revolt in the south against de Montfort's government. Lord William had gone from being Adam's prospective father-in-law to his enemy overnight, sundering the bond between Adam and Isabel. The raw pain of that wound cut at Adam still. But Joane, if she was aware of it, appeared not to care.

'It's not far now,' she said, as curtains of mist blew from the gathering darkness and hung all around them. They had ridden for another half-hour, as far as Adam could judge, when the track abruptly ended at a saddle between two slopes, where a clutch of twisted hawthorns bent their heads over a rough wooden cross. Around them, the misty twilight pressed close.

'I'm sorry,' Joane said, after a few silent moments. She climbed down from her jennet and edged into the shelter of the tree, beside the cross. 'I'm sorry – I think I've led us the wrong way.'

It was cold now, the damp mist soaking into them both, even the horses trembling and blowing for warmth. Adam dismounted too and secured the animals, then joined Joane beneath the tree. It offered no shelter, but at least they could see it. Otherwise, their surroundings were formless grey.

'When you asked about Isabel de St John,' Joane began, but then paused.

'Think no more of it,' Adam said quickly.

'No,' she said, 'I answered your question without thinking, and I'm sorry. Does she know that you survived the battle? That you were held prisoner?'

Adam shook his head, though he doubted Joane could see it. 'I had no way of sending her a message,' he told her. 'Hugh of Oystermouth left Evesham before the battle, and I told him to find her and . . .' He broke off. Only now could he admit to himself that he had not wanted Isabel to know of his defeat, his captivity. As if she might keep the memory of him pristine, unbloodied, and free.

Joane shivered too, pulling her cloak tight to her neck. Her tautly assertive attitude was merely a screen for her nervous anxiety, Adam recognised. He knew now how close to the brink of despair and exhaustion she had drifted in these months since Evesham. He felt ashamed of having thought ill of her. Without thinking, he reached out and took her into his embrace, clasping her close until her shivers subsided. She pressed her face into his shoulder, then into the hollow of his neck. He could feel his heartbeat grow faster, and then abruptly slow. One of the horses nudged him in the back with its muzzle, and Joane breathed a laugh.

'If we find your cousin . . .' Adam began.

Joane reached up, sealing his lips with her fingers. 'No,' she told him, almost whispering. 'No, let's speak no more of plans. Not now.'

She closed her arms tight around him, pressing her body firmly against his chest, and he wrapped his mantle around them both. How long they stood like that, sharing their warmth, he could not say.

A sound came from the mist, and the horses stirred and shook their bridles. 'Did you hear it?' Joane asked, raising her head.

The sound again, distant but gathering definition.

'A bell,' Adam said. And at his words the mist seemed to lift and thin slightly, and away in the gathering darkness on the far side of the hill slope he thought he could make out the shape of a tower.

'It's the compline bell!' Joane cried, pulling herself abruptly from his arms. 'The abbey – we're almost there!'

Adam helped her back into the saddle and then swung up onto his own horse. Over the crest of the ridge and down the far slope, they kicked their weary mounts into a trot as the sound of the bell rang out from the mist, guiding them to sanctuary.

*

Full darkness had fallen by the time they reached the abbey walls, and the gates were securely closed. Leaving Joane waiting with the horses, Adam dismounted and walked up to the gatehouse. He banged three times with his fist on the solid oak of the gate. No sound at first. Then, carrying eerily on the damp night air, he heard the sound of voices raised in steady song.

'Try again,' Joane said. Adam was about to use his fist when he noticed the heavy wooden mallet suspended on a chain beside the gate arch. Taking it, he delivered three loud knocks on the gate.

'Yes, yes!' a voice called irritably from within.

They waited a while more, and Adam made out the sound of shuffling footsteps from the far side of the gate. Then a small hatch opened and the hooded head of a man appeared beyond it, silhouetted against the glow of a lantern.

'*Deo gratias,*' the hooded man announced, in the same peevish tone. 'It is night,' he went on. 'No paupers at this hour. Come back in the morning!'

'Wait!' Adam cried, but the hatch had already swung shut. Clamping his jaw in frustration he reached for the mallet again. 'You in there!' he shouted at the boards of the hatch. 'We're travellers in need of shelter! I have a lady with me, and the night is cold!'

Behind him he heard Joane riding up closer and dismounting.

'Aren't monastic houses supposed to welcome strangers as they would welcome Christ Himself?' Adam cried in frustration. He gave another bang on the hatch with the mallet.

Abruptly the hatch opened again and the porter's hooded face reappeared in the lantern's glow. He was an old man, Adam saw, with a sourly wrinkled mouth. 'A *woman*, you say?' the porter said, with strained incredulity. 'You arrive at this hour with a *woman* at our gates?'

'I am Lady Hawise de Quincy,' Joane announced from the darkness at Adam's back. Her voice had taken on the cold note of command he had come to recognise, but for a moment he was baffled as to why she was using her younger sister's name.

'The Countess of Lincoln is my aunt,' Joane went on, 'and the Countess of Derby is my cousin. I request shelter for one night, and one only, and expect your abbot will provide it gladly!'

She stepped closer to the hatch and held up her hand, exposing the heavy ring she wore on one finger, set with a silver cinquefoil on blood-red enamel. The arms of her father, Robert de Quincy. The porter peered a moment more from the hatch, then slammed it shut. Adam made out rapid muffled speech behind the oak. Then the rasp of iron bolts, once and then twice, the thud of a drawbar, and the gate swung open on oiled hinges.

'*Bene veniatis domina . . . et dominus,*' the porter declared, bowing as he ushered them inside.

A lay brother took their horses, and they were conducted to the cell of the gate lodge – no visitors could be announced until the Holy Office was concluded, the porter explained, but he would inform the abbot and hosteller as soon as possible. He left them there, in the cold stone-walled chamber, with only a single rushlight to hold the darkness at bay. They stood waiting, their breath steaming, too cold to sit down. The austerity of the Cistercians, Adam decided, was no exaggeration.

'Where's the real Hawise de Quincy?' Adam asked quietly, when he was sure they were alone.

'My sister was taken into the wardship of our aunt,' Joane explained, in a rapid whisper. 'She really is the Countess of Lincoln, and a very grand lady too. Friends with the queen. She has little time for us, and I'm not sure where she's sent Hawise.'

But if Joane did not know, Adam thought, then the brethren of Dieulacres Abbey would certainly not know either, and it was safe to assume her identity. Far safer than telling the truth, anyway.

Joane was twisting the ring around her finger. 'That reminds me,' she said. 'Did Earl Humphrey ask you for anything, after the funeral at Combermere?'

'He did,' Adam said, as the memory returned to him from beneath a host of other considerations. 'He wanted to know whether your husband had given me something while he was dying . . . he didn't tell me what.'

Joane nodded. 'His ring,' she told him. 'The de Bohun signet ring, with the device of a golden swan set upon it. It's been in their family for six generations, and the earl gave it to Humphrey as his heir. Now he wants to give it to his grandson instead.'

'I remember seeing him wearing it,' Adam said, his brow furrowed as he cast his mind back over the long weeks of his captivity. 'But . . . I did not see what he did with it. Most likely that fool of a physician stole it.'

'A shame,' Joane said, with a wry smile. 'I'd hoped you might have it, secretly. No doubt Earl Humphrey would be indebted to anyone who returned it to him.'

They waited a while longer, listening to distant voices come and go. Joane shuffled her feet to keep warm. 'There's something else you should know,' she said, trying to stop her teeth chattering. 'I was going to tell you earlier, but . . . well, it seemed best to wait until Derby.'

Adam nodded for her to continue.

'There are men still in rebellion against the king,' Joane told him. 'Some of Lord Simon's supporters, and others who've joined them since Evesham. I overheard Hamo L'Estrange and his friends talking of them. De Montfort's son, Simon the Younger, has placed himself at their head, and they're mustering their forces at a place called Axholme. They call themselves the *Disinherited*, and they've vowed to remain in defiance of the king until their lands are restored . . .'

'And where is Axholme?' Adam broke in. His heart was beating quickly.

'I don't know,' Joane said, with a grimace of apology. 'In the north somewhere, in a marsh I think – I've heard it called an island.'

'I'll find it,' Adam told her. 'I'll find it and join them . . . as soon as you're safe in your cousin's household.' This was what he had craved, he realised. Allies to stand with him, and the strength to fight back.

But before they could say more, footsteps crunched on the gravel outside and the light of a lantern flooded the stone cell. Two monks entered, in copes and hoods, and prostrated themselves on the flagstone floor.

'*Hospes eram, et collegistis me*,' one of them intoned.

An older monk had accompanied them, and introduced himself as the hosteller. 'The abbot bids you welcome to our house, Lady Hawise,' he said to Joane, not looking at her directly. 'He is currently detained, and begs that he be allowed to greet you properly tomorrow, and perform the maundy then, in accordance with the rites of our order.'

'Of course,' Joane said.

'In the meantime, my brothers will conduct you to the oratory, that you might offer prayer, and beg forgiveness for the sins of your journey.'

The abbey was a place of darkness, and wavering shadows on stone. The two hooded monks led Adam and Joane by lantern-light from the lodge and along a short cobbled lane to the oratory chapel. At the door they sprinkled them both with holy water. Bowing, Adam and Joane approached the altar and knelt. The air was fiercely cold, but spiced with aromatics. Candles burned upon the altar, giving little heat.

For the sins of your journey, Adam thought. He presumed they meant things like travelling on a holy feast day, or on the Sunday before it. Travelling at all, in Joane's case, especially accompanied only by a single male servant. Certainly they would not refer to breaking out of a castle prison and murdering the jailor.

Despite the chill, Adam felt the prickle of sweat upon his brow. He should find a priest before he went to his bed that night, he told himself, and make confession. Beside him, Joane knelt in silent prayer. He wondered what sins she had in mind.

After they had prayed a while one of the brother monks went to a lectern and began to read from the Gospels. Adam barely heard his droning voice. He was suddenly extremely tired, so weary he could barely keep from slumping back onto his heels. Beside him Joane was wavering as she knelt, her eyes closed. Adam heard her let out a brief snore, which startled her back to wakefulness.

But soon it was over. The hosteller gave them both the kiss of peace, and led Joane away to her lodgings in the abbot's house. Adam, as a mere servant, would sleep in the common guest chamber.

Conducted back through the darkness and the stone chill, he was shown to a straw pallet in the corner and left there with a mug of water and a basin, a single rushlight burning low beside him. There was just enough time to drink and to splash his face before the light burned down and the blackness closed in around him.

He lay on his back, seeing only a faint plume of his breath above him. The straw and the rough woollen blankets prickled, but soon they grew warm with his body's heat. Disconnected images and sensations floated through his mind. The name *Axholme* written on parchment. The golden swan upon Humphrey de Bohun's ring. The nape of Joane's exposed neck as he spied on her through the thornbushes. The touch of her fingers on his lips.

Then the sensation of falling, the rope sliding through his fingers, and the plunge into blackness.

He swallowed heavily, jerking awake again. His mind reeled for a moment, and he remembered that he had still not managed to make confession. *Forget it*, he told himself. Forget it, you survived.

You survived.

Chapter 5

It was still dark when he woke, stony blackness all around him, and it took a while for Adam to remember where he was or what had happened to bring him here. A bell was ringing, cold and clear in the thin night air. He recalled that the big monastic houses kept the office of matins several hours before dawn. Figures moved in the dark, footsteps shuffling.

He lay still as long as he could, huddled down into the nest of rough blankets to conserve the heat, and when he opened his eyes again a faint light was leaking into the chamber. His first movement was agony, all the aches and injuries he had sustained the day before erupting in a blizzard of discomfort. Barely stifling a cry, he let the pain subside before crawling from his bed.

Dawn was still an hour away, he estimated, but a pale greyness was filtering into the chamber. Adam dipped his fingers into his water basin, wincing as he felt the crackle of ice, and scrubbed his face. His bladder was full, and he could ignore it no longer; pulling on his shoes and fastening his belt, he threw his mantle around his shoulders and paced, shivering, to the arched entranceway.

The door creaked open, and he breathed the tight cold air of morning. The abbey yard was in shadow still, but the sky above was clear and blue with the approaching dawn. There was a feel of snow in the air.

Crunching over the frosted paving of the yard, Adam quickly identified the stables, the thatch steaming with the heat of the animals within. A midden lay close by. A pair of monks crossed the yard, their white cowled habits wraithlike in the early gloom. Drawing his mantle closer around him Adam went to the midden, unlaced his hose and braies and emptied his bladder with a sigh of relief.

When he was done he edged open the stable door and peered inside. The warmth of the animals was like a balm, the familiar sweetish smell a blessing. There were only a few horses in the stalls, alongside Joane's pony and packhorse and Adam's rouncey. A boy rose blearily from his bed of straw, wiping his nose, and stared open-mouthed. A servant, Adam guessed, rather than a novice monk. He waved the boy back to his slumbers and eased the stable door closed.

In daylight it was easier to make out the abbey's arrangement, although the church with its high tower, the cloister and the other main buildings stood in the inner precinct, concealed behind a wall and gate. The outer wall was high enough that from the stable yard Adam could see nothing of the countryside beyond. If snow had fallen over the moorlands in the night, he thought to himself, then their onward journey to Derby would be more difficult and hazardous still.

Just inside the guest-chamber door there was a wooden ladder that scaled to the upper lofts; Adam had noticed it in the shadows as he left the building. He went back there now and climbed quietly up the rungs. As he had hoped, an upper window looked out to the south, and when he pulled open the shutters he gained a view over the abbey wall. No snow at least, though the surrounding land glittered with blue frost. To the east the horizon was glowing with the approaching dawn, between the darkly mottled moorland and a shelf of heavy cloud. A small river twisted and rilled down the dale from that direction, and Adam could almost feel the ice in the water. On the far bank lay a meagre-looking village, where the road from the abbey gates crossed a ford. Beyond the village the road climbed to the south, towards a ridge. And coming over the ridge, etched clear and black against the sky, was a line of horsemen.

Adam narrowed his eyes, leaning into the embrasure of the window. He counted six riders at first, then two more, all of them appearing across the brow of the ridge and dropping down the slope towards the village. He could make out the lances they carried, and almost thought he could see the sheen of mail. These were no pilgrims, no travelling merchants. They were coming to the abbey as well, that was clear, and with a jolt of anxiety Adam was certain of their purpose.

Dropping back down the ladder, he ran across the yard to the stables. Once again the lad started from his straw, but this time Adam ordered him to his feet. 'Saddle and tack those,' he told the boy, pointing to the packhorse and jennet. The boy appeared not to understand him at first, but when Adam took the bridle and headstall of his rouncey and fitted the bit, the lad caught his meaning and set to work.

Adam flung the saddle over the back of the horse as it blew and pawed the dirt. 'There are riders coming,' he told the boy as they worked, speaking clearly in English. 'Where from, do you know? *Who are they?*'

Again the lad appeared not to understand. Was he deaf, or an idiot? Adam repeated himself, and the boy nodded. 'Abbot sent a runner to Chetleton, gone midnight,' the boy said, his words thickly accented. 'To the sheriff's men, mebbe?'

Of course, Adam thought, as the ice of realisation flowed through him: the abbot had not been 'detained'. He and Joane had been betrayed. There was no time. The riders would be at the gates at any moment.

His body burning, sweat flowing down his back, he scrabbled a coin from his pouch and passed it to the boy. 'There'll be another for you if you have them all prepared by the time I return. *Finish? Understand?*'

The boy peered at the bright silver in his palm, as if he had never seen such a thing. Then he grinned and nodded.

Outside, birds were swooping overhead as the bells began to ring for lauds, the sunrise office. Heaving breath, Adam jogged across the outer yard to the cobbled lane that led past the oratory to the gateway of the inner precinct. The abbot's lodgings lay somewhere close by, he knew. He could only hope that Joane too had woken early.

Two monks were coming through the wicket gate beside the larger doors as Adam hammered to a halt at the end of the lane. He shoved one aside and grabbed the other by the neck of his cassock, pushing him back through the wicket gate.

'Abbot's lodgings?' he demanded, breath burning in his throat. 'Where?'

The monk's hood had dropped back; he was barely more than a youth, his eyes wide and his mouth working as he struggled to speak. The other monk was shouting and gesticulating wildly. His young companion managed to point to his left, where a large stone building stood just inside the precinct wall. Adam released him, and ran.

A low door to the kitchen swung open as he approached. A servant appeared in the doorway, summoned by the noise; he saw Adam and tried to close the door again, but Adam rammed his shoulder against the boards and forced it open. Tumbling through, bundling the yelling servant aside, he crashed into the abbot's kitchen. Cooks and scullions scattered before him in the hearth's glow. One threw a ladle at Adam's head, and he dodged it just in time. Then he was through the chamber and along the passage to the hall.

A weapon, he needed a weapon. But the abbot's lodgings held nothing warlike, and he had no time to return to the kitchen again and search for a blade. He was standing in the middle of the chamber staring around himself when he heard the creak of the stairs and a figure descended from the chamber above.

'Adam! What's happening?'

Joane was already dressed. *Thanks be to God*. She was dragging her cloak around her shoulders as she came down into the hall, and Adam stammered out what he had seen. A heartbeat, the shock of it blanching her face, then she nodded and ran to the door. She drew aside the bar, dragged the door open, and Adam ran past her into the daylight. She passed him at the wicket gate, Adam holding the passage against anyone who might try to stop them, then he followed close at her heels down the lane to the outer yard.

Outside the stable the three horses stood saddled and tacked, and the stable boy was breaking the ice in the water butt with a knotted quarterstaff. Grinning with gratitude, Adam took another coin and tossed it to him, then threw down a third and snatched up the staff as the boy dropped it. Swinging into the saddle of the rouncey as the boy scrabbled for the silver in the stable-yard dirt, Adam grabbed the bridle of Joane's pony and held it steady as she set her foot in the stirrup and mounted. The packs were already loaded onto the third beast, the straps secured. Adam kicked with his heels and urged his horse forward into a trot.

The gates were closed, barred and bolted, and as they rode closer Adam saw the old porter dash from his lodge and plant himself, legs braced, before them. A pack of his fellow monks were running from the inner precinct to assist him.

'Open, and stand aside!' Adam yelled, brandishing the quarterstaff as he drew his horse to a stamping halt.

For a moment defiance flared in the old man's eyes, and he pressed himself back against the gates. Then Adam kicked his feet from the stirrups and jumped from the saddle, quarterstaff raised to strike. He saw the realisation slackening the monk's features. This was no groom before him, the old man saw, no mere servant but a trained fighter. A knight, tournament-skilled, at home in the world of violence. His jaw slackened, then he quailed and darted back into the sanctuary of his cell.

One kick drove the first bolt open. A blow from the staff opened the second. Adam heaved the drawbar across and dragged the gate wide. Joane rode her jennet through at once, drawing the packhorse behind her. Adam swung back into the saddle – *Christ's mercy*, his body ached – and followed her.

A glance to the left, into the first blaze of dawn sun, and he saw the band of riders already fording the river and coming up the slope towards the abbey. He heard one of them shout.

'This way!' Joane cried. She dragged at the reins of her pony and urged it into a canter up a path that followed the abbey wall and then stretched northward over the brown hillside beyond. Adam was already following her. He heard the distant snap of a crossbow and his back hunched instinctively. The bolt struck the wall near the gate, but already he had ridden out of range.

They were scaling the path now, Adam kicking wildly with his heels and wishing fervently that he was wearing spurs. Up ahead of him Joane steered a weaving course on her sprightly jennet, towing the packhorse in her wake. A quick glance behind, and Adam saw the eight riders streaming after them from the abbey gates, lances stabbing at the dawn sky. Ahead the ground rose to looming brown moorland, bog and heather. Cloud was coming down from the heights, and the breeze was suddenly damp and growing stronger.

Head down, Adam rode into the teeth of the wind as Joane fled before him and the riders came up in pursuit. Behind him, the bell of Dieulacres Abbey was still ringing as the monks and lay brothers gathered in the yards and the cloister, shocked and baffled at the chaos that had disturbed the sacred tranquillity of their precincts.

None noticed the solitary boy in a straw-speckled smock, running towards the village as fast as his legs could pump, a grin on his face and three bright silver pennies clasped in his fist.

*

They were up onto the high moorland before the rain struck them. Needle sharp and icy, it came hissing from the lowering sky and drove their heads down over the streaming manes of their horses. The rain blanked the landscape around them too, and for the time it might take to hear mass they rode blindly in a featureless grey waste. The rain had eased by the time they gained the next height, and there was no sign of their pursuers.

'Probably turned back to seek the abbot's hearth,' Adam said bitterly, and shuddered beneath his damp cloak and hood. He scanned the surrounding slopes and vales anyway, alert for the slightest glimpse of man or beast. Sheep stood in clumps along the valley sides, pressed together for shelter among the heather. Otherwise they were alone.

'Who do you think they were coming for, you or me?' Joane asked, casting the fold of shawl back from her head.

'I doubt news of my escape could have outpaced us,' Adam said. 'The stable lad told me they were sheriff's men. Is L'Estrange still sheriff here?'

'He'll still come after me, whether he's sheriff or not,' Joane said quietly. They rode on down the far side of the ridge and along a boggy runnelled vale, letting the horses pick the surest path. Clouds covered the sun, and Adam was unsure of their direction.

'It may be that they were looking for somebody else,' Joane suggested. 'Or perhaps the abbot had been warned to be alert for strangers on the roads . . .?'

'Maybe,' Adam said with a shrug. 'Do you care to go back there and ask them?'

Joane shot him a hard glance. Both of them were still stunned after their rapid departure, soaked, and saddle sore after the previous day's ride. Adam could sense the clumsy words massing between them, the accusation and argument. It had been Joane's idea to seek shelter at the abbey, her plans that had led them there. She had trusted in her aristocratic privilege to keep them safe, and that trust had proved misplaced. To have come so close to recapture, after everything Adam had endured in his escape, seemed intolerable now. He sensed that she blamed him too. Every passing moment was freighted with statements they would come to regret. But to remain silent seemed to stretch the tension between them even tauter still.

And as they rode, Adam's mind was drawn back to that other horseback escape, months ago on a hillside in Wales, when a rainstorm had shielded him and Joane from their pursuers. To that, and to the hours that followed, when they had so briefly become lovers. A memory of summer, a more hopeful season, and far away now. This northern moorland in the grip of winter was a bleaker, harder place, and the long grim shadow of Evesham's slaughter lay across them still.

'Stop,' he said, drawing his horse to a halt. They were crossing another ridge, through thickets of stunted alder, and before them a stream snaked along the valley floor. Joane rode on a little and then slowed and turned. Her expression was sour with resentment.

'We have no idea where we are,' Adam told her. 'We don't even know which direction we're travelling. We need to stop and rest, and eat.'

'We're riding north,' Joane said, with a brittle note in her voice. 'Can't you see the sun, over there to our right?'

Adam squinted into the dull sky, and picked out a faint gleam through the clouds. 'It's January, and close to noon,' he said. 'The sun will be low to the south. We're riding east.'

'Well, what of it?' Joane said, after a heartbeat. 'The further east we travel, the closer we get to the Earl of Derby's lands, and people who might aid us.'

'That stream down there,' Adam said, pointing into the vale. 'That must flow southward, towards the lower country. We should follow it, if you want to reach Derby before nightfall. But first we need to rest.'

'Very well,' Joane said, and sighed as she dismounted. She led the pony to the nearest alder clump, tethered it and seated herself on the damp turf. She waited in silence as Adam fetched what remained of their provisions from the packhorse: a little cheese wrapped in linen, half a loaf of stale bread, and a flask of wine. Passing the flask between them they drank the last of the wine as they ate, and then Adam went down to the stream and refilled it with cold fresh water.

'You could have fled the abbey much more quickly alone this morning, without coming back for me,' Joane said when Adam returned. She was sitting with her arms around her knees, drenched in resentment. 'I should thank you, I suppose.'

'As you like, my lady,' Adam said, without a glance at her. There was a flint and steel among the supplies on the packhorse, and he was considering making a fire to try to dry their damp clothes. But the smoke might disclose their position to anyone still tracking them.

'I know you have not been long a knight,' Joane said with harder emphasis, abandoning her effort at gratitude. 'And we are hardly engaged in any chivalrous pursuit, but you might try to behave with more graciousness!'

'Is that so?' Adam replied, turning on her. 'And I know you have not been long a widow, and were not long a great lady of the realm, but you might try not to treat me as your servant!'

She glared back at him, her face flushed with indignation. Just for a moment Adam was struck by her beauty, as it rose with the sun of her rage. Then she laughed, a mirthless snort. 'Are you not my servant?' she asked.

'I am your friend, I believe, my lady. But I see you have no need for friends, in your current situation. Only your powerful relatives are of use to you now.'

He untethered the horses and climbed back into the saddle. 'We should travel while we have the light,' he told her.

Joane nodded briskly, and accepted his hand as he helped her to mount. 'Until Derby, then,' she said. 'After that, I release you from any obligation, and you may go wherever you please.'

As they rode onward, tracking the stream as it wound down the valley, Adam felt his heart racked by black despair, and his soul crushed to ashes. If Joane felt the same she gave no sign of it, and kept her face turned from him.

*

The first wolf howled as they descended a stony incline between slopes clad in ashwoods. Adam turned to see Joane tense in her saddle, pulling her cloak tighter to her neck. The horses had heard the sound as well. Their ears pricked up, and they trembled and chewed the bit as they walked. Below them the twisting stream had cut a deep cleft in the limestone, spilling between the rocks in rivulets and spiralling brown pools. Already the light was beginning to fade, the dark alder thickets along the banks of the stream appeared black in the gathering shadow.

'We'll not reach Derby before nightfall, will we,' Joane said.

It was not a question. Adam shook his head, his fingers touching the medallion at his throat.

'If we had taken the path eastward instead we may have reached a manor or village that would offer us shelter for the night.'

Like the abbey of Dieulacres, Adam thought. But he said nothing.

'As it is, we've passed no human habitation at all . . . This is a wasteland, a solitude . . .'

Distantly the wolf's howl came to them again, and Adam heard Joane's words cut off as she caught her breath. Now the rain had stopped, all warmth had leached from the day. The air was cold as stone, as ice water.

'We'll find something,' Adam said. His words sounded unconvincing even to him. 'Even a cave or a hollow. We can build a fire and keep warm . . .'

Abruptly he fell silent, drawing on the reins. His horse halted in the middle of the stony track, and Joane's pony and the packhorse came to a stop behind them.

Up ahead, barely ten paces down the trail, a man stood in their path. He had appeared so suddenly that he could almost have risen from the ground. He was the colour of the ground too, and the surrounding trees and rocky slopes, dressed in grey and dun wool with a dirty sheepskin over his tunic.

'Getting dark,' the man said. His voice was all burrs and jags. He held a bow in his hand, but he made no move to pluck one of the arrows from his belt and set it to the string.

Adam narrowed his eyes, staring back at the man, trying to fight his nervous apprehension. 'Who are you?' he demanded. 'Why do you stand in our path?'

He was uncomfortably aware that he had only the knotty quarterstaff he had taken from the abbey stable to defend himself, and to defend Joane too. The man in the sheepskin had a lean and dangerous look. He was smiling, but there was a glaring intensity in his eyes that robbed his expression of all goodwill.

'Adam!' Joane said in an urgent whisper.

Adam flicked a glance to his left and saw three more men emerging from the shadows of the alder thicket. They were dressed similarly to the first, in greys and russets, with hoods over their heads. All three held bows, drawn with arrows nocked. All were aiming at Adam.

'Hop down, lad,' the man in the sheepskin said. 'Do it prompt, and we'll have no need to peck out your eyes.'

Adam's hand tightened around the staff, the wood digging into his rope-burned palms. If he moved fast enough, he thought, he could reach the man on the path and knock him down before the archers could loose more than an arrow each. He shortened his reins, lifted the staff to his shoulder like a mace, and breathed in.

He heard Joane's scream even as he dug in with his heels. The rouncey leaped forward at once, and the first arrow whipped the air just behind Adam's back. The second struck the animal in the haunch, just as Adam was screwing the reins around to confront the threat behind him. The rouncey let out a pained whinny, flinching and kicking with its back legs as it turned.

Behind them, three more men had come galloping out of the alders and down the track, all mounted on shaggy cob ponies with spears and falchions in their hands. The first rode up beside Joane and seized her by the cloak, dragging her from the saddle before she could resist. Another threw his spear at Adam as he rode.

The rouncey was wounded, and Adam fought to stay in the saddle as the animal circled and shied. He could not see where the man in the sheepskin had gone; all his attention now was on the riders. Bunching the reins in his left fist he kicked wildly with his heels, urging the wounded horse towards Joane, who was still struggling against the man who had seized her.

He swung the staff down, breaking it across the face of one of the riders, then leaned back in the saddle to dodge the thrust of a spear. Another arrow struck his horse in the neck, and the animal reared back on its haunches. Its back legs gave out and it tumbled; Adam kicked his feet from the stirrups at the last moment and threw himself clear.

Rolling on the stony dirt, he staggered upright. He still had the splintered stump of the quarterstaff clasped in his fist. He saw the bows drawn in the shadows of the alders, the two men on ponies flanking him. He saw Joane with her neck in the lock of a man's elbow, a dagger in his fist aimed at the side of her head.

Then a blow to the back of his knees swept his legs out from under him and he fell. His hands were empty as he clawed himself back to kneel. A booted foot appeared before him, then another. When he raised his head he saw the keen tip of a hunting arrow, poised at the full extent of a drawn bow and only a handspan from his face.

'Now drop and lie still,' the man in the sheepskin rasped, holding the arrow steady. 'Or I'll split your brains with this.'

Chapter 6

Flames lit the bowl of the valley, smoke and flying embers rising into the early dusk, and the flickering light turned the caves in the cliffs above the river into the empty eye sockets of a giant's skull. Their captors stood all around them in the shadows.

A taller man turned from the fire to address them. 'You know who I am?' he said.

Adam and Joane stood silently, their wrists bound before them. Neither had said a word this last hour, as their captors had led them down the river gorge to this forsaken place. A few of the men gathered in the circuit of the fire's glow laughed, or muttered crude suggestions. Their leader held up his hand to silence them.

He was a big man, with a broad chest and the thews of a wrestler. His beard was red as autumn heather, and bristled around his jaw below a shaved upper lip. He was better dressed than his men, and wore high doeskin boots that rose to his calves, bound around with a multitude of straps and laces. The only weapon he carried was a short knife in his belt, of the sort a huntsman might use to flay a carcass.

'Well then,' he said, his fists on his hips, 'since you're my guests I must introduce myself! Men call me Red Reynard, and I am lord of this dale and all the country round. I give no homage to any man, and hold what I have by the strength of my arm.'

Adam glared back at him, unblinking. He knew well enough what this man was. A leader of robbers and reavers. A *wolfshead*. He had heard the man's name mentioned back at Nantwich, he remembered now. Beside him, Joane stood stiffly upright, her face blank of all emotion.

'And these friends around me here are my retinue,' Reynard went on proudly, gesturing to the gathering of rough men in the firelight. 'Your woolly captor over there is Ivo of the North, and beside him Long Thomas and Jakke the Liar . . .'

Adam moved only his eyes as he glanced at the men indicated. All appeared much alike in the twisting shadows. He caught the glint of steel, the burr of thick wool, the shapes of cruel smiles and hard eyes.

'. . . and there you see young Haukyn, and John Silence – do not look at John Silence, my lady, for he is a vicious man and torture is his only joy . . .'

The rest of the names fell into the firelight, like bizarre and unwanted gifts: Earless Wynn, Dabbe Alcok, John the Scot . . . Nearly two dozen in all, but their chief implied that many more lurked in the fastnesses of the dale and the surrounding moors.

'And now you know us,' he said, tipping back his head so his bush of a beard jutted in the firelight, 'you must tell us who you might be.'

But still Joane kept silent, and Adam knew that he must do the same.

As Reynard had spoken, his men had been unloading the packs from Joane's baggage horse, opening them and casting the contents down in the firelight where all could see them. Gowns and fur-trimmed robes spilled in the dirt, fine linens and silks heaped beside them. Men prised at the catches of jewellery boxes and levered them open. Adam watched Joane from the corner of his eye. Only once did she flinch, and her throat tighten, as she saw one of the thieves pull out a book with a tooled leather cover and leaf through it. Her father's Psalter, Adam knew; one of the few possessions she treasured. The man sneered and threw the book aside.

'Ah, but this is no common goodwife's clutter,' Reynard mused, surveying the pillaged goods. He turned back to Joane and took a long stride towards her. 'I think you are a noble's wife or daughter, though you dress so lowly. What is it, my lady, are you fleeing your rightful husband? Or the marriage your father has arranged?'

Before Joane could flinch away from him he seized her by the chin and pulled her head up.

'Take your hands off her!' Adam said, desperate to draw the man's attentions from Joane if he could.

Reynard's gaze flicked from Adam to Joane and back again. He smiled thinly, and his face appeared to darken. 'Oh?' he said. 'Or what, heh?'

Then he stooped quickly, grabbed Joane by the neck and planted a kiss on her mouth. His men roared their approval.

'So what are you then?' the brigand asked, pacing across to stand before Adam. 'The lady's protector? And what protection can you give her, armed only with a stick? Did you think she might be assaulted by hares?'

Again the men laughed. Their mood was growing hotter and more boisterous.

'Instead here she is, exposed to every indignity,' Reynard said, leaning closer to breathe the words into Adam's face. He stank of woodsmoke, raw meat, and badly tanned hides. 'And what more does this night hold, do you imagine?'

Adam just stared back at him, and behind the crude arrogance he saw a keen and ruthless intelligence in the man's eyes. Anything he said now would be a mistake.

'But truly you are blessed by the Virgin!' Reynard said, stepping away from him abruptly and swaggering back towards the fire. 'For you are, as I say, our guests. And until we can get an idea of who you are, and who might pay the most for your ransoms, you shall be . . . *unmolested* here.'

Adam heard Joane exhale. He could almost sense her shudder. He wished suddenly and fervently that he was properly armed and mounted, dressed in mail with gilded spurs at his heels and a good sword in his fist. Then, he thought to himself, he would scatter these brigands like chaff before the hooves of his war-horse, and relish cutting them down.

'But do not think to abuse our hospitality,' Reynard added, looking back at both of them with a hard grimace. He drew the short knife from his belt and levelled it at Adam, the steel catch-ing the light. 'If either of you try to flee,' he said, 'we'll peel the skin off you both, and leave your flesh for the wolves to devour!'

He gave a curt gesture and his men closed in around their prisoners, two of them gripping Adam by the shoulders and another two taking Joane by the wrists.

They were led down the valley another few miles. In the dark-ness it was hard to judge the distance, but as his eyes adjusted to the dimness Adam made out great spires of rock towering out of the bare trees on either side, like the fangs of a beast. Beside them the river rushed and spilled, but it was lost in deep shadow now. The air had grown colder, and Adam tasted ice on every breath. He was almost glad when his captors shoved him off the track they had been following and directed him to climb, up through the blackness beneath the trees.

Stumbling up a slope, loose scree sliding beneath him, bram-bles and tree roots grabbing and catching, Adam emerged before the mouth of a cave, or an arch of natural rock. Beyond it was a dark space where bodies huddled and muttered around a smoking fire, then a deeper cave that led into the cliff. Here the brigands directed Adam and Joane to sit. The man called Long Thomas cut their bindings, making sure they felt the sharpness of his knife. There were straw pallets laid for them at the edge of the firelight, and soon afterwards a shrouded woman brought them barley cakes warm and ashy from the embers, and a mug of sour ale to pass between them.

'We should tell them nothing,' Joane said, in a whisper barely louder than breathing. She was speaking in French, which their captors were unlikely to understand. 'If they don't know who we are, they won't know who to ask for our ransom.'

Adam nodded as he ate, then took the mug from her and drank. It was almost fully dark now, the cold of the cave pressing on them like something physical, something heavy enough to steal their breath.

'I'm sorry for leading us here,' Adam said. Saying the words unstoppered his anguish, and he felt the wretchedness of their situation almost overwhelm him. Then a surge of black rage gripped him. 'If they harm you, I'll kill every one of them. *Red Reynard* and all the rest. Even if I die in the process, I swear it in God's name . . .'

Reaching out in the dark Joane took his hand, rubbing her thumb over his calloused knuckles. 'It was nobody's fault,' she said quietly. 'I'm just glad I'm not here alone.'

*

Dawn crept over them in a wash of silvery light. Adam sat up and opened his eyes, barely conscious of having slept. All around him in the cave were other bodies, both men and women bundled in thick blankets and furs, dogs lying between them, some of them rising into the daylight, stretched faces yawning.

Beside him Adam saw Joane lying deep in sleep, her eyelids dark and her mouth partly open. Her hand lay with fingers slightly curled, and he remembered that she had reached out to him in the dark, and they had lain with hands clasped until sleep took them at last. He watched her for a moment, filled with a yearning desire, but then felt suddenly grimy and churlish, ashamed of his reaction.

There seemed nobody to stop him leaving the cave, so Adam scrambled to his feet, stamped the feeling back into his legs, then pulled a blanket around him and picked his way between the sleeping forms to the cave mouth. It was bitterly cold, and a smoking fire did little to warm the air. Three sentries were watching him, one of them the hard-eyed man called Ivo of the North. All had bows strung. Careful not to provoke them with any sudden movements, Adam filled a mug with water, took a warm loaf from the woman who tended the fire and returned to find Joane.

All through that day they remained in the cave, the outlaws and their women coming and going. Nobody said anything to Adam or Joane, and they slept that night more deeply, if no more comfortably.

The next morning Adam opened his eyes to see Reynard kneeling beside him.

'Get up,' the brigand chief demanded. 'You're to come with us.'

Adam frowned a question, his mind still hazy from sleep. He reached for Joane to wake her too, but one of Reynard's men seized his wrist.

'The woman stays here,' Reynard said. 'To ensure you behave.'

They left the camp, and within the hour they were making their way further down the valley, Adam walking between a dozen men armed with spears and bows. A toothed wind roared up the river gorge, shaking the bare trees and whining around the high rocks.

'Where are you taking me?' Adam asked. The man ahead of him turned and growled at him to remain silent. It was the wolfish Ivo of the North, and accompanying him were the hollow-faced Long Thomas and the youthful Haukyn. Another man too, with the bridge of his nose crushed and bloodied, and two black eyes.

'You did that,' the man said with a vicious sneer, stepping close to Adam and stabbing his fingers at his own broken features. The man on the horse, Adam remembered, who he had struck in the face with his staff. He felt reckless now Joane was not here.

'What did you expect?' he said to the man with the broken nose. 'A kiss?'

For a heartbeat the man bared his teeth, reaching for the knife at his belt. But Long Thomas let out a bark of laughter and cuffed Adam on the shoulder, and young Haukyn stifled a chuckle. Even Ivo of the North had a wry smirk as he glanced back.

Another twist of the gorge, and they scaled a narrow dirt path that climbed through the trees to a rocky eminence. From here they had a fine view over the curve of the valley, where the slopes opened and the river curled in braids over stones and shingle. Reynard crouched in the cover of a hawthorn thicket with Ivo of the North, gesturing for the men behind him to stay out of sight. The hawthorns provided a little shelter from the chill breeze, but the air was cold enough to chap the skin.

When they had watched and conferred for the time it would take to say a paternoster, Ivo returned and seized Adam by the elbow, dragging him up towards the rocky ledge. 'Not a sound, young sir,' he whispered, 'or I'll slice out your tongue.'

At the ledge they lay flat on the cold stone and peered across the valley. There were riders below them, just over two bow-shots distant and picking their way across the sinuous shallows of the river. Two carried spears and resembled huntsmen, but the leading pair were serjeants in wide-brimmed iron helmets, with shields slung on their backs.

'Know them, do you?' Reynard asked Adam in a low rumble.

Adam shook his head curtly. They may have been the same horsemen that had pursued him and Joane from Dieulacres, but he could not be sure. He was not about to tell his captors, either way.

'Reckon they might know you, eh?' Reynard added.

Adam felt sudden fear cramp in his belly as Reynard got to his feet. His captors were about to sell him, he thought; they would negotiate a ransom with these men right here and now. Doubt-less they believed that Joane was the more valuable prisoner, and they would hold her back for a higher price.

He made a move to scramble down from the ledge, and felt Ivo's knife nudging into his side. '*Doucelike*,' the man said between his teeth. 'Do nothing to startle us, and we'll see no blood.'

'You there!' Reynard cried to the men below him, in a booming voice that raised an echo from the far cliffs. 'Declare yourselves!'

He had a strung bow in his hand, and at his words a dozen other archers had appeared from the thorn thickets and bare trees on both sides of the gorge, bows bent and arrows nocked. They had waited until the men advanced into range.

The leader of the mounted party halted, raised his hand and then nudged his horse on a little further until he stood on the stony riverbank. Those behind him had slowed and halted too as they gazed at the slopes around them.

'We seek fugitives!' the serjeant cried back, standing in the stirrups. 'On our master's orders!'

'You'll find none here,' Reynard called. 'Only free men, and fierce ones. Best turn your little band and ride away!'

'We must search this valley,' the serjeant shouted, sound-ing almost apologetic. 'Or our master will send more men to do it.'

'Your master – whoever he might be – will need an army if he wants to come here,' the outlaw replied, thrusting out his chest and his jaw so his beard bristled.

'Are they de Ferrers men, d'you think?' Haukyn asked in a gruff whisper. 'Or do they come from the Peak?'

Long Thomas shook his head and gestured for him to keep quiet.

Craning his head as far as he dared, Adam watched the mounted men in the valley. He was sure now that these were the same rid-ers that had pursued him and Joane from Dieulacres. But there were too few of them. There should be at least eight, but he could only count four in the valley. They were acting strangely too, circling their horses with no sign of wariness.

'It's a ruse,' he said suddenly. 'They're biding their time; there are more of them . . .'

He felt the knife jabbing at his ribs, but managed to twist and glance behind him. Slopes brown with winter bracken and leafless trees rose over the valley, outcrops of bare rock here and there, and the higher slopes above them were barren against the hard bright sky. Adam squinted, staring, and caught a movement in the drabness.

'There!' he said.

A shout from behind him, and then movement erupted on all sides. A crossbow bolt snipped through the bare foliage overhead. Another found its mark to Adam's right; he heard the cry of pain and saw a body drop. Ivo had released him, cursing as he snatched up his bow, and Adam scrambled away from him.

'They're behind us!' Reynard yelled. 'Everyone at them!'

A second crossbowman rose from the cover of the bushes about twenty paces up the hillside, aiming his loaded weapon at Reynard's men. Haukyn had been first to bend his bow, but he was shooting from a crouched position and his arrow sailed high over the trees. Adam heard the snap of the crossbow, then he was on his feet and running up the slope through the thorny thickets. The crossbowman was stooped in the cover of the hawthorns, spanning his weapon. Another man appeared on the higher slope, an archer. The man's bow moved as he tracked the figures below him, then he released the arrow.

Reynard, Ivo and Long Thomas were already shooting back. Arrows and bolts whipped through the air as Adam forged his way upwards. Abruptly he stumbled into a patch of clear ground; the crossbowman he had seen moments before was somewhere above him, but Adam could see his comrade only a few long strides to his left. He saw the man raise his loaded weapon, aiming at Haukyn on the hillside just below him. Gasping for breath,

Adam swerved on the slope and charged to his left, before the man could shoot.

The crossbowman noticed him at the last moment and swung his aim. Too slow; Adam's shoulder rammed into him and knocked the crossbow upwards just as he squeezed the trigger. The bolt flashed past Adam's face, then he was down and rolling with the bowman trapped beneath him. They fell hard onto the stony slope, Adam grappling the weapon from the man's hands. One swing, and he brought the stock of the crossbow cracking into the side of the man's skull. Then he flung it aside.

A falchion was scabbarded in the man's belt and Adam seized it and drew it free. The crossbowman was alive, but writhing in pain. Adam raised his head and scanned the bushes, the blade in his fist.

'Stay!' a voice bellowed. They were all around him now, Reynard and Ivo with swords, Haukyn and three others with bows bent and arrows aimed at Adam's head. The fight was over. John the Scot and a party of archers had driven off the mounted men on the riverbank, wounding two of them and capturing their horses. The other crossbowman and the archer had either fled or fallen.

Adam raised his left hand, palm spread. Holding the falchion with his extended arm he reversed the blade, then presented it to Reynard.

Only then did he realise that he was grinning fiercely.

*

'I discovered some things, while you were gone,' Joane said, later that day as they sat in the cave once more. 'I overheard the women at the cooking fire talking with the men who remained here.'

She was massaging Adam's hands with a sour-smelling paste one of the women had given her. He had scratched and grazed himself more than he had realised during his fight among the thorn thickets. He nodded, urging her to continue. It seemed easier to talk now, although they kept their voices low and spoke in French.

'From what I can tell, most of these people fled here during the wars, after their homes were ravaged,' Joane said. 'Some of them fought for Earl Robert when he was plundering Lord Edward's lands, but they took to the hills when he was imprisoned a year ago. Now they say he's been released, and accepted the king's mercy.'

'He's been pardoned?' Adam said, startled.

Joane nodded. 'Around Christmastide last, when the king was at Northampton. Now he's supposedly the king's man, but nobody seems sure of his true allegiances. As I am unsure of theirs.'

'You still think your cousin would offer you help and refuge?' Adam asked her.

'It's still the best hope I have,' she replied, wiping her hands on a rag. She reached into her girdle, glancing quickly to either side to make sure she was unobserved, then opened her hand and showed Adam the enamelled signet ring she had hidden when they were captured. 'If we had some way of getting this to my cousin, wherever she might be,' Joane whispered, 'she would surely aid us, I know.'

The shape of a man blocked the light from the cave mouth, and Joane quickly hunched and concealed the ring in her girdle.

'You, come with me.' Adam recognised the voice of Ivo of the North. He nodded, then followed the man out of the cave and into the daylight.

They found Reynard standing at the brink of a precipice, beyond the arch of rock. The brigand chief was leaning casually against the gnarled roots of a tree growing from the cliff beside him, and gazing into the burnished light of early evening as the sun went down over the valley. Patches of snow on the higher moorlands glowed pale in the coming dusk.

'You must think I'm a rough man,' Reynard said, turning to Adam with his bushy brows lowered. 'But I'm no fool, eh? There are some of my company who think you and your woman must be runaway servants, who've murdered their master and mistress and stolen their clothes and horses. But no, I said. The woman has the manner of the highborn, and that can't be feigned. And you – well, you dress as a common churl, but fight like fighting's your trade. Am I right?'

Adam shrugged. He had not yet discussed with Joane whether they should maintain their silence or not.

'Be straight with me,' Reynard said, leaning from the waist until he gazed into Adam's eyes. 'Man to man, and you will not suffer for it, I swear upon the Host.'

'Very well,' Adam told him. 'I will say nothing of my companion – her identity is hers alone to keep. But I'm a knight, as you suspect. My name is Adam de Norton, and until a few days past I was a prisoner at Beeston Castle, after I was captured on the battlefield of Evesham.'

Reynard stared a moment, then his eyes widened and a smile split his face. 'So!' he said. 'I knew there was more to you . . .' He raised a stubby finger. 'If you escaped from Beeston you're a slippery one indeed, and I should bind you with the thickest cords . . . But you're saying you were one of Simon de Montfort's men?'

'I fought at his side, and I saw him cut down by our enemies.' Adam felt an unexpected surge of pride running through him as he spoke, and tears prickled in his eyes. He had not spoken of Lord Simon in that way for a long time, nor even thought of the man without misgivings. He blinked, mastering his emotions.

The outlaw chief breathed deeply, filling his chest as he gazed into the valley. 'They say this Lord Simon fought for the rights and liberties of common men,' he said. 'I've also heard he died a martyr for Christ, and those who pray to him have known miracles. Is that so?'

'I know nothing of such things,' Adam replied.

'No – if you've been in prison all this while there's much you won't know.'

'But you see,' Adam went on, 'there's nobody who will ransom me, and all the lands and wealth I held has been taken from me. So I'm worth nothing to you, and by keeping me you're harbouring a king's enemy.'

Reynard grinned. 'Ha, clever!' he said. 'But this is my country, and the king's writ don't run here. Besides, something tells me your lady companion is no ordinary runaway, and may be worth something to us yet. Should we let you go, and keep her instead, do you suggest?'

Adam felt the heat rise to his face. 'If she stays, I stay too,' he declared.

'And if we released you both, where would you go?'

'There are men holding out, I'm told,' Adam said. 'Men who've been disinherited like me, who refuse to submit to the king. I would go and join them. They're at a place called Axholme – do you know of it?'

'Aye, I've heard the name,' Reynard said, nodding. But he grew suddenly grave. 'The Isle of Axholme – a few of our local men went off to join the rebels there. But they came back again soon enough.'

Adam felt a chill crawl up his spine.

'Lord Edward went up north with an army just before Christmastide,' Reynard said. 'He marched right up to the Axholme dikes and demanded the rebels surrender to his peace. Word is, they did so. The rebellion's over,' he said, shaking his head. 'You're a month and more too late.'

Chapter 7

It was Candlemas, the Purification of the Virgin, when the friar joined them. He appeared as the first flakes of snow began to fall between the bare trees, and in his grey Franciscan habit he was almost invisible until he neared the first of the sentries. Adam heard the call of challenge, and a moment later caught sight of the pale figure, his raggedly tonsured head bare and his hands tucked inside his cassock as he walked. Already a crowd followed after him.

Reynard's gang had shifted camp the day before, crossing the river on a weir to a village of thatch and stones hidden in the winter woodland. Their number had grown; there were more than fifty men now, many with wives and families. The cold was bitter, but the appearance of the friar summoned a mood of festivity among them.

His name was Thomas of Jesmond, Adam soon learned, and he came regularly to visit Reynard's people, to preach and to take confessions. Adam was still sorely conscious of the weight of sin upon his soul. He had yet to atone for the death of Gaspard de Rancon back at Beeston, or for the duplicities he had been forced into since. But as he watched Brother Thomas moving between the huts of the village, pausing here and there to address groups of people, Adam remembered what the relic-pedlar at Nantwich had told him. It was the Franciscans who were spreading the story of Simon de Montfort's martyrdom, and his impending sainthood.

'Speak to him then,' Joane told him, as they whispered together in the hut doorway. 'Tell him . . .'

'It's not too much to risk?' Adam asked.

'Reynard knows who you are already – we can surely trust a holy friar to keep our secret.' She drew the ring from its hiding place in her girdle and pressed it into Adam's palm.

But as he approached the man, Adam shared none of Joane's confidence. Despite his cassock and the wooden cross he wore as a pendant, Thomas of Jesmond appeared little different to the brigands around him. He had a gnarled smile, a wiry beard grown into grey bristles, and spoke with a strong and almost alien accent from somewhere in the far north. For a while Adam watched him as he preached, hearing only the strange music of the man's voice as it rose and fell, singing of the wonders of Christ's power and glory.

'I wish to give confession and be absolved,' Adam told Reynard. He had never confessed to a wandering friar before. Some, he knew, did not hold that a mendicant's absolution carried the full force that a priest could deliver. But he was glad when Reynard gave his nod and gestured for him to approach the man.

A straggle of others were doing the same, each of them filing forward to kneel before the friar as he sat at the base of a dead tree and to mutter of their sins and lapses. Haukyn was among them, and John the Scot. Adam noticed Ivo of the North and John Silence leaning by the chapel wall, watching proceedings. Ivo had a look of weary contempt.

'Approach,' the friar said, and Adam saw that he was next in line. He walked forward, sensing the hush falling around him. Many, he knew, would be eager to try to overhear what he was about to confess. He knelt, smelling the mingled scents of filthy sheep's wool and ale dregs that lingered about the friar's clothing. Raising his hands he clasped his palms in prayer and leaned forward, until the friar's hooded head almost covered his own.

'*Benedicite, pater.*'

His breath steamed as he spoke, and he heard the rasp of the friar's breathing just above him as he went through the opening prayers and the declaration of faith. 'I have killed a man,' he said hurriedly, keeping his voice to a whisper. 'I have broken from prison, and killed a man who tried to stop me . . . I have lied about my identity . . .'

He paused a moment, then dared to lift his eyes. Thomas of Jesmond was gazing back at him, his eyes brightly intent. He nodded just slightly, urging Adam to continue. Adam had the uncanny sensation that he knew exactly what he was about to say.

'I was captured at Evesham, fighting for Lord Simon de Montfort,' he went on. 'That was why I was held a prisoner, and why I had to escape.'

He heard a low grunt from the friar. The nod of encouragement again.

'Now I am held captive here . . . the lady with me is the cousin of Margaret, Countess of Derby. The ring between my palms will prove her name. If you could take it to her . . .'

Another grunt, more definite this time. His eyes closed, Adam felt the rough calloused hands of the friar briefly enclosing his own.

'*Ego te absolvo*,' Brother Thomas said, signing the cross above Adam's head. 'Perform night vigil before the holy altar, at your next opportunity, and give thanks for your deliverance,' he said. When Adam opened his eyes he was sure he saw the friar's quick wink, but in the shadow of his hood it was hard to be sure. But when he opened his palms, Joane's ring was gone.

*

For the next three days the valley was eclipsed by snow. In the little village Reynard's robber band huddled in their huts, around their smoky hearths, and men went out in pairs into the whiteness to hunt rabbits, gather firewood and collect supplies from neighbouring settlements. How they got the supplies Adam never learned.

Joane had developed a mild fever and spent much of her time rolled up in her blankets and a mouldering sheepskin robe, shivering and trying to sleep. Two of the women from the camp attended her, while Adam sat at the door of their hut, gazing into the black and white of the valley. Several times he imagined making an escape from the village, he and Joane together stealing away under the cover of the snow. But in her current state of illness that would have been impossible. Besides, the outlaws might be snowbound, but they kept sharp-eyed men on watch around their camp.

On the fourth day the clouds cleared and the wintry sun shone. Ivo of the North and three others brought in a brace of deer they'd shot down with their arrows, and that night there was feasting and celebration. Joane and Adam sat in the hut door and watched the men dancing and capering around the fire. Haukyn and two of the camp women brought them wooden platters of meat smoking hot from the roasting spit, and mugs of fresh-brewed ale.

'This is good,' Joane said, almost gasping as she tore at the hot flesh with her teeth. She swigged ale. Her lips and chin shone with meat grease. 'By God, I'd forgotten how wonderful fresh food can taste!'

Adam nodded, eating too avidly to reply. He had eaten nothing but hard bread and winter barley porridge for what seemed like weeks. Even these scrags of poached venison, half burned and half raw, tasted like manna from heaven.

'I feel better already,' Joane said, and wiped her brow with her sleeve. She took another sip from her mug. 'Do you think the friar . . .' she began, dropping her voice.

'Best not speak of it,' Adam broke in quickly. He had noticed the figures approaching out of the smoky evening gloom. It was Haukyn again, with John the Scot and a couple of the younger men of the company. One of the women too, a girl who sat and stared wide-eyed at Joane, just as the men stared at Adam. There could be few among them, Adam guessed, who had not learned of his identity. Few who did not wonder about Joane's true name and status.

'What was it like?' Haukyn began, lifting his chin in an effort at proud insolence. 'At Evesham, when they killed the Earl of Leicester. What was it like?'

Adam took his time replying. He chewed, drank and swallowed. 'Have you seen a battle?' he asked.

Haukyn shook his head. He was probably only a year or two younger than Adam himself. 'Just a few fights, like the one in the valley, before the snow.'

Adam nodded. 'But you've seen the paintings in church, of the blood and flames of Purgatory?'

The young man nodded, and his throat gave a jerk.

'That was what it was like.'

'And did they cut him to pieces, truly?' one of the other young men asked, his breath steaming.

'Did they cut off his pizzle and feed it to King Henry's dogs, like they say?' the wide-eyed girl wanted to know.

Joane flinched with disgust, and one of the other men gruffly told the girl to be silent. 'But you saw it, you were there?' Haukyn went on, with fervent enthusiasm. 'Did the stormclouds cover the sun and the thunder roll, like the friars tell us, as they did when the Lord Christ Himself was slain?'

'They did,' Adam told them, and remembered well the sudden black wind and the thunder. He had not considered, at the time, that it was a message from heaven. Just for a moment, he allowed himself to think that the stories might be true.

Once the fire had burned down and the others had left them, Adam and Joane crept back into the dark fug of the hut. Joane took Adam's hand, unsteady in the dark. The two women who attended her were already asleep and snoring. 'Should you have told them those things?' she asked, drawing him close.

'Better that they know,' Adam replied. 'And it may help us, in time.'

Stepping over the sleeping women, they found Joane's mattress and Adam helped her to pull the blankets around herself. 'You feel better now?' he asked.

'I think so.' She took his hand again, her touch lingering, then she kissed him.

One of her sleeping attendants stirred and mumbled, and Adam drew back from Joane, then felt his way to his own mattress beside the door. Pulling the blankets around his ears he lay in the darkness, and a little later he heard Joane whisper something in her sleep. In the far distance, he could hear the wolves howling.

*

Two days later, the friar returned. Adam emerged from his hut at first light and saw the man walking up the narrow village track, wraithlike in his grey cassock. Thomas of Jesmond paused a moment, gave Adam a gnarled smile, then continued walking. Adam saw him enter the walled enclosure around Reynard's hut.

He did not see the friar again that day, but shortly after noon Adam and Joane were summoned to Reynard's presence. The brigand chief was waiting for them, one booted foot propped on a bench. Several of his senior men were with him, Ivo of the North and Jakke the Liar among them. In silence they waited for their leader to speak.

'Our friend, the good friar Thomas,' Reynard began, 'tells me that this lady here is kin to the Countess of Derby.' He gestured at Joane, and grunted from deep in his chest. 'How he came to know this, and how the countess came to discover it, I do not ask.

But she's sent him back here with a message. Release the captives unharmed and unmolested, she says, and she'll grant us forgiveness and clemency, and commend us to her son the earl.'

'Him? The *Devil of Derby*?' Ivo said with a sneer. Several others in the company muttered what sounded like objections. Reynard held up his hand for silence.

'The countess is known to me,' he said. 'And I trust her word. Many years I served her late husband, as huntsman. I know she is generous too, and the friar suggests that we may be rewarded for our mercy . . .'

'So we wait on rewards now, from the tables of the mighty?' Ivo broke in.

'We should tell this countess to show us her silver and gold, before we release her kin!' Jakke cried.

'God's teeth, quiet yourselves!' Reynard said, his face colouring. 'Have we not discussed this already? I like this no better than you, but we gain little by holding these captives, and could gain a lot by letting them go free.'

Joane broke her silence suddenly. 'I would speak well of you to my cousin, I promise you that,' she said, in a high clear voice. Several of the men glared at her, startled. 'I know you've suffered, some of you,' she went on, 'and known injustice . . .'

Her voice faltered as growls of dissent rose from some of the men. 'What do you know of us, or of injustice, *ma dame*?' Ivo sneered.

'I'll speak for you as well,' Adam broke in. 'And if I can meet with this Earl Robert de Ferrers, I'll make sure he rewards you.'

Reynard nodded brusquely. 'So,' he said, 'it's decided.' And he turned and swept his gaze across the faces of his followers, as if daring any of them to challenge him. Ivo of the North and Jakke the Liar met his eye for a moment, then both of them nodded, and it was done.

The following day at dawn, Haukyn and Earless Wynn and three others led the captives down the track into the valley and then up the river a mile or two. There were horses waiting,

Joane's jennet and packhorse among them, and in the packs were most of the clothes and possessions that had been taken at her capture. A couple of jewellery boxes and a pouch of coin had gone missing, but the Psalter was there in its silk wrapping, and that was all Joane cared to recover.

'Come,' said Haukyn, gruffly impatient with the importance of his mission. Once Joane and Adam were mounted – Adam on one of the horses captured in the fight in the valley – Wynn tied rags around their heads to cover their eyes. Then their captors led them forward on long reins, their mounts walking in file.

They rode a twisting route, up from the valley and over the hills. After a few hours, Haukyn allowed them to remove the blindfolds. They had ridden far from the camp by then, and were following a drover's trail across rolling country, brown and grey and featureless. Snow lay in patches on the heights, and smoke rose from the villages huddled in the dales. Anyone who saw them approaching was quick to flee and conceal themselves, and the trail and the surrounding landscape appeared empty of any life except the crows that cawed and cackled from the bare trees. By early afternoon they had reached a wider cart-road that led eastward towards wooded country.

'Keep on till you reach the crossroad,' Haukyn said, circling his horse back and waving for Adam and Joane to continue. 'Then take the righthand way, and you'll reach Duffield Castle by vespers.'

'Thank you,' Joane told him, turning in the saddle. Haukyn just nodded, his jaw tightening. He raised his spear in salute, gestured to the others to follow and turned to ride back the way they had come.

'Christ be praised!' Joane said under her breath, watching as their captors departed. She crossed herself. 'Christ and all his saints be forever praised!'

'Amen,' Adam said. Joy was vaulting through him now, and he could not hold back his delight. Joane caught his mood and laughed. A great shudder ran through her, as if she was releasing all the nervous terror and anxiety of the last sixteen days. She reached out and took Adam's hand, their breath steaming in the frigid air as the noise of their hilarity startled the birds from the trees.

'We need to keep moving,' Adam said as his laughter died. 'We don't want to be out on the roads after nightfall.'

Joane agreed, and they kicked their horses forward again in a rapid trot. A mile or two further they reached a crossing, where two rutted brown tracks intersected. A few huts and a smithy stood along the verge, and Adam confirmed that the righthand track would take them to Duffield. Another hour and they slowed to rest, then dismounted and walked the horses to the side of a stream in the shelter of a copse of trees.

There was a little food in one of the packs, dry barley cakes and a flask of water, just enough to hold off hunger and thirst.

'By God, how I long for spiced wine!' Joane said as she ate. 'And a soft bed, with feather mattresses! And a bath! A hot bath, with herbs floating on the surface, and somebody to rub my back . . .'

The image appeared in Adam's mind. Heat rose to his face and he quickly looked towards the stream, where the horses were drinking. He had given little thought to how either of them would be received when they reached the court of Countess Margaret de Ferrers. Little thought to how his relationship with Joane might develop, now they were free. And he had only a short while to consider it.

'I must ask a favour of you,' he announced, more stiffly than he had intended.

'Oh?' Joane replied. She gave a quick apprehensive flinch, as if she had expected this, and feared it.

'When we get to Duffield,' Adam began. 'I cannot act as your groom any longer. Not as a common servant, I mean. If you think it best that I conceal my identity then I will, but I cannot be other than a knight.'

'Yes,' Joane said, her brow creasing. 'Of course, that would be best.'

'I have no land, and no lord,' Adam went on, the conviction in his heart strengthening his words, 'I have no sword and no cause, and I am judged a traitor to my king. But, if it pleases you, I will pledge and bind myself to your service.'

Joane studied him as he spoke, tipping back her head. For one ghastly moment he thought she was about to laugh, and his voice dried in his mouth. But then he saw her blink, and the colour rise to her cheeks. 'I . . . don't know,' she began. 'I don't know how to take a pledge of homage, that is . . .'

Before she could say another word Adam dropped to one knee before her in the frosted grass. He raised his hands, palms clasped. 'You take my hands in yours,' he told her. 'If you wish it, that is.'

Hesitant, a nervous smile flickering, Joane enclosed Adam's hands in her own. He felt the heat of her palms, the subtle pressure.

'Hear this, my lady,' he said, firm and clear. 'I will bear faith to you of life and limb, and become your man, so help me God, and do you homage and bear faith to you of all folk.'

Similar words he had spoken, eighteen months and more past, to the king. Similar words he had spoken to Simon de Montfort and again, lying in his heart, to Lord Edward. But this time, he thought, he meant them entirely and truly.

'Stand,' she told him, and when he did so she kissed him to seal the pledge. There were tears in her eyes as he drew away. 'All this time you've stood by me,' she said, a slight waver in her voice. 'You could have left me and made your own escape but you did not . . .'

'I would not. And I never will.'

'Stop,' she said, holding up her hand. 'I do not know if I can promise anything,' she told him. 'But know that I mean this now. Know that I accept your faith, as God sees me . . .'

And as Adam heard her words he felt that acceptance bloom inside him. This was not just pretence, he realised. They were not just acting out a scene from a chivalric romance.

Abruptly Joane's voice cut off. The horses had ceased drinking and had turned their heads to look back towards the road, and now suddenly and very loud there came the thudding of hooves. Adam glanced across the meadow, and with a jolt of alarm saw the six riders kicking their horses into a gallop as they closed in around him and Joane. The leader's solid jaw jutted from his mail coif, and all had spears and lances raised. Adam reached for a sword that was not there.

'There's one of them!' the leader shouted, pointing his spear at Adam. 'Cut him down!'

'No, no!' Joane cried, running towards the mounted men. Adam stood his ground; the horsemen would be upon him in a heartbeat, and there was nowhere to run.

Then he saw the pennon on the leading rider's lance. Mottled red and gold *vair*. He heard the words that Joane was shouting to them. He raised his hands as the riders circled him with lances levelled, and fell to his knees.

*

The castle appeared as they crossed the ridge, in the last light of the day. The huge stone keep rose above the trees, with the curve of a river beyond. Then the road descended into woodland, and by the time they arrived before the outer gates dusk had fallen. The six riders kept their cordon around Adam and Joane, their lances high as they rode. The leader in the mail coif was John de Tarleton, a household knight of Countess Margaret de Ferrers. He had explained only that his mistress had sent them out to patrol the roads in search of the released captives, and that Joane at least was expected.

Adam had grown suddenly very weary over the final miles of the journey. This was safety, he told himself as they rode beneath the castle's timber gatehouse, and into the bailey beyond. After so long being a captive, so long in danger, this place was his first chance of security in many months. And yet he knew that he was still a fugitive, and harbouring him was as much a crime for a countess as for a cottager. He would have to tread carefully here, and remain on his guard.

Up the paved slope the horses rode in file, their hooves clinking off the cobbles. They passed over a drawbridge and beneath the arched stone gateway of the inner bailey. Steps descended from the keep's forebuilding, and waiting there in the light of torches was a group of finely dressed people. Adam recognised one of them: Joane's first cousin Elizabeth, the widow of Baron Marshal, who he had met at Hereford the year before. The older lady at the centre would be her mother, he guessed. Countess Margaret de Ferrers, the mother of Earl Robert of Derby.

'Cousin,' the countess said as Joane dismounted, in a clear and carrying voice. 'It really is you! I confess I was expecting some impostor to present herself before me. Although in your present guise you might have fooled me even so.'

Joane climbed the steps to greet her cousin, taking her hand and kissing it. Already the group of other women and chamber maids, guards and servants were retreating towards the warmth of the keep.

After securing the horses and passing them to a pair of grooms, Adam hurried to follow Joane and the others up the steps. John de Tarleton called something after him, but he ignored the man. He needed to present himself to Lady Margaret, or make sure he was there when Joane was ready to present him.

'You, wait,' de Tarleton called again, his voice leaden.

Adam reached the top of the steps and crossed the threshold into the arched entranceway of the forebuilding. He got a brief glimpse of firelight shining on stone, the backs of Lady Margaret, Joane and their party as they moved away along the passage, and then the heavy inner door swung closed before him.

Standing in the darkness, Adam felt the cold of the night at his back.

Chapter 8

Joane de Bohun rode from the woods on her spirited jennet, a peregrine falcon perched on her gloved hand. Behind
her came her cousin Elizabeth with her own bird, and then
Elizabeth's two younger unmarried sisters, and around them a
host of mounted grooms, bearers and falconers with dogs running beside them. Adam heard their laughter as the ladies rode
across the sward towards the postern gate. Behind them the
fringes of the woodland were still bare and brown, but in the
early spring sunlight the sward was speckled with primroses.

'A paradise for women, this place,' John de Tarleton said, pacing along the rampart walk to join Adam. He rolled each phrase
around his mouth and spat it out. 'Things'll change, mind, once
Earl Robert returns.'

'He'll be coming back soon?' Adam asked.

'Aye, soon enough,' de Tarleton replied. 'He'll spend Holy
Week and Easter with the king, at Windsor or Oxford. But after
Hocktide he'll ride north once more.'

'And what happens then?'

'What happens then,' de Tarleton said, 'is not for the likes of
us to know.'

Leaning from the rampart embrasure, Adam watched as Joane
and her friends rode up to the postern and across the lowered

drawbridge. Moments later he heard the ringing of hooves from the stable yard.

Six Sundays had come and gone since his first arrival at Duffield. Tomorrow was Palm Sunday, the beginning of Holy Week, and the castle and its inhabitants were alight with the promise of Easter and the end of the Lenten fast. John de Tarleton, of course, showed little sign of jollity. He was a dour and taciturn northerner, one of only a handful of knights among the garrison, but Adam had come to trust the man and even to like him.

John it had been who first attended to his needs when he came to the castle, providing him with two sets of rather worn but clean clothing in the de Ferrers livery of yellow and red, trimmed in black. A gambeson and hauberk too, and a simple sword and belt from the castle armoury. Now Adam at least resembled a fighting man, and de Tarleton and the other knights were content to treat him as one of their own. His name, he had told them, was Adam de Sutton, and he had been a household knight of Humphrey de Bohun until Evesham. Now he served Lady Joane, Sir Humphrey's widow. The duplicity chafed at his pride, but it was necessary, and none had sought to enquire any further.

Over the weeks since his arrival Adam had seen Joane frequently, but had seldom spoken to her. Countess Margaret insisted on a strict segregation among her household; noble ladies of her family were not to mingle with men at arms, or even knights. Adam slept on the floor of the hall with de Tarleton and the others, or in the chamber in the bailey, and spent his days riding at the quintain, sparring with sword and shield, and standing watch at the gates and ramparts. It was good to be once more training at the profession of arms, and Adam relished the slow return of his strength and skill, the steady rebuilding of his prowess. But to be sundered from Joane, after the days they had spent together, pained him more than he had expected.

As the weeks had passed and the first warmth of spring softened the air, Adam had plenty of opportunity to explore the surrounding country. Duffield Castle stood at the heart of a great swathe of woodland and heath. And all around were manors and estates held by tenants and vassals of the Earl of Derby. Adam had often heard of the de Ferrers family, and knew they were great magnates, but had never before realised the full extent of their holdings.

'At one time,' John de Tarleton had told him, 'the Ferrers lands stretched right across the north Midlands and over the moors to Lancaster on the west coast. Young Earl Robert held five castles too, until he fell out with the king and threw his strength behind Simon de Montfort. Not that turning rebel availed him much.'

Adam remembered the story Hugh of Oystermouth had told, about the earl's disputes with the leaders of both sides in the war, and his imprisonment in the Tower. The Devil of Derby had a talent for making enemies, it seemed.

'What sort of man is Earl Robert?' he asked.

De Tarleton sucked his cheek, frowning. 'Not one to accept slights with good grace, I'd say that. He's tried to build his own independent fiefdom hereabouts, but he's not wily enough at the game. Not yet anyway. The king's pardoned him for his treachery, but not restored his lands or castles. Earl Robert might have done better,' de Tarleton went on, cracking a rare smile, 'to have paid more heed to his mother's counsel!'

Lady Margaret de Ferrers, Adam had learned, was as formidable as her reputation suggested. Daughter and principal heiress of Joane's uncle, the late Earl of Winchester, she was now Dowager Countess of Derby and hereditary Constable of Scotland, and she wore her titles and prestige like mail armour. A statuesque, unsmiling lady of between forty and fifty, the countess was accompanied everywhere by her man of business, who was engaged in numerous lawsuits on her behalf concerning lands and property. Adam could well understand why Joane had been so eager to gain her protection and assistance.

Turning from the ramparts, he took a few steps down the stairway that descended to the castle bailey. The neighing and stamping of horses came from the stable yard, and a moment later the party of ladies and their servants appeared around the corner of the keep. Joane was still laughing, turning to say something to her cousin Elizabeth. The falconers strode behind them, carrying the hooded birds of prey. Joane looked, Adam thought, entirely at ease, heedless of all and any trouble in the land. She had always loved to ride freely and to hunt with birds, and life at Duffield was a liberation for her. She looked younger too, as if she had shrugged off the mantle of years that had settled over her since her marriage to Sir Humphrey. Perhaps even since her first meeting with Adam. Perhaps, he thought to himself, she had simply put all of it behind her.

He stood on the stairway and watched them pass. Only at the last moment did Joane glance back and notice him. For a heartbeat she held his sharpened gaze. Then she followed her friends into the keep.

*

There was feasting the following day. Holy Week had commenced, but the kitchens had a broad interpretation of the Lenten restriction on meat-eating: platters of roast goose sat alongside the huge eel pies, the crayfish in jelly, the herrings and mackerel rolls, and the grilled fish from the countess's own ponds. There was spiced almond porridge too, buttered eggs and pastries, and white loaves still warm from the oven, all of it served in the cavernous hall of the great keep to the music of vielles and flutes.

'Who's the guest?' Adam asked. He was seated halfway down one of the side tables, below the countess's almoner and chaplain, and the stewards and marshal of the household.

'Reginald de Grey,' replied de Tarleton as he chewed, inclining his head towards the man who sat at the high table on the dais.

'Constable of Nottingham Castle, and Keeper of the Peace in Nottinghamshire and Derbyshire. His late father held the post, until last month.'

Adam had seen the nobleman and his retinue arriving at the castle earlier that day, but had not recognised his banner of banded blue and white set with a red bar. De Grey was a lanky man of around thirty, who wore a black moustache and a sardonic smile. He and one of his men sat at the countess's right hand, while Joane and her cousin Elizabeth sat at her left. The wall above the dais was painted with heraldic shields bearing the red and gold arms of de Ferrers and de Quincy, linked by the family horseshoe badge. A haze of blue smoke hung above the hearth, lit by the sunlight through the high windows.

De Grey and those around him were drinking heavily of the countess's spiced wine, and as the dinner went on their voices rose. Leaning in the direction of the high table, Adam tried to pick out the words. Soon enough he did not have to make much of an effort. But then one phrase caught his ear, and his senses quickened into alarm.

'. . . escaped from the prison, and is now a fugitive!' de Grey declared. 'To be considered, of course, as a felon and king's enemy. You haven't seen anything of him here, I suppose?' he asked, with a clear note of insinuation.

'Why ever would we?' the countess replied. 'What did you say his name was?'

'Henry de Hastings,' de Grey replied.

Adam's breath rushed from him.

'Ah yes, I know of him, or of his father,' Countess Margaret said. 'His estates lie around Coventry, I think. Or are they in Norfolk? Far from here, in any case. Wasn't he supposed to be Thomas de Clare's prisoner?'

'He was, yes,' de Grey said. 'But he escaped from Beaudesert Castle, by subterfuge I believe.'

'One hears of all sorts of people escaping from prisons nowadays,' the countess said airily. 'Did not Simon de Montfort's son, the one who surrendered at Axholme, slip away to France recently?'

'I believe so, my lady,' de Grey replied, with a bow of his head. 'Certainly the king needs better jails, or better jailors. There have been far too many escapes, and too many traitorous and lawless men roaming the land, infecting others with their treason . . .'

Adam's heart was beating fast and heavy in his chest, and the heat of the fire was making his face burn and his body run with sweat. Staring down at the platter before him, he felt his guts churning. Fear, he thought, but anger too.

'But we do not speak of such matters here, you know,' Margaret said, in a peremptory tone. 'As you know, my son has been admitted to the king's grace and peace, and pardoned all those trespasses alleged against him. In the matter of the Earl of Leicester we remain neutral – but, as my son-in-law was slain at Evesham and his widow shares our board, I ask that you refrain from further opinions.'

'My lady,' de Grey said, bowing his head once more. But Adam caught the taint of scorn in his words, and the sly smile on his face.

'De Grey's been granted Wirksworth, and a fistful of Earl Robert's other manors besides,' John said, leaning to breathe his words hotly into Adam's ear. 'Lady Margaret hates him as she hates a leper, of course. Always amazes me that folk like that can sit and dine together.'

'But speaking of lawless men roaming the land,' de Grey continued, raising his voice, 'my informants tell me that you've lately been in communication with a gang of them. *Red Reynard*, their leader is called. As Keeper of the Peace in these shires, of course, I intend to ride against him and his band of robbers and malefactors soon enough.'

The countess sipped her wine, taking a moment to respond. 'I believe I know the person in question,' she said. 'He was once chief huntsman to my late husband, in fact. Not at all a disreputable man, and quite a resourceful one. If you do intend to oppose him, I would be cautious. And take a *very* large force of soldiers – foreigners, ideally, who have not yet learned to fear our dales and the men who inhabit them.'

'I also hear from my informants,' de Grey said, ignoring the countess's comment, 'that you recently made a sort of pact with this outlaw, Reynard, after negotiating for the release of certain captives?'

The hall had fallen silent now, everyone fixated on the conversation at the high table. Countess Margaret glared back at de Grey.

'Perhaps, indeed,' de Grey went on, smiling, 'the beautiful young lady beside you there was one of them?'

Joane sat stiff and unblinking in her high-backed chair, her face white. Even the musicians had ceased their playing, and the only sounds were the crack and hiss of wood burning in the hearth, and the shuffling steps of the squires as they collected the empty bowls and spoons.

'My cousin Hawise de Quincy has certainly never been a captive,' Countess Margaret said, feigning a casual tone. 'And I would suggest that your spies are telling you fables. I suggest you punish them for their impudence.'

Joane flinched slightly at the words. She and her cousin had agreed to continue the subterfuge of her identity, until the matter of her inheritance could be addressed. But Reginald de Grey was grinning, tapping his fingers on the table.

'Your cousin Hawise de Quincy,' he said, almost speaking over his hostess, 'is currently at Donington Castle, as a ward of the Countess of Lincoln. I happen to know this, as I passed through that place not a week ago and saw her there.'

Margaret de Ferrers inhaled sharply, her lips pressed into a hard line.

'So *this* lovely lady,' de Grey said, opening his palm towards Joane, 'must be a different cousin altogether, I suspect. And no doubt in need of a man's protection . . .'

Adam felt de Tarleton's hand on his shoulder, clamping him to his seat. He had been about to stand up, already calculating the number of strides to the dais, and whether he could reach it before anyone stopped him. Whether he could draw his sword and slam it through the smirking de Grey's throat before the man said another word.

'You forget yourself, Sir Reginald,' the countess declared. 'And when my son returns he will hear of your base incivility in my hall.'

'Ah yes, your son,' de Grey said. He drew the napkin from his shoulder and tossed it on the table. 'Speaking, as we were, of prisoners . . . Let's hope he manages to get back here without being arrested and thrown in the Tower once again, eh?'

He stood up suddenly, shunting his chair back behind him. Wavering for a moment on his feet, he picked up his goblet and drained the last of his wine. 'I've claimed your hospitality long enough, my lady,' he said to Margaret. 'And it's a long road back to Nottingham. Call for my horses!' he shouted down the hall.

'Peace, lad. Calmly now,' John said quietly, keeping his grip on Adam's shoulder.

De Grey and his knight left the table and stepped down from the dais, Countess Margaret glaring at him in speechless fury. But before he turned to leave de Grey took a few steps along the dais until he stood facing Joane. Reaching out quickly he snatched her hand, dragging it towards him and kissing her whitened knuckles.

'I know well who you are, lady,' he announced as he released her. 'And I know what you *need*. It is not good for a young widow to remain long unwed . . .'

'Enough!' Adam cried, forcing himself to his feet against de Tarleton's steadying grip. He vaulted across the table and stood beside the hearth, his hand on the hilt of his sword. His heart was thundering, his body primed for violence.

'Oh, a champion!' de Grey said with a smirk. His own knight, a beefy square-jawed man, had manoeuvred himself between him and Adam.

'Stand away!' Countess Margaret cried as she got to her feet. Her voice rang in the silent hall. 'All of you – I have seen and heard too much of this!'

De Grey, his smile not slackening, turned to her and bowed. Then, screened by his protecting knight, he circled the hearth on the far side to Adam and strode towards the door.

Adam watched him go, barely conscious of anything else around him. When he looked back towards the dais Countess Margaret was already pacing towards her private chambers. Joane and the other ladies hurried in her wake.

John de Tarleton appeared behind Adam. 'You heard her,' he said, in a rough low tone. 'Bread and water for you for the next week, I suspect. But there's not a man here would fault you.'

*

'I couldn't thank you before, for rising to my aid,' Joane said hurriedly, when they met on the stairs. It was the following day, and Adam had been summoned to Countess Margaret's private chambers. 'I was so embarrassed . . . the way that man looked at me made me feel sick. Like he was stripping me naked, in front of everyone . . . I'm sorry you were punished for it.'

'It's nothing,' Adam said quickly, taking her hand. 'At least, no worse than we knew when we were Reynard's captives!' He grinned, and Joane gave him a bleak smile in return. But she drew her hand away and stepped back from him, leaving the turn of the stairway open for him to pass. 'My cousin's waiting for you,' she said, and he noticed that she was unable to meet his eye.

Perplexed, he left her and climbed the stairway to the door of the countess's quarters. A valet opened the door and ushered him into the long, high-ceilinged chamber beyond. Adam's glance took in the costly furnishings, the panelled and painted furniture and embroidered upholstery, the great canopied bed on its curtained dais at the very far end. Embrasures to one side let in light through tall arched windows. Countess Margaret was standing before the middle one, the pale wash of sunlight casting her features into profile. As Adam appeared she turned and gestured for him to approach.

'Your actions yesterday were foolish,' she said, before he had even made his bow. 'De Grey was already leaving – what did you hope to achieve?'

Adam held her gaze. She was dressed in red and gold, with a white silk barbette drawn tight around her throat and beneath her chin. 'I acted by instinct, my lady,' he said. 'I thought nothing of the consequences.'

'You certainly did not,' Margaret said, but she appeared mildly pleased with his candour. Several of her chamber ladies sat nearby, deeply engaged in their sewing, and boys in scarlet tunics stood against the wall opposite the windows. She gestured to one of them, who brought her a goblet of wine. She did not offer Adam any refreshment.

'My cousin Joane has told me a little about you,' she said, turning back to the window. 'About your true identity, that is. She tells me that you held land of the king, a manor or two, and lost it all when you were captured at Evesham. You escaped from Beeston Castle, presumably intending to join the rebels at Axholme.'

'That was my hope, lady. But I was too late.'

'Yes, well,' the countess said, narrowing her eyes. 'We may have a good use here, soon enough, for daring young men quick to leap to violence, who think little of consequences. If you wish to fight for your inheritance, you'll need allies. My son too has been robbed of his lands, you know – of Tutbury and Chartley castles, and the Honour of the Peak . . . Unless the king makes adequate restitution, Robert will return here and set about reclaiming them by force of arms.'

'My lady,' Adam replied, 'how would he do so? To make war on the king he would need an army, but he has only a handful of knights here—'

'My son can gather an army, have no fear!' the countess broke in, raising her voice. 'He need only raise his banner and sound his trumpets, and the Ferrers men will come flocking from every dale and hill, with horses and arms, eager to give him good service!'

She pursed her lips, eyes gleaming. Adam glanced at the seated ladies, still plying their needles. None appeared to be paying any attention to the conversation.

'And there are others too who may be of use,' the countess went on. 'That brigand Reynard and his company, for example. Joane has spoken in their favour, and I've heard that you recommend them as well. Men like that could prove very effective, given the right incentives. Which is one of the reasons I was so very gracious in my dealings with Reynard over your release.'

Adam sensed there was another matter that the countess wanted to discuss, something that might affect him directly, but did not want to prompt her. It came soon enough.

'My cousin, Joane,' the countess said, her tone shifting abruptly. 'She cares for you, you know, and she's very grateful to you for remaining at her side during your travails. However, there is something you do not know about her.'

'My lady?' Adam asked, his voice thickening in his mouth.

'As she is the widow of a baron, a great magnate,' Margaret explained, 'Joane's remarriage is in the king's gift. Do you know what that means?'

Adam shook his head. He felt his heart beating heavily.

'It means that she cannot wed again without the king's permission and licence. In her case, however, the king has transferred the gift to her former father-in-law, the Earl of Hereford. At present my man of business is engaged in complex negotiations regarding the return of Lady Joane's inherited estates. These negotiations would be adversely affected by rumours of an unlicensed connection with a landless and penniless fugitive knight. Do you understand?'

Adam said nothing. His throat was clenched tight.

'My cousin Joane is *not for you*,' the countess said with emphasis. 'And you would do well to remember that, and avoid any further chivalrous notions. Once my son arrives we will have use for you, and can help you in return. Until then . . .'

She paused, then made a gesture of dismissal. Adam remained standing for a few long heartbeats, until she glanced sharply back at him again. Then he bowed his head stiffly, turned, and paced to the door.

He had clattered back down the stairs and was striding along the passageway when he noticed Joane waiting in the alcove of a slit window. He paused, glaring at her with his face burning.

'You should have told me,' he said.

'I thought you might desert me if I did,' Joane replied.

Adam held a breath, feeling the bitter yell trapped inside him. The countess's words turned in his mind. *Not for you.*

'You might have been right,' he said.

He took a step towards her and she shrank back into the alcove. As if she feared him, and thought he would strike her. As if, Adam thought, he were no better a man than Reginald de Grey. He stretched out his hand, gulped a breath.

Then he turned on his heel and stalked away from her, through the doors of the keep and down the steps without looking back.

He should keep walking, he told himself. Out of the main gates, and out of the castle altogether, never to return.

But he knew, as the flame of his anger burned down to embers, that he had nowhere else to go.

Chapter 9

Robert de Ferrers, Earl of Derby, returned to Duffield Castle as the first green leaves appeared on the trees, and he came with a cavalcade. His harbingers and outriders had been sent ahead to warn of his arrival, and by the time the horses of his retinue were sighted from the walls the road leading to the castle gate was lined with cheering tenants and servants, and the walls were decked with flags.

Countess Margaret was waiting beneath the stone arch of the inner gatehouse, a ring of iron keys in her hand, ready to pass the keeping of the castle to her son. Joane and Lady Elizabeth stood behind her, with Adam and the knights of the household far to the rear. Adam had a good view all the same, as the young earl's mounted retinue swept across the outer bailey and clattered up the slope to the gate.

De Ferrers rode under his banners of mottled red and gold *vair*. Mailed knights went before him, and flanked him on either side. They parted as they reached the gateway and formed a lane, pennoned lances raised, for Earl Robert to ride up and greet his mother.

'About time,' Countess Margaret declared, handing the keys to him.

Two men ran to help the earl from his horse. Robert de Ferrers dismounted with an audible groan, then walked through the gateway into the sunlight. The Devil of Derby was in his mid-twenties, and at first glance he made an unimpressive figure. He was short and very fleshy, almost fat, and his sallow face wore a peevish expression. He walked with a rolling bow-legged gait.

'Christ's wounds, I need a bath and a change of clothes,' de Ferrers cried. 'I swear that saddle's almost rubbed another hole in my arse!'

'*That would take some doing*,' John de Tarleton muttered from the side of his mouth. Adam stifled a laugh. Then he saw the two riders who had walked their horses in through the gates after Earl Robert.

One was a handsome, muscular man with a round head and dark hair, a few years older than the earl. The other was Henry de Hastings.

'De Norton!' de Hastings called, as he caught sight of Adam. 'Is that really you?'

'*Norton?*' de Tarleton grunted, his mouth twisting.

Sir Henry had already swung down from the saddle and was crossing the yard, grinning as if Adam were some long-sundered friend or relative. At the last moment he appeared to notice Adam's threadbare clothing and cheap sword, and collected himself. Instead of an embrace he clapped Adam on the shoulders.

'I heard you'd slipped away from Beeston!' he said. 'Is it true you killed that bastard de Rancon?'

'Not intentionally,' Adam said. John was staring at him with a deep frown.

'Well done,' de Hastings said briskly, thumping Adam's shoulder again. 'I'll have to tell you the tale of my own escape some time! Now that's a . . .' He broke off, distracted, and abruptly strode away to greet somebody else.

By now the cobbled courtyard was thronging with men and horses, more of them pressing in through the gates. Voices of men and the stamping of hooves, the jingle of bridles and the creak of leather filled the air. Robert de Ferrers and his mother were already climbing the steps of the keep.

Suddenly Adam heard a woman's cry, and glanced around sharply to see Joane running through the crowd. Darting between the standing horses and the armoured men, she reached the gateway. Another young woman had appeared there, riding in on a slim palfrey. Joane ran to her side and greeted her.

By the time Adam reached them, he had recognised the woman on the horse. He had not seen her since Joane's wedding to Sir Humphrey, eighteen months and more ago. This, though, was the real Hawise de Quincy, Joane's sister.

'Oh, it's you,' Hawise said simply, as Adam bowed before them both. 'I remember you.'

She must be sixteen or seventeen now, Adam estimated, and glowing with youth. Not only that; he saw the light flash in her eyes, and turned to see the round-headed nobleman who had accompanied Earl Robert smiling back at her.

'Have you met Lord Baldwin?' Hawise was asking her sister, as a groom helped her down from the saddle. Her bright auburn hair hung in braids from beneath her fillet. 'He took me from Donington and carried me away with him!'

For a moment Adam stood alone in the swirl of the crowd, feeling strangely bereft. He had become used to the relative calm and peace of Duffield. Even come to regard it as a sort of home. Now it was full of other men, and all the noise and fury of the world had come rushing back.

'*Preudhommes!*' Earl Robert shouted, standing on the steps above the yard with legs braced, fists on hips. 'Twenty days ago I left London, and every night since then I have passed in one of my own manors. And I have met with nothing but loyalty and good service!' He sounded slightly out of breath, his voice straining for volume.

'Many of those vassals and retainers who accommodated me on my journey have followed me here to Duffield,' he went on, jutting a stubby arm to indicate the extent of the crowd before him. 'With me too I have brought my good friends Baldwin Wake, Lord of Bourne,' he indicated the round-headed man, 'and Lord Henry de Hastings.'

De Hastings gave a bow, while Wake merely nodded.

'I have spoken with the king at Westminster,' the earl went on, prancing on his toes, 'and with Lord Edward, and I have not been satisfied by their assurances!'

A low growl came from the crowd. 'The king has seen fit to pardon what he calls my *trespasses*,' de Ferrers cried, 'in return for my homage and many a rich gift . . . But still he insists on keeping from me the honours and castles that are mine! Just as they have refused to return the lands and estates of Lord Baldwin and Lord Henry here, and many more besides. But the days of cringing and hiding are done! Soon,' he said, his voice rising to a cracked yell, 'we will see justice restored to this realm of England!'

Cheers from the crowd. Stamping feet, and the clash of lance butts against cobbles. Two steps above the earl, his mother Countess Margaret stood with her hands clasped before her. A slight, chilly smile crossed her face, but she said nothing.

*

By late April the woods of Duffield Frith were in fresh green leaf. White blossom covered the apple orchards, and bluebells grew beneath the trees. As the common people dragged harrows over their new-sown fields, Earl Robert de Ferrers announced a round-table joust for his friends and retainers, to be held in a broad clearing a few miles from the castle, on the feast day of St George.

The knights and their servants assembled the afternoon before, raising their tents and pavilions around the margins of the clearing. Banners streamed, and pennons flew from every lance.

Yellow and red were the livery colours of de Ferrers, Wake and de Hastings alike, but there were a host of other heraldic tinctures and blazons, many of them bearing the horseshoe emblem of Earl Robert's affinity. Just as the countess had said, the Ferrers men had answered the call.

For the first time since his escape from Beeston, Adam felt within him the stirrings of a new sense of vigour and purpose. It was not just the dappled sunlight and the fresh grass, the promise of coming summer. Nor the scenes of armoured men and horses, tents and banners that evoked the world of the tournaments he had known when he served Robert de Dunstanville. The joy he felt reborn within him came from the feeling, lost all these months, that at last he was in the right place. He was using his own name once more – John de Tarleton and the others had easily pardoned the deception. And now at last he might have a chance to seize back control of his fate. For beneath the festivity that surrounded him, there was a mood of steely purpose. This was an army, summoned for war.

But even as he considered that, a chill passed over him, and his joy faded as if a cloud had covered the sun. He remembered the vast array of royal forces at Evesham, and for a moment he saw again that scene of terrible slaughter. Few of the men here would have witnessed anything like it. Would they even know what they faced?

'There'll be more of them, in time,' de Tarleton told him, responding to Adam's expression of dismay. 'Most can raise additional men from their estates. Then there are the masterless men in the dales. And John D'Eyville up in the north – you know of him?'

Adam shook his head. On the far side of the clearing the servants were piling logs over smoking charcoal, and musicians were beginning to play. Already the succulent smell of roasting meat was rising on the smoke of the cooking fires.

'D'Eyville's not a man I would serve,' John went on, 'but he leads a strong affinity in Yorkshire. He was one of those who held out at Axholme, along with Lord Wake.'

He nodded towards a nearby group of men, where Baldwin Wake stood beside his horse, talking with Henry de Hastings. The two barons had been living at an isolated manor in the Frith these last weeks, rather than at Duffield. Wake in particular, Adam had noticed, was a vigorous fighter and a superb horseman. He had held a barony in Cumberland, and rich lands in Lincolnshire, but unlike de Ferrers he did not flaunt his prestige. Captured first at Northampton and then at Kenilworth, Wake had escaped imprisonment twice, only to yield to Lord Edward's terms at Axholme. Clearly he was not a man to concede defeat lightly.

A trumpet sounded from across the grassy sward, and at once the banners and pennons swirled into motion. Knights mounted their horses, squires and grooms passing them their helmets and lances; the trials were about to commence.

Adam set his foot in the stirrup and swung himself up into the saddle. His horse was still the serjeant's cob that Reynard had given him when he left the outlaw camp. A decent enough mount for general riding and training, but it lacked the dense muscle and hot blood that gave the true destrier its formidable agility in the melee, and thunderbolt speed at the charge. Nevertheless, mounted on his second-rate horse and wearing second-rate borrowed armour, attended only by a groom of Earl Robert's household, Adam was determined to do the best he could. Many of the knights gathered for the jousting were strangers to each other; during these initial trials they would show off their paces, riding at the quintain so all could judge their prowess and ability, and choose those whom they would challenge on the following day.

Already the first riders were spurring their mounts along the course. Over the smooth grass of the clearing they broke into a flat gallop, lances dropping as they rode. One by one they slammed their lance-points against the shield-shaped target on the quintain, then tried to dodge the swinging counterweight as it whipped around behind them. Most were successful; some were not.

'Ah!' John de Tarleton cried, then hissed through his teeth. Other men just laughed. One of Earl Robert's vassal knights had slowed at the moment of impact and been struck on the back of the head by the counterweight, which slammed him forward out of the saddle and over the mane of his stumbling horse.

With the next contender, the laughter turned to cries of acclaim. At the first touch of the spurs, Baldwin Wake's champing black destrier launched itself forward into the charge. Red streamers trailed from Lord Baldwin's saddle and helmet as he careered down the course, his lance raised. At the last moment he brought the weapon down, striking the target so hard and clean that the wooden shield was blasted into splinters. Cheering burst from the spectators as he left the quintain's counterweight whirling behind him.

'It's a bold one who'll challenge him on the morrow,' John said.

'Or a rich one,' Adam replied, 'who doesn't mind losing his horse and armour.'

One of the heralds came running over, gesturing with his white baton, and Adam hefted his lance and rode down to the far end of the course. Carpenters were busy fixing a new target to the quintain, slapping grease over the pivot, and making sure it turned swift and true. All along the course and around the far end men watched and waited. Adam could see some of them laying wagers.

He was hot in his armour. His horse was restive, pulling at the bit and pawing the turf. Another man rode up the course ahead of him, veering wide of the quintain and only just clipping the target. Groans and jeers from the spectators. Then the herald was before him again, raising his staff and letting it fall. Adam spurred his horse up to the start of the course, reined it in, then at the trumpet note urged it forward into a trot.

Down the course he let the cob gather pace steadily, keeping the reins short. With a horse like this, he knew he had to
conserve every bit of speed and power until exactly the right
moment. The lance juddered in his grip, but he held the shaft
angled upwards, his elbow raised. Hooves drummed the turf
below him, and the ranks of watching men flashed past on either
side. Then the quintain was before him, the wooden target looking suddenly very small.

A long breath, then Adam exhaled quickly and brought the
lance down. *Aim for a point a horse's length behind the target* . . . At
the same moment he let out the reins and dug savagely with his
spurs. The horse bolted forward, stretching its neck as it kicked
up the turf. Adam barely felt the lance strike. He was up at the
end of the course before the quintain finished swinging.

Cheers all around him. He slowed his mount and brought it
around in a tight circle, then passed his lance to his groom. The
acclaim was like wine to him, and he was grinning as he drank
it down.

'You rode like a champion today!' Henry de Hastings declared
that evening, slapping a heavy palm onto Adam's shoulder. Adam
had ridden twice more that afternoon, and on his second pass his
lance had smashed the wooden shield to shards, just as Baldwin
Wake had done earlier. 'Wouldn't you say, Baldwin?' de Hastings
went on. 'De Norton here showed us the true school of war, the
tournament style, eh?'

Lord Baldwin just raised an eyebrow and inclined his head.
They were sitting together on long trestle tables and benches
beneath the trees, close to the cooking fires where the venison
smoked and spat. Above the treetops the moon was full and fat
as a cheese in the dark blue sky, hazed by the rising smoke. All
along the tables sat knights and men at arms, boisterous as they
chewed on meat and tipped back wine, their voices and laughter
almost drowning out the scraping of the vielles and the hooting
of the shawms.

'But you should see him on the field of battle!' de Hast-
ings said, still clasping Adam's shoulder in a clamping grip.
'At Lewes he fought bravely, and at the taking of Rochester.
Together we held the burning bridge at Newport – what a
night that was! – and at Evesham we fought at the side of Lord
Simon himself!'

'Your friend is quite the paladin, Sir Henry,' Wake said, smiling. He raised his cup of wine in salute to Adam. 'You did well.
Even on that serjeant's stot you were riding today.'

Adam tried to accept the praise, and not let his discomfort
show. De Hastings had summoned him to sit beside him at the
table, and seemed intent on holding him up as a great war-
rior and comrade at arms. Already he had told the company of
Adam's flight from Beeston – almost as daring, he claimed, as his
own escape from prison. It felt, Adam thought, as if he were Sir
Henry's trophy, taken in battle, to be shown off with pride. Or
perhaps de Hastings was just praising him as a way of goading the
others at the table?

For all the supposed unity among those gathered at Duffield,
Adam knew there were strong rivalries and feuds between
them. In particular, between those like de Hastings and
Baldwin Wake who had fought for de Montfort, and the affinity
of Robert de Ferrers, who had followed his more independent course. Earl Robert might call himself lord here, but not
everyone was willing to accord him the mastery. Taking another
slice of venison, Adam dipped his head as he ate.

'This is not the place to speak of Simon de Montfort,' another
voice broke in, from along the table. 'Who, we should remember, tricked Earl Robert, and then seized him and imprisoned
him unjustly!'

The speaker, Adam noticed, was the knight who had been
knocked from his horse by the swinging quintain earlier that day.
He was a couple of years older than Adam, dressed in fine wool
with a jewelled brooch at his shoulder.

'I'll speak of him if I choose,' Henry de Hastings said, his voice thick with wine. 'A great man! A hero of England, by Christ – who died fighting for the liberties of us all. Even for the likes of you, de Grendon!'

'If your Lord Simon was so beloved of God,' the knight said, sounding equally lit by drink, 'how was it that he was defeated at Evesham? How was it that he was killed, and his body chopped to bits?'

A few of his companions growled their agreement.

'Lord Simon was defeated by Edward, the king's son,' Adam said abruptly, his annoyance with Sir Henry finding a fresh target, 'and by Roger Mortimer and the Earl of Gloucester. You were defeated by a quintain!'

A moment of startled silence followed, and then roars of laughter from along the table. Henry de Hastings slapped the board with delight, and Baldwin Wake's broad face creased with hilarity. The knight, Ralph de Grendon, was pale with fury as he glared back at Adam. After what had happened earlier that day, this new humiliation was too much to endure.

'My horse stumbled!' he declared, then as the laughter doubled he stood up suddenly and stabbed a finger at Adam. 'You insult me!' he said. 'You insult me in public, and I challenge you to single combat on the morrow!'

Henry de Hastings let out a cry of pleasure. 'Single combat!' he said with relish. Had he desired this all along? 'A challenge – good! What do you think, Baldwin, shall we lay odds?'

Lord Wake pondered, stroking his smooth cleft chin. 'He'll need a better horse, if the fight is to be fair,' he said.

'Then give him one,' de Hastings said, 'and I shall arm our champion.'

Ralph de Grendon was already complaining that this was unfair; one of his friends reminded him that he had challenged a man, not his horse or equipment.

'Be careful tomorrow,' Henry de Hastings said to Adam, dropping his voice as he leaned closer. 'De Grendon's been foolish, but now his honour's at stake. He'll be sure to fight like the devil.'

He picked up the wine jug and refilled Adam's cup. As he did so, Adam noticed the heavy ring he wore on his right hand. The golden swan caught the light from the roasting fires.

'You like it?' de Hastings said, noticing Adam's glance. He put down the jug and turned his hand so Adam could see the ring clearly. 'Sir Humphrey gave it to me, when he was on his deathbed,' he said. 'He intended that I pass it to his father, but I thought I would keep it for a time. Apparently,' he went on, gazing at the ring as he flexed his fingers, 'the de Bohuns claim to be descended from Godfrey de Bouillon, who in turn was descended from the Swan Knight of ancient legend. This was his ring originally, so they say. I don't know about that myself, though they certainly prize such things highly, as a matter of family honour.'

Adam recalled what Earl Humphrey had said after the funeral mass, his offer of aid if the ring were returned to him. Joane had suggested the same, at Dieulacres. It might be worth a lot to Adam too, he realised. But he was perplexed; he did not recall de Hastings having visited Sir Humphrey's chamber while they were at Beeston. Perhaps he had crept in there in the dying man's final days? Perhaps, indeed, he had simply stolen the ring while Humphrey lay insensible?

'Oh, but you think he should have entrusted it to you instead, is that it?' Henry said. His voice had dropped further, and taken on a cruel edge. 'You really think that he, an earl's son, would have placed his trust in a man of your degree?'

Adam felt the heat rush to his face, the sense of affront mingling with an odd sensation of shame. Yes, he realised, he had thought exactly that.

'Here,' de Hastings said, grabbing at the ring and twisting it on his finger, 'I'll give it to you . . .'

For a heartbeat Adam thought he was sincere. Then de Hastings grinned again. 'Or perhaps I will not, just yet,' he said. He closed his hand into a fist, and kissed the golden swan. 'Perhaps I'll wait,' he said, 'to see what service you can offer me in return!'

*

Before sunrise Adam was up and preparing himself for the day ahead. He had slept badly, in the little tent he shared with John de Tarleton and two other knights and their squires. But the morning freshness restored his spirits. Dew lay on the grass and the trees all around were filled with birdsong even as the grooms exercised the horses and servants gathered fodder and water, and the first smoke of their fires rose to the glowing blue sky.

At first he thought the horse was intended for somebody else. It was a fine stallion of the palest grey with dark legs and mane, its hide brushed to a silvery sheen and the veins standing out proud on its neck. It was named Blanchart, so the youth leading it explained, and was sent by Lord Baldwin Wake.

'And who are you?' Adam asked.

'Gerard de Bracebridge, sir,' the youth replied. He was around fourteen or fifteen, but his long neck and wide eyes gave him a boyish look. 'My father is a tenant of Henry de Hastings,' he went on, 'who says I am to act as your squire. He sends this as well.'

The packhorse behind him was loaded with armour in oxhide wrappings. A full mail hauberk with coif and gloves, and leg chausses. A new shield too, with a blank leather face.

'Is it true that you were knighted by Lord Simon de Montfort himself?' the squire asked, as Adam looked over the horse and armour.

'I was,' Adam replied, without sparing him a glance. He had known a squire named Gerard once before, he remembered.

Long ago, at Pleshey Castle. He had been the death of him as
well, as surely as if he had laid the killing blow himself. He felt a
dull stir of apprehension in his chest.

'Then it's a great honour to serve you, sir,' Gerard said,
blushing slightly. 'I only hope that I too can prove as worthy,
when the time comes for valour—'

'Yes, of course,' Adam said curtly, cutting him off, then
gestured to the squire to help him dress.

Once Adam was clad in the new mail hauberk, John and the
other knights watched with taciturn approval as the squire fastened the sword belt over the armour, and Adam mounted the
saddle of the grey destrier. The animal stirred beneath him, and
Adam felt the power of its flowing muscle. He could not hide his
pleasure.

'Now you look ready to take on de Grendon,' John said with
a terse nod.

First Adam needed to exercise the horse, and get the measure
of his new charger. For the next hour he rode, out along the
woodland paths and onto the broad pastures nearer the castle. It
was a joy to be back in the saddle of a trained warhorse, carrying
the weight of armour on his back and a shield on his arm, and
his spirits soared as he urged Blanchart into a gallop over the
close-cropped grass. The stallion was brisk at first, nervous at his
touch, but soon came to understand him and respond instantly
to his command.

By the time Adam returned to the clearing where the jousts
would be held, the carpenters were erecting a tall wooden viewing stand with a canopy raised above it. A line of ponies stood
in the shade of the trees nearby, and a covered litter. Adam saw
the flash of fine fabric, and heard the voices of women. Countess
Margaret and her ladies had arrived to view the day's sport. As
he walked his sweating horse across the clearing, Adam turned
in the saddle and scanned the gathering for a glimpse of Joane.
But he did not see her.

Another woman was waiting for him when he returned to his camp.

'Lady Hawise,' he said as he dismounted. Joane's sister gave him a cool smile. Surrounded by stamping horses and grimy, unkempt serving men she appeared immaculate.

'I have something for you,' she said, turning to one of the maids that accompanied her and taking a folded square of green silk. She offered it to Adam on spread palms. 'I did the claws and tongue in red, as I had thread left over,' she explained.

Adam took the silk and let it unravel between his hands. It was a lance pennon with three long streaming points, sewn with his heraldic arms of a golden lion rampant on a green field. The beast looked fierce and lively, capering in the air with its bloody tongue snaking from its jaws. 'Thank you!' he said at last, almost too moved to react.

'I did one for Lord Baldwin too,' Hawise said. 'But his was quite simple.'

Adam smiled back at her. True enough, Baldwin Wake's arms of two red bars and three red roundels on yellow would have given Hawise's needle little play. 'I thank you from my heart,' he said with a bow, and passed the pennon to his new squire to attach to the head of his lance.

'My sister should have come to wish you good fortune,' Hawise told him, 'but she's too stubborn. So I wish it on her behalf.'

Speechless again, Adam could only bow again in acknowledgement. But Hawise had already turned away, and was returning across the sward to the raised wooden platform, her maids following behind her. From the far end of the clearing the trumpets were blaring once more, startling the birds from the surrounding woodland. The sun was above the treetops, and the day's combat was about to commence.

Chapter 10

Other challenges, other champions, came and went, and it was nearing midday by the time Adam faced Sir Ralph de Grendon.

His grey stallion was primed and hot-blooded as he rode up to the canopied viewing platform. Robert de Ferrers sat on the high seat, with Countess Margaret and her ladies flanking him, beneath the red and gold drapery and the hanging horseshoe badges. The Earl of Derby was not riding that day; he was troubled by the same gout that had afflicted his father, so John had explained. But he stood and hobbled to the railing at the front of the stand as Adam approached, raising his palm.

'The first to unhorse his opponent shall be victor,' the earl said, 'and honour satisfied. We want no death or maiming this day – marshals, see that both combatants respect my ruling.'

Joane de Bohun sat with her sister in the shade of the canopy. Now that her identity was no secret she had resumed the dress of a widow, but the severe charcoal grey and black only accentuated her stark beauty. She too stood and approached the railing – Adam saw Countess Margaret's disapproving glance. Without a word, Joane drew a blue silk scarf from inside her sleeve and passed it to one of the attending boys. Adam knew that Joane hated the joust, and feared tournaments in general – her father,

Robert de Quincy, had been killed in one when she and Hawise were children. Knowing that, her favour meant all the more to him. He took the scarf from the boy, looped it, and tied it around his upper arm, knotting it tight over his mail.

The trumpet sounded, and Adam turned his horse and rode back into the sunlight, over the scarred and muddied stretch of open ground where the combat would take place. Somewhere a drum rolled and pulsed.

Ralph de Grendon was already waiting for him. His white shield bore two scarlet chevrons, and his warhorse was decked in a red and white caparison. Adam might have hoped that his adversary would be drawn and ill after a night's drinking, or unnerved by his humiliating performance of the day before. But de Grendon on the field of combat looked every inch the capable knight, goading his horse with his gilded spurs to keep it fiery, his squire standing by with a painted lance in each hand. A sword was at his side, and a heavy iron mace hung from his saddle. Inside the steel oval of his mail coif, his face was bunched into a furious scowl.

Adam moved up to the far end of the course, Blanchart champing and restive beneath him. His squire came up beside him and gave a last tightening tug to the buckles of the stallion's girth straps. Then he handed Adam his shield, and the lance with Hawise's green and gold pennon secured beneath the tip.

One of the marshals paced across the open course, his baton raised. The drumming ceased. In the shade of the trees, around the sunlit margins of the field and beneath the canopied viewing stand, the spectators fell silent. For three heartbeats there was only distant birdsong, and the deep breathing of the horses.

The baton rose, then fell, and the marshal ran for safety as the trumpet screamed.

De Grendon kicked his horse into a gallop at once, determined to avenge his slights of the day before. Adam held back a moment, shoving his legs straight into the stirrups, heels down, and firming himself in the saddle before giving a light touch with his spurs. Blanchart needed no more encouragement, and surged forward at once. The distance between the two riders closed in only a few heartbeats.

Adam had faced men in the joust countless times, but it never got any easier. Always this same rush of nervous energy, then the chill that ran through his body as his oncoming opponent drew nearer and the socketed tip of his lance swung downwards. He kept the reins tight, holding in the energy of his steed until the last moment. A brief gulped breath, the practised hunch of the shoulder behind the speeding lance shaft, then he let out the reins and felt the surge of muscle beneath him. The last distance vanished with shattering speed as the horses blazed past each other, a hand's breadth apart.

His opponent's lance struck Adam's shield, and the force drove him back in the saddle. His own weapon had clipped de Grendon's shield too, and glanced aside. *Poor aim.* But already he was hauling at the reins, drawing the plunging warhorse into a tight arc to face his challenger again. Screwing his head around, the mail links crunching at his neck, he saw de Grendon turning as well, the red and white caparison billowing around his horse's legs. Both of them still had their lances intact; their second charge would be at closer range.

Now that he had stood the first blow, Adam felt the warmth of combat in his blood. Reflexes took over, and he kicked with the spur and charged at once with his lance held high. The green and gold pennon whipped the air as he closed in on de Grendon, and the other knight barely had time to wrestle his horse around and get his shield up to protect himself.

Blanchart closed the distance in three galloping strides, and Adam brought his lance down to slam against de Grendon's shield. Even with such a short charge the impact bent and cracked the weapon's shaft and gouged a line across the shield's red chevrons. De Grendon dropped his own lance and pitched sideways on his saddle, kicking one foot from his stirrup. For a moment it appeared that he would topple. This time, a roar of acclaim rose from the spectators.

Flinging away the broken shaft of his weapon, Adam dragged back on the reins, pulling Blanchart into a cantering turn that carried him clear of the other rider. Circling back, he drew his sword.

The two horses snaked around each other. De Grendon had righted himself in the saddle and got his foot back into the stirrup. 'Your master, de Montfort, died excommunicate!' he yelled, his face blazing as he swung the iron-flanged mace up from his side. 'His soul burns in the fires of purgatory! Soon you will share his fate!'

Adam made no reply. The man was goading him to an uncontrolled attack, but he kept his nerve. Shortening his reins once more he dragged Blanchart into a crabbed sidestep, turning his unshielded side towards his enemy. Muscles burning, he dropped his arm and forced himself to slump in the saddle, as if he was injured and retreating. De Grendon let out a cry of triumph, then raised his mace and charged.

Screwing the reins, Adam turned his horse quickly to face the oncoming rider, spurring Blanchart into a surging counter-charge. With only a few long yards of hoof-battered turf between them the two riders converged, Adam bringing his shield up just in time as de Grendon slammed down with his mace. The heavy iron punched against the shield facing and Adam turned the blow, then twisted in the saddle as the two horses passed. Swinging from the waist, he slashed with his sword and caught de Grendon between the shoulders, buffeting him forward.

Another wrenching turn, the grey stallion's forefeet rearing, and Adam was riding up on de Grendon's right. The other rider was still sprawled forward in the saddle, and Adam struck him again with the pommel of his sword, then let the weapon drop to swing by its wrist strap. Reaching downward, he seized de

Grendon's right leg and pulled his foot from the stirrup, then urged Blanchart forward. Letting the destrier's momentum carry him, he dragged the other knight with him. De Grendon let out a strangled cry, trying to strike at Adam with his mace, but he was unbalanced and twisting in the saddle now. He kicked, his spur raking across Adam's mailed thigh, but as the two horses pulled apart he was helpless to stop himself toppling from the saddle. At the last moment he kicked his other foot from the stirrup and rolled sideways, plunging from the horse's back into the trampled dirt.

*

It was after vespers when Joane came to find him. Adam was sitting on a folding stool outside his tent as his groom attended to the horses and his squire cleaned his armour. He stood up as he saw Joane approaching through the smoky afternoon sunlight.

'My sister shamed me this morning,' she said as she joined him. 'I should have come to speak to you myself.'

'It didn't matter,' Adam replied with a shrug. 'You granted me your favour, my lady. That was the important part.'

Joane smiled and inclined her head. It must have cost her, he knew, to sit and witness a joust and mounted duel, knowing that her father had died in a tournament melee.

'I've never seen you in combat like that,' she said. 'I could hardly bear to watch . . . but I couldn't look away either. It was terrible, and yet compelling. I see now why men love to fight.'

'Wiser men learn to fight only when they must,' Adam said.

'Still, you won,' she said, and raised an eyebrow. 'And these are the spoils of victory?'

She gestured to the armour and equipment laid out on the ground before the tent. Gerard the squire glanced up from his polishing and bobbed his head in an approximation of a bow. The hauberk and mail chausses that Adam had won from Ralph de Grendon were slightly too large for him, but he could have the castle armourer adjust them. His battered shield needed to be refaced, and painted with his arms. A fresh lance, with Hawise's silk pennon attached once more, stood before his tent. Laid on a folded blanket, a new sword and a pair of gilded spurs gleamed in the sun: gifts from Earl Robert de Ferrers and Countess Margaret, to show their good grace after Adam defeated their vassal knight.

'I want to keep the horse that Lord Baldwin loaned me,' Adam said. 'I'll exchange it for the one I took from Ralph de Grendon, if I can.'

'You should ask my sister.' Joane gave a wry smile. 'She has Lord Baldwin's attention, I find. I have to watch her like a zealous nursemaid,' she went on. 'I even wonder if they've already . . .' She broke off.

'I would say Hawise knows her own worth,' Adam told her. He remembered her that morning, so self-assured as she came to visit him. 'Anyway,' he said, lowering his voice, 'she has you as a model of virtue.'

Joane glanced quickly at him, and Adam worried that he had gone too far. But then he noticed her hiding her smile as she turned away.

'Countess Margaret will leave us at the beginning of the month,' she said, in a more public tone, as she gazed across the sward. 'She has a safe conduct to go to the king's court, in Oxford or Northampton or wherever he might be, and make her case for her son's inheritance. Her daughter Elizabeth's too.'

'You'll go with her?' Adam asked, his voice catching.

'No,' Joane said with a shake of her head. 'Margaret wants Hawise to accompany her – to keep her distant from Lord Baldwin, I think – but my presence would be . . . difficult. I shall remain here.'

Adam tried to conceal his relief. Even with relations between him and Joane so strained, the thought that she would leave Duffield altogether had brought a stab of anguish.

'Then again,' she went on, lowering her voice once more, 'there is so much talk here of war and fighting. I believe Earl Robert seriously intends to challenge the king, whatever his mother might achieve at court. Who can say where safety lies?'

A voice called across the field; one of the countess's chamber ladies, summoning Joane.

'I must leave you,' Joane said, with a note of apology. Already, her expression said, she had spent too much time with him.

'Wait,' Adam told her, and took her quickly by the hand. They had drawn away from the tents a little, and the servants were being careful to ignore them. 'Henry de Hastings has Sir Humphrey's ring,' Adam said in a low tone. 'The swan badge of the de Bohuns. I saw him wearing it.'

Joane's eyes widened. 'Will he give it to you? Or to me?'

'Not without something in return,' Adam told her. 'But what that might be, I cannot say.'

A look of silent agreement passed between them. Then the summoning voice called again, and Joane tightened her hand in Adam's before releasing him.

'My lady, your favour,' Adam said, snatching up the blue silk scarf as she walked away.

'Keep it,' Joane told him. 'You may need it again soon.'

*

By the time Countess Margaret and her travelling household made their departure from Duffield, the fine skies of late April had shifted to overcast grey.

'I almost wish I was staying,' John de Tarleton told Adam, as they waited in the castle courtyard for the countess to appear. He was one of only four knights who would be escorting her on the journey to the king's court. He cast a chilly glance around the palisade walls and the gateway, and the armed men who remained to guard them. 'If the king's army comes here,' he said, 'Earl Robert's best hope would be to retreat to the woods and dales. You don't want to get caught in a siege in this place. Not with the numbers our foes can muster.'

'Perhaps it won't come to that,' Adam said. 'Perhaps the countess will persuade the king to grant what we all desire?'

John just snorted a laugh. It was possible, they all knew. But unlikely.

'A word of advice,' he said, as he set his foot in the stirrup. 'If things turn bad, you might want to make for Kenilworth.'

'Lord Simon's castle?' Adam asked. De Montfort's army had been marching towards the stronghold the year before, when they were cut off by Lord Edward at Evesham. 'Does it still hold out?'

De Tarleton nodded. 'The garrison have only grown in strength, these last months,' he said. 'And it's a far better sanctuary than Duffield. Perhaps I'll see you there, further down the road?'

Adam thanked him. But in his heart he knew that, for all he had said to Joane about the wisdom of peace, he relished the prospect of open warfare. The chance to decide things on the battlefield, and take revenge for all he had suffered and all he had lost, was undeniably alluring.

'Just make sure you look after her,' Adam told John, gesturing toward Hawise de Quincy, who sat on her pony wrapped in a travelling cloak and looking utterly miserable.

'You can be sure I will,' John told him. 'Lord Baldwin's promised he'll rip out my guts if even a hair on her pretty head is harmed!'

But now the countess descended the steps from the keep, bade farewell to her son and mounted her horse. A trumpet sounded as the castle gates creaked open, and the travelling household began filing out. Adam raised his hand in farewell to John; he would miss the gruff northern knight. As the castle yard emptied, Joane embraced her sister, and the two of them parted. She glanced in Adam's direction as she walked back towards the keep, and he saw tears on her face before she wiped them away.

'Fewer ladies about now,' said Henry de Hastings as he came from the stables. 'Good thing too.' He sniffed and looked at the sky. What had happened, Adam wondered, to de Hastings's own wife, and the children he had spoken of back at Beeston? He seemed to have entirely forgotten about them.

'Now,' de Hastings said, addressing all those who remained in the yard, 'this shall be a place for men, heh? A place for noble deeds and valiant struggles!' He let out a cracked laugh as he swaggered away.

But for ten days more Earl Robert and his allies did not stir from Duffield Castle. Daily the earl's knights, and those of Wake and de Hastings, exercised on the meadows around the castle, and went out to hunt in the surrounding woods. In his mother's absence, Earl Robert had indeed turned the castle into a boisterous, masculine place. Every night he sat up late, drinking in the great hall with his closest friends, their boastful shouts and the coarse sound of their laughter echoing from the open windows. Joane and the few remaining wives and other ladies occupied the countess's chambers, and seldom emerged. Henry de Hastings was often closeted with the earl, Adam noticed, while Baldwin Wake remained more often apart from them. Everyone was waiting, guarding their nerves, honing their steel, while above them loomed the clouds of impending war.

Rumours reached the castle, carried on a damp and threatening breeze. The king had ordered his nephew, the Earl of Cornwall's son, into the north to grieve and subdue his enemies and to crush the sparks of revolt. Henry of Almain was only a young man, but he was accompanied by John de Balliol and Warin de Bassingborne, two of the king's most capable captains.

Together they had established themselves at the old de Ferrers fortress of Tutbury, and put garrisons at the crossing points of the Trent to forbid passage to anyone without a safe conduct. Reginald de Grey, the Constable of Nottingham, was also mustering troops to oppose the rebellion.

Heavy rain was drumming against the shutters when a figure appeared at the doorway of the great hall during dinner. It was a herald in mud-spattered drab with spurs at his ankles, his cries cutting through the ebb of merriment around the tables. The seneschal gave a curt gesture, and two guards escorted the man up to the dais where he could make his report to Earl Robert. A deep hush fell, stirred by hurried whispers.

'So, the enemy is in the field!' Baldwin Wake said loudly, overhearing the herald's words. He looked ready to spring up at once and seize his sword. The men on the lower tables were shouting now, calling for the news to be spread among them all. Earl Robert gestured for the herald to speak.

'Reginald de Grey's bringing siege engines from Nottingham,' the herald told them. 'He intends to join Henry of Almain and his forces at Derby, and then march north against us – they could be here in only a few days.'

'What strength do they have?' somebody demanded.

'Greater than ours,' the herald replied grimly.

Henry de Hastings, Adam noticed, appeared unmoved by the news. But Earl Robert de Ferrers was transformed. All his boisterous jollity had drained from him, and he looked greyish and flabby, as if he might be sick. Could it be that he had truly believed his enemies would never move against him? That the king and his commanders would simply give in to his demands without a fight? Adam too felt the sickening lurch of realisation; this bold new rebellion, the strike for justice in which he had placed all his hopes, was vanishing like smoke before his eyes.

'Where is John D'Eyville?' somebody else asked. 'Where are all those who pledged to support us?'

'Still in the north,' Baldwin Wake replied promptly, 'ravaging the manors of the king's supporters. And we should go and join them there. If our foes are combining their forces, so must we. Our only hope now is in a union of strength.'

The hall was filled with a clamour of voices, every other man standing up from the tables to shout and to question, to demand further news or angrily to oppose the views of others. Some of the women had appeared at the far doorway as well, drawn from their secluded chambers by the uproar. Adam noticed Joane among them. But he kept his attention on Earl Robert. The plump young nobleman was lord of this castle, and of most of these men. Only he could decide what was to be done.

Abruptly the earl got to his feet, steadying himself on the edge of the table. His expression had changed once more, the greyish pallor darkening and his features bunching into a thunderous scowl. He had not been sick with fright at all, Adam realised. This was the Devil of Derby, and his rage was only now beginning to burn hot. Standing beneath the heraldic frieze on the wall, he waited for the noise to subside into silence. Then he spoke, in a cracked yell that carried to the far doors.

'My friend Lord Baldwin is correct,' he told them all, leaning forward with his fists braced on the table. 'We shall not wait for our enemies to assemble and trap us – instead we march to join Sir John D'Eyville and his northern host. Then, together, we shall turn and destroy all those who raise their heads against us!'

'But what of your mother's journey to petition the king, lord?' a voice asked from the hall. 'Should we abandon all hope of peace?'

'*Peace*?' de Ferrers snarled. 'Let no man speak that word to me. We shall have no more of peace – let Satan take it! All of you,' he declared, raising his arms to encompass the hall, 'must prepare at once to leave. Every man, every woman and child. Strip this place – take everything! We leave nothing but an empty husk for our enemies. A burning husk!'

Gasps from the hall. Adam remembered what John de Tarleton had told him: Duffield may have a strong stone keep, but its timber palisades would not long stand a siege. To destroy it, though . . . He had seen castles slighted before, to deny them to the enemy. At Monmouth, and at Usk a year ago. But for Robert de Ferrers to consign his own castle to destruction carried the taint of madness.

Already panic was taking hold, men running and shouting, bellowed commands rising above the tumult. Staring across the hall, Adam sought out Joane among the figures gathered at the doorway. But she was already gone.

*

Duffield Castle was burning as the army marched out, two mornings later. Earl Robert had ordered the cellars of the keep packed with straw, barrels of lard and kitchen grease, and the last men to leave had kindled a blaze that soon roared up through the timber floors of the building. As the earl's followers filed across the bridge and swung north up the river valley, flames were jetting from every slit window, and a great black plume spread across the valley.

Joane rode with the hood of her travelling cloak pulled over her head. Two maids accompanied her, and four grooms to manage her packhorses; Countess Margaret, before leaving Duffield, had made sure that her cousin was properly attended. Adam brought up the rear of the little retinue, with his own squire and groom trailing behind him.

'You have to leave here,' he had told Joane, the day before. 'Leave now, before Earl Robert moves north. I'll escort you wherever you choose to go.'

'How can I?' she had replied. 'How can I, with an enemy army approaching? Reginald de Grey is with them. Perhaps even

Hamo L'Estrange. I cannot fall into their hands, Adam – I would
rather take my own life!'

'Don't speak of such things!' Adam demanded. He wanted to
tell her that he would defend her, whether against the preening, predatory Sir Reginald or against L'Estrange, Joane's former
guardian. But such boasts would sound hollow now. 'There's still
time to flee . . .'

'No!' Joane had told him firmly, and in her eyes Adam had
seen a certainty that he could not hope to match. 'I'll leave here
with Earl Robert, Lord Baldwin and everyone else. The north is
surely a safer place anyway. You swore once to be my knight, did
you not?'

Adam could only agree.

'Then you'll follow me now – wherever God's will should
direct us.'

'Of course,' Adam had said, his voice thickening. 'Wherever
God's will directs.' He had no other choice, he realised, aside
from forcing her to accompany him in the opposite direction.
But that would take them both into the path of Reginald de Grey,
Lord Henry of Almain, and all their forces. Better the dangers
of an army at war than the chance of becoming a captive again.

But as they marched off up the river valley, that army resembled
a straggling band of refugees, the fighting men almost outnumbered by grey-faced servants and snivelling women and children.
Their carts and packhorses were piled high with furniture, silver
plate and table linen, bedding and kitchen implements. There
were beasts with them too, flocks of sheep and cattle driven along
in the wake of the army rather than left to fall into the enemy's
grasp. The dogs and stragglers trailing behind them stretched the
column for miles along the muddy road.

Whenever he turned in the saddle Adam saw the squat black
rectangle of the keep behind him, spilling flame and smoke
across the sky. Pale ash rained across the wet earth. The sight
chilled him, like a premonition of evil.

Chapter 11

'Blind puppies!' Henry de Hastings said. 'Where are we to find such things?'

'Why does the earl want blind puppies?' Adam asked. He scarcely wanted to know.

'Treatment for his gout, according to the physician,' Sir Henry replied. They were in his campaign tent, pitched in a damp meadow beside the road. 'Blind puppies boiled alive, and the swollen limb bathed with the waters. Either that or a paste made of baked owls.'

'Baked owls?'

De Hastings rolled his eyes and grinned. As usual, the rigours of military life suited his temperament. Few others shared his enthusiasm; Earl Robert de Ferrers certainly did not. The stresses of the march so far had caused the gout in his legs and feet to flare up alarmingly, and he was in a frenzy of angry pain.

'Mostly he blames the Jews,' de Hastings said, with a wry tone. 'He does hate them incredibly, I find. It seems their money-lenders in Lincoln and Nottingham press him for old loans, and refuse to advance him further coin to pay his men!'

Adam listened, disturbed. Robert de Ferrers had attacked the Jewish community of Worcester two years before, he remembered, and those had been less desperate times. He hoped the earl would not act on his hatred this time.

A long march from Duffield, on roads flooded by the late spring rains, had brought them to Shirland, the *caput manor* of Reginald de Grey. Once again fires flared along the horizon, and black smoke rose in trails across the low sky. Earl Robert had taken over the manor house while his men ransacked the surrounding settlement, killing any man or beast they could find. Tomorrow morning the house too would burn.

One of Sir Henry's squires brought cups of wine, and Adam sipped gratefully as he stood at the entrance of the tent and gazed out across the encampment. He heard distant shouts, wild laughter, and the lowing of beasts.

'Did you know, tomorrow is the second anniversary of the Battle of Lewes?' Henry de Hastings said, joining Adam at the tent's mouth. Gerard the squire was loitering just outside, listening intently. 'I believe you and I are the only men here who fought that day,' Henry went on. 'A great victory for Lord Simon – and for you too, of course.'

Adam nodded. He had gained the honour of knighthood at Lewes, after his capture of the Earl of Hereford. Henry de Hastings had not distinguished himself: he and the London militia he had commanded had been driven off the field by Lord Edward's first charge. But such things could be easily forgotten now.

'Did Humphrey de Bohun ever pay you the balance of his father's ransom?' de Hastings asked.

'He did not,' Adam said. The thought summoned dark memories. Again he saw the dying man on his bed at Beeston, and felt the chill of the father's words in the chapel at Combermere.

But Henry seemed amused. 'And that's why you want this, I suppose?' he said, and raised his right fist. The golden swan ring caught the last of the daylight. 'Doubtless Earl Humphrey would be grateful if you returned it to him. But if it's money you're after, you'd be better off asking de Bohun's widow.'

'Joane doesn't have any money,' Adam said. 'All her lands were taken from her.'

'Countess Margaret, before she left to seek the king,' de Hastings said, with a knowing smile, 'agreed with Lady Joane and her sister to share the inheritance of their late kinsman, Earl Roger of Winchester. Lands worth something over a hundred and thirty pounds per annum each. Baldwin Wake told me of it, and he got it from Hawise. Although we can be sure he needed no additional inducement where she's concerned.'

'They hold these lands now?'

'Not quite, no,' de Hastings said. 'There's still some legal difficulty about the inheritance, that the countess and her men of business need to arrange with the king's financiers – and that might be a knotty issue, now her son's in active rebellion. But with those holdings and her share of Sir Humphrey's dower lands, your Lady Joane could well become quite a wealthy prize for any man.'

'She's not *my* Lady Joane,' Adam said, as his mood grew bleaker.

De Hastings chuckled, then slipped the ring from his finger and closed it in his fist.

*

The following day they marched north beneath tumbling skies. Adam had not yet spoken to Joane of what Henry de Hastings had told him. Perhaps, he thought, he had best keep silent about it.

'Was the battle at Evesham much greater than the one at Lewes?' Gerard asked as they rode.

Adam glanced back at the squire. He shook his head. 'Just bloodier.'

'And it's true that you saw Lord Simon fall at Evesham?' There was an eager impatience in his voice, and Adam was reminded of the young outlaw Haukyn, who had asked very similar questions. He nodded.

'I'm sure God must have wished him to be martyred, as an example to us all,' Gerard said, and Adam saw him glance piously at the sky. 'But it must have been glorious to stand with him that day, and at Lewes too . . . I can only pray that I see such a fight!'

'Pray that you do not.'

Gerard blinked, dismayed, and Adam regretted his angry tone at once. He was remembering his previous squires – Benedict, slain at Evesham, and Eustace who had died in a skirmish. He promised himself that he would not let this Gerard de Bracebridge share their fate. But he remembered that he too had been eager for battle, at this young man's age. He too had vexed his master with foolish questions and idle prayers.

The end of the day's march brought them to Chesterfield, a market town in the crook of two rivers, surrounded by the rolling wooded country of northern Derbyshire. Baldwin Wake had been lord of the place, before his lands were seized and granted to Lord Edward's wife Eleanor. Now he had returned, to claim his property.

Adam rode on ahead of the marching column as it approached the settlement, Gerard cantering behind him. Together they crossed the timber bridge and rode up the slope into the centre of the town. Adam's long experience of the tournament circuit had taught him the necessity of finding good billets, before anyone else got to them. He knew the questions to ask, the demands to make, and the sums to offer. By the time the rest of the army came crawling up from the bridge to flood the town with men and beasts, Adam had already secured stabling and fodder for his horses, and accommodation for both Joane and himself: two upper rooms in the house of a cloth merchant, with high gable windows overlooking the Old Market and the Church of All Saints.

The Earl of Derby soon established his household in the largest building in town, also facing onto the market square, while Baldwin Wake and Henry de Hastings found lodgings close by.

The remaining knights and squires spilled through the narrow streets, pushing into houses and claiming what rooms they could find, evicting the occupants where necessary. Others raised their tents in the broad expanse of the New Market to the west, or in the meadows beyond the town.

Joane and her maids arrived to find Adam waiting outside the house together with the cloth merchant, who greeted her with such profuse gallantry that she might have been the Queen of England herself, or at least Countess Margaret de Ferrers. Joane passed him a few extra silver pennies as she crossed the threshold.

When he returned from ensuring his horses were properly stabled, Adam climbed the narrow stairway to the upper chambers. He and his squire and the grooms would be staying in the larger rear chamber, sleeping on mattresses on the bare wooden floor. Joane had taken the front one, smaller but better furnished, for herself.

'Can I come in?' he asked from the doorway. Joane was sitting on the bed brushing her unbound hair. Her maids had gone out to fetch food and hot water, and she was alone. A long glance, then she nodded and he stepped inside.

Adam crossed to the window at the gable end of the room. Swinging back the shutters, he looked over the churchyard below him and the open space of the market, crowded now with carts and packhorses, servants and grooms milling as their masters shouted orders. Evening was falling, the last rays of sun slanting from beneath the low clouds to cast flashes of shifting light across the throng. Men were running from the streets and alleys on the far side of the market square, Adam noticed. Riders followed them, carrying lances. A knight on a caparisoned horse appeared, lit by a flash of the sun. His mail hood was thrown back to expose his black hair, and a red and yellow banner flew above him, studded all over with fleur-de-lys. Adam heard the cheers, the voices calling out. *'D'Eyville! D'Eyville!'*

On the far side of the marketplace Adam picked out Joane's two maids, cut off by the swirling crowd. Trumpets were blowing, men shouting their greetings.

'What's happening out there?' Joane asked.

'Sir John D'Eyville and the northerners have arrived,' Adam told her. He watched them a moment longer, then turned to address her. 'You did not mention that your cousin was arranging lands and properties on your behalf.' He felt the anger stir within him as he spoke, and could not keep it from his voice.

Joane paused with her comb. Her hair hung across her face, rich dark copper in the evening light. 'Should I have done?' she said lightly. 'You sound as if you are accusing me of some deception or other.'

He turned to face her, propping himself against the window sill. 'I did not know that your situation had changed, that's all.'

'Well, now you do,' she told him, her voice hardening as she tossed the comb onto her bed and shoved the hair from her face. She glared at him, her eyes grey-green and fierce. 'And now surely you understand why I could not have risked falling into the hands of that worm Reginald de Grey, or any other man of his sort, who would have seized me and married me for my inheritance. But I did not expect to have to justify myself to you, Adam de Norton.'

'You don't,' Adam said, remorse curdling inside him. Unable to meet the fire of her eyes, he turned once more to the window. The tide of newly arrived men had filled the marketplace now. The knight who rode beneath the fleur-de-lys banner – John D'Eyville himself, Adam assumed – had dismounted and was talking to Henry de Hastings, flexing his legs after a long time in the saddle. Baldwin Wake appeared and the two barons embraced like old friends. The men accompanying D'Eyville looked mud-spattered and weary, but their shouts and laughter, the clatter of their strange accents, were raucous in the gathering shadow of evening.

Adam looked back towards the bed, and felt the distance between him and Joane charged suddenly with possibility. He remembered another time, in a hut on a distant hillside, when they had so briefly been lovers, and knew with a flash of certain intuition that she too was thinking of that moment. They were truly alone now, as they had not been since their arrival at Duffield. He knew what he had to do, and could no longer delay acting.

'If you do not wish to marry against your will,' he said, his voice thickening, 'then make it impossible.'

Taking two steps from the window he dropped to kneel before her. 'Marry me,' he told her. 'We can do it here in this town, this evening or tomorrow. We can be wed in the sight of God, before witnesses, and no other man can dispute or deny it.'

He seized her hands as he spoke. For a long moment she looked at him, wide-eyed, her chest rising as she drew a breath. Then he saw the sorrow welling up in her eyes, the anguish, and knew he had been wrong.

'Do you understand nothing?' she said, her voice thin and parched. 'Did you hear nothing of what my cousin told you? My remarriage is in the king's gift, and the king has awarded that right to Earl Humphrey . . .'

'Forget them!' Adam said, his words caught in a snarl. 'Forget your cousin, and the king too, and may the Lord of Hell take Earl Humphrey!'

'No, *no*,' Joane was saying, her gaze dropping to her lap. She pulled her hands from his grasp. 'Don't you see? If we marry without licence *they will ruin you*, Adam. You're a rebel, a king's enemy . . . Earl Humphrey's enemy too. They will grieve you and persecute you and drive you either to prison, exile or the grave! You will never recover your lands, *never.*'

'I don't care,' Adam heard himself saying, but his mind was filled with the roar of hurt pride and the shame of his error. 'We can be exiles together – go across the seas. We can go to France, or Italy, the Empire . . . I can make a living on the tournament circuit, as Sir Robert once did . . .'

Even as he spoke he felt the fire of conviction dying within him.

'Stop,' she ordered him. 'Stop this madness now.'

Abruptly Adam stood up, his head reeling. 'Very well,' he told her, bitterness washing through him. 'If I am no better a man to you than Reginald de Grey . . .'

Joane was standing too. For a heartbeat they faced each other, his fists clenched and her fury blazing. 'Everything I have done,' she said, through her teeth, 'everything I have appeared to be these last months has been to protect you from exactly this. Do you not understand? You think I've enjoyed being so remote from you, so cold? But how could I have done otherwise, Adam?'

Her voice cracked. Angrily she swiped a tear from her cheek. 'Leave me,' she commanded. 'Leave me now, before we say more that we will regret.'

Without another word Adam turned and slammed from the room. Rattling down the narrow stairway he called for Gerard to follow him and strode out into the street. He suspected that Joane was watching him from her high window, but he did not look up.

The town was more crowded than ever, the narrow lanes and alleys that led from the old marketplace choked with men and almost consumed with darkness. Lanterns and rushlights glowed from the open doorways, casting reeling shadows. Adam pushed his way through the throng, his fist tight on the hilt of his sword. He was horribly aware of how stupid he had been, how crude in his attitude. Joane had been entirely correct, entirely just. He had acted like a foolish boy, and the memory of his own words sickened him.

'De Norton!' a voice cried. Henry de Hastings appeared from the crowd, walking with a grim-faced knight of his own age. 'We're going hunting tomorrow, Sir Gregory here and me,' de Hastings said. 'Baldwin Wake has a good chase not two miles from town. Will you join us?'

'Gladly,' Adam told him. The thought of a ride in the open woodland, far from the town and from Joane, was deeply refreshing. 'I don't have a hunting spear or bow though.'

'No matter, we have several. We muster by All Saints, before sun-up. Should be a good band of men with us.'

'I'll be there,' Adam told him, and managed to smile.

The smile faded as he walked on a little way down the narrow street that led towards the New Market. The stables were down here, and he thought he should check on the horses again before night fell. Gerard was yawning as he stumbled along behind him; the young squire had spent a long day in the saddle, and Adam sent him back to the house to rest. He would need him fresh and fit if he wanted to take him along on the hunt tomorrow.

There were several other men in the stables, grooms attending to the horses, and knights and squires ensuring their animals were well treated. Adam made a brief assessment of each of his own mounts and Joane's too, then gave a penny to the groom for food and ale and told him to have the best two riding horses ready by first light. He was tired himself, he realised, and the argument with Joane had sapped both his spirits and his strength.

He was halfway back along the lane when he heard the singing, and paused.

A solo voice, and he knew it at once. The words were unknown to him.

Welsh, he realised.

A low gateway opened off the lane into a yard behind the stable buildings. There were alehouse benches and tables drawn up in the yard, and a crowd of men gathered there drinking and slamming the tables in time to the singer's choruses. The singer himself had his back to the gateway, and Adam could not see his face. But he recognised the plump figure, the round head capped with a thatch of pale hair. Standing to one side he waited until the song was done and the cheers echoed around the yard. Some of the drinkers pressed forward to slap the singer on the shoulders, and one shoved a mug of ale into his fist.

'Hugh of Oystermouth,' Adam said, stepping up beside the man.

The singer turned, startled, then his round face blanked with surprise. 'By the chin of St David!' the Welshman said. 'By the Virgin's tears . . . is that really Adam de Norton?'

Adam grinned, and suddenly the two of them were embracing as Hugh gulped back laughter. 'How?' he cried as they parted and gazed at each other. 'How did you come to be here? I thought you were dead!'

'And I thought you were far away,' Adam told him. He had last seen Hugh of Oystermouth, once his herald and Robert de Dunstanville's herald before that, in Evesham on the morning of the battle. Adam had sent him off with a message for his betrothed, Isabel de St John. He had seen or heard nothing of his friend ever since.

'Come, sit here,' Hugh cried, leading Adam to one of the vacant benches. He still had his mug of ale, and poured another for Adam from the jug. 'I looked for you,' he said, speaking rapidly. 'I looked for you at Axholme, back in December last, thinking you may have joined the rebels there . . .'

'I was in prison, at Beeston,' Adam told him. He took a swig of the ale; weak and acrid, but at that moment it tasted like the finest mead to him. Quickly he sketched an account of all that had happened to him: the slaughter at Evesham, Robert de Dunstanville's death, then his captivity and escape and his months at Duffield.

'I knew that Robert was slain,' Hugh said, his mirth sinking to bleak reflection. 'That is, I was told about it . . . A few men escaped the battle, you know, but it was hard to know what to believe. Nobody could tell me what had happened to you. I feared the worst, and hoped for the best . . .'

'But how are you here now?' Adam asked him. 'You're with D'Eyville's men?'

Hugh nodded, with a rueful grimace. 'I am currently employed by Sir Osbert de Cornburgh, one of his knights,' he said, and gestured discreetly towards the far corner of the yard. A large man was sprawled full length on one of the benches, an ale mug still clamped in his fist even as he snored. 'He was at Axholme and wanted a herald and clerk, so for my sins and for want of bread I joined his retinue.'

He shrugged eloquently. Clearly there was little more to say about Osbert de Cornburgh.

'But tell me,' Adam said with sudden urgency, seizing Hugh by the arm. 'Did you return to Basing after you left Evesham?'

'I did!' Hugh said, widening his eyes. 'Oh, you don't know, of course . . . I saw Isabel de St John, and her father Lord William too. I returned to the lady her paternoster beads, as you'd commanded, and told her that she should pray for you. At that time I thought you likely dead, and your soul in the balance . . .'

'What did she say?' Adam demanded. The answer might be too much to endure, but suddenly he needed it more than anything.

'She said, my friend,' Hugh said, smiling, 'that she had done nothing but pray for you since last she saw you, and would continue to do so. She said that you remain in her heart, and always will, and she will consider herself your betrothed until God restores you to her. And I must say, her father was quite moved as well.'

Adam slumped back on the bench, speechless. For a moment his mind was full of white light and whirling darkness, and his heart felt too big for the cage of his chest. For all that he might have wished, he had never dared to hope that Isabel would keep their promise of betrothal intact, even after her father had turned against Simon de Montfort, and even after the news of Evesham. But she had done so . . . He grinned suddenly, then his mood plummeted. All this time, he thought, all these months, she had been faithful to him while he had betrayed her in thought and deed. He had allowed himself to become fixated on Joane de Bohun, and had strayed from the true path of happiness. Hopeless fantasies had corrupted his soul.

'You appear dumbstruck, my friend,' Hugh said, concerned. 'Granted, it was eight months and more since I was at Basing. Things may have changed?'

'I have been a great fool,' Adam said quietly. 'A great fool, and a sinful one. All this time and I never sent word to her. All this time, in ignorance . . . I'd forsaken her. I've broken every vow I ever made! To Isabel, to Robert . . .'

'Why to Robert?' Hugh asked, frowning.

'I told him I would find Belia and tell her of his last words,' Adam explained. 'But I made no effort to do it. I wouldn't even know where to find her. London, maybe, with her brother . . .?'

'She's in Nottingham, in the Jewish quarter,' Hugh broke in. 'I met her there as I journeyed north last autumn. Wilecok and his wife are living there too, as her servants.'

'Nottingham?' Adam said, aghast. The town was only a day's ride from Duffield. He could have gone there at any time over the last three months.

'She has a child, you know,' Hugh said quietly. 'Robert de Dunstanville's child.'

Of course. Belia had been pregnant when last Adam saw her. 'I need to find her,' he said, dropping his voice. 'As soon as I can. As soon as I can quit this army and this mad campaign . . .'

Suddenly the thought of Earl Robert de Ferrers and his deranged rantings, his vainglorious postures, filled Adam with repugnance. Henry de Hastings was little better, and Baldwin Wake was a mere adventurer. No, he thought, he must go to Nottingham, and then somehow return to Basing, and to Isabel.

'What of my lands?' he asked Hugh. 'Did you learn who holds them now?'

But Hugh could only shake his head. 'Sadly, I did not,' he told Adam. 'But Lord William mentioned that the king's supporters in the region had seized many of the estates of those they called *rebels* . . . I believe Hugh de Brayboef and his son Geoffrey were among them. Perhaps they took the chance to possess your manor once more?'

Yes, Adam thought, he did not doubt that the de Brayboefs would snatch that opportunity; Hugh de Brayboef had once been his stepfather, and had claimed Adam's estates after his mother's death. Geoffrey, he remembered, had once been betrothed to Isabel. But William de St John was de Brayboef's overlord; if Adam could only get back to Basing, speak to the man, make peace with him . . . Suddenly everything seemed very clear, the fog that had filled his thoughts for so long driven off by the breeze of renewed purpose.

'There's a hunting party tomorrow,' he told Hugh. 'We're leaving from the church before first light – will you join me? We can talk more then.'

'I'm not sure Sir Osbert will be in a fit condition for hunting, come the morrow,' Hugh said wryly, glancing at his slumbering master, 'but he can probably do without my services for a few hours!'

*

Slipping off his shoes at the door, carrying his sword and belt in his hand, Adam climbed the stairs to the upper rooms as quietly as he could. Every wooden tread creaked loudly beneath him. He doubted that he would be able to sleep – his mind was still rioting with the news that Hugh had brought him. But he needed calm and rest all the same. Calm, rest, and solitude.

'Adam?' a low voice said as he reached the head of the stairs. The door to his own room lay to his right. The other, to Joane's room, was partly ajar. 'Is that you?' She was breathing the words.

He eased open the door, then closed it behind him and set his sword down beside the threshold. For a moment he was about to tell her all that he had learned from Hugh. But then he did not.

'Where are your maids?' he said, his voice low in his throat.

'I sent them to sleep downstairs,' she told him. In the faint light through the gap in the shutters he saw that she was sitting on the bed, her hair loose, dressed only in her white linen chemise. He waited near the door, his heart grown still in his chest, and she stood up and crossed the floor to join him.

'I wanted to say,' she began, then her voice cut off. She made a sound, midway between a sigh and a gasp of exasperation. 'I don't want you to leave me,' she said. 'Not now . . .'

Suddenly they were pressed together, their embrace urgent and feverish as they kissed. In his mind Adam heard a clear voice telling him of the madness of what he was doing, the sin of it. Then it was gone, in the loud rush of his blood. Joane was drawing him towards the bed even as she tugged at the laces of her chemise, even as he dragged at his hose and fumbled with his braies. She laughed quickly, stifling his irritated cry with her lips.

'Slowly,' she told him. 'We've got all night.'

Chapter 12

Voices woke him. The snap and yowl of hounds. The first light of the coming dawn was seeping between the shutters, and outside the hunting party was assembling in the square beside the church.

'*No, not the dogs,*' Joane mumbled into the bolster. She was speaking from a dream. Adam raised his head and gazed at her, his brow puckering. Her eyes blinked open and she gazed back at him. From outside came the bleat of a hunting horn.

'They're going out to the chase,' Adam said quietly. 'I told Henry de Hastings I'd go with them. I should leave . . .' Even as he spoke, the events of the previous evening flooded his mind. Hugh of Oystermouth. Belia. *Isabel.*

'Stay a while longer,' Joane said, her hand at the back of his neck. They had slept naked, and he propped himself on one elbow, pushed back the quilt and admired her. She smiled. 'My husband never did that,' she told him.

'Your husband was a foolish man then.'

Her hair looked dark as ink in the morning twilight, flowing across the bolster and mattress, and the hollows of her body were pools of shadow. 'You're fond of some other things my husband never did,' Joane told Adam, and pulled him down to her kiss. 'I expect you learned them on your travels overseas? From those wanton women with whom you consorted?'

'None but the finest ladies,' Adam muttered, laughter catching in his throat.

The horn sounded again from the street. Distantly he heard somebody calling his name. He raised his head. Hugh would be waiting for him. 'I ought to leave, all the same,' he said. 'Otherwise . . .'

'Otherwise idle mouths may talk, yes,' she said. 'But wait for the sun, at least.'

He waited for the sun. Only when the first brightness edged the gap between the shutters did he swing himself off the bed. Joane took his hand.

'Come back quickly,' she told him, a sudden urgency in her voice.

'I'll return before noon,' Adam said.

He turned from her as he dressed, knowing that if he glanced back even once the day would be lost. In the other room Gerard was already awake; he rose with a start as Adam entered, then blushed and looked away.

'Get dressed and come with me,' Adam ordered him curtly. He splashed his face with water from the basin, fastened his sword belt, then picked up his riding boots and went down the stairs.

Fresh sunlight spilled into the hall through the open door. As Adam laced his boots the cloth merchant brought him a chunk of bread and a mug of ale to break his fast; the hunting party had left not an hour beforehand, he said. 'Lord Baldwin's woodland chase is a bare two miles distant,' he explained, flinging out an arm towards the low morning sun. 'One of my boys can guide you there.'

Adam thanked him, knocked back a mouthful of ale, then strode off towards the stables with Gerard following him. Finally the clouds had parted, and the day was warm and springlike, the sky bright blue and the puddles and cart-ruts gleaming. It was the Saturday before Pentecost, and the town was already alive with the preparations for the week's biggest market. A flock of geese waddled across the marketplace, steered between the stalls by two small girls with sticks. Nearby, pigs stood grunting in a muddy pen. A heavy wagon emerged from the main street, drawn by oxen. Another came behind it, both of them filled with sacks of wool covered with canvas to protect them from the rain.

Only now did the first sensation of guilt soak through Adam's mind. He heard again Hugh of Oystermouth's words from the previous evening. *You remain in her heart, and always will . . . she will consider herself your betrothed until God restores you to her.* Suddenly all the warm contentment that had bathed him was gone, and in its place was cold black disgust. Even knowing that Isabel still waited for him, he had betrayed her once more. How could he ever think of returning to her now? But how could he ever think of forsaking Joane?

At the entrance to the lane that led to the stables he almost faltered, and reached out to the crumbling plaster of the wall to steady himself. He had barely slept all night, and fatigue was dragging at him. The ale he had swallowed was sour in his gut.

'Sir?' Gerard said, taking his arm. 'Are you unwell?'

Adam shook him off, too tired to be gracious. 'Go ahead and ready the horses,' he said. 'Bring them round. I'll wait for you here.'

Leaning back against the wall, he watched the slow progress of the wagons across the marketplace. He yawned widely. Images of the night before returned to him, memories and sensations, and he smiled as the guilt and disgust fell away from him. The lowing of beasts jolted him from his private reverie. Cows filled the narrow lane between him and the stables; a drover was thwacking at their bony hindquarters, driving them onward.

Adam's attention drifted back to the scene in front of him. The big wagons had almost crossed the muddy expanse of the marketplace. Idly he wondered why the wagoners had gone to the trouble of covering their loads with canvas, when the rain had passed and the sky was cloudless blue. As he watched, the leading wagon came to a halt only a few long strides away from him. The canvas covering twitched aside, and just for a heartbeat Adam saw a grimy face staring back at him from the shadows among the woolsacks. He frowned. The grimy man raised a finger to his lips, then grinned.

Startled out of his weary daze, Adam pushed himself away from the wall and reached for his sword. A scream came from away to his left, beyond the wagons. Then a bellow of rage. Something came whirling towards him, and he dodged just in time as an axe spun past his head. The blade struck the wall just behind him, the steel biting deep into the lath and plaster.

'*Almain! Almain!*' The stillness of the morning was shattered by a hundred angry voices. Adam squinted into a reeling chaos of shadows and splintered sunlight. Men were running, horses and other animals bolting into wild and sudden motion, and for several speeding heartbeats Adam could not tell what was happening around him.

A pulse of terror, then of fury. He let out a cry as he drew his sword. 'To arms!' he called, though he did not know who could hear him. 'Everyone, to arms – the enemy are upon us!'

The wagons, he realised. The attackers were coming from the wagons. They were throwing off the canvas covers and scrambling from beneath the woolsacks, axes and wickedly glinting falchions in their fists. A serjeant dressed only in braies and undershirt stumbled blearily from a house that fronted the marketplace, and one of the men from the wagons swung at him with an axe. One savage downward chop split the victim's face open and dropped him instantly.

A roar from his left, and Adam glanced around just in time to see a man in a gambeson charging at him with a spear levelled at his chest. Gripping his sword in both hands, Adam waited until the attacker was almost upon him then swung his blade in an arc, driving the spearhead aside. A swift backhand slash, and his attacker went down, sprawling in a muddy puddle. Blood brightened the water around him.

A mailed rider cantered across the marketplace, the hooves of his mount kicking sprays of wet dirt. He brandished a naked sword in his raised hand. 'Awake, traitors, awake!' the horseman yelled. 'In the king's name, you are all dead men! Death is here . . . *Death is here!*'

Adam saw it all too clearly now. The forces of the king's nephew Henry of Almain had not delayed at Duffield after all. They had stormed north like thunder in the wake of Earl Robert's march, pushing on through the night to reach Chesterfield and catch the rebel army unawares. They had smuggled men into the town in market wagons to spread chaos and terror, and now the rest of their troops were swarming in through the streets and lanes. The battle seemed over before it had even begun.

On foot with only a sword, no shield or armour, Adam knew he had little hope of cutting his way through the melee to the house where he had left Joane. Dazzled by the low sun, sweat stinging his eyes, he looked back towards the stables. No sign of Gerard with the horses; the lane was still blocked by milling panicked cattle. His only chance would be to take one of the other alleys leading from the market, get behind the houses and work along the yards and garden plots to the rear of the house. Did the cloth merchant's house have a back door? He could not remember.

Half a bowshot to his right was the mouth of a narrow alley. Another glance towards the stables, then he ran across the open ground and plunged into the opening. Darkness all around him, and for two heartbeats he was running blindly. Then the alley opened out, and he saw the far end blocked by a chaotic press of fighting men. Light fell from the slot of blue sky overhead, picking out raised faces, glinting steel. The combatants all looked

alike, nothing to distinguish one side from another. '*A Ferrers!*'
one man shouted, trying to rally his supporters. '*Almain! Almain!*'
another yelled back. '*King's men!*' The confined space resounded
with the clink and rasp of steel, the breathy cries of anguish, the
screams of pain and fury.

Something fell from above, a jug flung from an upper window to shatter amid the melee. Adam smelled the sharpness of
ordure. He threw himself back against the wall, protected by
the overhang of the upper storey, and edged towards the pack of
struggling men.

He could pick out the fighters now: one of them was Osbert
de Cornburgh, Hugh of Oystermouth's new master. The northern knight stood with his back to an open gateway, dressed only
in his braies and undertunic but hefting a sword and shield. He
bellowed as he fought, staggering and swinging wildly, his face
still flushed after his night of drinking. Adam plunged towards
him. '*A Ferrers!*' he cried.

He was into the fight at once, cutting and thrusting to either
side. With his left hand he grappled and punched, shoving himself forward as the press of men opened before him. This was a
kind of fighting he knew well. But without a shield or a helmet,
steel whirling all around him, he felt horribly vulnerable. A blade
flashed past his head, and the side of a spear gashed the back of
his hand. He felt the impact of a club on his shin and cried out in
pain. A man turned, screaming in his face through brown teeth.
Adam drove the point of his sword into the softness of the man's
belly. The steel went in deep, and the man's scream died as he
choked and coughed bright blood over Adam's chest and neck.
Turning, he dragged his blade from the wound.

When he looked again, Osbert de Cornburgh was down. Two
men with maces pummelled his body, even as the knight raised
a hand for quarter. Stooping, Adam snatched up the the fallen
man's shield by the strap and slammed his left forearm into the
grips. Two blades struck the facing at once, but already he was

shuffling backwards, staying low in a fighting stance, towards the gateway that de Cornburgh had been guarding. He jabbed with his sword, short controlled cuts from behind the shield. For a few rapid heartbeats he stood alone against his attackers, keeping the gateway behind him.

Then a rush of pounding footsteps and bellowing voices, and half a dozen armoured bodies pushed past him. They were mailed serjeants with shields and iron helmets, led by a knight in the red and yellow livery of Robert de Ferrers's household. Adam yelled with relief. Already the newcomers were ploughing into the close-packed mass in the alleyway. Blood sprayed the alley walls.

But this was not Adam's fight. Without another thought he was through the passage behind him and into the muddy yard beyond. A rapid glance took in the midden, the henhouse, the shoulder-high wicker fence on the far side, and the huddle of ragged militiamen clutching spears and falchions in trembling hands.

'You!' Adam said, pointing his sword at them. 'Whose men are you?'

'Yours, sir?' one of them suggested. He was a skinny man with grey stubble, and his eyes flickered between Adam's face and the blood on his blade.

'After me, then,' Adam said. Without another glance at them he ran to the fence and threw his shoulder at it, crashing through to the far side. Three of the militiamen followed immediately behind him. Together they crossed a narrow kitchen garden plot, stamping through the lettuce beds, then scrambled over a fence of wooden planks. Adam was trying to remember how far away the cloth merchant's house was. Could he recognise it from the back?

'Halt! Halt and declare yourselves!' voices screamed. He faced a thicket of spears, levelled swords and drawn bows. One of the militiamen following him yelped and dropped back on the other side of the fence. The skinny one slumped to his knees in the dirt, wheezing for breath, and vomited loudly.

The garden beyond the fence was full of armed men, and Adam and those following him had jumped down into the middle of them. He raised his hands, holding his sword and shield clear of his body. If they were king's men, he was dead.

'De Norton, isn't it?' a voice said. Adam released his breath in a gasp, recognising the red chevrons on the man's shield. Ralph de Grendon, Earl Robert's vassal. So these must be Earl Robert's men. But de Grendon's sneer did not appear welcoming.

'Who are those men with him?' one of the serjeants with de Grendon snapped, jabbing his spear towards the puking militiaman. 'Is he leading them?'

'Maybe he's trying to capture Earl Robert?' another cried. In their voices Adam heard the madness of confusion and shock, of betrayal.

'I swear to you,' he called back, keeping both arms raised, 'I'm on your side. Ralph de Grendon here knows it . . .'

'Aye well,' de Grendon said. 'We could use another sword, sure enough.'

Only now did Adam notice the second group of figures, gathered around the rear door of the house. These were better dressed, clerks and clergymen among them; one was Earl Robert's private physician. A few women too – Adam searched for Joane in their number, but in vain. Then he saw the body on the makeshift stretcher.

Robert de Ferrers looked dead at first, but then raised his head and peered around him. A linen shroud covered most of his torso. Sounds of fighting seemed to come from all directions.

'What's wrong with him?' Adam asked. 'Is he wounded?'

'He's just been *bled*,' Ralph de Grendon snapped back. 'For his *gout*. The leech takes his blood every day at sunrise.'

'The lord Robert is weak, but he'll recover soon,' one of the clerks said, overhearing them. 'We must carry him to safety, and ensure his rest is undisturbed . . .'

Adam could barely restrain his bitter laughter. The Devil of Derby was an invalid, crippled by his own doctor, if not by his hereditary illness. And now de Ferrers began to writhe and thrash about on his stretcher, throwing aside the linen shroud and swatting at the men carrying him. 'Christ's teeth, why are we waiting here?' he demanded. 'Don't you know I'm in pain! I'm sick! My body is burning, by God's death!' He let out an anguished cry, as the physician bent over him and pressed a wetted cloth to his brow. 'Get off me, leech!' de Ferrers bellowed. 'What are you, a Jew? Are you trying to murder me? By the Blessed Virgin's teats, let's *move!*'

'All together then,' de Grendon ordered. He seemed to have taken charge here, and Adam was content to follow him. 'We go ahead and clear a path across the marketplace to the church. When we've driven the enemy back, the physician and his servants will carry Lord Robert to safety . . .'

'You're taking him to the *church*?' Instantly Adam glimpsed the bloody massacre around the altar of Evesham Abbey. 'There's no safety there!'

'He'll be safe if they don't know he's in there,' Sir Ralph replied, stepping closer to snarl in Adam's face. 'Enough talk — we go now, while we still can.'

They formed up, those in armour and carrying shields pushing to the front. At once they were moving, clattering through the darkened house and out into the glare of morning sunlight. Adam followed in their wake, still clutching de Cornburgh's battered shield. He had no intention of fighting for Robert de Ferrers, but this was taking him in the direction he wanted to go.

Outside, the marketplace was a battleground. De Grendon and his serjeants charged straight out into it, roaring their defiance. Trumpets sounded to the south, beyond the church. There were more enemy troops coming from that direction. Knights followed behind them, armoured men on caparisoned horses with pennoned lances and banners. Adam saw the banded blue and white banner of Reginald de Grey waving above the chaos.

De Grendon's armoured serjeants quickly carved a path from the door of the house to the porch of the church opposite, scattering the lightly armed plunderers. Then they turned, butting their shields edge to edge, and with fierce shouts defied the enemy to break their line. Adam was still hanging back at their rear. Already he could see the physician and his servants bringing the stretcher forth, carrying it low as they jogged towards the church. Women screened it on all sides – it was clear now why they had been brought along.

'That's right!' the physician called out, in a tremulous voice, 'all the women must go to the church! Women only!' he cried, raising a finger.

Turning, Adam scanned the facades of the houses behind him. He picked out the right window – too far away, on the far side of de Grendon's line – and just as he did so the shutter opened and Joane glanced down and saw him.

'Stay there!' he yelled. 'I'll come for you!'

But before he could move, a blast of trumpets and a clatter of hooves on cobbles came from behind him. Turning, Adam saw another band of mounted knights, all in mail with lances in hand, appearing from a street on the far side of the marketplace. This time their pennons were yellow and red – John D'Eyville and his retinue had armed themselves and entered the fight. Cheers went up from de Ferrers's men. But the knights were not massing to join them; D'Eyville's riders reined in their mounts only long enough to scan the chaotic tumult before them. Then, at a command from their leader, they dragged their horses around and spurred them away down one of the other side streets.

'They're fleeing! The bastards are deserting us!' one of Earl Robert's men cried. His words were almost drowned out by a fierce roar as the enemy saw their foes in flight, and redoubled their attack. Arrows and crossbow bolts flickered overhead, striking shields and the walls of houses. One of the men flanking de Grendon went down, then another. Then all was pandemonium.

Adam had retreated to the doorway behind him, waiting for a chance to dash across the open ground towards the house where Joane was lodged. Now he saw all possibility dissolve before him. With a wordless yell he raised his sword and charged out into the melee.

A man came at him with a falchion and Adam slammed him aside with his shield, stabbing out at a second attacker and driving him back. The man tripped and fell, and Adam leaped over him and ran onward. Somebody had fired the neighbouring buildings, whether by accident or on purpose, and black smoke billowed against the bright morning sky. The marketplace was cluttered with broken stalls and animal pens, bodies sprawled in the churned mud between them. A pig ran past, squealing wildly. Geese battered the air with their wings. And everywhere men were fighting, locked in furious combat. Adam saw two ragged figures rolling on the ground, breathlessly jabbing knives at each other. This was no longer a battle, but a slaughter. The cries of the combatants — '*Almain! Almain!*'. . . '*A Ferrers!*'. . . '*King's Men!*' sounded like the shrieks and wails of the damned in hell.

He reached one of the abandoned wagons. Wounded men had clambered into it hoping for safety, and the wagon-bed streamed with blood. There was blood on the back of Adam's shield as well; his left hand was cut badly, although he still could not feel it. Pulling himself up onto the tail of the wagon, the wounded shrinking away from him, Adam turned and stared through the smoke, the glancing light, the chaos of reeling bodies and prancing horses. Every window around him seemed to hold an archer or crossbowman. Then, through the frenzy, Adam saw his squire

Gerard mounted on his palfrey, dragging the panicked grey destrier by a leading rein.

'Gerard!' he cried, raising his sword. 'Over here! To me!'

But the squire was staring in every direction but his own. He was hunched in the saddle, face blanched by fear as he fought to keep control of the horses. A moment more, and the squire released his grip on the rein, set spurs to his own horse, and galloped wildly towards the nearest side street.

'Adam!' came a cry from the opposite direction, and with his heart clenching in his chest Adam saw Joane running from the doorway of the house, pulling a shawl over her head. He leaped down from the wagon, and at once bodies slammed into him, two men in gambesons trying to wrestle him to the ground.

'Go back!' he yelled, hoping Joane could see him. He punched one of the men with the pommel of his sword, and raked his blade across the neck of the other. A strike with his shield put the man down. But now there were riders cantering across the open ground between him and Joane, led by an armoured knight on a horse caparisoned in blue and white stripes. Adam saw the face in the oval mail coif, recognising the cruel features, the black moustache. Reginald de Grey was giving orders to the footsoldiers that came running up after him. When the horses parted, Joane was struggling in the grip of two of de Grey's serjeants.

Adam opened his mouth to cry out, willing himself to charge forward and free her. But suddenly the stench of blood was flooding his mind; his own blood, and the blood of other men. The gore dripping from the wagon tail. The red streaks on the blade of his sword. Blood was all around him, and in his mind he saw again the carnage of Evesham, the savagery of the slaughter. Mouth gaping, he sucked down air and tried to quell the reeling horror in his mind. A wound had opened inside him, his strength and resolve were pouring from it, and he could not staunch the flow. He looked back towards Joane, and saw that she was lost.

Then all his courage and honour, all his pride in knighthood, was lost too and he was running, head down and sick with terror. He threw aside his battered, arrow-pitted shield and would have dropped his sword too were it not secured by the wrist strap. He was running solely for survival, for anything but death and drowning in the tide of blood that seemed to rush at his heels.

Down the funnel of an alleyway he ran, trying to put the marketplace behind him. The alley broadened into a lane dropping towards the river and the mill. But it was thick with other fugitives, panicked men fleeing in terror, and the enemy were hot behind them and slaying without mercy.

Adam tripped, sprawling over a fallen body. A shadow blocked the sunlight. A brawny man in a leather jack stood over him, a notched falchion gripped in both hands. He raised the weapon, grinning through crooked teeth.

Before the blade came down, the man's knees buckled. Adam glanced up, teeth clenched in terror, and saw the head of an arrow, bright red with gore, jutting from the man's throat. The body fell heavily across him.

Shoving the corpse aside, Adam saw a pair of red deerskin boots wrapped with thongs up to the wearer's thighs. He raised his head, and saw Reynard with bow in hand, his beard flaring in the morning sun.

'If you want to live another day,' the brigand said, 'follow me.'

Part Two

Chapter 13

In the dappled evening sunlight they moved beneath the trees, fast and silent as famished wolves in their garb of grey and dun. At the edge of the cleared ground they crouched, waiting, concealed.

The manor house looked placid under its thatch, a kitchen block to one side, stables, barns and dovecots on the other, fences penning the herb garden and orchard, the sties and the byres. Smoke rose blue into the deepening summer sky. This manor had been held by the D'Eyvilles, until the king seized their lands and granted it to Newstead Priory instead. But the prior's men would not be enjoying it for long.

Somewhere a dog began to bark. A cry from the far side of the grounds, like a bird's call but harsher, louder. Then another, from the opposite perimeter. Adam heard the cries, and recognised the signal. The manor was surrounded on all sides. A man in a hood rose from concealment. Two more followed, bows already flexed and arrows nocked. Adam went after them, running in a low crouch with his sword in his hand. All around him, the attackers flowed from the edge of the woodland in a rushing wave.

A head appeared from behind one of the garden fences, then the figure of a man rose, startled, and let out a cry. He turned at once and began to run back towards the house. An arrow struck him in the thigh, and he staggered and fell.

Adam leaped the first low fence, crossed the muddy yard of a cattle byre and leaped the second. Other men followed him, and together they made for the door at the far end of the house. A manor servant was running for the same door; he reached it just ahead of Adam, yelling as he crossed the threshold and slamming the heavy oak behind him. Adam heard the rattle of the locking bar, but before it could fall he rammed his shoulder against the door and burst it open.

Staggering, he was across the threshold and into the gloom of the house. The servant had fallen, knocked down by the door as it swung back. Blinking, Adam made out another figure ahead of him. A man with a crossbow spanned and loaded, straightening as he brought the weapon up to aim. Adam threw himself to one side. The crossbow snapped, and the bolt struck the wooden lintel of the door. One of the men behind Adam bent his bow and shot through the doorway, and the crossbowman screamed and dropped his weapon as an arrow struck him in the shoulder.

It was over. Heaving breath, Adam strode forward into the house, along the passageway between the pantry and buttery, towards the hall. The leading wave of the attackers had already burst in through the main door and quelled all resistance there. The gloomy space beneath the high ceiling rafters echoed with shouting voices, cries for mercy, and the crash of tumbled furniture and smashing crockery.

Adam sat down on a bench and laid his sword across his knees. His heart thumped in his chest; the crossbow bolt had been a very near miss, and he was only now feeling the effect. This was the third manor they had attacked, since he joined the outlaw band. So far they had faced little resistance, and lost no men. Only a few of their victims had died or been badly injured. As Reynard said, it was more lucrative than capturing wayfarers on the common highway. But Reynard was not their leader.

'Here, look,' Haukyn said, flinging open a chest. 'Clothes and woollens – you need them.' He took a fistful of folded garments and tossed them to Adam. They were supposed to hold all of their plundered goods in common, but in practice nobody cared about the smaller things. Adam looked at the clothes, selected a new yellow tunic and a pair of hose, and threw the rest back into the open chest. He had left Chesterfield only with what he stood up in, but disliked arraying himself too generously in the takings of these plundering raids.

Shouts and cruel laughter came from the yard behind the house. With the folded clothes under his arm Adam went out and stood in the rear doorway. The victim was the prior's bailiff. A gang of men, Silent John and Ivo of the North among them, had armed themselves with birch rods and were making the bailiff run between them, grinning and joking as they struck at his knees and his head. 'Fiends! Enemies of Christ!' the bailiff squealed as he ran back and forth and the birch rods thwacked his limbs. 'Ow! Foes of God . . . May your souls burn in torment! May you never be absolved! Ah!'

For now, Adam knew, they were playing. Soon the real violence would begin.

Shoving himself from the doorway, he walked back around the side of the house. Outside the kitchen Reynard was sitting on the well coping, paring meat with his knife from a large ham he held in his lap and cramming it into his mouth.

'What are they doing back there?' the brigand asked as he chewed.

'Tormenting the prior's bailiff.'

'Hah! Good,' Reynard said, with an approving nod. 'You gave him a few hearty whacks yourself, I hope?'

'I did not.'

Reynard swallowed, pointing his knife at Adam. 'You still think you're better than us, eh?' he said. 'Let me tell you something. In this world there are only the hunters and the prey. If you don't act like the one, folk might think you're the other. You see me?'

'I prefer not to persecute holy men, or their servants,' Adam said.

'They persecute us!' Reynard declared. 'All these clerks and canons, these monks. They persecute us with their tithes, don't they? Anyway, Sir Nicholas is grieved at the prior and his folk for accepting his family's estates from the king.'

Sir Nicholas was the cousin of the Yorkshire baron John D'Eyville. He was also the accepted leader of this band. A cry came across the yard, and Adam turned to see the man himself stride out of the house. He resembled his cousin, with black hair and a fierce look of displeasure on his face, but dressed in a forester's russet and drab.

In the near distance a figure was running. The bailiff, Adam noticed; he must have broken from the ring of his tormenters and fled. Two of Reynard's men went after him, bows in hands. With casual ease they nocked arrows and prepared to shoot.

'Let him go,' Nicholas D'Eyville snarled. 'He won't find anyone to help him before tomorrow noon, and we'll be far from here by then.'

The bailiff ran onward, into the soft light of the summer evening. Reynard snorted in disgust; obviously, he would have preferred to make the man suffer a little longer. 'If I'd thought you'd turn so soft-hearted,' he told Adam, 'I mayn't have plucked you from that bloody mess at Chesterfield. For all I owed you for speaking to the countess on our behalf.'

Reynard had only been in the town that day by chance, he had told Adam. He had led a dozen of his followers down from the hills, but had been in two minds about joining Robert de Ferrers, despite the pardon the earl had offered. Instead he had trailed his army north, keeping clear of Robert's scouts and observing

his behaviour. Reynard had entered Chesterfield that morning to
visit the market, and see if he could arrange a meeting with the
earl. The mistake had almost cost him his life. But it had saved
Adam's.

A month had passed since then, and Adam had remained with
Reynard's band, wandering with them deep into the royal hunting forest of Sherwood. When the brigand band had joined the
larger company led by Nicholas D'Eyville and his fellow rebels,
Adam had acted as a link between the disparate groups.

Long the haunt of outlaws, renegades and masterless men,
the woods and heaths of Sherwood were now home to a great
number of fugitives, knights whose lands had been seized by the
king's men, and footsoldiers who had fled after Chesterfield or
the fall of Axholme, their number swollen by common thieves
and reavers. All, supposedly, were equal under the same pledge
of brotherhood.

But not all considered themselves allies.

'Listen to them,' Haukyn said, sneering. He and Adam had
volunteered to stand sentry watch that night. Behind them the
manor house glowed like a firelit beacon. Nicholas D'Eyville
and his friends had broken into the supplies of wine and ale
from the buttery, and the night was filled with coarse roaring
revelry.

'Only a month away from their feather beds,' Haukyn went
on, leaning on his spear, 'and every one of them thinks himself
the king of the greenwood!'

Adam snorted a laugh. The wiry young outlaw had changed
since their first meeting, back in the winter. He had matured,
it seemed. And although none of Reynard's band trusted Adam
entirely, they regarded him in better favour than the other renegade knights and serjeants whose company they kept. And
Haukyn at least seemed to like him. It was a small comfort.

'Not so long ago, they'd be hanging the likes of us from the
trees at the first chance,' the young man went on grimly. 'Now

they call us friends. Like as not they'll be trying to hang us again before long.'

'You don't think much of their pledges of brotherhood then?' Adam asked.

Haukyn cleared his throat and spat into the darkness. 'Maybe there'll be peace one day,' he said, with a strangely wistful tone, 'and things'll go back to how they were before the wars. Maybe the king'll grant us all his mercy, and a general amnesty. Then we can go home and work our lands, find wives and raise families . . . Maybe. Till then, I'll trust no bastard in belt and spurs!'

Adam's brief chagrin rose and then died. Haukyn was right. He could put no faith in Sir Nicholas D'Eyville and his knightly friends either.

Over the last month, news had filtered slowly into the fast-nesses of Sherwood from the world outside. Fugitives and survivors of the attack on Chesterfield had told the full tale of the destruction of Earl Robert's army. Travellers waylaid on the highway had filled in the rest. The earl himself had been captured quickly enough, while trying to hide under a pile of woolsacks at the back of the church. Now he was a prisoner of the king once more, loaded with iron chains and taken off to London. John D'Eyville had cut his way through the enemy and ridden to safety; he and Baldwin Wake had returned to their fastness in the marshes and fens of the Isle of Axholme, in defiance of the king and his mercy. Of Henry de Hastings there was no word.

No word either of Joane de Bohun, or Hugh of Oystermouth. The king's nephew and his troops had retreated south, leaving a garrison at Chesterfield. Reginald de Grey had returned to Nottingham Castle. And now the king was summoning all his loyal knights, barons and magnates to muster at Warwick. The full military might of England was about to fall on the stronghold of Kenilworth.

All of it felt so far away. And yet, some days, Adam felt in the air the reverberation of distant events, like the roll of thunder across the summer sky.

'Will you go to Nottingham then, if you get the chance?' Haukyn asked abruptly. Adam had almost forgotten he was there, it had grown so dark.

'If I can. There's a woman there I need to find.'

'Your lady, is it? The same that you travelled with, back in the winter?'

Adam took his time before replying. It was possible that Joane was in Nottingham; often he had considered slipping away from the camp to go there and find out. His pledge to D'Eyville meant little to him, but he suspected that Reynard would come after him if he did. No, he thought, while the delay chafed at his nerves he would need to know exactly where Joane was being held before he could act decisively.

'There's another,' he said. 'A Jewish woman . . .'

'Jewish?' Haukyn said, and made a sound in his throat. 'Can't say I've ever seen one of them. They do say that Jews is beastly folk, though, and drink the blood of Christian children, and . . .'

'Fools say those things,' Adam told him sharply, conscious that he had believed such lies himself once. 'Anyway, I need to find this woman. A promise I made to a friend.' For a moment he recalled Robert de Dunstanville's request, as he lay dying on the field of Evesham. He had carried the guilt of that neglected oath for too long.

But the guilt of his cowardice at Chesterfield was harsher still. He had fled the fight, neglecting all his vows of knighthood, and since then he had considered himself vile. He had deserted Joane as well, leaving her in the hands of the enemy as he scrambled to save himself. Sometimes he considered that it might be better if he never saw her again. Never saw Isabel either. Perhaps in truth this desperate outlaw life in the woods and wastelands was all he deserved.

He was about to speak again, but realised that Haukyn had become strangely still and alert. His scalp prickled; the young brigand had senses like a hunting hound, and he had detected something moving on the track that emerged from the woodland.

Swinging his spear up, Haukyn aimed it into the darkness. Adam curled his fist around the hilt of his sword. Hurried footsteps, coming closer. Then the shape of a man forming from the blackness. Adam drew his sword.

'Halt there!' he said, keeping his voice low. 'Who are you?'

'A friend,' another voice replied. Adam could make out the paleness of the man's raised palms as he paced forward. 'A friend from Nottingham, with news for Sir Nicholas!'

'What news? – we share all here,' Haukyn said.

As the newcomer advanced closer Adam saw he was a weaselly little man in dusty servant's clothes. A spy, he assumed, that D'Eyville paid to bring him intelligence. The man leaned forward to brace himself on his knees, breathing hard. He must have run the last distance through the night. 'If that's ale in that flask . . .' he said.

Adam picked up the leather bottle and passed it to him, and the man drank deeply and then smacked his lips. 'Very well,' he said. 'There's a party setting out from Nottingham, three days from now. A king's clerk, travelling north to meet with the Bishop of Durham.'

'Well guarded, then?' Haukyn said.

The man nodded. 'But he'll be carrying coin, to raise troops from the bishop's estates to serve at the siege of Kenilworth Castle. He'll be coming up the Great Highway, through the forest.' He took another drink from the flask, then tossed it back.

'Wait,' Adam said as the man strode towards the manor to pass on his news. 'Is there a woman in Nottingham, a nobleman's widow, arrived about a month past?'

In the dark he caught the flash of the man's eyes, his smile. 'There are women aplenty in Nottingham, friend,' he said. 'You can take your pick!'

*

Three days later, he waited once more in the shadow of the trees. D'Eyville had arranged his men in three bands, along the highway a mile north of Ravenshead, where it crossed a brook and climbed a slope through dense woodland. The trees were cut back from the sides of the road, but long grass and scrub had grown along the verges, tangling between the old stumps thickly enough to conceal the figures lying in ambush.

It was June, the summer solstice approaching, and the day was growing warm. Insects hung in shafts of light between the trees. Adam sat with his back to a stump, and swigged warm water from his flask. A cart went by, carrying a load of charcoal north towards Mansfield, but if the carters spied the men waiting in the trees and roadside bushes, they gave no sign of it. It was past noon by the time the birdcall signal came from the watchers to the south. Moments later, the sound of thudding hooves and jingling harness grew more distinct. Craning his head a little from his place of concealment, Adam peered down the road and saw the group of riders approaching.

There were a dozen men on horseback, at least half of them armed. Four laden packhorses and a light baggage cart came with them. They crossed the brook, the hooves of their horses splashing loud through the shallows, then bunched together and slowed as they climbed the slope. Two mailed serjeants rode in the lead; they were halfway to the summit, passing through the deepest shade of the trees, when the cry went up.

Archers appeared from cover on both sides of the road, stepping from behind the trees and darting from the scrub along

the roadside verges. 'Drop your weapons!' the men screamed as
they rushed forward. 'Throw them down!'

Adam drew his sword as he rose from cover and ran leaping through the heather banks onto the road. He heard the
hollow thud of arrows striking the sides of the baggage cart.
A horse screamed as it went down, shot through the neck. At
the top of the slope Nicholas D'Eyville and two of his comrades had ridden out on horseback, swords drawn, to block
the way ahead.

Half of the mounted serjeants had dropped their weapons at
the first challenge. The king's clerk – a young man in a tunic of
fine blue wool, his cloak secured by a gilded brooch – lifted his
hands at once, his face blank with fright. Adam seized the bridle
of the clerk's horse, his sword levelled at his throat.

Sudden hoofbeats from behind him. Two of the escorting men
had turned their mounts and were riding back down the slope,
D'Eyville and his friends spurring after them. Bows hissed, and
one of the galloping horses went down in a fountain of dust, pitching the rider forward over the flying mane. The second horseman,
a knight in a mail hauberk and surcoat, rode straight at one of
D'Eyville's men, who stood in his path. The big palfrey kicked out,
knocking the outlaw down with a hoof, then the rider screwed his
reins and brought the horse around as he drew his sword.

Adam ran up to the rider's left side. The knight twisted in
the saddle, trying to aim a cut at him, but Adam reached up and
seized the hood of his mail coif, which lay back upon his shoulders. The horse jolted forward, Adam keeping his grip on the
steel links and dragging the rider from the saddle. The knight
toppled backwards over the horse's rump, and Adam leaped
back as he crashed down into the dust of the road.

Reynard ran over to join them, an arrow nocked to his bow.
The fallen outlaw lay groaning where the horse had kicked him
in the chest.

Standing over the downed knight, Adam set the point of his blade to his throat. Only then did he recognise him. Blood flowed from the man's nose, reddening his clenched teeth, but his brow tightened as he gazed up at Adam.

'You?' he said.

'Barely more than a month, and already you've changed sides?' Adam replied.

'There are no *sides*,' Ralph de Grendon said. He was wincing as he tried to move. 'Earl Robert's a prisoner, and his lands forfeit. I sought the king's mercy, and it was granted. As for you . . . Rebels have turned to robbers, I see!'

Nicholas D'Eyville had swung down from his horse. 'Traitorous dog!' he said.

'Hang him from a tree!' growled one of the other rebel knights.

'I know my loyalty better than you,' de Grendon spat. 'You think you can preach to me? You – a band of thieves on the highway? You have no honour left – none of you!'

'He should hang, I agree,' Reynard said.

'He's my prisoner,' Adam said. 'I captured him, and I'll ransom him.'

'We hold all our captures in common, you know that,' D'Eyville said, with casual menace. He strolled over to de Grendon. 'If my man over there dies of his injury,' he said, gesturing to the fallen outlaw, 'then we'll hang you, understand?' He spat at him, then strolled on.

One of the serjeants had broken his neck when his horse went down; the others, with the king's clerk and the second escort knight, were soon stripped of their weapons and armour and securely bound with cords.

Ralph de Grendon still lay where he had fallen. He gestured to Adam. 'Listen,' the knight hissed through reddened teeth. 'Preserve my life, and I'll tell you something of worth.'

A glance at D'Eyville, then at Reynard and the other out-laws. Then Adam knelt quickly beside de Grendon. 'Speak,' he said.

'The woman . . .' de Grendon began, then spat blood. 'De Bohun's widow . . . Reginald de Grey has her at Nottingham. He keeps her closely confined in the castle . . . He's bought the grant from the Earl of Hereford.'

'What grant?' Adam demanded, stooping closer.

'Of her marriage, you fool,' de Grendon said. 'He means to wed her before Michaelmas next!'

*

It was the early hours of morning, just light enough to see the ground between the trees, when Adam slipped away from the camp.

D'Eyville and his band had spent the night in a glade of the oak woods, as it was pleasanter to sleep in the open air than the close confines of a smoky hut. In the middle of the glade they had built a fire, and roasted venison over the flames while they drank the fine Gascon wine intended as a present to the Bishop of Durham. Reynard and his men sat on the far side of the blaze, tipping back mugs of ale taken from the soldiers' supply. There were new arrivals among them, come from the lands across the Trent. And they brought news: John D'Eyville and Baldwin Wake, with the men from Axholme, had stormed Lincoln and almost captured the castle. The cobbled streets of the town, so the newcomers eagerly reported, had run with blood.

'And now my cousin's gone south, you say?' Nicholas D'Eyville asked, prodding at the fire with a stick. The roasting meat dripped and sizzled.

'Aye, with Lord Wake and all his company too.'

'We should join them,' somebody else said. 'Make a greater band, and hold all the eastern shires to ransom!'

Adam had paid little attention to the men's tales. He heard only the harshness of the voices, the harshness of the words, and felt a cold sickness inside him. He had managed to persuade D'Eyville not to hang Ralph de Grendon immediately, but the man kicked by the horse was suffering greatly, and might be dead by morning. Adam had no power to prevent further dishonourable acts. More than ever, he knew he had to get away from this place.

As the fire burned down and the last ghosts of smoke spiralled up towards the new moon, the men stretched themselves on their beds of heather beneath the trees. There were sentries around the perimeter of the camp, but with the warmth of the night and the sweet languor of the wine, few would be keeping a sharp watch. In any case, Adam thought as he rose and quietly gathered his sword and his small sack of possessions, the sentries would be looking outwards, not in. Silently, moving in a crouch, he crept across the margin of the glade and into the deeper shadow of the trees. A few men muttered or stirred in their sleep, but none challenged him.

Ralph de Grendon was still awake. Adam saw the flash of his eyes in the darkness as he approached. The captors had stripped the knight to his chemise and bound him to the base of a tree. Pacing up silently beside him, Adam drew his knife.

'You'll go north,' he whispered, kneeling beside him. 'And give me time to get clear first. Swear it.'

'I swear,' de Grendon said.

Adam cut his bonds. He pressed his palm to the man's shoulder, but the knight made no sudden movement, no lurch for freedom. Instead he remained sitting against the tree, not even moving his arms. Adam nodded once, then sheathed his knife and stood up. He barely heard de Grendon's whisper of thanks as he crept away.

Easy enough to slip past the sentry; the man was slumped against a tree ten paces away, snoring gently. Lifting each foot with care, holding his sword away from his body, Adam slid through the weave of darkness and moonlight. The blood was thumping in his neck. An owl hooted, so loud and distinct it almost sounded like a human call. Adam stilled his breath and waited. Then he stifled a laugh, and moved onward.

He was well out of sight or hearing of the camp when he halted suddenly, his spine stiffening. Over the past month he had come to feel at home in the deep woodland, and regard it as a sanctuary. Now he remembered the tales of his childhood, the deeper fears that grew from them, and felt himself surrounded by a hostile world. His eyes had grown accustomed to the deep darkness beneath the trees, but as he stared around himself the ivy-grown trunks were the bodies of giants, the banks of heather and nettles a vast serpent coiling over the forest floor. Sweat prickled his brow, and with a superstitious flinch he touched the medallion of St Christopher at his neck.

Then the darkness moved ahead of him, and he heard the crush and snap of brittle twigs underfoot. Adam's hand darted to his sword as the shapes of men rose from the black woodland all around him.

'No need for that,' Reynard said quietly. 'We're coming with you.'

Chapter 14

At first light they emerged from the woods and into the open heathland. It was a perfect summer morning, filled with the sound of birdsong, and only the faintest taste of woodsmoke on the air suggested human habitation. They had walked in near silence through the darkened woods; now, out in the clarity of dawn, they continued in silence until the sun appeared above the trees to the east. Only then, as they paused to rest and get their bearings, did Adam speak.

'You tired of Sir Nicholas's company, then?'

'He'd have tired of ours, soon enough,' Reynard replied. 'And matters would have come to blows, as they ever do. Besides, there was no way he'd divide that fat purse of silver we captured equally between all.'

'And where is the fat purse of silver now?'

Reynard grinned, and patted the sack he carried at his side, beneath his ragged cloak. Not all of his men had accompanied him; Ivo of the North, John Silence and two or three others had remained behind. Had they agreed to the separation, Adam wondered, or even been aware of it?

'I was about to bid them a soft farewell anyhow,' Reynard said, with a twitch of his head. 'We'd have gone without you, except that you were making such a lot of noise crashing about in the bushes and freeing that prisoner of yours, it seemed only fair that we thank you for covering our exit.'

'Where will you go now?' Adam asked. He was still unsure whether the brigands would force him to accompany them further.

'Back to the dales, where we belong,' Reynard replied, and jerked his head away from the rising sun. 'Far from these quarrelling lordlings and their great matters. You?'

'I go to Nottingham,' Adam told him, trying not to let his relief show. As the light grew he could make out the line of the Great Highway crossing the heath, only half a mile distant. Reynard had led them here on purpose, he realised.

'Then your road lies there,' the outlaw said, with a brisk gesture. 'We shan't detain you.'

He made as if to turn away, and Adam glanced around at those who accompanied him, clearly visible now in the gathering light of dawn. Haukyn gave him a brief nod, and John the Scot raised a hand in farewell. Once he had hated these men, Adam realised, and feared their leader. Now it was painful to part with them.

'You remind me of somebody,' he said to Reynard. 'Somebody I once knew.'

The outlaw paused and peered back over his shoulder. He gave a wolfish grin. 'And this person came to a great and gallant end, no doubt? Well never fear, I'll not be doing likewise.' He drew a long breath, squinting into the sun. 'Dying well's easy,' he said. 'Living well – now that's the real test of a man. But you've reminded me of something too . . .' He reached beneath his cloak, into the sack he wore slung around his shoulder, then brought out a smaller bag and tossed it towards Adam.

'Your share,' Reynard said.

*

The sun was climbing the sky as Adam approached Nottingham. He had fallen in with a band of packmen and pedlars who were travelling to the weekday fair; at first they had been wary of him, in his dun hood and cloak, his smoke-smelling earth-hued garments, and of the sword-sized bundle he carried slung over his shoulder. But he had assured them that he posed no threat, and they had wordlessly agreed that he could share the road with them.

'A fine morning, goodsir,' one of them said as they walked, falling into step beside Adam. 'Look here – the baby tooth of Little St Hugh! Proof against the jealousy and malice of others, and yours for only a penny!'

Adam glanced at him. He recognised the round fur hat and the wandering eye.

'Ignore him,' a thick-set packman said, sweating under his load. 'That one's been trying to hawk his tat to us since we left Mansfield.'

'Uncharitable cur!' the pedlar cried, his eye veering wildly. 'For charity is the milk of virtue, goodsir, as I'm sure you've heard. And what could be more virtuous than this certified relic of St Maurice? A fingernail, to bring wealth . . .'

'You had a relic of Simon de Montfort once,' Adam broke in. 'A scrap of his shirt. Do you still have it?'

'Saint Simon, would that be?' the pedlar gasped. His head jerked from side to side; Adam was unsure whether he feared being overheard or was simply excited. 'Well, yes, I did . . . and I'm sure I could find it again. Or did I sell it to a man in Derby?'

'We'll have no talk of Simon de Montfort here!' the sweating packman called. 'That rogue caused enough bloodshed while he lived! *Saint*, indeed – he was excommunicated, and died a traitor's death!'

Adam stiffened, his hood concealing his angry glare. The pedlar had fallen into fitful muttering, while the packman and his fellow travellers strode on down the long slope that led to the town.

They went in through the Cow Lane Bar – or so the packman called it – and at once the noise and activity of the town consumed them. The church bells had only just rung the hour of prime but already the narrow street was crowded and the air filled with the smoke of the morning kitchen fires. Adam had managed to detach himself from his fellow travellers, but the relic-pedlar dogged his steps, ducking and weaving in his wake. He had appointed himself guide to Nottingham's sights, and pointed them out as they walked.

'That's the French town, goodsir, and over there's the English burg. And that way's the Shambles, and there's the Poultry. And that dead ahead's St Peter's Church, sir. You might just catch a look at the castle, away beyond it there on the mount.'

'Where do the Jews live?' Adam asked, pausing and turning to him abruptly.

'The J-Jews, goodsir?' the pedlar replied, with an anxious stutter. 'Why would you . . .? Well, they live in the Jewry, which is down yonder by Warsergate, which backs onto Swine Green, I suppose especially to punish them for their heathen ways, sir, as swines disgust them particularly . . .'

Adam narrowed his eyes as he committed the directions to memory. His first task would be to find Belia and discharge his vow to Robert de Dunstanville. Then he would have to set about locating Joane and liberating her from the custody of Reginald de Grey – altogether a more difficult undertaking, but one he needed to accomplish as soon as possible. Michaelmas was far off yet, but after deserting Joane in Chesterfield Adam was driven by the need to redeem himself.

He walked on, following the swell of the crowd. A short way further, and a turn or two of the street brought him into a confined square packed with stalls and hucksters, mud and straw underfoot and the air rich with the stink of dung. Cries cut through the clamour of other voices: 'Pies all hot, all hot!' and 'Ale fresh! Ale fresh!'

'The weekday market, goodsir,' the pedlar explained, with a shrug.

Fishing into the small bag Reynard had given him, Adam brought out a sliver of silver. Most of the coins in the purse had been cut into half and quarters. The pedlar took it gladly, but with a questioning glance.

'Tell nobody you've met me,' Adam said. 'And leave me be.'

The pedlar nodded, and his expression sharpened to a very knowing smile. 'Oh yes, Sir Knight, I will,' he said, and held up the half-penny. 'But I do recall meeting you once before, I think. Close to Beeston, it was. Match this, and I might not.'

Frowning, Adam rifled the purse until he found another half-penny, and gave it to the pedlar. The man wished him good day, and melted into the crowd. Hopefully, Adam thought, he would be as good as his word. But he could not risk believing him.

He paid a quarter-penny for a meat pie and a cup of ale to break his fast, then found a barber who had set up his stall outside the wooden posts of the Guildhall and paid another piece of silver for a shave and a trim. Sitting on the stool while the man worked, he studied the passing crowds. So many faces, he felt almost unnerved. So many bodies packed together. The last time he had been surrounded by such a throng was in the marketplace of Chesterfield, moments before it erupted into bloody violence. He closed his eyes, and for a heartbeat saw the streaming gore, the flash of blades. Then the barber wiped his face and Adam pulled his tunic back on, glad to be on his way.

Walking slowly, casting glances up the side streets, he steered a path back towards the area that the pedlar had indicated. He found it quickly enough. A narrow lane deep in shadow, with old houses backing onto a stretch of ancient crumbling wall. He had only taken a few paces along the street before a man emerged from a side alley with the distinctive identifying panels of white linen sewn to his mantle. Now that he was here, Adam was unsure how to proceed. He had no idea how many Jews lived in Nottingham, or whether any of them might know Belia.

Perhaps, he thought with a lurch of despair, she had already left the town and returned to London?

Opposite the alley he leaned against the wall and waited. The sun angled down the street, and the noise of the marketplace echoed between the houses.

'You are looking for somebody?' a voice asked.

The man had appeared beside Adam without him noticing. He was small, with a cocked head and an eye as bright as a sparrow. One side of his face was marked with a burn scar, and his beard did not grow there. At his voice Adam had stepped away from the wall, reaching instinctively for the sword he carried in the bundle over his shoulder.

'Forgive me for startling you,' the man said. He was speaking in French, rather than the English of the common people. 'But we have reason to be wary of strangers here. Especially young men who appear to be carrying swords.'

'My apologies,' Adam said, easing his hand from the concealed hilt. 'I'm looking for somebody, it's true. Belia, a Jewess. Sister of a man named Elias, who lives in London. Do you know of her? She has a child, I think.'

'You're a friend of this Belia, then?' the man enquired. Only now did Adam notice the pointed yellow skullcap he wore. Elias had worn one very similar, he recalled.

Adam nodded. 'I have a message for her,' he said.

The man held up a finger, bidding him to wait, and paced across the street and into one of the narrow alleyways opening between the larger houses. Returning a short while later, he gestured for Adam to follow him. He led the way to a wide gateway further up the street, and along a covered passageway. Two young men stood up from a bench to bar the way, but at a gesture from the man with the scarred face they stepped back. Adam glanced at them as he passed. His guide did not appear to be a threat, but the young men had the look of fighters. He wondered whether he was being led into danger here, and how quickly he could free his sword. The knife in his belt would be quicker, he thought, and a better weapon in a confined space.

At the far end the passage opened into a gloomy yard, and the scarred man gestured for Adam to remain there while he disappeared into the house. Adam sat on the coping of a small well. He could smell food cooking nearby, and the distant reek of a tannery. Somewhere a baby was crying.

When the figure appeared in the doorway opposite he got to his feet at once. He had not been expecting to find her so soon.

'So it really is you,' she said.

She took a few steps forward into the yard. A maid followed her, carrying an infant wrapped in a shawl.

'Belia,' Adam said, laying down his sword. He stepped towards her, then abruptly she ran to him and embraced him fiercely. But when he stepped back her expression was grave and racked with sorrow.

'How long has it been?' she asked. 'A year?'

Adam nodded. 'I'm sorry. I was a captive, and then . . .'

'You don't have to explain,' she told him. She had changed in the months since their last meeting. She had been dressed in widow's weeds when Adam first met her, years before, and now she wore the same clothing of black and grey, but she appeared to have aged by more than twelve months. Her hair had grown ashen, and her face was hollowed, but the warmth and wisdom of her gaze remained.

'I know what happened at Evesham,' she said, seizing his hands. 'I know Robert died there. Were you with him?'

'I was,' Adam told her. So many times he had imagined this moment, and the discharge of the debt he had carried for so long. Shame had kept him away; shame, and fear of how she might react. 'I was with Robert,' he said, 'in his final moments. He was badly injured, a wound in the belly, and knew he was dying. He said . . . he spoke your name. As his last word. He wanted you to know that.'

Belia closed her eyes and stepped away, covering her face. For several slow heartbeats they stood silently. 'I knew,' she said at last. Tears roughened her voice. 'I saw him, standing beside my bed one morning. A vision. It must have been that very moment. I knew, then, that he was gone. But I thank you for telling me of it.'

The baby stirred in its swaddling, and let out a cry. Belia turned at once to comfort the child. Adam had a brief glimpse of a round red face, a plump fist. 'Your child?' he asked.

'Robert's child, yes,' she told him. 'Robert's son. Six months old now, and already as strong as his father!'

The baby wailed suddenly, and very loud. The nursemaid began to bob and coo.

'This is my brother-in-law's house,' Belia told Adam as she helped comfort the infant. 'I've lived here for nearly a year now. Wilecok is in Nottingham too, with his wife and child – did you know that?'

'Hugh of Oystermouth told me,' Adam said, nodding. Wilecok had been Robert de Dunstanville's groom and servant, and Adam had known him well. It would be good to see him again. He had noticed Belia's twitch of displeasure at the mention of Hugh's name; clearly she had not parted from him on good terms.

'But why are you here, Adam de Norton?' Belia asked, cradling the baby in her arms. 'Why now, of all times? So soon after the news from Lincoln.'

Adam's brow furrowed. 'Lincoln?'

'You don't know?' Belia's expression hardened, and for a moment she could not look at him. 'You really don't know what your friends did in Lincoln, not ten days ago? The men who call themselves the Disinherited?'

'Tell me. I've heard nothing of it.' But even as he spoke Adam remembered the fireside stories, only the night before. Baldwin Wake and John D'Eyville and the men of Axholme had attacked Lincoln. And now he was to learn what they had done there.

'They invaded the town, and the castle,' Belia said, her clipped voice chopping the words. 'Then they went down into the Jewry and attacked our people there. Just like they did in London two years ago – and the scum of the town joined in with them, as always. They dragged the Jews from their houses and butchered them – men, women, children too. Near a hundred and sixty slain, so we hear, their bodies left naked in the streets. Then they sacked their houses, smashed the document chests and burned the records of loans and debts. For *money*, Adam,' she said, with furious disgust. 'Your friends did this because they *owed money*, and did not want to pay!'

'They are not my friends,' Adam said. But the words choked in his mouth.

*

In an upper chamber of the house, dishes of nuts and pickled cheeses were laid on a circular table. Adam was not hungry, but sipped from a cup of watered wine just to appear polite. This was not a sociable occasion.

'And you say he was once a follower of the cursed de Montfort?' one of the assembled men asked, gesturing towards Adam. 'Like the devils who attacked Lincoln? A king's enemy, then, and a fugitive. Even to shelter him is a crime!'

Adam made to speak, but Belia subtly gestured for him to remain silent. Her brother-in-law Menahem was a stout, powerful-looking man in late middle age, dressed in finely cut clothes. He appeared to have taken against Adam from the first, for all his duties as a host.

'True enough,' said the man with the burned cheek. His name was Bonefay, and he was the owner of the neighbouring property; the two young men who had guarded the passageway were his sons. 'And yet,' he went on, 'our sister Belia claims he has been a good friend to her.'

'He risked his life to save mine, in London,' Belia told them. 'He saved others too – he and Robert de Dunstanville. He is not our enemy, Menahem. Would he be here, if he were?'

The third man was much older, bent and grey. He was the Rabbi Chaim, Adam had learned. The younger woman accompanying him was his daughter, Chera.

'Certainly, he came peaceably to us,' the rabbi said. 'We should respect that, in these troubled times. And besides . . .'

'But he wishes to oppose Sir Reginald de Grey,' Menahem broke in. Adam had already told Belia of Joane's confinement in the castle, and his intention to liberate her if he could. 'The king's constable, and our chief protector! Should we give shelter to one who plans such evil?'

'Not evil!' said Chera, the rabbi's daughter, with a brisk shake of her finger. 'If the constable intends to marry the lady by force . . .'

'Not possible. The ruling of Magna Carta forbids it.'

'A rule broken often enough, Menahem, like all of them,' said Bonefay. 'Besides, what power would she have to refuse, in those circumstances? Without a friend or supporter . . .'

'This Lady Joane,' the rabbi asked Adam, narrowing his eyes. 'Her name was de Quincy before her marriage, you say? Would she be descended from the Dowager Countess of Winchester?'

Adam thought for a moment; Joane had boasted often enough of her family connections. 'Her granddaughter, I think,' he said.

'The countess was a good friend to our people in Leicester,' the rabbi said, nodding wisely, 'when the accursed Simon de Montfort first came to these shores. One of the few, among the higher nobility. That at least might count in her favour.'

Menahem was about to add something, but Belia cut him off. 'Dispute all you like,' she declared. 'This man is my friend, and I will vouch for him. If you wish to expel him, you must expel me too.'

The rabbi laughed. 'There speaks one of true heart!' he said. 'And who could argue with that?'

'Very well,' Menahem agreed, grudgingly. 'Perhaps the Christian can stay in my Pilchergate house, with the others. But only for a few days. And God alone knows what will happen then.'

As the three other men retreated to the far end of the chamber and conducted a brief muttered debate, Belia leaned towards Adam. 'In three days' time,' she told him in a low voice. 'It is the Eve of John.'

Adam nodded. The night before the Feast of St John the Baptist was always a time of revelry and disorder, of bone-fires and wake-fires lit in the streets, of music and dancing. A night when the wilder passions of the mob could be unleashed.

'After what happened in Lincoln, we fear a similar attack here,' Belia said. 'So you'll understand why so many of us are wary of strangers . . .' She gestured towards her brother-in-law and the other men, who appeared to have reached a conclusion. 'But Menahem will shelter you, for now – he's a good man, for all his stern attitudes, and I'll see that he does.'

*

The next day was the Jewish Sabbath, and Nottingham was crowded for the great Saturday Market. Adam wore his hood pulled low, glancing quickly around him as he moved through the streets. He had a better guide this time, at least. Wilecok had been living in Nottingham with his wife and child for nearly a year, and already acted like a native of the town. As he led Adam through the throng in the main marketplace he greeted the traders, the grifters and hucksters, even the beggars by name, speaking back over his shoulder as he went.

'Yes, Lady Belia's a good mistress, right enough, for all she's a Jew – suffice it to say, many think ill of them, as I did once myself, shame though it be . . . But now God has opened my eyes, so to speak! Even her sister's husband's not a bad sort. Now step careful here, master, mind the turds . . . Yes, it's true I was once thinking to go back to London, but Nott'n'am's a decent town, especially since I'm a family man now. I'm opening an alehouse, a right goodly one, me and my wife, did Lady Belia tell you?'

Adam shook his head. Wilecok and his Gascon wife lived with their infant child in a narrow house owned by Belia's brother-in-law. Adam was lodging there too now, in the cramped upper chamber; he had not realised how much he missed the faces of his past. But it was strangely disconcerting to find a man who had spent so long on the tournament circuit now deeply bedded in domestic contentment.

'And it's good to keep the connection to Sir Robert, you know,' Wilecok went on, rubbing the grey bristles on his chin with a grimy knuckle, 'with his little boy being here and all. How we miss him, every passing day! Though that's nought to you, of course, who was with him in his last hour . . .'

They were nearing the western end of the marketplace now, where the cattle traders had their pens and stalls. Across the roofs to his left Adam could make out the walls and ramparts of the castle.

'Can we get in there?' he asked, catching Wilecok's arm.

'The castle? Not unless the constable's men drag you there in irons.'

'Have you seen him? Reginald de Grey?'

'He rides in and out, with his retinue,' Wilecok said, with a dismissive gesture. 'But if you want to know if I've seen Lady Joane de Quincy, or whatever she's called now – no, I ain't!'

They walked over to the castle all the same, or as close as they could get without attracting attention. The outer gatehouse was a massive structure with twin towers, a drawbridge and portcullis. Another gatehouse stood beyond it, and a walled keep to its left on a high rocky summit. Open ground, cleared of houses and trees, surrounded the castle on all sides. No chance to approach without being seen from the ramparts. No chance to slip through the gates or scale the walls without being shot down by the patrolling crossbowmen. Over the gate flew Reginald de Grey's banner, blue and white stripes with a red bar across the top.

Somewhere inside that fortress, Adam thought, was Joane. And his hopes of getting her out seemed to have evaporated completely.

The following morning he went with Wilecok and his wife to the Church of St Mary's, close to their house. It was a balm to his soul; he had not heard mass properly since leaving Duffield. After the service he lingered in the crowd outside the doors and looked at the faces around him. Most were ordinary townsfolk, plump and prosperous, emerging from the gloomy solemnity of the church to chatter and gossip in the warm sun. It was only three days until St John's Eve. Were these people really likely to turn on the Jewish community of their own neighbourhood, as those in London had done years before? Perhaps not, Adam thought. But if Nicholas D'Eyville decided to emulate his cousin at Lincoln, and led his gang down from the forest . . . Or if John D'Eyville, Baldwin Wake and their followers chose Nottingham as their next target . . . Adam remembered what he had seen in Westcheap and the London Jewry all too well. He remembered Belia's bitter words: '*and the scum of the town joined in with them, as always*'. . .

As if summoned by the grim recollection, a pair of young men appeared on the far side of the street. One was Bonefay's elder son, Yosi, and both were dressed in the patched mantles of the Jews. At once a stir ran through the crowd outside the church, the warm goodwill hardening and souring into aggression.

'Shame on them!' somebody in the crowd shouted. 'Showing their heathen faces here on the Lord's Day!'

Adam felt a tight grip on his arm. Hissing between his teeth, Wilecok ordered him to remain silent, to do nothing. Yosi and his friend passed rapidly, heads down. A barrel-chested man stooped and flung a clod of manure after them.

'What will happen, on John's Eve?' Adam asked, speaking quietly. 'Will there be trouble here?'

'May the Blessed Virgin prevent it,' Wilecok said. Beside him, his Gascon wife was muttering fiercely in her own language, cradling their child in her arms.

'But it's possible?' Adam went on.

'There are fools and devils enough in any town, and this one's no different,' Wilecok said with a squint and a nod. They were walking away from the church now, letting the crowd thin behind them. Adam knew that the Jewish community, here and elsewhere, employed Christian servants and retainers like Wilecok to guard them and their property in times of trouble. He did not doubt the man's loyalty to Belia, at least.

'Anyway,' Wilecok went on, 'it's the king who's supposed to protect the Jews, and the constable's the king's man. I believe Rabbi Chaim's been up to the castle this very day to request sanctuary within the walls for his people on St John's Eve.'

'Was it granted?' Adam asked with sudden interest.

Wilecok nodded. 'Mind you,' he went on, raising a twisted finger, 'it'll be up to the likes of me and a few sturdy others to barricade the doors and windows and stand guard outside them. No St John's revels for the likes of us, suffice it to say! But such is the price we pay for our loyalty and good service . . .'

But Adam was no longer listening. As they walked back towards the house his mind was turning, his thoughts spinning, and he tried to hide his smile. Suddenly Nottingham Castle did not seem so impregnable after all.

Chapter 15

They left the house before sunset. Already the streets thronged with gangs of people awaiting the festivities ahead. Wood lay heaped outside the churches and chapels, and at every intersection, ready to be kindled into the fires that would fill the evening sky with whirling sparks and burn until the midnight hour.

Heads down, hoods raised, they moved fast. Adam had not counted their number, but there must have been at least a score of them, children included, and more fell in along the route. They carried no weapons, but most had bundles of possessions, or heavy ironbound boxes and chests. Adam carried his sword and belt, with the purse Reynard had given him, rolled in sacking and slung across his shoulder beneath the enveloping mantle. It had been Menahem who had handed him the hooded garment with its identifying patches, but he had kept his grip on it for several heartbeats, staring Adam in the eye. He had been against this from the start, and still opposed it fiercely.

'We are not smugglers, or thieves!' he had shouted, during the angry debate the day before. 'Our faith is not a ruse, and should not be used as such by any outsider!'

'This puts us all in danger,' another man had agreed. 'What if this stranger is discovered among us? What if he commits some crime? We would be culpable, and rightly so!'

'I intend no wrong, I assure you,' Adam had told them. 'Just get me into the castle, and I'll cause you no further trouble . . .'

'Oh, and we should take your word for this? The word of a Christian rebel? Ha!'

'Peace, Jacob, please,' Belia said. 'I've told you, I know this man. Adam de Norton is a friend, and I owe him my life. This is no evil thing he proposes . . .'

In the end it was Belia's older sister who tipped the balance in his favour, arguing with her husband to grant his permission. But still Adam felt the weight of the community's disapproval settling over him as he shrugged himself into the enveloping mantle. Belia and Yosi, Bonefay's son, had helped him to arrange it around himself in the customary way. They did not need to remind him to keep his head down, to keep silent, and to follow where the others led. Once inside the castle he would be on his own; for now, his life belonged to them.

Reginald de Grey had sent a party of armed men led by a pair of serjeants to conduct them to the safety of the royal fortress. Sufficient to ward off idle attackers, but Adam knew that they could do little to defend against a concerted mob. Nor, he suspected, would they even try.

The serjeants led them along the narrower streets and alleys, avoiding the main thoroughfares where the crowds gathered. Down a lane behind the high wall of the churchyard, they crossed a broad street where men lounging at the corners yelled abuse after them. Adam bristled, wanting to turn and glare back at them, but he suppressed the urge. His discomfort mounted even so. Belia was walking just ahead of him with her sister Hester, the rabbi's daughter Chera and the maidservant carrying her child; the women glanced back at intervals, as if to check he was still with them.

Then, as they darted across another crossroad, Adam caught a glimpse of the castle ramparts down the street to his right. He saw the great gateway, with the towers and drawbridge. 'Wait!'

he called to the women ahead of him, fearing a mistake. 'Where are we going? The castle's that way . . .'

'The likes of us don't go in through the main gates!' Mena-hem's voice said from behind him, with a note of scorn.

'There's another entrance,' Belia told Adam, dropping back to walk beside him. 'A postern gate leading to a tunnel that climbs up through the mount. It's used to bring supplies to the inner ward. They'll take us in that way, where none will see us.'

Sure enough, the two serjeants were leading the Jewish group towards the southern flank of the castle, which dropped sheer to the riverside. Bare rock showed through the scrub cover-ing the slopes, darkening now as the sun sank to the west. As he approached the shadowed bulk of the mount, Adam glanced upwards and recalled the cliffs of Beeston, and the terrifying descent. He lowered his eyes quickly, letting the hood cover his face.

There was a mill down by the riverside, and beyond it sheds and huts clustered around a wooden wharf. The ragged column of shrouded figures passed the mill and the huts, and came to a halt in the deep shadow beneath a rocky bluff. Caves pitted the surface, the entrances hollowed from the sandstone.

'Quickly now, come on,' one of the serjeants said, stepping aside and gesturing curtly. Belia and the other Jews filed past him into the cave mouth, and Adam followed, keeping his head down. There was a wooden gateway mortared into the rock, heavy tim-bers studded with iron; stepping over the threshold, Adam felt the damp cold of the stone passageway closing around him. One of the castle servants checked off the refugees as they passed, grabbing each roughly by the shoulder and calling the number to a man behind him, who scratched lines on a tally board.

The tunnel led upwards, away from the light. One of the ser-jeants went ahead with a candle lantern and the other followed at the rear, but those in between them stumbled in darkness and reeling shadow. Adam's feet caught on steps cut into the rock floor. Muffled breath, footsteps, the shunt and stagger of bodies, all echoed in the stone throat of the tunnel.

Discomfort crawled through Adam's body, sharpening to a pulsing sense of panic. He sensed the weight of the rock above him, around him, pressing in on all sides. Like he had entered a tomb, he thought, and they would never emerge alive . . . They passed through another heavy wooden gateway, where a brutish-looking serjeant leered at them in the fierce glare of a lantern, as if he were taking possession of them. Adam heard the squeal of hinges and the heavy thud behind him, then the grate of an iron lock.

Then, abruptly, there was daylight ahead. The hooded figures were scaling a wooden ladder that rose into blueish twilight. Adam followed them, climbing upwards into a vaulted stone chamber. By the light filtering in through the barred windows he made out stacked bales and kegs, straw piled between them. This place would be the lodging of the Jewish refugees for the night, until they heard that the danger had passed and they could return to their homes. The second serjeant lowered a heavy trapdoor over the mouth of the ladder shaft and slammed an iron bolt across to seal it.

'Wait here with us,' Belia told Adam, drawing him down to sit beside her at the margin of the group. 'It's an hour or two yet until nightfall.'

Adam sat with his back to the stone wall, pulling the mantle around him. The serjeants and their guards had departed now, but he did not want to risk drawing any attention to himself. Instead he sat still and silent, running through what he had learned of the castle and its internal arrangement.

This storeroom was part of the inner ward, a circle of ramparts and towers on the top of the mount. The middle bailey below it was far larger; that was where the sheriff had his own chambers and kept his court. Beyond the gateway and moat lay the outer bailey, where the castle garrison was quartered. But where might Joane be held? Would Reginald de Grey be keeping her close to him, in the middle bailey? Or might he consider the inner ward with its strong towers and chambers a more secure lodging?

Adam turned the questions over in his mind as the light steadily faded. Menahem and Chaim shared the food and drink they had brought with them among their congregation, who ate by the glow of rushlights. Adam, seated at the far edge of the group, felt them shrinking steadily away from him. When it was almost too dark to make out the huddled figures, he stood up quietly and crossed to the open doorway. In the next chamber he stripped off the mantle he had been wearing. Carefully he folded it around his sword and belts, then stashed the bundle between two dusty kegs where it would not be seen. As he got to his feet a figure appeared from the darkness.

'A moment, Adam, before you leave us,' Belia said.

He turned to face her, and she placed her hand flat on his chest. 'You know,' she said in a whisper, 'that I only agreed to help you for Robert's sake.'

'I know that, yes. And I thank you all the same.'

He caught the slight motion of her head as she nodded. In the darkness her scent was very noticeable, stirring memories inside him. 'But I'm grateful you told me . . . of his end,' she said. 'These things are painful to hear, but become sweet in time. The memory of him has been all that's sustained me over these months.'

Adam took her hand, feeling a sudden tightness in his throat. 'I wish I could have come to you sooner,' he told her.

'No matter.' She squeezed his hand, then kissed him lightly. 'I hope you find your love,' she said. 'You may not deserve her, but you can help her avoid a worse fate. Go now, the hour is here. And if we don't meet again . . . May God's mercy guide you in the darkness.'

*

The first door he tried was barred from the outside, but the second opened freely. Adam breathed a prayer of thanks as he slipped out into the twilight dimness. Before him was the oval courtyard of the inner ward. Darkened buildings enclosed him on all sides, and a great stone tower rose directly ahead of him. Beside it was an arched gateway, where a lamp burned in an alcove. Figures were passing back and forth through the gateway, entering and then leaving carrying bales and bundles.

Summoning a casual air, Adam fought down the swell of nervous agitation. He could see now that the figures were castle servants, valets and porters, and they were bringing kegs of wine and ale and great sides of mutton and beef from another of the storage chambers. Supplies for the kitchens of the middle bailey, Adam realised. Reginald de Grey would be hosting a late supper for his guests, while they awaited the lighting of St John's fires.

'Let me help you,' he said, stepping up behind one of the men as he emerged from the storeroom. The man was toting a heavy barrel – pickled herrings, by the smell of it – and Adam took one end.

'Thanks, friend,' the servant said, barely glancing at him. Together they carried the barrel towards the gateway. Beyond the stone arch Adam could see the middle bailey some distance below, the great hall already lit by lamps.

'Always the usual rushing and bellowing, eh?' the servant said, waddling slightly as he walked with the barrel. 'And when do the likes of us get to eat our fill?'

Adam laughed wryly. He had known such things himself, when he was a young squire in the household of the Earl of Hereford. As they passed through the arch he glanced at the gates and was relieved to see that they were wedged open. Clearly the inner ward was not usually sealed at night, as he had feared it might be. That would make his task a little easier.

On the far side of the gateway a stone ramp descended to the side of a rock-cut ditch, crossed by a timber bridge. Peering across the ditch towards the middle bailey, Adam saw figures gathered in the spill of light from the great hall. Sir Reginald de Grey had clearly invited many friends to join him on this festive night, and each had brought their own retinue of followers. Not surprising that the castle servants appeared so unperturbed at finding strangers among them. Adam breathed another prayer. So far, God had favoured his scheme.

The hall was a huge stone building with a leaded roof and tall arched windows. Voices came from within, the boom of laughter and the skirl of music. Sir Reginald and his guests were keeping late hours; most probably they would remain at the feasting tables until the bone-fires and wake-fires were blazing.

Once he had helped the servant deposit the barrel of herrings in the kitchen courtyard, Adam had no trouble strolling back towards the hall. Sentinels lounged in the porch, but none moved to stop Adam as he passed between them. Inside, long tables and benches were set between the pillars, thronged all the way to the dais at the upper end. The central fire was unlit, but every pillar was ringed with candle-sconces and the heat and the smeech of burnt tallow thickened the air. Servants clustered behind the benches, and Adam moved between them along the nearer side aisle. He paused to reach between a couple of bent backs and snatch a bread roll from the table, then a cup of wine. He had not eaten since that morning, but he could barely swallow. The wine was sour, and he drank it down.

He was halfway down the hall when he saw her, and his breath caught. She was sitting up at the high table on the dais, and just for a moment as he gazed at her Adam felt utterly transfixed. Joane's expressionless face was waxen and gleaming in the candles' glow. She resembled an effigy of herself.

And there beside her, seated at the centre of the table, was Reginald de Grey, Constable of Nottingham. His black moustache twitched as he smiled and bantered with the man on his other side. Of course, Adam thought – *of course* de Grey would want Joane here with him, displayed before his guests. His captive. His *betrothed*. A surge of anger ran through his body so intense he feared those around him would notice.

But the men at the tables and their servants were distracted by a new amusement. A troupe of tumblers or jesters had entered the clear space between the tables, with musicians and singers accompanying them. One wore a tunic and hose stuffed with padding so his limbs and body bulged grotesquely. He capered before the dais, his arms tangled with reddened bandages, while two assistants tried to pull him down onto a bed they carried between them. Two more jesters were throwing sacks of straw about, bouncing and kicking them. Music twanged and jangled, and a pot-bellied jongleur broke into song. With a jolt of amazement, Adam realised that the song was about Robert de Ferrers.

'*The Earl of Ferrers he gathered his host,*' the singer bellowed, pumping his fist to the rhythm.

> '*He swelled up his pride and made many a boast!*
> *In Chesterfield town he thought to give battle,*
> *When he piled up the woolsacks to make him a castle!*'

To a gale of laughter, the man in the stuffed clothes blundered and blustered, tumbling among the sacks. He was supposed to be Earl Robert, Adam realised. The bandages on his arms were intended to represent bloodletting. He was trying to join in the raucous amusement of those around him, but horror racked him as he remembered what had really happened that day.

Up on the dais Reginald de Grey was smiling along with the farce. The man beside him was Warin de Bassingborne; Adam had seen him in the battle at Chesterfield, and on the field of Evesham before that. On de Grey's other side, Joane sat motionless and unsmiling. Then she turned her head, and with a shock Adam realised that she was staring directly at him.

> '*But he soon was dragged forth by our Lord of Almain,*
> *Who led him to Windsor, bound by a chain!*'

Adam met her gaze. Her expression barely shifted, just a slight widening of her eyes as she recognised him in the throng. For a long moment – three heartbeats, then four – they held the stare, and Adam felt the distance between them narrow to nothing. Then Joane blinked, and looked quickly away.

'Well done! A bold show!' de Grey cried, clapping as the jesters bowed before him. He threw a small purse of coin and the pot-bellied singer caught it deftly and bowed again. The others were running around the tables, snatching food and drink. Some of the guests started throwing food at them as they ran.

Adam had hoped that he might be able to approach the dais and the high table undetected, but he saw now that it was impossible. Only servants in de Grey's livery stepped up to the dais with their silver wine jugs, ewers and towels. Behind the table stood a line of the constable's household squires and valets, awaiting any order he might give. De Grey himself was scanning the crowd in the hall, still smiling but with a quick attentiveness. Adam shrank back behind one of the pillars. Would the man recognise him as the young knight who had challenged him at Duffield months before?

'Yes, de Ferrers is a fool, and ripe for mockery,' Warin de Bassingborne was saying, speaking loud enough for Adam to catch his words. He sounded slurred, slightly drunk. 'But what did your charming guest think of the performance? She was at Chesterfield herself, if I'm not mistaken?'

A hush fell. Adam realised that he was holding his breath. Everyone within hearing distance of the high table had turned now to look at Joane. Colour rose to her cheeks, and her lips tightened.

'The Lady Joane was there indeed,' Reginald de Grey said, with a smile. 'I plucked her from amidst the butchery myself. If I had not done so, well . . .'

'I'm most grateful to you, my lord,' Joane said. Her voice sounded strained, unnatural. 'As you know, I find the behaviour of these rebels and enemies of the king sickening. Had I not been compelled to accompany them, I should have forsaken them entirely . . . But now I feel safe and secure, under your protection.'

'Well said, by God!' de Bassingborne cried. 'And that from the widow of one of de Montfort's leading supporters!' He threw out his arms to the crowded hall, as if to beseech their applause.

'And soon,' de Grey announced, standing and raising his goblet, 'she will be my wife! How I long for it!'

'As do I, my lord,' Joane said. 'With all my heart.' And for the first time, she smiled.

Chapter 16

He waited in the shadows as the fires burned. Anger burned in his heart too. Anger for the greasy, prattling Reginald de Grey. For his braggart friend, de Bassingborne. For the foolish capering clowns, and their mocking display. And for Joane, for all he tried to quell it. Surely she had not meant the words he had overheard her speak. But they had cut him even so. Had she intended him to hear them?

Flames leaped towards the night sky. The servants must have kindled the bone-fires out in the bailey yard shortly after Adam entered the hall, and now they were burning fiercely. Reginald de Grey had ordered his minstrels out of the hall as well, to entertain the festive throng around the fires with the music of shrieking vielles and thudding tabors. Some of the castle servants had already broken into a dance, staggering as they circled the fires. Sparks whirled overhead, flickering around the ramparts.

Adam had left the hall with everyone else, while Joane was still seated at the table on the dais. He watched the porch carefully, squinting as every figure emerged into the firelit yard. He was still standing there, seething to himself, when he heard her voice addressing him.

'You there, servant, bring a lantern,' she said.

He turned sharply, and saw Joane standing at the edge of the firelight with two maids accompanying her. She must have left the hall by a rear door.

'Quickly now,' she told him, with a snap of command in her voice. 'I wish to return to my chambers. All that noise and merriment has given me a headache. I need a lantern to light the way – fetch one!'

Impressed by her quick thinking, Adam nodded briskly and crossed to the porch, taking one of the candle lanterns that hung just inside it. He could not bear to look at Joane as he rejoined her. She set off at once, across the cobbled yard towards the wooden bridge and the ramp that Adam had descended earlier.

'You're lodged in the upper castle, my lady?' Adam asked, muffling his voice. He held the lantern high, walking ahead of her. 'The inner ward, I mean.'

'You know I am,' she replied curtly. 'Now walk more briskly, please.'

He smartened his step, across the bridge and up the paved ramp towards the upper gateway. Already they had departed from the noise and laughter of the crowd around the fires. The two maids that accompanied Joane fell behind them.

'Did you mean what you said back there?' he asked, not turning his head.

'Of course not,' she whispered. 'I say what I must, or my life here becomes more unpleasant. Why are you here?' There was anger in her tone as well.

'To get you out,' Adam told her. 'Will you follow my directions?'

'I might,' she said, after a pause. She dropped back a few steps as they turned at the top of the ramp and passed beneath the stone arches of the gate. The porter was still slumped on his stool – he raised a wizened face to the lantern's glow as Adam passed, and nodded.

In the dark oval of the inner ward Adam hung back and let Joane go on ahead. She led him to a stairway that climbed to the chambers on the upper floor. Gesturing for her maids to go on ahead of her, she fumbled with the purse on her belt, as if to find a coin. 'There's a chapel beside the tower, behind you,' she said under her breath. 'Wait for me there. I'll come as soon as I can.'

Then she exhaled, as if in exasperation, and ran up the stairs after her maids.

Adam found the chapel easily enough. It was no more than a stone cell between two storage chambers, a rushlight burning on the altar in the recess at the back. Setting his lantern down, he knelt on the tiled floor and prayed. After a while, as he felt the cool of the night tightening his back, he got up and retreated to a stone bench just inside the doorway, where he sat huddled in the corner. His mind was in ferment, his blood racing. Even so, he had slipped into an uncomfortable doze by the time he heard a footstep on the tiles. He opened his eyes as Joane dropped to sit beside him.

'Those maids watch my every move,' she said, in a breathless whisper. 'I ordered them not to wake me until noon tomorrow, but I had to wait until they were snoring.' She had brought a large leather bag with her, and wore a dark cloak over her gown. Good walking shoes too – again Adam was impressed by her foresight. But for a moment he was overwhelmed by the sense of relief. She had not forsaken him.

'I swear I've hardly slept a night through since I was brought here,' Joane said quickly, with a shudder. 'I just lie awake, praying for God's mercy, trying to think of some way out of here . . .'

'I deserted you at Chesterfield,' Adam broke in, his words tumbling. 'I thought there was nothing I could do. When I saw de Grey's men take you . . .'

'But you came back for me,' Joane told him, with emphasis. She took his hand. 'You came back, and that's what matters now.'

'And you truly meant nothing of what you said, back in the hall?' Adam went on, unable to hold himself back.

'*Nothing,*' she replied, and shivered again. 'I've been a prisoner here, you understand? No more.'

Still Adam felt a chilling sense of unease. He drew a breath to ask more, but Joane placed her fingers over his lips.

'Wait,' she said. 'We have little time. Tell me what you intend to do.'

So he told her, briefly and directly. Joane said nothing at first. Then she gave a single nod, snatched up her bag and got to her feet.

Outside, the yard was drenched in moonlight. They moved stealthily, keeping to the blackest shadow around the walls, and when they reached the door Adam eased it open, alert for the squeal of a rusted hinge. The storeroom beyond was dense with shadow, but a spill of faint moonlight fell from the open door. Reaching down blindly Adam found the folded mantle, his own sword and belts wrapped inside it. Laying his own possessions aside he unwrapped the garment and passed it to Joane.

'Only one?' she said in an anxious whisper. 'What about you?'

'You're the only prisoner in this place. Nobody knows I'm here. But they counted the number of Jews entering last night, and they'll count the same number leaving at dawn.'

'But how will you get out?' Joane asked.

'There'll be a way,' he told her. In fact he had given little thought to that aspect of his scheme. And what had seemed a simple matter in daylight, from outside the castle, seemed altogether less simple here, wrapped in night's darkness with guarded ramparts and towers on all sides.

'I'll find you,' he told her, gripping her by the shoulders. 'As soon as you're safe – I'll get out myself and I'll find you.'

And then? he asked himself. But he had no answer to that question.

Quickly Joane pulled the oversized mantle over her dark cloak, and drew up the hood. From the next chamber Adam could hear snores and muttering voices; Menahem, Belia and the others would be spending an uncomfortable night on their beds of straw. And now Joane would be joining them, silent and unseen.

She embraced him quickly. 'Make sure you get away,' she told him, with an edge of her old note of command. 'I can't be alone out there.'

Then she slipped from his arms and vanished into the darkness.

*

The fires had burned down to embers by the time Adam returned to the middle bailey. Castle servants, grooms and men at arms, a few dishevelled women among them, sat around the margins of the glow with costrels and cups of ale. Dogs slinked in the shadows. Somewhere a minstrel scratched a tired dirge on a vielle, while another tapped at a tabor. Adam moved between them, carrying his scabbarded sword over his shoulder. None gave him a glance. The gates were firmly closed and the drawbridges raised, and there was no cause to fear or suspect strangers here. His empty stomach growled, but there was no food to be had.

Reginald de Grey and his friends had retired for the night. The constable's chamber was on the far side of the yard, adjoining a round tower at the angle of the wall. Adam could see candles burning within, and guessed de Grey was sitting up late, perhaps over a game of chess. Hours remained of the night. There was plenty of time to consider his exit.

What would Robert de Dunstanville have done, in this situation? Waited for dawn perhaps, and merely walked out of the gates as soon as they were opened, as if he were a visiting knight attending his own business? Perhaps. But Adam knew that Robert would have aimed for something greater. He would have had some scheme, some cunning stratagem, to create a diversion and cover both his own escape and Joane's departure from the upper castle. Only a bold stroke, Adam told himself, would succeed.

But he was weary, and hungry, and could find no inspiration in the smoky friendless dark. Instead he made his way to the stables, in the lee of the wall. Stepping over the groom sprawled asleep on the threshold he entered the familiar close warmth of the stalls. Most of the horses were still awake, restless and unnerved by the fires and the noise. Their eyes gleamed in the shadows, and they shunted in their stalls. Here and there other men lay asleep in the straw – the stable was as good a place as any to find a rough billet. In one empty stall Adam glimpsed a tangle of limbs, a woman and at least two men lying in drunken sleep. He moved on, picking his way carefully in the darkness, towards the saddle-and-tack room at the far end.

As he passed one of the last stalls the horse within stirred and stretched its neck forth, whinnying. In the dull glow from the fires outside, Adam made out the shape of the animal's head, the silver gleam of its hide. For a moment he scarcely believed it possible; then he had no doubt.

'*Blanchart!*' he whispered. He rubbed the horse under the jaw, and felt the breath blowing warm into his hands. Clearly the animal recognised Adam too. Of course, Reginald de Grey would have captured the silver-grey stallion in the rout at Chesterfield, and brought it back here to Nottingham with the rest of his plunder. Adam had not intended to leave here with a horse, and if he had wanted one then an ordinary riding palfrey would be less obtrusive. But now he knew what he had to do. God, he thought, had prompted him.

From the tack room he fetched a light riding saddle, with bit and bridle. A pair of plain steel spurs as well. One of the grooms sat up from the straw, and Adam motioned that he needed no assistance. First he rubbed the horse down with a currying comb, near blindly in the darkness but working by touch and familiarity. Then, as silently as possible, he fitted the headstall and saddle, buckling the girth straps. By the time all was done he was surprised to notice the faint grey light of approaching dawn seeping into the stable. In two or three hours the sun would rise.

Fatigue was weighing his limbs, but there was no time for sleep. Leaving Blanchart munching hay at the stable byre, he went back out into the bailey yard. Moving very slowly, placing each foot with care, Adam approached one of the fires and took a stick from the embers. The end was still glowing, red through the ashen grey, and he cupped it in his hands as he carried it back across the yard. Beneath the window of the chamber block was a low wooden shed filled with straw. One last swift glance to ensure nobody was watching, and Adam blew gently upon the brand. When the first flame appeared he stooped and thrust it deep into the stacked straw. Then he ran, quick loping strides back across the yard to the stables. He was braced for an alarm, a voice raised in challenge, but there was only the deep silence of the early hours.

A bell rang the hour from the distant friary, answered a moment later by another from further still. In the heavy gloom of the stable Adam sat on the straw. He prayed that his ruse had worked, that the flame would not be noticed until it had taken a good hold. For a long time he sat, tensed and waiting. Guiltily he recalled telling Menahem and the other Jews that he would cause no trouble in the castle, commit no crimes. At least, he considered, the stables were far from where the Jewish group were quartered. They could not be blamed for what was about to happen.

The first shout from outside. Adam sniffed, and caught the scent of fresh smoke on the morning air. *Up now.* All weariness poured out of him as he leaped to his feet. He was leading the saddled horse from the stable as a handbell sounded the alarm, shockingly loud as it clanged through the silence.

'Fire!' somebody was yelling, coarse and cracked. Adam had only to glance to his right to see the blaze over the stable-yard wall, the flames leaping up the side of the chamber block. 'Fire!' the voice yelled. 'Everyone up! Everyone bring water!'

Some of the people slumped in the yard cheered and laughed blearily, thinking this was some new entertainment for St John's Day. A serjeant ran between them, kicking and striking at them, rousing them from slumber and drink.

'Bring out the horses!' Adam cried, calling back towards the stable. 'Bring them all out, before the thatch takes fire!'

Everywhere was chaos and confusion as the smoke from the blaze filled the yard. Figures ran and collided, some of them toting buckets of water from the well. When he rounded the corner of the stable yard Adam saw a band of men beating wildly at the flames with blankets and brooms. But the fire was roaring now, rushing almost as high as the eaves of the chamber block.

Steering a path through the confusion, he led Blanchart towards the gatehouse. The stallion was nervous, terrified by the smoke and the heat of the flames, primed at any moment to kick or to bolt. Adam clasped the animal's head as he led it along, rubbing its muzzle, trying to reassure it every time it tugged against his hand.

Behind them, the grooms and stable servants were bringing out the other horses and casting them loose into the yard. The animals scattered, galloping and whinnying, adding to the confusion. In front of the gatehouse, a pair of serjeants stood and stared, baffled and slack-jawed.

'Get the gates open!' Adam commanded. He had fastened his sword belt around his waist; hopefully, he thought, he might at least look like a knight. 'Let the men outside in to help fight the fires – do it!'

Others had the same idea as Adam, and added their shouts. At least they could escape the fire, if nothing else. A man on the gatehouse battlement was blowing a trumpet. A moment later a heavy thud came from within the entranceway, and the studded gates swung back. A long low creak as the counterweight fell, and the drawbridge at the far end of the gate passage began to descend.

As soon as the bridge was down, men came running in from the lower bailey. Adam pulled Blanchart back from the rush. He glanced to his right, across the yard towards the chamber block. The fire in the straw shed was sinking now, doused to billowing black smoke, but other fires had broken out in the thatch of the adjoining buildings. Figures emerged from the smoke, and among them Adam recognised the moustached face of Reginald de Grey. He was stumbling, dressed only in a linen chemise covered in smuts. Two of his servants helped him as he staggered to safety.

Swinging up into the saddle, Adam kicked his heels and the destrier surged forward at once. Breasting the tide of incoming men, the horse rode straight out through the gate passage and across the drawbridge, hooves drumming on the timbers. Across the outer bailey Adam urged his mount into a canter.

'Open up!' he called to the men at the outer gatehouse. 'I'm carrying an urgent message from Lord Reginald de Grey!'

He reined to a halt before the gates, Blanchart stamping and champing the bit beneath him. Once again he shouted, standing in the stirrups, until the men in the gate towers heard him. A nervous few moments passed – Adam had no idea what he would do if his passage was barred now – and then the porters hurried forth to unbar the gates. As the outer drawbridge descended he was already nudging Blanchart forward into the gate passage, and the road was open before him.

*

The first sun was capping the roofs of Nottingham as the bells rang the hour of prime. Adam stood in the cool shadow of the mill beside the river, the grey horse placid at his side. The sky above him was bright and busy with swifts, but he could see the trails of black smoke still traced against the blue. Somehow he could still smell the burning too, as if the singe of it had worked into his clothes.

As the sunlight descended from the high walls of the castle to the scrub-covered crags of the mount, the first of the hooded figures emerged from the mouth of the cave. Adam remained where he was; he was close enough to observe them, but not to be seen by anyone accompanying them. The first few figures passed his place of concealment; he was certain that he would be able to pick out the one he was waiting for. He saw Menahem, his hood thrown back, and his wife behind him. Then, a few moments later, he saw Belia and the hooded figure that walked at her side.

He let them pass him, ensuring that none of the guards from the castle were escorting them, then he led the horse from the lee of the mill into the morning sun. Joane turned abruptly, as if she sensed him there. She looked back at Belia, who paused.

It had worked, he thought. Somehow, against the odds, his scheme had worked and Joane had escaped the castle. She seemed barely able to believe it herself; she walked slowly, as if drugged or half asleep, and only when she was a few paces from him did she begin to hurry. Adam slipped his foot into the stirrup and stretched out his hand. She ran the last few strides, and he seized her and pulled her up behind him.

Belia stood and watched as Adam turned the horse towards the ford further upstream. The last of the Jewish group had trailed past her now, and she was alone in the dawn light. Reining in his horse for a moment, Adam raised an open palm. A salute, or a farewell. She answered him with the same gesture. Then he shook the reins, nudged with the spurs, and rode onward.

Half an hour later they were riding across the open water meadows south of the river, Blanchart cantering swift and easy to an open rein. Joane sat at Adam's back, her arms clasping his waist. The morning mist veiling the meadow grass was lit by the sun, the town and the smoke-shrouded castle were behind them, and they were free once more.

Chapter 17

'You would scarcely imagine,' Joane said as she rode, 'that there was war anywhere in this land.'

Adam, walking beside the horse, could only agree. The broad track they were following crossed open countryside drenched in sunlight. Beyond the ditches and verges overgrown with cow parsley, smooth-limbed beech trees cast their shade along the hedgerows. On the far side, the land spread away in a herringbone pattern of strip fields, ripening wheat and barley, lush meadow and pasture. In the middle distance, a line of haymakers worked across the top of a meadow, their scythes whisking in unison. Their womenfolk came behind them, gathering and sheaving the last of the hay crop. The air was filled with sunlit pollen, birdsong, and the lazy drone of bees. Yes, Adam thought, it was hard to believe that this land had ever known conflict.

But war was out there, all the same. And they were journeying towards it.

Joane had told Adam all that she had learned during her month's unwilling stay at Nottingham. King Henry, she had overheard, had gathered all his strength for the siege of Kenilworth. At every market cross the summons had been read: every loyal vassal and tenant was to come to Warwick, with horses and arms and all their power, ready to march against the fortress, to crush and subdue the king's enemies and force peace upon England at last.

'So he'll be there already?' Adam had asked.

'Most likely, yes. With all the barons and knights of England, supposedly.'

'So, then . . . where should we go?'

They had spent the previous day in a small village a few hours' ride south of Nottingham, a cluster of thatched houses around a humped stone church, where Adam had paid for a room with a bed, stabling for his horse, and food and drink enough for a day and a night. Both he and Joane were too exhausted for gentility. He had given her the bed, and stretched himself across the threshold to sleep, his sword at his side. But they had not been disturbed, no riders had come from Nottingham hunting them, and nobody in the village seemed to care who they might be. It had been almost blissful. But Adam's mind was troubled, and his heart too.

'When you were de Grey's guest . . .' he had asked her, that first night.

'His *captive*.'

'When you were de Grey's captive, did he . . . You were not mistreated, at all?'

'No,' Joane told him firmly. 'I was held against my will, but not molested. Reginald de Grey is a crude and boorish man, but he's still a knight. He treated me courteously enough.'

She was hiding something, Adam could tell. There was an evasiveness in her attitude, in the curt edge of her words. And after a month in the company of Nicholas D'Eyville and his men he had few illusions about the behaviour of knights. But he knew enough not to push further. Not yet. If she wanted to speak of what had happened, she would do so.

For all her joy at her deliverance, there was a reserve in Joane now that Adam had not known before. Not the assumed hauteur of their journey to Duffield. It felt instead as if she were afraid of him, or afraid of any intimacy with him. Only once had he embraced her, on the evening of their escape, and she had drawn back from him after only the barest contact. He might have been offended, but there was too much he did not know. It pained him, but he could find no way to speak of it that would not risk opening the wound even further.

They had not decided on a destination when they left the village that morning, but they took the road that led them in the opposite direction to Nottingham. In all her time there Joane had not learned the whereabouts of her cousin, Margaret de Ferrers.

'Perhaps she's at Kenilworth too?' Adam said as he walked. 'If the king is going there, with all his court?'

'You want to go there, don't you?' Joane said. 'To the castle, to join the garrison. You want another chance at victory.'

Adam was about to deny it. But it was true, he realised. The only hope of justice for men like him lay in a united defiance. Only by holding out against the king could they force him to grant them a just peace. And Kenilworth Castle was the only place in the kingdom where such a stand might be possible.

'It's the most powerful fortress in England, so they say,' he told Joane.

'How long could it hold out against all the might of the king's army?' she asked.

He had no answer to that. But even as she spoke he had become more determined. This last month had shown Adam all too clearly how vulnerable he was, how slim his chances on his own. Better to seek shelter inside the walls of the besieged castle than to skulk and hide in the forests with Nicholas D'Eyville, or Reynard and his gang. And if the king could not take the castle, Adam thought, then he might be forced to negotiate instead. He might even be compelled to grant an amnesty and return the lands of the disinherited. That possibility alone was tantalising.

'Will you come with me?' he asked.

Joane thought for a time, letting the horse carry her steadily onwards. 'It seems I have nowhere else to go,' she said at last. 'Besides, as you say, my cousin may be with the king's court.'

Adam nodded; if that were so, they might find themselves on opposing sides of the walls of Kenilworth. But that was a matter for another occasion. For now, he was content only to walk with Joane riding at his side. She had found a broad-brimmed straw hat, and wore it over her linen cap to shade her head and neck.

The horse's hooves thudded steadily on the dry dirt of the road, and the bridle jingled. As a trained warhorse, Blanchart was too hot-blooded and mettlesome to be ideal for riding long distances. The horse carried Joane easily enough, and could carry them both for short stretches; still, Adam wished he had taken a less distinctive animal from de Grey's stables, and one cheaper to maintain.

The day grew warmer, and around noon they paused and sat on the grass in the deep shade of a beech tree, eating and resting. They had a costrel of freshly brewed ale from the village, with bread, bacon and curd cheese.

'There's something I should give you,' Joane said, more relaxed now as they finished their meal. She fetched the leather bag she had brought with her from the castle; it contained clothing, a purse of coin and a few bits of jewellery and cosmetics, and her precious Psalter. As she drew the book from the bag, Adam saw that it was shrouded in green silk. Joane unwrapped it, spreading the cloth before Adam. A golden lion danced upon the green, flourishing scarlet claws and tongue.

'The pennon!' Adam said. 'The one Hawise made for me.' He took it and ran the smooth silk between his fingers.

'I made sure to take it from Chesterfield,' Joane said. 'I told Sir Reginald that it was a keepsake of my sister's . . .'

'Thank you,' Adam said. 'I can only hope I might find a lance to display it on.' He smiled ruefully.

They lay back in the soft grass, lulled by the warmth of the day. Joane was smiling too, as if her spirits had been restored now they had put many miles between them and her former captor. Perhaps, Adam thought, that was all that had oppressed her? If so, the further they could travel, the better.

'We should move on,' he said abruptly, sitting up. While Joane untethered Blanchart and led the horse back to the road Adam went to a brook that flowed on the far side of the trees to bathe his hands and face and fill a flask with fresh water. When he returned he saw that a band of other figures had joined Joane on the road.

Blanchart was tense, neck arched and ears erect. Joane, sitting in the saddle, appeared scarcely more relaxed. The newcomers were on foot; there were six of them, one pushing a barrow. They must have moved fast to appear so suddenly.

'Aha, and here is the young lady's escort!' a man who appeared to be the leader of the band exclaimed. His voice was instantly familiar, but for a moment Adam could not place him. 'I had thought, seeing such a fine destrier,' the man went on, grinning widely, 'to find a bold knight, a Galahad, appearing from the bushes. But . . .'

'I am a knight,' Adam said, bristling slightly as he strode through the grass to the roadside. He laid his hand on the hilt of his sword. None of the newcomers appeared to be armed with anything but walking staves.

'Ah, forgive me, I see that you are!' the man said with a bow. Something in his eye, in his tone, struck Adam as false, calculating, perhaps dangerous. 'Your travelling clothes spoke of a lower station. But your lady of course is no village maid, for all her rustic headgear!'

Joane leaned from the saddle, rubbing the horse's neck to calm it. Blanchart blew loudly and pawed the dirt. Suddenly Adam knew where he had seen the man before.

'You were at Nottingham,' he said abruptly, before he could stop himself. 'In the castle hall . . .' He caught Joane's sharp glance.

'We were!' the man said, still smiling. He had been the singer, Adam realised. The large fleshy man with the barrow had mimed the role of Robert de Ferrers, and the others had been Sir Henry of Almain and the assistants. 'Gervase of St George, my lord,' the singer said, plucking off his peaked cap and bowing again. 'Leader of this company of humble jocatores and makejoys!'

He was a small man, gaudily dressed, with prominent teeth and a pot belly. 'So you too were at Nottingham the evening before last?' he enquired. 'I confess I did not recognise you, but the crowd was large, thanks be to the saints!'

Adam could see the man glancing at Joane, once and then twice. Had he marked her out already as the distant and austere figure that had sat at Reginald de Grey's high table?

'You sang a song about Robert de Ferrers,' Adam said, drawing the man's attention away from Joane. 'Where did you learn it?'

'Oh, very pleased to hear that you enjoyed it, lord,' the man said. 'It was my own composition! Based, of course, on stories we hear upon the roads. A mere jest . . .'

'We have songs of Lord Simon de Montfort too,' said the big man with the barrow, in a surprisingly deep full voice.

'No, we do not!' Gervase cried, raising his hand to silence the man. 'No, Nubbe! These good people do not wish to hear of treachery and impiety!'

The big man merely dipped his head. Already Gervase had turned back to Adam. His look of needling enquiry was unsettling. 'And where might my lord and lady be bound, perhaps?' he asked.

'We're travelling to Kenilworth,' Adam said, taking the bridle of the horse. Joane shot him an even sharper glance. 'My liege lord is there, with the king's retinue,' Adam went on, oblivious, 'and we'll be joining him.'

'Saints be praised!' said Gervase. 'We too are bound for Kenilworth!'

Adam's heart plunged. Joane let out a hissing breath.

'Yes, the greatest assembly of barons and magnates in the land,' Gervase went on, 'all of them rich, and longing for entertainment too, no doubt! Well then, we can travel together, heh? You can be our protector. In these disturbed times no road is safe, goodsir. No, even here we fear the onrush of these *Disinherited* devils . . . or the D'Eyvilles, aptly named . . . Even Red Reynard is rumoured to be stalking hereabouts!'

'We might be travelling faster than you,' Adam said briskly, already leading the horse forward.

'Ah, we move at quite a pace ourselves,' the singer cried, gesturing for his company to follow as he strutted after Adam. 'Besides, we know the way!'

The big fleshy man heaved his barrow forward; it carried all the company's possessions, Adam guessed. At a gruff word of command, what Adam had taken to be a heap of furs lying on the road drew itself up onto four legs and began shambling forward after the barrow. It was a bear, Adam realised. He had not seen such an animal back at Nottingham, he was sure. A thin and very ragged girl in a grimy linen coif led the beast along by the chain around its neck, whispering to it. But Gervase snatched a stick from the barrow and began smacking the animal around the hindquarters, urging it forward.

'Must you torment the creature?' Joane asked, turning in the saddle. 'It appears placid enough.'

'Oh yes, never fear my lady, he is very placid,' Gervase of St George declared. 'His claws and teeth were drawn long ago – we must feed him with a spoon! But he's so very slow, you see, if we don't urge him on. And he's so hairy, he scarcely feels the blows.'

The bear let out a mournful roar and began to shamble a little faster. The thin girl patted its head, whispering to it fervently as she tugged at the chain. The big man pushing the barrow forged steadily forward, as placid and shambling as the bear.

'What did you say your name was, again, lord?' the singer asked Adam.

'I did not,' he replied. 'But I am . . . Sir Adam de St John.' Immediately he regretted his choice. The singer's own name had suggested it, Adam realised.

'And you're travelling to join your lord's household at Kenilworth, you said?' the man went on. 'Might we learn his great name, perhaps?'

'His name is Lord Humphrey de Bohun, Earl of Hereford,' Joane said abruptly, before Adam could think of an answer.

'Oh, a fine lord, and a great magnate. One of the greatest, to be sure!' the singer exclaimed. 'And we would count it a great honour and a blessing, sir, to gain an introduction to his court . . .'

Adam was barely listening to him. He looked at Joane, who returned a level gaze, cold and hard. She had given that answer on purpose, he realised. A deliberate allusion to her former husband's family, in return for his allusion to Isabel's. In silence they continued along the track, Adam leading the horse and keeping his distance from Gervase and his company of jongleurs, unwilling to be drawn into any further conversation.

'Did you have to tell that man all of our business?' Joane asked, when they had drawn sufficiently far ahead to be out of even the keenest hearing.

'Would you prefer me not to have given any answer at all, or to lie? He looks shrewd enough to know an untruth when he hears one.'

'Exactly,' Joane said, stooping in the saddle to whisper harshly. 'And he knows me as well, I'm sure of it. Maybe he knows of you too. He's saying nothing now, but you can be sure he'll sell

the information at the first chance he gets. And now he knows
we're going to Kenilworth! No doubt he'll tell somebody there
of your identity.'

'We'll remain with them for now,' Adam said decisively. 'They
know the roads, and we'll appear less conspicuous travelling in
a group. But tomorrow or the next day we'll slip away and out-
pace them to Kenilworth.'

Joane nodded, but appeared unconvinced.

They ended their day's journey beside a bridge that spanned a
winding river. It was still an hour until sunset, and Adam would
have preferred to press onward, but Gervase assured him that it
was still ten miles or more to Leicester. Their lodging place lay
beside the bridge and the river wharf; an alehouse and smithy,
with a long barn-like building where travellers could sleep on
straw. They passed an uncomfortable night, and were on the road
again by daybreak.

There were plenty of other travellers sharing their route now.
As they passed beneath high bluffs crowned with the overgrown
ruin of a castle, an armed retinue clattered by with pennons
on their lances and warhorses in their train. No doubt, Adam
thought, they too were headed for Kenilworth, to join the king's
muster. He kept his head down, and calmed Blanchart's twitching impatience.

'I was thinking, as I lay sleepless,' said Gervase of St George,
scratching idly at the flea bites on his neck as he strutted along
beside Adam, 'of the night before we departed Nottingham. You
were there, I think, in the castle? You'll have seen the terrible blaze,
I suppose? An accident, they say – St John's Eve can be hazardous,
with the fires and the merriment. Poor Brun was quite singed –
we were obliged to leave him chained in one of the sheds – and I
hear that Lord Reginald's betrothed vanished that night as well!'

'Vanished?' Adam asked, feigning a nonchalant air.

'Indeed, my lord. Some say she might have simply flown off
with the smoke! Others that she absconded with a mysterious

young man seen leaving the castle before dawn . . . But those stories are surely mere romance, as all the witnesses claim that this young lady was truly devoted to Lord Reginald, and had acted like a wife to him in all ways for a month and more!'

'Really?' Adam said, and the word almost choked him. He did not dare glance at Gervase, fearing the look of crafty enquiry in the man's eye. He did not dare glance at Joane either, who he knew had overheard. Instead he just gazed at the rutted dirt of the road ahead of him.

Before noon they reached Leicester, rolling in through the northern gate and along the High Street. The town was crowded, and Adam saw many armed men and many a knight's pennon among the throng. Gervase led them to a hostelry he knew well, but even there they could secure only a single chamber for the whole company. The rest had been taken by the Earl of Leicester's men.

'The Earl of Leicester?' Adam asked, startled.

'Not the old earl, that's to say,' the hosteller explained, wiping his hands on a rag. 'Not the one who died – the traitor, that is. This is the new earl, the king's second son, Lord Edmund. He's Earl of Leicester now. And soon to be Earl of Derby too, so they say!'

Adam had intended to leave the town again that afternoon, getting a half day's start on Gervase and his company. But Blanchart had loosed a shoe and needed the attentions of a blacksmith, and Adam was stiff with weariness after two days on foot. It seemed that God or fate wanted them to remain in Leicester.

In the common hall that evening Gervase and his company soon made themselves comfortable, striking up tunes on their vielles and tabor. The hosteller did not allow them to bring the bear inside, however, and they left it chained in the stable. The benches were filled with Lord Edmund's retainers and servants, who laughed and clapped along to the song about Robert de Ferrers, with Nubbe reeling between them as he acted his part.

Adam sat with Joane at the end of the lower table, a jug of wine and two cups between them. All afternoon they had been skulking about the town, avoiding each other as much as avoiding the attention of other travellers. Now they were compelled to be together once more.

'Was it true, what he said?' Adam asked at last.

Joane scarcely bothered to feign ignorance. She opened her palms, not meeting Adam's eye. 'Of course not,' she said. 'That is . . . of course I did what I could to seem compliant. To give Reginald no reason to distrust me, or to mistreat me.'

'And he did not mistreat you, you said?' Adam went on, his voice hardening. He was being foolish and knew it, but he could not hold himself back. 'So you gave him what he wanted willingly, is that what you mean?'

'No, listen to me!' Joane cried, her face reddening. 'Reginald de Grey had no interest in my flesh. Do you understand? He wanted my lands and the prestige of my name, that's all. And that's all I offered to give him, so he would leave me alone and not torment me. And if I did so in public, so others would see it, I was only protecting myself. God knows I had nobody else to do it for me!'

Both were breathing hard, with barely a hand's breadth between them. Adam felt the heat rise to his face as well, with the stir of sickness in his gut. How foolish he had been, how insulting. He understood it all now. 'I'm sorry,' he said. 'Please forgive me, I was . . .'

'I know,' Joane said, her voice softening. 'I've wanted to explain everything. I could see you were suffering, but I too have my pride. You see that?'

Adam nodded. He felt suddenly freed of a burden of anger and shame he had not even known he was carrying. Another gust of noise came from the hall, a volley of palms slapping tables.

'We need to get away from here,' Adam said. 'Tonight.'

'I agree. We leave now, and gain half a day on them.' She motioned with her head towards Gervase, now darting around the hall with the thin bear-girl, collecting coins. 'Go to the stables,' she said. 'I'll meet you there.'

From the door, Adam watched as Joane made her way across the hall. She reached Nubbe, now seated again with his moon face sweaty and glowing, a cup of ale in his fist. Stooping at his side, Joane whispered something in his ear.

Out in the darkened stable, Adam brought Blanchart from his stall and fastened the saddle and tack. The horse was rested, newly shod, and seemed eager enough. Adam had got directions from the smith earlier that day: he knew of the gap in the town wall, above the riverbank, where a man on horseback could leave the city after the gates closed at curfew. He knew he should cross the river and take the left-hand road once he'd passed Austin Friars; that would take him to the ancient track called the Fosse Way, which led by the straightest route towards Kenilworth.

As he led the horse to the stable door Adam noticed the bear, sitting in a dark corner, secured by a short chain. The beast raised its head and let out a lowing complaint. Through the timber wall, Adam could hear cheering as a new song began. This one had a new singer as well; he recognised Nubbe's bass tones.

'Now he is slain, that flower of fame,
Who knew so much of war.
The Earl Montfort, his cruel death,
The land will deeply mourn!'

The silence that had greeted the first lines erupted almost immediately into angry noise. Startled, Adam took a step closer to the wall. He could hear Gervase's raised voice now, yelling above the clamour. 'No, Nubbe, no! Not that one – not here!'

Joane hurried from the connecting passage, carrying her bag. 'Quickly,' she said, and motioned towards the gateway of the stable. But still the singing voice rolled on, deeper and richer still as it rose over the shouts, the crashing of benches and the thumping of fists.

> 'Those by his side for justice died,
> So England might be free.
> But by his death, the Earl Montfort,
> Gained the victory!'

Throwing her bag over the saddle, Joane advanced towards the corner of the stable.

'What are you doing?' Adam demanded in a harsh whisper. 'Be careful!'

'It's quite safe,' Joane said, with a tremor in her voice that belied her words. 'I saw the girl do it, several times.'

Gently she approached the bear, which nuzzled towards her, lowing. With a deft movement she unlatched the chain from its ringbolt in the wall, then stepped away. The bear thrashed its head, clattering the loose chain, then reared up onto its hind legs. Standing as tall as a man, it advanced into the stable. A low grinding roar came from its toothless mouth.

Adam was already leading Blanchart out of the open stable door. He swung up into the saddle, then leaned to pull Joane up behind him. She was grinning, joyful with her accomplishment. Turning in the saddle they saw the bear drop to all fours and walk from the stable, the chain swinging from its neck. It veered to one side, towards the door that led to the common hall. As the beast vanished inside the building, Adam kicked with the spurs. Blanchart began to move, trotting across the stable yard and out into the darkened and shuttered street.

Behind them, they heard the hum of noise from the hall shattered by the first shrieks of terror.

Chapter 18

From the creaking limb of a chestnut tree, Adam stared at the distant castle. The keep was the size of his thumbnail. He shifted on his perch, grasping one of the branches above him and craning upwards. Through the leaves he surveyed a mile or more of open country. The sun was low, the evening air clear. To the left of the castle ramparts Adam could make out the sheen of water. A lake, or spreading mere, and another to the right. Before them he could see a pallisaded outwork or barbican, and a causeway that ran between the lakes to the castle gatehouse. Squinting, he could just pick out the flag on the highest tower of the keep, red against the blue sky. Months after Lord Simon's death at Evesham, the banner of de Montfort still flew above Kenilworth Castle.

A bell was ringing for evensong, and away to his right Adam picked out the tower of the priory. Between it and the castle there were tents and horse lines, baggage wagons and rows of mantlets, the big wicker screens used to shield archers. Adam's breath caught as he scanned the scene; he had known that the king was summoning a great force to Kenilworth, but he had not anticipated its true size. At first it seemed one huge encampment, wrapping the castle on the sides not cut off by the lake. Then, as he looked closer, he determined that there were three separate camps, perhaps four, covering the main approaches to the fortress.

Squinting against the glare of the low sun, he picked out tall wooden frames erected to face the castle: gibbets, he thought at first with a stir of cold horror. Was the king threatening the garrison with execution if they did not surrender? Then, gazing more carefully, he saw that they were the frames of siege engines: towering trebuchets and mangonels. He could even make out the tiny figures of men working on the machines, swinging the great beams into place and lashing them together. Soon their work would be done, and the engines would commence their battering assault.

The bough beneath him let out a protesting wail. He had seen enough. Clambering down to the lower branches Adam dropped to the ground and retrieved his sword and belt. Across the sunlit open ground and over a ridge, he dropped down into the thicker woods that clad the banks of a meandering river. Stepping carefully, he made his way through the green shade beneath the leaves until he reached the bank, then followed it upstream towards the small wooded islet opposite the glade where he had left Joane and the horse. This was the same river, so the alewife in Bretford had told them the day before, that after many miles looped around Evesham. They had no need to follow it so far; just to Stoneleigh Abbey, the woman had directed, and they would find Kenilworth away to their west.

The islet appeared ahead of Adam now. On its nearer side, the bend of the river formed a pool shaded by willows. The evening sun fell in bands between the trees, illuminating the depths of the water; a movement in the shallows, and Adam halted instinctively. A shape broke the surface, sleek and gleaming: a woman's head, then her shoulders and upper body rose from the water, her unbound hair streaming in a dark red tide down her back. Joane wore only her linen chemise, the wet fabric clinging to her body. Adam knew he should look away, but for a long moment he could not. She had her back to him; unobserved, she bent and splashed her face with water, then pulled the streaming length of her hair over one shoulder. As she turned to wade back to the riverbank Adam crouched, concealing himself behind a thicket of ferns.

Even after what had happened between them in Chesterfield, he still could not define the true nature of their relationship. Was Adam her lover now, or merely her escort? Her companion, or just her rescuer? The thought that very soon they might have to choose different paths – Joane's to the king's siege camp, his to the beleaguered walls of Kenilworth – was painful. But at least, he told himself, the torment of frustration and uncertainty would be at an end.

He waited as long as he could, then he started forward once again, careful to make enough noise to forewarn of his approach. By the time he reached the glade she was seated on a mossy log, dressed in a fresh chemise and combing out her wet hair.

She had been feeling unwell earlier that day. Adam thought it most likely the after-effects of the sun; after leaving Leicester they had journeyed south-westward with little or no shade from the blistering glare. Even wearing her straw hat, Joane had been worn down; they had been compelled to rest through the hours of midday, and travel only in the relative cool of evening and the early morning. At least she seemed to have recovered now. In fact, sitting on her log with her unbound hair glowing copper red in the shafts of the evening sun, Joane looked radiant with health.

'You found the castle?' she asked.

'I did,' Adam said, and pointed. 'Two miles that way. The king's forces are camped all around it. They're still building their siege engines.'

'Did they see you?'

He shook his head. 'But they'll have sentries guarding the perimeter, and bands of men patrolling the area all around. There are three or four separate camps, each with their own defences. Almost as if they expect to be attacked themselves.'

Adam took a drink from the flask. The ale they had bought at Bretford was already tasting sour in the heat. Perhaps drinking from the river would be better? Now he came to think of it, Adam found the idea of immersing himself in cool fresh water almost overwhelmingly attractive.

'I've been thinking,' Joane said, attempting a casual air. 'If Earl Humphrey is with the king, he'll just send me straight back to Nottingham, under guard. Or summon Sir Reginald to come and fetch me.' She paused in her combing and gave Adam a searching look.

'So you'd need to locate Countess Margaret without being detected, and before Earl Humphrey locates you,' Adam replied, his brow furrowed.

'But if my cousin isn't there, or we choose the wrong camp . . .'

Their scheme, which had seemed so simple as they journeyed towards Kenilworth, now seemed impossibly difficult. 'A shame we couldn't have remained with those minstrels a while longer,' Joane said with a sigh. 'We could perhaps have slipped into one of the camps unnoticed with them. Still, I don't regret what we did. I wonder if the bear survived?'

'You gave him a chance of freedom anyway.'

They had not discussed what had happened back in Leicester. Gervase of St George and his company would no doubt be detained there for a while, but would catch up with them before long.

'We could wait for another large retinue to pass, and join them,' Adam said. 'But the longer we wait, the more likely we are to encounter people who know us.'

'I'm beginning to think that I might be safer inside the castle myself,' Joane said. Then she gave a brisk nod, as if her mind was resolved. 'We wait until after nightfall, I suppose?'

Adam considered for a moment. 'No,' he said. 'They'll be more vigilant then, and we could easily get lost in the dark. We'll rest while we can, and find a way through their lines at first light, before sunrise.'

He noticed Joane smiling at him, as if she found him amusing. A heartbeat's affront, then he smiled too.

'You sound so much like Robert de Dunstanville at times,' she said. 'He too was a man of strategies.'

Not that it helped him, in the end, Adam thought. But did not say it.

He bathed in the river, then as the sun went down he secured Blanchart in a hidden glade close to the bank, and gathered long grass and ferns to make beds for him and Joane. 'Just make the one,' she told him.

He did as she directed, keeping his mind from the implications of his task. Only when he was lying down, covered with his cloak, did she come and stretch herself beside him. It was twilight, the gentle sound of the river in the gathering darkness a constant accompaniment.

'This may be the last night we spend together for some time,' she said in a whisper.

Adam made a sound in his throat. His heart was beating fast.

'I should thank you, for bringing me all this way,' she went on, propping herself on an elbow. 'I have not been the easiest of companions, I expect.'

He made the slightest sound of disagreement, but before he could speak she dipped her head and kissed him. Then she pulled off her chemise.

'We don't have long,' he told her.

But she made no reply.

*

At first light the sky was filled with larks and the loop of the river flowed with mist. They found a cattle trail leading up from the riverbank, close to where they had camped, and followed it west into open pastureland beyond.

The sun was not yet above the trees when the enemy caught them.

'Adam!' Joane cried, turning in the saddle. She was pointing at the line of riders emerging from the woods at the top of the slope. Six of them, Adam counted, the leading couple with spears raised as they broke into a canter. Two more had crossbows, and were leaning in the saddle to span their weapons as they rode. Within moments, Adam knew, they would be surrounded. Joane had already jumped down from the horse; Adam leaped into the saddle and pulled her up again behind him. No need for discussion now. As soon as his feet were firmly in the stirrups she pressed herself against his back, arms wrapped tight around him, and clung on as he dug with the spurs and the warhorse erupted into motion beneath them.

Cries from their pursuers, and the distant snap of a crossbow. Hooves drummed the turf as Blanchart crossed the pasture at a gallop. Ahead was another fringe of trees, with strip fields beyond. No escape for them there. Adam dragged at the reins and the horse veered towards the broken ground and thickets further to the left. But even the powerful destrier was labouring under two riders, and the lighter horses that pursued them were gaining ground rapidly.

'We can't outrun them,' Adam said over his shoulder. 'I'll turn once we're into the thickets – jump down there and make for the river, and I'll try to hold them off.'

'No!' Joane cried, tightening her grip around his chest. 'There are too many of them!'

She was right, and Adam knew it. The men chasing them were lightly armed scouts and skirmishers, but he had no armour or shield himself, no lance. Besides, they had crossbows: they would shoot his horse first, and then shoot him. No option but flight remained; hunching forward in the saddle he dug harder with the spurs and tried not to hear Blanchart's heaving breath.

Now they were riding between thickets and stands of trees. The horse leaped a ditch, coming down hard and almost throwing Adam from the saddle. He screwed again at the reins, the destrier's hooves kicking up mud as it turned sharply. Behind him Adam heard a cry, and glanced back to see one of the pursuing horses stumble and fall. Five remained. The two crossbowmen had shot their bolts and were riding too hard to reload.

Another swerve, doubling back across the ditch. Joane pitched on the horse's back, almost sliding off. Her hair had come loose from its binding and streamed behind her as they rode. Adam drew his sword.

One of the pursuers had jinked back across the ditch to try to cut off the chase; Blanchart barrelled into horse and rider at full pace, slamming the other animal back onto its haunches even as Adam aimed a wild cut at the rider's head. The man screamed as he toppled from the saddle, his horse staggering beneath him. Joane was screaming too, her grip digging into Adam's chest. But they were clear again, the pursuit spilling away behind them as the other riders tried to turn, to rally and follow them once more.

Joane had recovered her balance, and clung on grimly as Adam urged the horse back across the open pasture. Somewhere ahead of them now lay the outer perimeter of the closest siege camp. It occurred to Adam that the men chasing them might have deliberately herded them in that direction. He could not risk looking back now. He knew they were close.

'Adam, there!' Joane cried, pointing to the left. Adam snatched a sideways glance, and hope died in his chest. There were more riders, and these were wearing armour and carrying shields and lances.

He began to laugh, his breath heaving bitterly. How easy this had seemed once. How impossible it had turned out to be!

Then the mailed riders charged through the pursuing horse-men, cutting them from their saddles. A knight in full mail was leading the charge, and his red shield bore three gold crosses shaped like daggers. Adam recognised the blazon. *Gules, three crosses fitchee or.* But for a moment he could not place it. The knight slammed his mace over the head of a fleeing horseman; the man toppled, his foot catching in the saddle, and his body was dragged behind his careering horse.

'De Caldwell!' Adam shouted, the name rising to his memory at last. 'Sir Gregory! I was with you at Chesterfield!'

'You were?' the knight yelled back as he shortened his reins. His face was grim inside the steel oval of his mail coif, his brow cleft with a prominent scar. He had been with Henry de Hast-ings, Adam remembered, and had left town with the hunting party on the morning of the attack.

'Drop in behind us and follow if you can, then,' Sir Gregory cried as he spurred his horse. 'We're here for the cattle, not for you!'

Now Adam could see the herd of long-horned cows driven along in the wake of the horsemen. The animals were moving fast, lowing as they went, the leading ones dragged by rope halters and the rest goaded by mounted men with sticks. Gregory de Caldwell and his men were on a cattle raid, Adam realised; the cows would have come from the Prior of Kenilworth's pastures.

'We follow them?' Adam called over his shoulder.

'Yes!' Joane said at once. 'Yes, go – go!'

Adam was laughing as he spurred Blanchart forward. If the cows had not been so troublesome, the raiders would already have been back inside the castle walls by now. As it was, fortune had favoured Adam with a rare opportunity. He was determined to take it. Urging the lathered warhorse to another burst of speed, he rode on after the herd of lowing beasts.

Over the ridge they saw the castle before them. The great mere lay to the left, gleaming in the morning sun, and a smaller pool to the right. Between the two stretches of water, a road ran across a broad straight causeway to the castle's main gates. The barbican on the landward side was ringed with earthworks and palisades. But before it, as Adam rode down the slope through the dappled shade of the trees, lay the royal siege lines.

De Caldwell was roaring as he charged, his mace raised high. He had two other knights with him and three serjeants, all in armour and mounted on warhorses, but the rest of his raiding party were servants and mounted grooms. Their route back to the barbican gate was sealed off by rows of big wicker mantlets intended to shield archers. But the raiders were charging at them from the rear, using the captured beasts to drive a path through them. Maddened and bellowing, the herd of cows stampeded forward and crashed the wicker screens aside, the defenders scattering. Exultant, the mounted men followed in their dust.

Arrows spat from the air. Adam kept his head low as he rode. Beside him one of de Caldwell's men jerked upright in the saddle as an arrow punched through the neck of his gambeson. Another went down in a spray of dirt, his horse shot through the leg. Several of the cows had been hit as well, but the arrows sticking from their haunches just drove them forward more vigorously.

In a swirl of dust and arrows, a volley of yells, Blanchart was through the gap in the mantlets and cantering up the last stretch of road to the barbican's timber gateway. De Caldwell was already there, turning his horse to ensure the precious cattle were safely herded home. The serjeant with an arrow in his neck galloped past, and the last of the servants flogged the cows in behind him. Then Adam followed, raising his hand to de Caldwell as he passed.

Onward, across the open space of the barbican and over a wooden drawbridge, they rode forward onto the causeway. Sunlight flashed off the water to either side. Joane was still clasping Adam's waist, caught by the wild fury of their ride. Ahead of them lay the red sandstone walls and ramparts of Kenilworth, the powerful inner gatehouse with its twin towers immediately in front of them, and the huge stone block of the great keep rising beyond it. Above the keep, de Montfort's red and white banner flew proudly against the morning sky.

One last canter, Blanchart regaining strength now the end was in sight, and they were across the causeway and through the gates. Along the vaulted gate passage and under the teeth of the two raised portcullises, they emerged into the bailey and were safe within the circuit of the walls.

Adam slowed the weary destrier to a walk, then dropped gladly from the saddle and helped Joane down after him. She embraced him, grinning. Was this what she had wanted all along?

Only then, as she released him, did Adam turn and look at the scene before him. The bailey was filled with tents and crude shelters, cattle pens and byres. A vast number of people too, thronging the scrubby parched grass between the walls. One glance took in smithies and laundry vats, cooking fires and brewing tubs. To one side was a makeshift slaughteryard, where butchers were already at work. Blood flowed in runnels, and the axes hacked down into glistening red flesh, cutting through the bone.

'Adam!' a voice cried, and Hugh of Oystermouth came striding from the midst of the chaos. 'Again you return from the dead!'

Joane had slipped away at once, drawing her shawl over her head to conceal herself. John de Tarleton appeared from the crowd too, the Lancashire knight's long face creasing into a smile as he saw Adam. But before either John or Hugh could reach Adam's side, another voice called from the rampart walkway above the gatehouse. 'De Norton, is that you? I've been expecting you this last month!'

Adam turned, looking back towards the gates. There, standing against the bright sky with his thumbs hooked in his sword belt, was Henry de Hastings.

*

The great chamber of Kenilworth filled the upper storey of the keep, rising a full forty feet to the roof beams. Deep window embrasures pierced the massive thickness of the walls on all sides, but their narrow openings let in only scant daylight. The chamber was gloomy, and it was crowded.

Trestle tables stood on three sides, each seating six men. These, Adam knew, were the leaders of the garrison, the defence council. A few clergymen and civilians sat among them too. Behind stood other knights, and squires and serving men waiting attendance on their masters. Hounds slunk between the tables and stretched their paws across the rushes beneath.

Adam knew some of the men around the tables from Chesterfield, or from de Montfort's great gathering at Hereford long before. A few more he had met since his arrival only a few hours ago. But most were strangers. He felt their eyes on him, the weight of their appraisal. Some regarded him with curiosity, some with suspicion, others with cold and open hostility.

'Step forward,' one of them called, standing up from the table and beckoning. He was an older man, gaunt and grey, and his hair was shaved into a clergyman's tonsure, although he wore a sword belted at his side. 'Step forward, and declare yourself before the assembly.'

Advancing between the tables, Adam stood in the open space at the centre of the chamber, his scabbarded sword in his left hand. He cast a glance to either side, taking his time. Then he bowed, slow and deliberate, towards each of the tables in turn.

'I am Sir Adam de Norton, messires, of Selborne Norton. I come to you as an ally, and a friend. Many here know me well.' He bowed once more, but kept his eyes on the men at the high table. He noticed a few of them nodding in approval. He might wear plain steel spurs and the dust-stained clothing of a common wayfarer, but he knew how to behave as a knight.

'Who speaks for this man?' the swordbearing clergyman asked.

'I do,' Henry de Hastings replied promptly, standing up. 'Sir Adam is a valiant soldier, who fought at Lewes and at Evesham, at the side of Lord Simon himself. And at my side, on the bridge at Newport. I was imprisoned with him at Beeston, and he rode with me to Chesterfield. None could fault his valour.'

Adam could only nod his thanks, and felt the heat rise to his face. He had grown unaccustomed to praise, and from a man like de Hastings it was strangely moving.

'I know him from Duffield,' another man called. He was a knight of around forty, with a lined face and piercing blue eyes; Richard de Amundeville, Adam remembered, had also been at Chesterfield. 'You rode well in Earl Robert's tourney,' Sir Richard said, addressing him directly.

'Then he's not a spy from the king's camp, come to sow dissent amongst us?' the man at the centre of the high table asked, rubbing his bristling black beard. 'Where's he been since Chesterfield? Making his peace with our enemies, perhaps, like plenty of others?'

The bearded man was heavily built, broader even than de Hastings but fleshy with it. He resembled a butcher more than a knight. Adam pitied the horse that had to bear his weight.

'I've travelled a long road,' Adam replied, careful to show neither anger nor fear. 'For now, I can only give you my word.'

'Let him swear the same oath as all have sworn, then,' said the older knight, de Amundeville, 'if he is to be one of us.' Several of those around him growled in agreement.

The tonsured man had already risen from the table, holding a book wrapped in ivory silk. 'Take the Holy Gospel in your hands,' he instructed Adam, 'and pledge before men and God that you will be one with us until the end, and you will never desert or betray the community of this castle.'

A hush fell as Adam stepped forward and took the book. He raised it, kissed the tooled leather cover, and then held it before him as he repeated the pledge.

'And if you should break this oath, may every man's sword be turned against you, and may you die a traitor's death,' the clergy-man intoned. 'Swear it.'

Adam did as he was instructed, speaking the words clear and steady for all to hear. As he spoke his stomach churned briefly, and a cold sweat broke on his brow. He had sworn so many bad oaths over the last year and a half. As the cheering erupted around him, he hoped desperately that this was not another.

Chapter 19

Beyond the castle walls the mere spread away westward into the middle distance, placid blue beneath a cloudless morning sky. Along the nearest shore stretched the siegeworks of the enemy. From his vantage point on the keep's highest rampart Adam could clearly see the tents and pavilions of the besiegers, a great pale crop of them spreading across the fields like mushrooms after rain, speckled with the brighter colours of banners and pennons. The three massive trebuchet catapults that stood above the bank of the mere were almost complete now, each mast-like throwing arm standing upright from a cage of scaffolding. Already they exuded menace.

But Henry de Hastings appeared oblivious to any threat. Leaning from the battlements of the keep, he peered down into the bailey at the spreading encampment of huts and animal pens that Adam had seen when he first arrived. 'Look at them,' he said, with the trace of a sneer. 'Like ants.'

'Who are they?' Adam asked.

'Tenants of the local manors, following their lords,' de Hastings said. 'Or people from the neighbouring shires and towns, driven from their homes since Evesham. If it were up to me I'd drive them from these walls too and let them fend for themselves, but there are soft hearts among us!'

With a grunt he climbed up onto the rampart wall and stood between two of the merlons, fists on hips. Above him the red and white banner stirred in the warm breeze. 'I confess, I thought you'd probably been captured at Chesterfield – or slain,' Sir Henry said over his shoulder. He tightened his lips into a thin smile that showed his teeth. 'England has become a cruel place these last years.'

And men like you, Adam thought, *have done nothing to make it any kinder.*

'That's Lord Edward's encampment, just over there,' de Hastings went on, gesturing towards the tents on the south bank of the lake. 'Roger Mortimer's men are camped to his left, just beyond the palisades of the barbican. You came through there this morning, with Sir Gregory and his cattle. Lord Edmund's camp lies to the north. And if you look that way, directly eastwards,' he said, turning and pointing, 'you'll see the priory tower. The king's camp is between us and the priory. Most of the great magnates are with the king there.'

Craning his neck, Adam peered out over the crenellations, but the priory tower was lost in the morning haze.

'Both of our main gates are kept open, day and night,' de Hastings went on, 'so we can sally forth at any time, and bid defiance to our foes!'

Adam had often heard that Kenilworth was one of the strongest fortresses in England. Seeing the place now, he could well believe that. At its heart was the great keep where he and Sir Henry were standing, a pugnacious-looking block of red sandstone, eighty feet high with buttresses at each corner rising to turrets. Directly below it lay the inner bailey, a paved oval whose curtain wall enclosed the hall, chambers, kitchens and chapel. The outer bailey surrounded it on all sides and held the stables and the cattle pens, the timber barracks and the storage rooms, and the civilian encampment that so annoyed de Hastings.

From this elevation Adam could see that the mere to the west and south was artificial, formed by damming a stream with the causeway that carried the road to the main gatehouse. Further embankments created pools and waterways to the south-east as well, and a flooded moat followed the line of the walls to the north and east. The castle was practically an island, surrounded on all sides by stone and by water, defended by both nature and engineering.

Henry de Hastings was still standing on the rampart, holding his bold posture as if he were lord of all that lay beneath his gaze. 'But I didn't bring you up here just to admire the view,' he said.

Adam glanced up at him, raising an eyebrow.

'You've seen the leading men of the garrison,' de Hastings said, with a contemptuous gesture towards the stair turret and the chamber below them. 'There are *factions* among them, naturally. Some are loyal and true, and fierce as devils: Gregory de Caldwell, and John de Clinton and some of the younger knights.'

Adam nodded, understanding his meaning: this was the faction that followed de Hastings himself.

'But then there are the others,' Sir Henry said with a scowl, clambering down from his perch on the wall. 'Nicholas de Boys, Simon de Pateshall . . . Richard de Amundeville's chief among them. Fainthearts and old women. I swear, for all their oaths and bold claims, they'd surrender this fortress for the merest nicety from the king!'

'Is there a single leader directing the garrison?' Adam asked.

De Hastings nodded. 'John de la Warre – a staunch man, if a stout one.'

The fleshy knight with the black beard, Adam thought; de la Warre was probably only in his mid-twenties, for all his formidable size, but the force of his presence must have impressed the older men around him.

'His father and namesake was Lord Simon's constable at Bristol, and is currently the king's prisoner there,' Sir Henry went on. 'Sir John was with Eleanor de Montfort at Dover, and she sent him here to strengthen the defence. Which he's done, admittedly . . . But he doesn't like me. Oh no, not at all!'

And doubtless, Adam thought, Henry de Hastings did not like having to serve under a younger man of lesser status. But from what Adam had seen so far, most of the other men holding Kenilworth were local knights from the neighbouring shires. Aside from de Hastings, there was not one baron among them. None had his reputation, or his prestige. None had his ferocious pride either.

'Oh, and there's a gaggle of town burgesses and merchants in the castle as well,' de Hastings added, and sighed through his teeth. 'Old supporters of Lord Simon, who've sought safe haven here. They're a faction of their own, and just as querulous and obstinate as de Amundeville's followers.'

Adam nodded, gazing down from the battlements. The castle which had seemed so large only moments before now seemed almost oppressively small.

'How many people are here, in total?' he asked, stepping back from the ramparts. The sun was directly overhead, and he was sweating.

'Well over a thousand,' Henry replied, 'although nobody's made an accurate count. Barely half that number are fighting men. The rest are wives and children, tradesmen and servants, clergymen, laundresses, even whores . . . And with these heroes, we must hold this place against the royal might of England!'

He seized Adam suddenly by the shoulder, dragging him close. 'But I can rely on you to back me, can't I?' he said. 'Help me gain the primacy here, the mastery. You have a reputation – you stood with me at Lewes, at Newport and at Evesham . . .'

I stood with Lord Simon de Montfort, Adam thought.

'Besides, if God grants us victory, and we force the king to bow to our demands,' de Hastings said, 'I'll reward you handsomely for your support!'

Then his eyes widened as a thought struck him. Raising his other hand in a fist, he showed Adam the signet ring he still wore on his finger. The ring bearing the golden swan of Humphrey de Bohun. 'And this too,' he said quietly, 'shall be yours. A token of gratitude, shall we say? Just be mine, and help me gain what is mine!'

It was only when Sir Henry had left him that Adam noticed Hugh of Oystermouth waiting by the turret steps.

'*Omnia dabo, si cadens adoraveris me,*' his friend muttered, gazing at the retreating figure of Henry de Hastings. Adam just frowned at him, sensing the loom of blasphemy.

'Well, if you want to fight against God and the king, best take the devil as your ally,' Hugh said.

Adam caught the note of pride in his voice, and wondered at it. Strange, he thought, that his friend had continued to support the cause of the Disinherited. The Welshman had no lands to lose, no inheritance to reclaim, and he had never shown any great liking for the barons of England.

'Why did you come here?' Adam asked him.

Hugh appeared puzzled by the question.

'Osbert de Cornburgh was captured at Chesterfield,' Adam said. 'You could find a new master wherever you choose, or even go overseas if you prefer. I don't recall you ever had any great love for Simon de Montfort, or for his followers.'

'True!' Hugh replied, and raised his eyebrows. 'And it's true I was divided in my mind about where I should go, after what happened in the north. You're right that I never loved Lord Simon. But I loved Robert de Dunstanville above all men,' he said, with sudden vehemence. 'I could not take service with any that had opposed him. Those bastards out there,' he said, stabbing his finger across the lake at the distant camps, 'were his enemies, and his killers are among them. And so they're my enemies too, as I see it. And if I can do something worthwhile here to bring justice to his memory and honour to his name, then I shall.' He nodded firmly, his jaw set. In all the years of their friendship, Adam had never seen him so fervent, nor as staunch.

'You feel the same, I'd have thought?' Hugh asked him, cocking an eyebrow.

'Yes,' Adam said. The simple clarity of Hugh's words was a balm to him, and he knew he meant it. 'Yes, I do.'

'Although,' Hugh went on, his expression clouding. 'Some of those here I find harder to endure. De Hastings for one, of course. You've heard about his mutilation of the royal courier?'

Adam shook his head, gesturing for Hugh to continue.

'It happened shortly after I got here,' Hugh said, lowering his voice and stepping closer, although there were only a few watchmen on the keep ramparts that might overhear him. 'A foraging party captured a messenger bearing letters to the king's garrison at Warwick. Several of the leading men here argued that the man should be released, but Henry de Hastings demanded that he be put to death . . . So he and John de la Warre compromised by cutting off the courier's hand and hanging it around his neck, then sending him back to the king – as a message!'

Adam sucked a breath between his teeth. He had always known that de Hastings had a streak of cruelty and wanton malice in him.

'Even the Devil of Derby would not have done such a thing, some are saying,' Hugh went on, still keeping his voice low. 'Though to be fair there were plenty who cheered it, all the same. Many here lust for bloodshed, and have a great fury against the king and all his followers.'

Despite the heat, Adam felt a chill rising from inside him. As he turned towards the stair turret, Hugh stopped him with a hand on his arm. 'If you don't mind my asking,' the Welshman said. 'The young lady accompanying you when you arrived this morning . . . I didn't get a clear look at her, was she . . .?'

'Joane de Bohun, yes,' Adam told him. He gave the herald a dark look, trying to deter further questions. But he knew what was coming.

'Because I did think, you see,' Hugh went on, oblivious, 'that your intention was to marry Isabel de St John, once you'd reclaimed your lands. Otherwise, I mean, why—'

'My *intention*,' Adam began sharply, cutting him off, but then found he could say no more. Hugh's face fell as he understood Adam's dilemma, and he exhaled in a sigh.

*

'Apparently it's true,' Joane said, 'that there really is no such thing as St Eloi's Sickness. Master Philip here has confirmed it.'

'Completely fictitious,' the surgeon agreed. 'A fable invented by charlatans who call themselves physicians, to explain what they cannot control.'

'You recall that physician at Beeston?' Joane asked Adam, with a scornful air. 'He claimed that Sir Humphrey was dying of it!'

'More die of the ministrations of those who try to cure them, I believe, than of the devil's malice,' Master Philip said, nodding. 'In the case of your late husband, my lady, I expect the physician had caused the wound to suppurate, due to a misreading of Galen, and was then unable to halt the process of putrefaction – he should have read Avicenna! . . . Now,' he said, with an abrupt shift of attention, 'let's begin the examinations.'

They were in a high-windowed storeroom adjoining the kitchens of the inner bailey. The walls were whitewashed, wooden shutters stood open to admit the daylight, and in the centre of the room, on several long trestle tables and a number of straw mattresses, was the makeshift infirmary of Master Philip Porpeis.

A copperish smell of blood, both dried and fresh, filled the air, diluted by acrid vinegar and the sweet reek of medicinal salves. Even with the deathly stink, the groans and cries of the wounded, the flies that circled in the shafts of light, there was a sense of calm and order here that the rest of the castle with its hordes of people and ceaseless turmoil entirely lacked. The tables were currently occupied by those wounded in the morning's cattle raid. Only one man had died so far, but there were nine injured, their wounds ranging from arrow strikes to sword cuts. One man, a groom, had been trampled by the stampeding herd, and the hooves had crushed his ankle and lower leg.

'This one we may have to amputate,' Master Philip said briskly, gesturing at the injured man with his stylus. Besides Joane and two older women, most of his helpers appeared to be kitchen boys and butcher's mates.

The victim on the table moaned and began to plead that he not be left a cripple. 'Stuff a rag in it, boy,' an assistant said, holding him down while another fetched the saw. Porpeis had already moved on to the next patient.

Adam had met the wry, neatly dressed surgeon the year before, on campaign with de Montfort's army; Porpeis was a clerk in holy orders, and had been physician to the late Bishop of Worcester, but had no scruples about dealing with blood or wounds. He had been acting as surgeon to the castle garrison this last month and more.

'I need honey,' he announced to all present, 'and I need cobwebs.'

'Cobwebs?' Adam asked. For a moment he recalled Robert de Ferrers, and the bizarre nostrums his physician concocted to treat his gout.

'Cobwebs are splendid for sticking wounds together,' Porpeis said over his shoulder. 'And honey both cleanses and cools injured flesh admirably. Now – this young man, I think, might live . . .'

As the surgeon paced over to the next table, Joane took Adam by the arm and drew him aside. Together they stepped through an open doorway into a small herb garden between the kitchen and the inner bailey wall. Sunlight angled down from overhead, shining on a bench where pestles and mortars and dishes of ingredients for salves lay ready. The air was dense with competing scents.

Adam had been forced to part with Joane almost as soon as they arrived within the castle walls. The memory of what they had shared only the night before, and in the early hours of the morning, returned to him now with overwhelming intensity. Joane was suddenly unable to look at him, and moved a pace away. He knew she was thinking of the same thing. But even here they were not alone; a pair of kitchen servants were teasing at the parched soil of the herb patch.

'Master Philip's already put you to work, then?' Adam asked.

Joane gestured at the workbench. 'Yes, he has me grinding pastes and mixing potions for him. I daresay in time he'll trust me to collect cobwebs too. I'll share lodgings with his people in the king's chamber, which should keep me from prying eyes.'

For a moment Adam was obscurely jealous. But no, he told himself, the dry clerical surgeon could have no designs on Joane. Even so, the arrangement did not please him. 'There are other ladies here,' he said. 'Should you not be given a place among them?'

The wives and daughters of some of the knights of the garrison had taken over one of the well-appointed solar rooms flanking the great hall; they were packed in there like a litter of puppies, Hugh had told him, with their maids and children, their chaplains and confessors. Several of them were quite highborn, though none as high as Joane herself.

She dismissed the suggestion lightly. 'I would not rob Margery de Pateshall or Alice de Nafford of their primacy in the ladies' bower,' she said, smiling. 'Besides, the fewer people who know of my presence here, the better.'

'But you'll be recognised, surely?'

'Henry de Hastings knows me, and maybe a few of the others who saw me at Duffield with my cousins,' Joane replied. 'But I barely resemble the woman I was then – men can be quite amazingly unobservant, I find.'

It was true, her appearance was different now. She was no longer the finely dressed lady who had sat beside the Countess of Derby on the tournament stand at Duffield. Now she wore a gown of plain ochre wool and a simple linen headscarf, no jewellery or fine fabrics adorned her, and the signet ring inlaid with the arms of her family was safe in the purse on her belt. Her beauty she could not conceal, and there was a haughtiness to her attitude that she could not overcome, but within the castle walls she could hope to blend in with the other women around her, the wives and daughters of the garrison.

Kenilworth, as they both knew, was the safest place for her at the moment. John de Tarleton had already told them that Countess Margaret de Ferrers had gone to Windsor to petition the queen. Even if Joane had found her way into the royal camp, she would have received no welcome there.

'So if you are not to be Joane de Bohun,' Adam asked her, 'who will you be instead?'

She raised her eyebrows. 'Nobody, perhaps? I've spoken to Master Philip, and he's agreed that I shall be introduced as his brother's widow. That should serve.'

Adam nodded, but felt the ache of their separation grow greater still. For a moment, despair rose like a dark mist in his mind. He tried to shrug it off; he had not slept well for many days, and he was hungry too. A smell reached him: roasting flesh, a sweet torment. For a moment he thought it came from the infirmary behind him, and his gut twisted. Then he realised that the odour carried from the kitchens on the other side of the herb garden. The garrison cooks were already roasting the beef that de Caldwell had captured at such cost that morning.

'For the dinner later today,' Joane told him, as she noticed Adam's questioning expression. Of course, he thought: it was the Feast of the Apostles, Saints Peter and Paul, an even greater festivity than St John's Day.

'We must attend, naturally,' Joane went on, smiling. 'The leading men of Kenilworth have decreed that all shall feast with them. And not even the king of England and his army will keep them from their meat!'

*

Meat there was in plenty, every trencher laid with fat beefsteak dripping in red juices and rich pepper sauce. Other foods in plenty too: casked salmon and oysters, fresh bream from the mere outside, spiced mutton rolls served with creamy mawmenny, herring pies dusted with cinnamon, cheese tarts and almond butter. Such great profusion, Adam thought, that nobody could imagine that the castle was laid under siege, and the king was encamped outside the walls readying his war engines. And that, he realised, was the point; the feast was a gesture of defiance, intended to demonstrate to their enemies that the defenders brimmed with ease and confidence in their provisioning, and could well afford to be lavish at table.

Lavish it truly was, as the squires and servants came and went from the kitchens with one dish after another, and for the first time in a great many weeks Adam felt himself relaxing into the comfort and good company. His own squire, Gerard de Brace-bridge, stood behind him at table, ready to lean in and cut his meat, or to refill his cup with wine or water. Gerard had found Adam shortly after his arrival at the castle that morning, stammering apologies for having fled the rout at Chesterfield. Adam had been quick to forgive him. He was only glad that the boy was still alive and unharmed.

John de Tarleton had offered them both lodgings in the north-east tower. He was sharing the upper chamber with another knight of the garrison, their four squires and six men at arms.

With so many people packed into the circuit of Kenilworth's walls, Adam was grateful for even the narrowest accommodation. He had found stabling for his horse that morning too, and attended to the animal's grooming and feed. He had not had time to bathe, or to change his clothes, but nobody appeared to care. For now, at least, he was content to relax and enjoy the feast.

No great lord occupied the high chair on the dais; instead the men of the defence council sat there in a state of equality. It was a boisterous gathering, rough at the edges, the hall packed with men and women of all ranks and stations. But all were united here, in their common cause.

After the tables were cleared there was dancing, great rondels and caroles in the open space of the hall, as the music skirled and the dancers kicked and scuffed the reeds underfoot. Dust eddied in the beams of sunlight falling from the tall windows. Adam saw Joane among the dancers, and got up at once to join them. One of the turning circles opened to admit him, and he clasped hands and moved with them, to the thump of the tabor and the lilting melody of the flutes and vielles. The rhythm picked up, some of the dancers breaking contact to clap or to shout.

Adam was breathing fast, the rich food and the strong wine propelling him onward. He saw Joane on the far side of the circle, her face flushed and grinning as she danced through the shafts of sunlight. Another turn, the circle splitting and reforming, and he was beside her, clasping her hand as the dance went on. She was lost in the joy of it, dishevelled and uncaring, sweat darkening her gown in patches and her hair swinging free. He heard her laughing, and he was laughing too.

The carolling ring broke up into couplets as the music changed, and together they danced the swallow and the hawk, swooping across the rushes towards each other and then veering away with barely a touch. As the dance went on their touches became more frequent, and they seemed to fall against each other more often. Everyone was clapping and shouting with the music, oblivious.

But all too soon, Joane made her retreat. A last smile over her shoulder, and she went back to join the other women at the far end of the hall. Adam bowed in her direction, then returned to the benches. The music had changed to a faster jig and a rattle of drums. Master Philip Porpeis, pulling up the skirts of his long tunic, was performing a solo dance in the middle of the hall, stamping and kicking up his heels as the circle of onlookers clapped and laughed.

'Our surgeon has an eccentric temper, I'm afraid,' another man said, seating himself on the bench beside Adam. 'And for one in minor orders,' he went on, lowering his voice, 'he is quite notoriously godless too!'

Adam turned to him, raising an eyebrow. The newcomer was fleshy, sallow of face but dressed in fine Lincoln scarlet, with gold rings upon his fingers. 'I myself,' the man said in a confidential tone, 'have heard Master Porpeis question the truth of the mass, and the miracle of bread and wine . . . Apparently he once said that there is no more soul in a man's body than in a chicken's carcass!'

He gave Adam a needling glance, as if he half suspected him of holding such heretical notions himself. Adam's scalp prickled, but he revealed nothing of his unease. 'As well that his care is for the body, and not the spirit,' he said lightly.

'Indeed so,' the man replied. 'I do not believe we have met, sir,' he said. 'I am Lambert FitzThomas, burgess of Kenilworth. And this is my companion, Stephen of Thurlaston.' He turned on the bench to indicate the even stouter man on his other side. 'He was burgess of Coventry, until the disasters of last year, when we were robbed of our property and driven from our homes by the enemies of Earl Simon, and forced to seek refuge here . . .'

'A sainted man, Simon de Montfort,' Stephen of Thurlaston broke in. 'A hero to all good Englishmen! The holy angels mourn him.'

Adam simply bowed his head in acknowledgement.

'Is it true,' FitzThomas asked, leaning to take Adam by the arm, 'that you fought at Lewes, and at Evesham?' His expression brightened at Adam's nod. 'The one battle the blessing of our nation, and the other its curse! Do you know, sir,' he went on ardently, 'one of my most prized possessions is a fragment of the hair shirt worn by Lord Simon on that fateful day, still stained with his martyred blood? May Christ and the holy angels protect him and praise him always!'

'Always and for ever,' Adam agreed. Stephen of Thurlaston echoed his words.

'I noticed,' FitzThomas said, leaning closer still, 'that you were speaking with Sir Henry de Hastings a moment ago. A valiant knight, certainly. A bold man – and a hotheaded one, as many agree. Some here have cooler tempers, and are more inclined to wisdom. I hope I give no offence?'

Adam merely shrugged, sensing the unwanted discussion shaping to a purpose.

'Perhaps we might hope,' FitzThomas said, 'that with all your martial accomplishments, you can aid us also with your good counsel and moderation?'

For all his smooth words there was a heaviness to his manner, an air of threat. As if he resented having to speak in this way. Such men, Adam assumed, would normally be accustomed to having others obey them without question.

'I would hope to give good counsel to those that require it,' he said calmly, narrowing his eyes slightly. 'And hold my peace with those who do not.'

For a moment, Lambert FitzThomas gazed back at him, perplexed. He seemed about to say more, but before he could speak a deep thud ran through the floor and the wall behind them. Adam felt it deep in his gut. Others had felt it too, and rapidly the motion of the dancers slowed and stilled, the music dropping into silence.

Another thud, dust filtering down from the roof timbers. Now all could hear the shouts of alarm from outside. FitzThomas and his friend had dropped to crouch against the wall, both peering upwards with wide eyes. 'What's happening?' the burgess cried. 'What is that?' But when the sound came again they all heard it plainly: the heavy crack of stone against masonry, and the screams that followed. Panic rippled across the packed hall, and any answer Adam might have given was drowned by a wave of terrified cries.

He reached for his sword, then remembered that Gerard had it. No sign of the squire. No sign of Joane either in the chaotic tumult of people. Some were running for the far end of the room, and the shelter of the kitchens and buttery. Others scrambled to the windows or spilled out through the open doorway into the bailey yard. Now all recognised what was happening. The king's engineers in the siege camps outside had finished assembling their mighty catapults; now for the first time they were demonstrating their range and power.

Pushing between the bodies at the open window, Adam stared out into the courtyard. A cry came from the eastern rampart, a shriek from the bailey, as a dark tumbling fleck crossed the sky.

Fugitives scattered, gazing upwards as they ran, veering and doubling back as they tried to gauge the path of the incoming missile. The stone struck the inner curtain wall, cracking the masonry. Another came down in a lower trajectory and demolished the crenellations above the gateway. Adam could only watch, immobilised by shock.

Then a great stone twice the size of a man's head came hurtling out of the brightness of the afternoon sky. It slammed against the wall of the great keep like a thunderbolt. Rebounding, it went plunging downwards at an angle, to plough into a man who stood transfixed in terror outside the door of the kitchens, smashing his body to a red ruin.

Chapter 20

'We have received a demand from the king,' Sir John de la Warre said, speaking over the heads of the other men. He held up the parchment so all could see the royal seal in the ruddy glow of the cressets. 'His Majesty swears that he will demolish this castle with his artillery, break down the gates and hang every man, woman and child within the walls, unless we submit to his power. He gives us until the Morrow of the Visitation to respond. He has further promised that he will not break off his siege until Kenilworth surrenders or it is taken by force, however long he needs to wait.'

'This is nothing new,' Richard de Amundeville said, standing up from his bench. Like almost everyone gathered in the great chamber, he was dressed in full mail hauberk and surcoat, his sword belted at his side. The smell of the feast was still upon them all, but they were armed for battle. The attack of the king's war engines had been a demonstration of force, lasting a mere hour or two, but even now the air seemed to quake with the threat of further violence.

'Why would the king send this friar to us with a message,' de Amundeville went on, 'unless he had some offer to make us?'

'He believes our hearts quail at the power of his catapults!' another man cried. John de Clinton had also been at Chesterfield, in de Hastings's company.

'There *was* another point to the message,' de la Warre said, raising his hands to silence the noise of question and complaint from the chamber. He turned to one of the men beside him, who stood to address the assembly. Simon de Pateshall was a dry, sharp-nosed man of nearly fifty, more like a clerk than a knight. His son John, similarly sharp-nosed and around Adam's age, stood at his shoulder. 'It seems,' Sir Simon began, looking down his nose, 'that the legate of the Pope, Cardinal Otto-buono, is on his way here, to join the king's household before the walls. The legate intends to negotiate a peace between the contending parties. If we do not submit to this peace, he threatens to excommunicate every soul in this castle, and deny us the grace of God.'

'There's some here who never knew that to begin with,' John de Tarleton said in a low mutter. He was sitting beside Adam on one of the benches towards the rear of the chamber.

Adam smiled. But his heart was troubled. For months he had felt the threat of excommunication hanging over him. He was still not sure whether the sentence passed on Simon de Montfort had extended to his followers, or if so whether it had ever been revoked. The threat was real, the fear palpable: even thinking about it brought a swell of cold terror, like steel pressed against his heart. He felt his soul balanced on the brink of damnation.

A clamour of angry voices filled the chamber. Henry de Hastings was standing, demanding to speak. The scowling Gregory de Caldwell jumped up from the table. 'Be still, you yapping dogs!' he bellowed. 'Let's hear Sir Henry, by Christ's mercy!'

'What I say,' Henry de Hastings told them, 'is that these threats only show our strength, and the weakness of our enemies! We are a multitude, armed and united by a common cause, and we hold the greatest fortification in the land. An impregnable fortress! If this Cardinal Ottobuono wants to come here, then let him do his worst. A legate who speaks only for the king, instead of speaking for God, is no true legate at all!'

'I agree entirely,' said the older man with the tonsure, standing up to address the assembly. Peter of Radnor was Archdeacon of Shropshire, but he too wore a mail hauberk and a belted sword. 'Let no man doubt the righteousness of our cause, or the strength of our faith!' he thundered, his voice echoing back from the high ceiling. 'For ours is a god of justice – the god of Saint Thomas Beckett, and of Saint Simon de Montfort!'

'*Yes! Yes!*' the multitude cried, pounding on the tables, and this time nobody called for silence. Richard de Amundeville was shaking his head, but clearly saw that he was outnumbered. When Adam glanced behind him he saw Lambert FitzThomas standing among the mob of other figures at the rear of the chamber.

Easy for these men to be complacent, he thought, within their powerful and well-supplied castle. But something else was stirring in his soul. The enthusiasm of the crowd was contagious, even if it was fed by false confidence. Yes, Adam thought, he knew this well. De Montfort was dead, and the king and his sons triumphant, but England's fury still burned hot and bright here at Kenilworth.

'So what answer do we give to the king?' John de la Warre called through the noise, his voice grating. 'The friar who brought the message is in the gatehouse, and awaits our decision.'

'Should we cut the hands off this one too, Sir Henry?' de Caldwell called across the room to de Hastings, grinning. 'Maybe cut out his tongue, for good measure?'

But de Hastings gave no response. Not even he would dare mutilate a holy friar.

'We must reply with bold deeds, not with empty words,' John de Clinton growled.

The yells of agreement filled the space of the chamber. 'We attack the king's artillery then,' Gregory de Caldwell said, stabbing the tabletop with his finger. 'If he threatens us with his engines, we threaten them right back!'

'*Yes! Yes!*'

Abruptly Adam knew what he had to do. Standing, he pushed his way forward until he stood in the cleared area between the tables. A hush fell.

'I am a newcomer among you,' Adam said, sweeping a level gaze around the men at the tables. 'Many of you do not know me, and some do not trust me. But let me earn my place here. If you will arm and equip me, I volunteer to join the attack.'

Henry de Hastings was frowning, uncertain. But many of the other men were agreeing with enthusiasm; they too were volunteering now, more than a score of them throwing up their hands and raising their voices. John de la Warre appeared grudgingly impressed.

'I too will go,' Henry de Hastings declared, standing up suddenly and planting his fists on the table before him. 'And follow Sir Gregory's lead, of course.' He inclined his head towards de Caldwell, who acknowledged him with a nod.

'Three days from now, then,' de la Warre said, 'on the night of the Visitation. Prepare yourselves well, and if God grants it we shall give the king an answer he cannot ignore!'

*

The night was black, and the air felt warm and thick as milk. Above the enemy encampment the last nail-paring of the waning moon cast little light. The raiding party had walked beside their horses across the causeway in darkness and muffled silence, shrouded like an army of phantoms. Now they assembled within the palisades of the barbican, throwing off their capes and hooded mantles and mounting their horses. The dark was filled with the creak of leather and the clink of harness, the whinny and stamp of beasts, the harsh breathy whispers of men. Impossible, Adam thought, that the enemy sentries had not yet heard them.

He was already sweating in his borrowed hauberk and mail coif, the padded linen aketon beneath soaked and clinging.

Blanchart stirred and twitched beneath him, the horse already sensing the approach of violence. Adam's squire, Gerard, moved around the animal in the darkness fumbling at the girth straps and bridles, breathing curses.

'*God is with us*,' a voice whispered from the darkness. '*God is with us*.' Peter of Radnor was passing between the mounted men, giving them his blessing. The clergyman would not be accompanying the raiders, but he had followed them across to the barbican and would pray for them until they returned.

Around Adam were near a hundred riders, though half of them were spearmen, archers and crossbowmen mounted on cobs and rounceys, and only two dozen were knights on proper destriers. But they were more than enough to rip apart Lord Edward's encampment, while the men who were to follow them on foot did the real damage to the trebuchets. All they had to do was to cross the open ground between the barbican and the siege lines, and find a way in through the wicker screens and spiked barricades before the enemy could muster the force to oppose them. Gregory de Caldwell had been out with his scouts on the two previous days, and claimed he knew the best approaches. In the warm saturating darkness, the men following him knew they were placing their lives in his hands.

'Remember,' said John de Tarleton from Adam's right, 'war first, then chivalry!' Adam muttered his agreement. They all knew what they had to do.

Their principal target was the largest of the trebuchets, standing at the forward edge of Lord Edward's camp. That was the only one with the power to pelt its huge stones right across the lake and the outer walls to strike the inner ward of the castle. In the three days since the demand for surrender, the great machines had remained inactive, the artillerists merely cranking the huge counterweights up and down to keep the cables and timbers supple. The following morning the brief truce would be over. But by then, Adam hoped, at least one of the deadly war engines would have been crippled.

This would be the first time since the Earl of Derby's tourney at Duffield that he had ridden properly armed and equipped for war. The first time since Evesham that he had ridden out to real combat, with killing steel. He felt at once entirely at ease, and utterly unnerved. Hanging from his saddle was a battle-axe that he had taken from the castle armoury; Robert de Dunstanville had always favoured the weapon, and Adam had often trained with one, but had never before used one in a fight.

A stir ran through the men around him, every rider shortening his reins and nudging his horse forward. Squires passed the knights their shields and lances; Adam took his from Gerard, and then walked his horse forward. Ahead of him, he made out Gregory de Caldwell turning in his saddle and raising his mace.

Out through the gateway in the barbican palisade, the raiders kept their horses to a walk at first, careful of the ground in the darkness and trying to preserve the silence. On the far side of the trenches, in the open ground before the enemy lines, they halted and mustered. Still no cry of alarm came from the sleeping encampment opposite.

Ahead of him Adam could make out the jagged shapes of the enemy siege defences, washed in faint moonlight. Beyond them, the trebuchets were clear to see, their great wooden beams lit by the watch-fires of the guards that surrounded them.

A dog barked from the depths of the night, then another. Then the first shout went up from the enemy lines, the first clamour of alarm. Gregory de Caldwell gave a cry. He set spurs to his horse, and the massed attackers surged forward after him, a torrent of steel in the darkness. Hooves thundered across the baked earth, raising dust, and the night air rushed around them as they charged.

Tight in the saddle, holding his lance upright, Adam could see almost nothing but the rider in front of him. Blanchart stumbled slightly, and Adam just had time to push himself back securely into the saddle before gouts of flame erupted along the defences. The riders ahead of him were silhouettes, and he was plunging into a gulf of darkness. Four heartbeats of desperate terror, fighting against the urge to pull at the reins and slow his charge, then the row of big wicker mantlets were directly in front of him, the firebrands of the defenders weaving between them. Arrows spat from the air, and he heard the snap of crossbows. The rider to Adam's left went down suddenly as his horse collapsed beneath him.

'Veer! Veer!' John de Tarleton was yelling. Adam heard the words through the thick padding of his coif, the dulled thunder of his blood and the beating of the hooves, and screwed the reins to the right. A flash of firelight, a volley of cries, and one of the mantlets toppled suddenly as a careering horse rammed into it. Adam spurred Blanchart into the gap, then heaved himself forward as the horse leaped an invisible obstacle and almost threw him from the saddle.

Suddenly he seemed to be alone, riding free across a dark plain, with only spats of fiery light at the margins of his vision. Two crossbow bolts had struck Adam's shield without him noticing; he saw them now, jutting from the leather facing. Swinging the tip of his lance down, he searched the reeling dusty darkness ahead of him for a target. He made out the high beams of the trebuchets away to his right. Then flames burst to his left, and a gang of men ran at him shouting and waving burning brands, the firelight edging the blades of their swords and the points of their spears.

Blanchart reared back from the fire, but Adam kept a tight grip on the reins and spurred the horse forward, veering again to attack the men directly. He drove his lance at one of them, spearing him and then dragging the weapon free. Blanchart was stamping and turning, kicking out suddenly. One flying hoof struck a torchbearer. The man fell, his shattered face horrible in the weaving flame. Adam swung the shaft of the lance over to his other side and stabbed at a second man. Another knight rode through them at the gallop, lance couched. The rest scattered.

Pale shapes of tents over to Adam's left. Horses cantering wildly, some with riders and others without. The night pulsed with noise, screams of terror and shouts of command, the roaring of the attackers, the high whinnying of the horses and the clash of steel in the darkness. Adam's face was covered with dust, and he could feel the sweat from his brow washing through it.

He was almost among the tents now. Burning coals spilled from a fallen brazier, lighting the running shapes of men. A figure reared up in front of Adam, seeming to spring from the earth. Somebody slashed at Blanchart's head with a falchion, and the horse shied. Adam drew back his lance then stabbed underarm, spearing the soldier through the throat. As the body dropped, the shaft of Adam's lance broke. He flung it aside, snatched the battle-axe from his saddle and hefted it in his right hand.

He was into the camp now, steering a weaving course between the tents. Up ahead another rider, one of de Hastings's serjeants, slashed down at a fleeing man in a chemise; the next moment his horse collapsed forward, its legs tangled in the guy ropes, and the rider was thrown across the mane. Figures dashed from the reeling shadows, knives raised.

'To arms!' somebody was yelling. 'To arms, curse you! Where's my God-damned squire?' Trumpets were bleating, sounding out over the noise, but the sounds were strangely muffled and distant in Adam's ears.

Another figure appeared suddenly to his right, an unarmed man in a linen coif emerging from one of the tents, his mouth open in shock. Before he could think, Adam brought the axe slashing down, and the curved blade bit into the man's skull. A tug and the weapon was free, and Adam was riding onward. *War first, then chivalry.*

'Form on me! Form!' the high cracked voice was screaming. 'Where's my damned squire, in Christ's name where is he?'

The attackers had blasted through the camp almost unopposed at first, but now it was swarming like a nest of angry hornets. Arrows and crossbow bolts fletched the darkness. One struck Adam on the back of the head, a glancing blow stopped by the iron skullcap he wore under his mail coif, but it felt like a hammer had clipped him. He was painfully aware of how vulnerable he was here. Blanchart had no armour, not even a fabric caparison. An unlucky bolt or a spear could bring the horse down, a tent rope or even a fallen body could trip him. The destrier seemed aware of the danger, and had shortened his steps to a brisk aggressive trot.

Another rider careered through a tent, his mount kicking and trampling the struggling forms under the canvas. A moment later, both man and horse were down in a flurry of dust. Beyond them Adam spied the yellow pennon of Henry de Hastings. He heard the bleat of a horn, short notes calling the rally, and turned Blanchart in that direction.

A gush of flame, a brazier thrown down igniting piled straw. In the glare Adam could see the larger tents on the far side, the great pavilions with pennons raised above them. *Lord Edward*. But he could see the mounted men too, the armoured knights with lances mustering to charge against the invaders of the camp. They were still unformed, and for a fleeting moment Adam considered charging in amongst them. No, that was death.

'This way! De Norton – with me!' It was Henry de Hastings, three other knights riding at his back. Adam dragged at the reins and pulled his snorting, lathered horse back towards the darkness at the far side of the camp. In his ears he heard the trumpet calls, the heavy battering of hooves as Edward's retinue knights began their countering charge.

'. . . can't stand,' de Hastings yelled, his voice a thin whine through the drumming in Adam's ears. 'There's too many . . . back to the war engines . . . rally . . .'

Adam nodded, or tried to, then drove Blanchart forward once more. A horseman appeared suddenly from the darkness to his right, screaming and raising a sword to strike. Twisting in the saddle he took the blow on his shield, then swung his axe in a tight underarm slash. He caught the horseman in the ribs, and felt the crunch as the axe blade cut through mail and padding and broke the bones beneath. Backhand he flicked the axe up again and smacked the flat of the blade into the man's coif. Then his attacker veered away and was gone.

A lance jarred against his back as he turned. No space to wheel and confront the new threat. Adam dug with the spurs, trusting to his mount to carry him clear. Armoured men on heavy horses all around him now, but in the dust-fogged darkness it was impossible to distinguish one side from the other. Head down, still feeling the pain of the arrow strike rattling around his skull, Adam rode in the direction of the great trebuchets, still standing against the black sky, lit by the fires beneath them.

A rending crash, a cheer and a blizzard of sparks. Something collapsed into a pit of shadow, but Adam could not make out what had fallen. Blanchart was hobbling slightly, injured in the left foreleg. 'There's one of them!' a metallic voice yelled. 'Take him! Take him, curse you! . . .'

Adam turned just in time to meet the attack, slamming his shield against the head of a lance aimed at his face. He turned the shaft aside, then lashed with his axe. The attacker was a mailed knight, ermine and rampant lions on his shield. Adam's chopping blow skated over the ermine and struck the man on the thigh, but did not break his mail. They were side by side now, horses jostling, Blanchart twisting his neck to bite at the other animal as the dust eddied up between them. The ermine knight had dropped his lance and was trying to draw his sword. Adam freed his axe and swung it again, standing in his stirrups to drive a hacking blow that caught the other rider between the shoulders. It seemed to have no effect. The man was wearing a coat of plates over his mail.

Sword drawn, the other knight stabbed at Adam's face. The blade grated across the mail of his coif. They were pressed too close to use the axe effectively now, the two horses snaking and twisting. Another stabbing blow bit into Adam's shield. He pushed against it, throwing his shoulder into the shield's curve. The ermine knight reeled back in his saddle, and Adam slammed his axe directly upwards like a spear, driving the top of the blade into the other man's throat.

Stunned, gasping for breath, the knight hunched forward in the saddle and tried to pull his horse away. Adam released his own reins and reached across, clumsy with the shield strapped to his arm, to seize the bridle of the other horse. His mailed fingers closed around the leather, and he clung on tight as the animal dragged against him. Then, as the ermine knight swayed upright in the saddle and lifted his sword for another strike, Adam slammed the axe down on the top of his head.

Sagging in the saddle, the man appeared to be unconscious but was still held in place by the high cantle and the stirrups. Hauling on the bridle of the other horse, Adam urged Blanchart forward with his knees. Blissfully, the horse responded at once and they were riding free, towards the darkness beyond the crushed man-tlets, the dropped firebrands still sputtering in the dust, Adam towing the captured mount and rider behind him.

Somewhere a horn was sounding the retreat. And in the dark-ness along the shore, two of the big trebuchets were burning, the flames reflecting across the black mirror of the lake.

*

The captured knight was a veteran, Adam discovered the fol-lowing day, close to sixty, with large grey moustaches. From the arms on his shield – *ermine, a chief indented azure, three lions rampant or* – one of the garrison heralds distinguished him as Walter de Horkesley, a knight of Essex. Adam had captured him single-handed, but both de Hastings and John de la Warre were insisting that all ransoms taken in the night raid had to be shared equally among the company. Adam could not insist otherwise; at present it looked like there would be no ransom at all. Walter de Horkesley was dying.

'That blow you dealt him broke his skull and drove the bone into his brain, as you can see here,' Philip Porpeis said, indicating the wound with his stylus. De Horkesley lay on the infirmary table, insensible as a dead man, ashen in his bloodstained chemise and braies. Clearly, in the chaos of the night attack he had armed in haste, and had not worn a steel skullcap beneath his mail coif. The surgeon had shaved the thinning hair from the man's scalp to expose the wound, then cleaned the gouged and livid flesh and peeled the skin away from the incision. Adam felt a clamping sensation in his gut. Never before had he closely examined the body of a man he himself had struck down. A sense of deep shame as well, and growing remorse. Walter de Horkesley was old enough to be his father. Perhaps even his grandfather.

'Will he live?' he asked Porpeis, his throat tightening.

The surgeon plucked at the short beard on the end of his chin, considering. 'Hard to say. If the brain is damaged then perhaps death would be a kinder fate. But I have removed the fragments of bone, as you see, and in a moment I will treat the wound with Ointment of the Apostles, prepared by the good Lady Joane, and then apply a compress and bind it. The patient feels nothing at present, of course. If he wakes from the stupor you knocked him into, then we shall see . . .'

'Where is Joane now?' Adam asked, glancing around.

'She was unwell, and I gave her leave to rest,' Philip said. 'Several others were feeling ill this morning – I suspect some of the food supplies are already spoiling in the heat . . .'

Adam had turned at once for the door, intending to go and find her, but the surgeon halted him with a hand on his shoulder. 'She should remain undisturbed, for a few hours,' he said, hastily but firmly. 'Besides, you need to rest yourself – sit, and let me examine that wound.'

The arrow that had struck the back of Adam's head during the night raid had injured him more seriously than he had thought; he had returned to find the padding beneath his mail coif soaked with blood. Now the top of his skull was wrapped in a linen bandage. Standing over him, Master Philip peeled away the dressing and studied the wound, sucking on his bottom lip. 'Well, you seem to be mending a lot better than Sir Walter over there . . . But you must avoid exertion, and any excessively hot emotions that might cause your head to swell!'

Adam knew he had been lucky, all the same. Several other men of the raiding party had been injured, some of them grievously, although only two men at arms and a spearman had failed to return, either killed or captured by the enemy. The infirmary was crowded with the wounded, Master Philip's assistants moving between them administering draughts, and washing and binding wounds. Groans and sobs filled the warm thick air, and the smell was becoming unpleasantly cloying.

The raid itself, however, had been only partially successful. One trebuchet had burned and another had been crippled, but after two days the king's engineers had repaired the damage to the second and were in the process of rebuilding the first. With all the resources of the kingdom of England at his disposal, the king was short of neither building materials nor manpower. For the besieged, any respite could only be temporary.

Soon enough, the great engines began to pummel the castle once more. From the battered ramparts Adam and the other men of the garrison watched them day after day, trying to gauge where each shot would fall, braced for each crashing impact. There were other machines to the north and the east, batteries of engines that sent their projectiles arcing across the pools and moats of the castle's water defences to smash at the outer walls and the north gate, and even to strike the inner walls and bailey and the base of the great keep. The spreading encampment of huts and animal pens that Adam had seen when he first arrived at the castle had almost entirely vanished now, the survivors dragging their beasts and all they could salvage of their possessions to shelter beneath the walls and towers. Anyone crossing the open spaces of the castle moved at a crabbed run, glancing fearfully upwards. And all the while the weather got hotter, the cloudless sky vibrating with blue intensity.

It took Walter de Horkesley nearly a week to die. There was no final spasm, no wracking pain. He merely ceased breathing, and Master Philip pronounced him dead. Adam found the body laid out in the small chapel of the inner bailey that evening, surrounded by flickering rushlights and the shadowed forms of men.

'We should ransom the corpse, at least,' Henry de Hastings said. He glared at the body, as if it had offended him by dying so soon.

'Fling it over the walls with a mangonel, more like,' Gregory de Caldwell said with a sneer.

'No!' declared Richard de Amundeville, taking a step forward. He gestured to de Horkesley's body. 'He was a knight, like us. A loyal man, who died for his king. He deserves to be treated with respect.'

'Is this a time for chivalry?' de Caldwell asked, sneering.

'When is it not?' de Amundeville replied, in a voice of low gravity. 'If we cannot maintain our dignity, what are we fighting for?'

'I agree,' said Adam, stepping forward into the circle of wavering light. Henry de Hastings gazed at him startled. 'I captured him,' Adam went on, 'and I dealt him the wound that killed him. I will honour his body, if none of you will.'

'Well spoken,' a deep voice said, and John de la Warre's huge shape loomed from the darkness at the rear of the chapel. 'I'll have no churlish acts here,' de la Warre went on. 'Not while I am captain of this garrison.'

'Very well,' de Hastings said. 'Let us be honourable men, then.'

They carried Walter de Horkesley's body from the castle that same night, wrapped in linen with his scabbarded sword upon his chest, laid on a bier with candles set around him. The night was still, the air warm, and the flames of the candles barely wavered as they crossed the causeway to the barbican. Out through the gate in the palisades, they set the bier down in the open before the enemy siege lines and then stepped away from it. In silence they waited, until a solitary rider came forth from the opposing lines and raised his hand in acknowledgement. Then they filed back inside the defences.

John de Tarleton found Adam the following day, sitting outside their shared quarters cleaning his mail and oiling his belts.

'You did well,' de Tarleton said. Praise did not come easily to him, and Adam was moved. But he merely nodded his thanks. From somewhere to the north came the thud of a trebuchet counterweight falling. Moments later, the crack of a stone striking the wall, and a woman's distant scream.

'Anyway, looks like the dead man's horse and saddle belong to you now,' de Tarleton went on. 'His armour too, if you want it. And these.'

He tossed a pair of gilded spurs onto the ground beside Adam; Walter de Horkesley would not be needing them now.

'Seems you've earned them,' he said.

Chapter 21

The assault began with a hail of arrows, arcing out of the dawn sky. Two or three found their mark. The rest of the men along the battlements of the northern wall kept their heads down. They knew all too well what the day would bring.

The crenellations were shattered in places, merlons crushed to rubble by the trebuchet stones, and the heavy timber hoardings that had covered the wall walks were a wreck of tangled beams and collapsed planking. But amidst the wreckage the defenders still sheltered, crouching behind the pitted masonry of the rampart and in the chambers of the towers and gatehouse. Sweating in their armour, they endured the arrow storm. The hours ahead would be fierce, and they needed to conserve their strength.

'You hear it?' one man asked, with a grimace.

The others around him lifted their heads, ears cocked. Several nodded. Adam heard the sound as well, as he crouched alongside them: a deep grinding creak, wood against iron, and the groaning of timbers.

For the last ten days, as the catapult stones crashed around them, they had watched the enemy siegeworks tightening around the castle. Lines of heavy mantlets to protect the king's archers and crossbowmen now surrounded the walls. To the north, the besiegers stood almost at the far lip of the moat. As the great trebuchets had hurled their stones in soaring arcs, the king's men had sent labourers forward to fill the moat with bundles of sticks and great wicker baskets full of earth and stones. Several times Gregory de Caldwell and John de Clinton had led night forays from the north gate to attack the besiegers and to burn or destroy their constructions. But the heaped causeway that now spanned the moat would not burn, and would have taken a small army of engineers to destroy.

And that, Adam knew, would be the avenue of the enemy assault. Because, while some of their men were busy filling the moat, others had been at work in the camp of Lord Edmund. From the walls the defenders had watched the huge timbers raised, the frame assembled and faced with wicker screens. The siege tower was as tall as a church belfry, rising in stages above a wheeled chassis, and thickly clad with wetted animal hides. Through the hours of darkness they had heard the grinding creak of the axles as the tower was moved towards the castle. Now a horde of men stripped to their braies were preparing to heave it the last distance, across the moat and up to the ramparts.

All the enemy archers, all their engines, were now concentrated on the stretch of wall that faced the approaching siege tower. But the defenders, too, had moved up their artillery in response. Two large perrier catapults and a mangonel stood in the bailey behind the walls, the crews hauling on the cables to send stones whirling towards the enemy lines. There were machines in the chambers of the north gatehouse too, and on the turrets along the wall.

As the withering hail of arrows began to slacken at last, Adam picked his way along the walkway towards the gatehouse, climbing over mounds of fallen rubble and the bent backs of other defenders. Over his mail coif he wore a broad-brimmed helmet with a bowl of blued steel, but still he kept his shield raised. Spent arrows rattled around his feet as he reached the doorway into the gatehouse. The shade was an immediate relief. As his eyes adjusted to the gloom he saw Richard de Amundeville in the upper chamber, and a younger knight named William de Naf-ford. A dozen archers and crossbowmen were hunched at the embrasures.

On either side of the chamber, flanking the portcullis mecha-nism, were two large constructions of beams and tightly plaited cords, each about the size of a four-poster bed. Adam had not seen bolt-shooting engines like these before coming to Kenilworth; springalds, they were called. As he entered the chamber the two crewmen were turning the windlass at the rear of one engine, drawing back the powerful torsion arms. The frame of the machine creaked as the tension steadily increased.

'How is it out there?' de Amundeville asked.

'Hard to see anything without getting shot,' Adam told him.

'Follow me,' the older knight said. 'There's a better view from above.'

They climbed the wooden steps to the gatehouse roof, where a dozen archers and slingers crouched along the rampart. Few of the enemy crossbowmen bothered to aim their bolts in this direction, so it was a marginally safer vantage point.

'If our foes were wise,' Richard de Amundeville said, 'they would attack one of the other parts of the wall while we're dis-tracted here.'

'Then let us thank God for our unwise foes,' Adam said.

De Amundeville grinned and nodded. Together they raised their heads from behind the merlons. From up here Adam could survey the enemy siege works, and the approaching tower. It was much closer than it had appeared from the wall; already the besiegers were heaving it forward across a platform of rough-cut logs they had laid on top of the debris filling the moat. With the advantage of height Adam found that he could see right across the mantlets and trenches to the spreading encampment beyond. Bright banners and pennons hung slack in the still air: Lord Edmund's red royal standard, and those of several other great magnates too. Adam picked out the white and blue stripes of Reginald de Grey: the Constable of Nottingham had also brought his forces to join the attack.

Enemy troops were gathering in columns, marshalled by their serjeants. Most were archers and crossbowmen, ready to climb up into the tower as it approached the wall and shoot down at the defenders cowering on the battlements. But many wore mail and padded gambesons, and bore shields and spears. Once the tower was close enough, a tide of armoured men would storm across the bridging timbers onto the castle ramparts.

Seeing such great numbers waiting to join the assault was unnerving. Adam wondered how they must be feeling themselves. The tower swayed as it approached, the beams of its construction creaking and wailing and the hides that covered it shuddering with the motion of the great wheels.

'It should take them most of the morning to push that monster across to the wall,' de Amundeville said, nodding towards the tower. 'Our best hope is to destroy it before it reaches us. But it would take a lucky shot indeed.'

Even as he spoke a thunderous crack echoed from the gatehouse chamber beneath them as the springald released its bolt. Adam flinched instinctively, and de Amundeville laughed as he slapped his shoulder. The bolt struck the hides cladding the siege tower, but the lumbering belfry did not slow its advance.

'I didn't have the chance to commend you, you know,' de Amundeville said to Adam, settling back to sit against the rampart. 'When you stood up to Sir Henry and de Caldwell like that.'

Adam remembered the night of Walter de Horkesley's death, and the debate in the chapel. 'It was no great matter,' he said.

'All the same,' de Amundeville said. 'Honour is becoming a rare thing here.'

Adam avoided his gaze, unwilling to be drawn any further into the conflict of factions. His throat was dry, his body drenched with sweat, and his head was beginning to ache with the heat of the sun. Pulling off his helmet he craned his neck, staring across at the mass of enemy troops waiting to begin the assault.

'Have a care, sir,' one of the archers at the parapet said, 'there's—'

Before he could say another word a crossbow bolt smacked into Adam's left shoulder, just below his collar bone. Red pain lanced through him as he staggered back from the parapet, and the sky whirled above him as he fell.

*

'A flesh wound, happily,' Master Philip said. 'Your mail took the force of it and the bolt barely punctured, although you'll have a fine bruise to remind you of it. You can still use your arm?'

'Well enough,' Adam said, wincing as he flexed the muscles.

'Good. You may need to use it briskly soon!'

They were in the bailey, sitting on a bench beside the gatehouse wall. Gerard de Bracebridge was doing his best to close the rent in Adam's mail, squatting to hammer at the rivets, with the tip of his tongue between his teeth. Adam himself was stripped to the waist, a linen bandage around his shoulder and chest. Now that the immediate danger had passed he felt ashamed of his wound; all around him were men injured far worse, and bodies were laid out in a row on the parched grass. He had been stupid to expose himself like that to the enemy.

Hugh of Oystermouth brought a skin of water and Adam leaned forward as his friend poured it over his head. 'God bless you,' he gasped as he wiped the water from his stinging eyes.

The crews manning the perrier catapults had dragged their machines back to try to aim the stones directly at the looming siege tower. Adam watched as six men drew down the lever arm of the nearest engine, placed a boulder in the sling, then with a shout hauled on the ropes and dragged the arm in a flinging arc.

The stone soared away over the wall, and Adam heard it splash into the moat. The men on the rampart were already yelling to the catapult crew to adjust their aim.

But now the enemy machines were shooting too. One stone struck the parapet, sending two bodies tumbling in a shower of gritty rubble. Another arced down into the bailey, narrowly missing one of the perriers. Adam saw Joane running from the inner bailey carrying a basket of bandages and salves; he almost called out to her to go back, but it was useless. Nowhere was safe inside the castle walls.

Passing her burden to Master Philip, Joane ran to assist the wounded lying along the inside of the wall. She did not so much as glance at Adam, and he wondered if she knew he was there. After nearly a month under siege, just about everyone in the castle appeared similarly filthy and ragged, unwashed and exhausted.

'Everyone to the walls!' a voice said in a brassy yell. 'Everyone to the walls – they're almost upon us!'

John de la Warre strode across the bailey towards the rampart stairway, his red surcoat flaming in the heavy sun and a red-painted great helm under his arm. Adam gestured to his squire, who fetched his tunic and padded aketon and helped him dress and pull on his hauberk. This time he would wear the coat of plates he had taken from Walter de Horkesley as well; it would be punishingly hot and heavy over his mail, but the protection was worth it. By the time he had tightened his belts and laced the broad-brimmed helmet over his coif, he could hear the renewed cries of alarm from the wall. Teeth clenched against the pain in his shoulder, he snatched his shield and axe.

Labouring up the wooden stairs to the rampart, Adam heard the double thud from behind him. Two stones arced overhead a moment later. As he reached the top three more projectiles came whirling in from the other side. Sweating under the weight of his armour, he ducked his head and made his way along the rampart walk. John de la Warre was there already, and de Tarleton, and

Simon de Pateshall's son John. From the gatehouse door came Henry de Hastings, sword in hand. All of them were assembling on the rampart that faced the oncoming siege tower.

It was juddering closer now, the hide-covered face bristling with arrows. Somehow the attackers had rigged a block and tackle to pull it the last distance to the wall, with cables running back to two teams of oxen on the far side of the moat. The stretch of rampart it was approaching had been demolished by the trebuchets, the parapet smashed flat and only an open rubble-covered wall remaining.

A sudden crack from overhead, and fragments of stone cascaded from the sky. A cheer, and cries of amazement; two flying rocks had struck each other as they flew, one from each side. Another moment and the cheers turned to screams as a plunging projectile struck the second perrier catapult in the bailey, killing three of the crew.

The tower began to creak as men scaled the broad ladders running up the open back. All were archers and crossbowmen, and as each gained the summit he took aim at the men on the wall below him.

'By God's death, there's hundreds of them!' John de Pateshall cried.

Arrows and bolts zipped and flickered around them, the steel heads biting at the stone of the wall and cracking into their raised shields. The closer the lumbering tower got to the wall the more bowmen scrambled into its upper storeys, shooting down at the castle's defenders. The whole massive construction swayed and groaned as it advanced. Adam risked a glance from beneath his arrow-studded shield and saw the first wave of attackers beginning to scale the ladders inside the ripped and ragged cladding of the siege tower.

'They're coming across!' he shouted.

'Forward!' John de la Warre cried, then pulled his red iron helm down over his head. Three crossbow bolts slammed into his shield, splitting the wood, and he hurled it aside and ran along the wall top, bellowing.

Adam was right behind him, de Hastings coming up at the far side. Together they converged on the point where the tower would drop its boarding bridge. They reached it just as the heavy timbers slammed down onto the shattered masonry of the rampart, and with a roar the assault group stormed forward.

Stepping up onto the brink of the broken parapet, Adam swung his axe in a low cut and chopped the legs from under the first man across. De la Warre was to his right, standing firm as an armoured giant at the centre of the wall and using his sword with both hands. Henry de Hastings was on the other side, hewing from behind his raised shield. Bolts spat down at them from above, and the enemy came on in a seething rush.

A spear rammed into Adam's shield, and another jarred against his kneecap. He hacked overarm, knocking a man down sprawling onto the bridge timbers. His feet were grinding broken stone and grit, and he was dizzyingly aware of the brink of the wall directly beneath him. One false step, one loss of balance, and he would plunge thirty feet to his death. A crossbow bolt deflected off his helmet, shoving the rim down over his eyes, and for four long heartbeats he was fighting blind, striking out furiously as he tried to remain standing.

The attackers were pushing forward in greater numbers. Adam took a step back, then another. Even John de la Warre had been forced to retreat. But now their own archers and crossbowmen were crowding at their backs, shooting between them straight into the faces of the attackers. A loud crack, and a bolt from the springald in the gatehouse tower speared three men on the bridge, pinning their bodies together and pitching them over the side. 'Now, now!' de la Warre shouted, his voice booming from inside his blazing iron helmet. 'Drive them back!'

A rush of heat from behind him, and Adam stepped aside just in time as two men pitched a brazier of hot coals at the men on the bridge. Smoke and whirling cinders stung the air. Another tide of men flowed up the ladders; they were bulky in their gambesons and mail, their sweat-drenched faces stretched in fear and fury. And the force of their attack was not flagging.

Clambering up onto the bridge timbers, Adam pushed forward with his shield and then hewed with his axe. The blade bit, sticking deep in flesh, and for a moment of lurching terror Adam thought he would be pulled over the brink by his victim's falling body. Roaring, he hauled back on the axe and it came free. Another bolt from the springald pierced a man through the chest. The boards of the bridge were slippery with blood, smoking in places from the cinders. A mist of gritty dust fogged the air.

'That's the way! That's the way!' John de la Warre bellowed, fighting the enemy back onto their bridge. 'Come on, my beauties – come and dance!' Arrows and bolts jutted from his mail, but he appeared invulnerable.

A brief pause, the wave of attackers cresting and then receding, and Adam almost shouted in relief. But they were just rallying their forces for a more concerted attack. He took two steps forward, legs braced on the streaming timbers.

Overhead, a dark shape parted the singed air. Adam did not see the catapult stone strike the top of the siege tower, but he saw the beams judder and then split. He heard the torrent of horrified screams as the whole construction began to collapse, spilling bodies. For a moment he was too startled to move. Then the timbers beneath him dropped sickeningly, and he saw the yawning gulf open beneath him, a pit of collapsing timbers and screaming men disappearing into the dust.

He threw himself backwards, feet skidding on the bloodied planking. John de la Warre seized his right elbow, and one of the archers caught him by the surcoat, and together they dragged him back from the brink as the tower and everyone inside it crashed to ruin beneath them.

Adam was lying on his back, spent arrow shafts crackling beneath him, heaving breath as the sense of lurching terror subsided and he realised that he had survived. Survived, and triumphed too. De la Warre was punching the air, bellowing defiance in the direction of the enemy. Adam coughed, tried to sit up. The archer who had dragged him to safety passed him a waterskin and he drenched his face with it, and as the liquid flowed over his parched and bloodied lips he thought it better than the finest wine he had ever tasted.

They had won, he thought. They had won, *for now*.

*

Scaling the narrow spiral stairway, he emerged onto the roof of the north-east tower and found a crowd already gathered at the ramparts: John de la Warre, Simon de Pateshall, Henry de Hastings and a score of wives, servants and men at arms. He hung back a moment, until de la Warre noticed him and gestured for him to approach. Ten days had passed since the attack of the siege tower. He had earned his place among them now.

'It's started,' Hugh of Oystermouth said, pointing out across the crenellations.

On a hillock to the east of the castle walls, just outside the range of the longest bowshot, a group of robed figures had assembled under the massed banners of the king and his magnates. One banner stood proud from the rest. Adam did not recognise it at first, but then picked out the crossed keys emblazoned upon it. The papal insignia, he realised. And the man standing beneath it, illuminated by the evening sun, was the papal legate himself, Cardinal Ottobuono Fieschi.

Since his arrival at Kenilworth the cardinal had been sending his messengers across to the castle gates under flags of truce, demanding the garrison's surrender in the name of Pope Clement and the Holy Church. In the name of God Himself. The garrison, unanimous for a change, had refused even to admit the messengers. Their own emissaries had returned with no acceptable terms. Now, it seemed, the legate's patience was at an end.

He stood in his red cope and golden mitre, flanked on either side by six bishops, each holding what looked like a tall white candle. Behind them were gathered a mass of knights and clerics, witnesses to the ritual.

'Can you hear what he's saying?' Adam asked.

'It's all in Latin anyway,' snarled an aging man at arms. 'Like in church. You can guess it ain't good, whatever it is.'

'The cardinal is fulminating the sentence of excommunication against us!' another voice said. Adam turned to see Philip Porpeis emerge from the stairs and pause to catch his breath. Behind him came Joane de Bohun.

'You shouldn't be here,' Adam told her, meeting her at the stairhead. 'It's dangerous . . .'

'I'm not afraid,' Joane said briskly, brushing past Adam and striding to the parapet to join the others.

Philip Porpeis hopped up between the crenellations and seated himself on a merlon, pulling the hanging sleeves of his mantle around him. He appeared to be enjoying himself. 'I've never seen this done, you know,' he explained to the men around him. 'Let alone seen it done *to me!*'

'You're not worried, master?' the man at arms asked.

Porpeis merely shrugged. 'It seems unavoidable. Many of the castle chaplains, you know, are hiding in the armoury, hoping to avoid the fatal words. But if one believes in these things, one must believe them *ineluctable*, surely?'

The soldier frowned, pulled off his linen coif and scrubbed his bald pate. All along the eastern rampart of the castle there were men gathered to watch the ritual. Women too, and children. They crowded the shattered remains of the wooden hoardings along the wall top, peering across the crenellations. All of them in silence.

'Can you make out the words?' Hugh of Oystermouth asked. In the distance the tiny figure in the red cope and mitre was gesturing with his left hand. His voice sounded like a metallic twanging on the breeze.

'I know the phrases well enough,' Porpeis said. 'He separates all of us, together with our accomplices and abettors, from the precious body and blood of the Lord Christ, and from the society of all pious Christians!'

The aged man at arms gasped and crossed himself; many of the others on the tower did the same.

'He excludes us from our Holy Mother the Church,' Porpeis went on blithely, 'both in heaven and on earth. He declares us excommunicate and anathema, and he judges us damned, with the devil and all his reprobate angels, to eternal fire until we shall recover ourselves from the toils of the evil one and return to amendment and to penitence!'

Adam had joined Joane at the parapet. She pressed herself against him as the surgeon spoke, and he felt her quick shudder. Instinctively he put his arm around her, not caring who might notice. He felt the chill of fear as well, striking through the day's heat. Excommunication was the most serious sentence that the Church could enact. Adam had known the threat of it before. He had blocked it from his mind, but he could not avoid it now. Every clipped Latin word that drifted across from the hill to the people lining the castle wall was a steel blade, murdering their souls. An iron door, closing off the path to salvation. A leaden chain, linking them to the devil, and to damnation.

'And now, you see,' Porpeis said, 'he and the bishops have thrown down their candles and extinguished their light – it is done! He has closed the book upon us.'

A bell tolled from the assembly on the hill, a single flat iron clang.

Adam heard Joane's indrawn breath, and she pressed herself tighter against him.

'Banners to the wall!' somebody shouted from the rampart below the tower. 'All banners to the wall!'

Already squires and grooms were running from the keep across the stone-pitted expanse of the bailey, with banners lifted on tall poles. Others were carrying pennoned lances. From all directions men were converging on the eastern wall, passing the flags up to the men on the ramparts above them.

Lances furled with silk were thrust up the spiral stair to the tower roof. Gerard came scrambling with them, and unfurled Adam's green pennon with the golden lion. Two of Henry de Hastings's squires appeared with his big yellow banner, the emblem of a red sleeve, a *maunch*, displayed upon it. All around the tower and along the wall below were a host of other flags: Richard de Amundeville's white lattice on blue, John de la Warre's rampant lion on cross-studded red, John de Clinton's blue and white set with gold fleur-de-lys, and Simon de Pateshall's red crescents and black bar. The banners of Simon de Montfort too, lord of the castle in death as in life. The twin-tailed lion flew in the breeze, above all the others.

Both men and women were laughing, yelling in rebellious disregard of the legate and the king and their sentence of damnation. Together they had survived the assault on the walls, and the worst the king's engines could throw at them. Kenilworth remained standing, and it remained strong. There was a wild freedom in that defiance, and Adam felt it too, dispelling all dread. Joane shook herself from his protective embrace, raising her fist as she joined the cheers.

Philip Porpeis had jumped down off the battlements, and two of de Hastings's squires were fastening a white linen cloth around his shoulders. 'Peter of Radnor refused, you know,' Sir Henry told Adam. 'He thinks mockery to be impious. But our bold surgeon here has no such scruples!'

'Is he drunk?' Hugh of Oystermouth asked, perplexed.

The squires knotted the sheet across Master Philip's chest, while another set a yellow bag on the top of his head and plucked at it until it resembled a mitre. Then they helped the surgeon clamber up and stand perched upon the battlements, facing the papal legate and the delegation of bishops.

'Ha, yes – now we have a legate of our own!' the old man at arms said.

'And ours is better than theirs!' cried Henry de Hastings.

Another cheer went up from the men in the tower, echoed by the multitude along the battlements. Philip Porpeis was swaying, the two squires clinging to his ankles to hold him steady. Somebody passed him up a greasy old tallow candle from the chamber below and he held it aloft. Already he was warbling out the Latin imprecations. Adam could hardly bear to listen.

But all along the walls the cheers were rising, the banners swaying as men brandished them in defiance. Master Philip continued his solemn chant, directing his mock excommunication at the legate, the bishops, the assembled magnates and the entire king's army gathered behind them. At the king himself too, and his sons. They could hear the yells of outrage and the jeers of abuse drifting across from the enemy lines.

'And so be it!' Philip declared, in a ringing tone, and then hurled his greasy candle into the moat below him. The cheers hammered at the sky as the squires helped him from the wall. In the distance, the cardinal and his bishops were already retreating.

'What happens to us now?' Adam asked in a whisper, almost as if he were talking to himself. 'We cannot confess, we cannot be absolved . . . We are damned, sinners unto death.'

'Then let's try not to die,' Joane said, twining her fingers with his. 'Not yet. Not here.'

Chapter 22

'*Argent, a saltire engrailed gules,*' Adam said, narrowing his eyes against the morning sun.

'That would be Sir Robert de Tibetot,' Hugh of Oystermouth replied, leaning beside him on the shattered rampart. 'Who's his challenger?'

Adam squinted towards the far end of the distant field, picking out a red banner covered with yellow spots. '*Gules, bezanty or.*'

'Alan la Zouche,' Hugh said with a nod. 'His brother William bears similar arms, *azure bezanty.*'

Adam watched as the two knights spurred their chargers across the field. The crack of lances drifted across the waters of the lake, and one rider reeled in the saddle. Hugh made a vague sound of appreciation. His skills as a herald were still finely tuned, unlike his eyesight; so many hours peering at manuscripts in scanty light had blunted his vision.

'Two more coming up,' Adam told him, craning his neck as he heard the trumpets. Then he grimaced. He needed no herald to identify the blue and white stripes of Reginald de Grey.

It was the middle of August, the Morrow of the Assumption, and so many knights had gathered in the king's siege camp that they were holding a round-table jousting tournament in the fields beyond the south-eastern pool. The battered wall of the castle was lined with spectators, but none cheered the victors. The day before, the king had held a great feast to mark the holy day, and the encampments all around the castle had pulsed with music and song. Adam wondered if Gervase of St George and his troupe of minstrels had been among the entertainers. Somehow the king's cooks had contrived to waft the smells of fine food over the moats and siege lines as well. The men and women of the castle garrison had eaten their pease pottage and bacon with little enthusiasm.

Beyond the tents of the royal encampment, and the bright banners of the tournament field, the land was the colour of dry straw. It had barely rained since mid-June, and so many local men had been summoned to labour for the king that there were few left to bring in the harvest in the neighbouring manors.

'Is it true,' Hugh asked as they watched the distant horsemen, 'that Henry de Hastings wanted to lead a raiding party out to burn the crops in the fields, and the other men of the defence council refused to allow it?'

Adam nodded. He had been present during that heated debate. 'Richard de Amundeville got his way, for once,' he said. 'As he explained it, the king can draw supplies from all across the kingdom if he needs them. All we'd accomplish by burning the crops hereabouts would be to starve the local people.'

'A wise argument,' Hugh said. 'Did you support him?'

'I did, though I was not alone.'

'Sir Henry loves you less with every passing day, I believe.'

Adam knew that well enough. But he had not come to Kenilworth to act as de Hastings's vassal, and while he often grew impatient with Richard de Amundeville and Simon de Pateshall, and their constant argument that the garrison should re-open negotiations with the king, he had to admit that they were not always wrong. Besides, the men of Kenilworth were no longer alone in their defiance; only days before, a messenger had managed to slip into the castle with news that John D'Eyville,

Baldwin Wake and their rebel band had occupied the fenland redoubt of the Isle of Ely. Now the king would have to divide his forces to counter the new threat.

'How long can we hold out here, do you think?' Adam asked, dropping his voice. Hugh had been appointed the castle's quartermaster, and would know the answer better than anyone.

'I would estimate another two months should exhaust our stores,' the Welshman replied. 'Kenilworth was provisioned to hold out for a full year, but the garrison was only supposed to number three hundred, and we have four times as many mouths to feed. Besides, we have too little salt.'

'Salt?'

'To preserve the fresh meat, you see,' Hugh explained. 'The animals that remain have to be eaten as soon as they're slaughtered, and nothing can be saved. We tried smoking the meat, but the result was . . . well, *unsavoury*.'

Two months, Adam thought. Four, perhaps, on half rations for all. Already the wine was almost exhausted, and both knights and commoners alike lived on coarse and flavourless fare. Joane had it slightly easier; the inner ward had so far been spared the worst of the bombardment, and many of the ladies kept their own private stores of provisions, which they were eager to share with the popular Master Porpeis, who in turn shared them with his own retinue.

But the castle was growing less habitable by the day as well. The walls and internal buildings were battered and scarred by the catapult stones, many of the roofs and the rampart hoardings brought down completely. In the fierce heat of midsummer the smell was becoming intense. Hundreds of unwashed people lived packed together in crowded airless chambers. Many used the inner ditch as a latrine, or hurled their ordure over the walls, where it baked and stank at the side of the stagnant moat. The refuse from the slaughteryard had gone the same way, and half the inner bailey ditch was a sickening swamp of rotting carcasses and animal bones, hazed with flies.

'Ah look, new challengers emerge!' Hugh declared as the trumpets bleated from the tourney field. 'Can you pick out the banners?'

Adam studied them with a frank lack of interest at first, then one caught his eye. 'There's one I recognise. *Argent, two chevrons rouge.*'

'De Grendon, I believe,' Hugh said. 'Did I not see him at Chesterfield, in the Earl of Derby's affinity?'

'You did,' Adam replied. 'I fought him in single combat, in the earl's tourney at Duffield.' At least now he knew that Sir Ralph had escaped from the outlaw camp in Sherwood. Seeing him appearing so boldly among the knights of the king's army was a shock, all the same.

The rider who came forth to challenge de Grendon was a still greater shock. '*Quarterly or and gules, a border vair,*' Adam reported in a flat voice, his mouth dry. 'Is that . . .?'

'John FitzJohn,' Hugh said, in a similar tone, then shook his head and whistled through his teeth. 'So he's been granted the king's mercy now then?'

A year ago, John FitzJohn had been one of the fiercest and most ardent followers of Simon de Montfort. He had fought at Lewes and Evesham, and before that had led the murderous attack on the Jews of London. Now, it seemed, King Henry was happy to accept the young nobleman back into his peace and favour. It was sickening.

Hugh blew a breath, puffing his lips. 'Just goes to show what's possible,' he said, 'with the right words, the right contrition. Even the worst of bloody-handed villains can become loyal subjects once more.'

He glanced quickly back over his shoulder towards the keep behind them, and raised his eyebrows. He did not need to say another word. Every former rebel knight who raised his banner in the king's camp sent a message to the leaders of Kenilworth's defenders. There could be forgiveness, the message said, and mercy for those who submit. But would that mercy be extended to all?

Abruptly Adam found that he had seen enough of the jousting.

There were two men waiting for him as he dropped down the stairs from the ramparts. He tried to evade them as he strode off towards his chamber in the north-east tower, but they moved quickly to intercept his course.

'Master FitzThomas,' Adam said with a curt nod, turning as they joined him. He was hot, and in no mood for niceties.

Despite the heat, the burgess wore a tunic trimmed with marten fur. His friend Stephen of Thurlaston was sweating heavily. 'Sir Adam, perhaps we might speak with you for a moment?' Lambert FitzThomas asked.

Adam inclined his head, and gestured for them to walk with him as he continued onward past the eastern stables. It was nearing noon, and the few people who might overhear them had retreated to the shade of the walls.

'Sir Richard de Amundeville thinks very highly of you,' Fitz-Thomas went on, slightly breathless. The man was nervous, Adam realised. 'He thought we might profitably discuss certain matters with you . . . You'll have noticed, of course, how many of the knights currently in the king's camp have recently changed their allegiance?'

'Betrayed their oaths, you mean?' Adam replied. Had they too, he wondered, noticed John FitzJohn out there? He had betrayed many an oath himself, but was feeling particularly inflexible. He also got the strong impression that these two men were not speaking for themselves alone.

'Oaths to Earl Simon, yes, and to the Community of the Realm,' FitzThomas went on, 'which all of us swore, in our time!'

'All of us,' Stephen of Thurlaston agreed, wiping sweat from his brow.

'But now, you see,' FitzThomas went on, 'with our current sufferings . . . Some of us wonder, in short, whether the defiant policy of Sir Henry de Hastings and his followers is the correct one. We wonder if you might add your voice to Sir Richard's and urge a more moderate approach?'

Adam halted suddenly, turning on his heel. The burgess stood his ground, his lips tightening. There was more steel to the man than it appeared. Even so, Adam had no time for him. 'Listen to me, I came here to make a stand for justice,' he told FitzThomas. 'To fight for the lands that are my birthright, and to regain my good name. Unless the king can offer me that – and he has not – then I remain as defiant as Sir Henry, and may God damn anyone who speaks of dishonourable surrender!'

'Of course,' FitzThomas said, with a humourless smile. 'We would not, I'm sure, wish to speak against anyone's *honour*.'

And with another tight bow of the head, he summoned his colleague and strutted away towards the stinking ditch and the gate of the inner bailey.

*

Clouds covered the moon, and the night was airless. In all of Kenilworth, only the rampart of the western wall which over-looked the great mere caught the breath of a breeze. It was the only undamaged part of the castle too; the king's engines either lacked the range or had not directed their shots that way. After dark, many of the civilians camped in the sheltered area just inside the wall climbed up onto the narrow walkway of the battlements, hoping for relief from the night's heat. Beyond the crenellations, the mere was dull under the clouded sky, the far shore lost to darkness.

Adam moved along the walkway, stepping over slumbering figures. There were a few sentries up here too, posted above the water gate that led to the fishing jetty. Night watch was becoming a prized duty among the garrison. Up here in the relative coolness, with the placid lake spreading before him, he could appreciate why.

He stood for a while, watching the shimmer of diffuse moonlight on the surface of the water. The mere had proved a good source of fresh fish over the last two months, although anyone going out in a boat in daylight became a mark for the king's archers and light catapults. Instead the castle fishermen had fixed stakes and traps in the shallows close to the bank. Adam saw a pair of them out with a punt, collecting their night's haul. His stomach growled, and he sent a brief prayer for fresh trout grilled over hot coals. The water plashed, a cooling sound.

'I hoped I might find you here,' a voice said from the darkness. Adam turned, startled for a moment, then eased out a breath as he saw Joane appearing from the shadows. 'Hugh of Oystermouth said you'd be keeping the night watch.'

She joined him at his vantage point, and they gazed out over the mere as the fishermen gathered their catch and returned to the lakeshore; beneath them they heard the creak and then the heavy thud as the postern gate opened and closed.

'How easy it would be,' Joane said as she looked out at the lake, 'to take a boat and slip away. Have you ever thought of that?'

Even as Adam denied it, he realised that he had just been thinking of that very thing. *May every man's sword be turned against me, and may I die a traitor's death . . .*

'Where would you go?' he asked her.

'Home,' she said at once. 'Back to Ware. I felt it was my prison once, but as I think of it now it was heaven itself. I am not the woman I was then . . . What about you?'

'All that I want,' Adam said, after a moment's consideration, 'is all that was taken from me. If I left here I would have nothing.'

'Is that really true? What of Isabel de St John?'

He glanced at her quickly, and caught her smile in the half-light. 'Hugh told me of her as well. And of the news he gave you, back at Chesterfield. I ought to be offended that you did not mention her yourself.'

Adam felt the shame unfolding within him. He tried to speak, but just as he had when Hugh questioned him about Isabel on the keep ramparts, he found he could say nothing.

'Often we cannot be the people we think we should be,' Joane said. She leaned against him, resting her head on his shoulder. For several long moments they stood like that, and Adam felt a strange contentment stealing through him. Everything was known now, he thought. Everything was forgiven. A waterbird crossed the mere, long wings beating in the darkness.

'There's something I've concealed from you as well,' Joane said, after a while. She took his hand and he turned to face her.

'Tell me,' he said, half dreading what she might say. Half elated too.

Before she could speak, a shout came from the darkness, harsh and sudden. Another answered it, from further along the wall. Moments later, the stillness of the night was shattered by the clangour of an iron bell, ringing from the arch above the postern gate.

'What is it?' Joane demanded, terror spiking her voice. 'What's happening?'

Adam had moved at once to shelter her. He stared back over his shoulder, along the rampart walkway, as figures rose from slumber. Then he looked out between the merlons.

'There!' he said, staring across the black water as the shifting patterns of moonlight formed into distinct shapes. 'They're on the lake,' he said, his breath tight. '*They're coming across the lake!*'

The noise of the watchman's bell had been answered now by a discord of clanging metal, yells from all along the wall answered from the bailey and the inner ward. Voices came from the lake as well, the first cries of command drifting eerily over the still waters.

'There are scores of them!' Joane said. Standing at her shoulder Adam saw the lake covered with boats and wide flat-bottomed barges, each one crowded with men. A shift of the clouds, and moonlight washed the scene before him, glittering off the helmets and spears. Oars rose and fell, and the enemy craft resembled black insects creeping across the glistening surface of the mere.

'Archers to the battlements!' Adam yelled over his shoulder. 'Crossbows!' Plenty were shouting the same thing. 'You have to get down,' he told Joane, taking her by the shoulders. 'This is no place for you.'

'No, I'm staying here,' Joane said, pulling herself from Adam's grip. 'Anyway, there's no way down, unless I jump . . .'

Men were scrambling up the steps onto the narrow walkway on both sides of them, archers and crossbowmen, slingers, and anyone who could throw a spear or heft a stone. Joane would not be able to get off the wall now even if she wanted to do so.

'Stay well below the parapet then,' he told her.

A sharp crack of timber came from across the water, and Joane flinched as a catapult stone arced overhead. Screams from behind them as it came down amid the darkened tents and shelters inside the wall. The enemy vessels were approaching faster now, the oarsmen no longer intent on silence, and Adam could clearly make out the light perrier engines mounted on two of the bigger barges. The lever arms swung down, then with a shout the crews hauled on the ropes and whipped the stones towards the castle wall.

But now the defenders massed along the rampart were responding, pelting the oncoming boats with arrows and sling-stones, yelling defiant abuse into the darkness. Screams from the lake as the men in the boats began to feel the bite of steel from the black sky. Adam grinned; normally this stretch of wall would have been lightly guarded at best, and the enemy might have expected an easy assault. Only the stifling midsummer heat, and the promise of cool breezes from the lake, had drawn so many to the ramparts. But for all their numbers, most of the people on the wall were poorly armed civilians. As he stared between the merlons, Adam picked out the shapes of ladders in some of the boats; they would try to scale the wall once they reached the shore.

'Adam, keep down!' Joane cried, grabbing at his arm. Only as she spoke did he notice the snick and clatter of arrows on the stonework. The attackers had bowmen among them too, and as their approach brought them within range they were returning the volleys from the wall. An arrow struck a man to Adam's left, just beyond where Joane was crouching. The shaft punched into his throat, and the man dropped the light crossbow he had been aiming and tumbled silently off the walkway into the darkness.

Adam was wearing no armour; the night had been too sultry for mail, or even a padded aketon. He had no bow, no spear he could hurl, not even a rock. Merely waiting, powerless, for the assault to come was near unbearable, but if the enemy got to the lakeshore and managed to raise their ladders against the wall, the defenders would need skilled fighters on the rampart to repel them. Standing at the merlon, he drew his sword.

Joane had snatched up the fallen crossbow from the walkway and spanned it. Straightening from the shadows, she braced the weapon against the stone parapet. Adam was about to protest, but there were plenty of other women on the wall aiding the defence, and he knew that Joane was a keen shot with a hunting bow. She aimed, released her bolt, then at once turned and stooped to span it again.

Cheering from around them now. The shredding clouds spilled another wash of moonlight, and Adam saw that the leading wave of boats had ground to a halt, still a hundred or more paces out from the lakeshore.

'It's the fishing traps!' a man beside him cried. 'The nets and stakes – they can't get through them!'

Adam stared, and saw that he was right. With a shout of laughter, he saw the leading boats nudging together in the water, men leaping into the chest-deep shallows to tug and haul at the lines of stakes. Howling in panic, many of the oarsmen were throwing themselves overboard as the arrows spat from the sky. Not just arrows either – a moment later a plummeting black shape struck the water between two of the boats, raising a plume of spray. More cheers from the wall – the crew of the big mangonel catapult in the north-western bailey had managed to slew their machine around and were hurling stones straight over the angle of the walls to fall among the clustered boats.

'They're trapped!' Joane cried, breathless with excitement. 'Praise God!' She lifted her loaded crossbow, braced it, and then loosed her bolt with a fierce snap.

Another missile crashed down into the shallows, narrowly missing one of the boats, and the oarsmen and the armoured serjeants beside them hurled themselves into the water in terror. Before the plume of spray had fallen, one of the perrier catapults on the barges swung and released its stone.

Adam saw the missile whirling against the moonwashed clouds. He opened his mouth to shout a warning, but was too late. The stone smashed against the merlon between him and Joane, and he felt the shards of broken masonry against the side of his face. The top of the parapet collapsed, stones tumbling inward across the walkway. Adam was on his knees, his face freckled with blood. Gritty dust filled his throat as he drew a breath to call Joane's name.

Two other men had crawled to assist her, but in the blackness and dust Adam could see nothing for a few panicked heartbeats. 'She's alive,' one of the men said. 'Careful now – she's bleeding . . .'

Then Adam blinked the dust from his eyes, and in the dirty shadow he saw Joane lying sprawled across the walkway, motionless in the shattered rubble, her face webbed with blood.

*

The first light was in the sky by the time he found his way to the reeking clamour of the infirmary. He had seen Joane taken down from the rampart soon after her injury, her body lifted in a blanket and passed from hand to hand to the stairway. One man said she had a broken leg. A woman claimed she had a broken skull, and would not survive the night. But she had still been breathing when Adam saw her last.

He had spent the following hours on the wall, in an anguished fury of prayers and curses, ready to repel an attack which never came. Only two or three of the flotilla of boats had managed to push their way through the maze of stakes and netting to the lakeshore, but the men aboard them had discarded their ladders and could only huddle against the base of the wall until the defenders drove them away. The rest of the boats and barges had backed oars and retreated across the lake, ignoring the cries of the drowning men they left behind them.

As light streaked the sky behind the looming castle keep, the shallows had been a hellish expanse of bodies and broken spars, tangled among the stakes. A few overturned boats still drifted, the hulls bristling with arrows. Nearly a dozen of the enemy had managed to scramble ashore and surrender, kneeling outside the postern until they could be taken inside as prisoners.

'Not as much of a slaughter as we might have feared,' Master Philip said, once Adam located him. 'On our side at least. Christ alone knows what the other side have suffered.' Taking Adam's arm, he guided him between the tables and mattresses, the bodies lying in the thick gloom. 'She's over here,' he said.

'Is she . . .' Adam started to ask, his jaw numb and his mouth dry.

'Oh yes,' the surgeon replied.

Joane was in the far corner of the chamber, on a trestle bed with a hanging drape screening it from the rest of the infirmary. Hugh of Oystermouth was already there, sunk into exhaustion as he dozed on a stool beside the bed. Linen bandages wrapped the top of Joane's head and her left foot. As Adam drew the drape aside her eyes opened and she gave him a thin smile. His heart swelled, and he dropped to kneel beside her.

From somewhere outside came the distant thump of a trebuchet. The enemy, foiled in their attack across the lake, had recommenced their bombardment.

'Of course, it was madness for her to be on that wall in the first place,' Master Philip was saying as he searched among a collection of jars and bowls on a table beside the bed. 'In her condition, of course, it could have been a greater tragedy . . . But with Christ's blessing, she has only a broken ankle and a contusion to the scalp. I considered giving her dwale, for the pain. But hemlock and poppy seed can loosen the womb . . .'

Adam had barely heard him speak. It took a moment for the words to reach him. He raised his head, his brow furrowed. Joane took his hand.

'I wanted to tell you,' she said. 'I was about to tell you . . .'

'What do you mean?' Adam said, turning to the surgeon.

Master Philip arched an eyebrow. 'Christ's mercy, man, do you not know?' He let out a scoffing laugh. 'The Lady Joane is with child. Just past her first trimester, I would estimate, although I'm no student of such things . . .'

Speechless, Adam looked back at Joane. He was still kneeling beside the bed, and she tightened her grip as she clung to his hand. Questions tumbled through his mind, too many to form into words. But when he looked at her, when he met her eyes, he knew that he need ask her nothing.

'What do we do now?' he asked the surgeon instead.

'Oh, rest for the lady, of course,' Philip said, applying ointment liberally to a linen pad as he spoke. For the first time Adam noticed how fatigued he appeared. 'No more strenuous activity! Frequent bathing, and a light diet. Avoid any excitement that might heat the blood and arouse the passions . . . And then we simply let the mysteries of nature take their course.'

Adam began to laugh, helpless to fight it down. He gazed back at Joane, and she began to laugh too, although there were tears in her eyes.

And before either of them could speak another word, a stone from one of the king's trebuchets demolished the roof of the infirmary and plunged everything into night.

Part Three

Chapter 23

The rain was falling as they butchered the horse. Adam forced himself to watch, the water dripping from his hair and running down his face. The animal was one of his own, the warhorse he had captured from Walter de Horkesley months before, and it was worth the annual income of a manor. But it had fallen sick from eating mouldy oats – the *blind staggers*, the grooms had called it – and now it was worth nothing but its weight in fresh meat, hide and bone marrow.

Dogs lapped at the blood flowing through the dirt. This was not the first horse to die in this way; many of the sumpter beasts and the rounceys had already been slaughtered for their meat. Each knight was permitted to keep only a single charger now; there was neither the grain nor the oats to feed more, and no hay or grass remained within the circuit of the castle walls. Adam thought of his prized Blanchart, safe in the stables on the far side of the bailey, and promised himself that he would never allow the same fate to befall the silver-grey destrier. But what would happen when the last of the feed was gone? What would happen when the garrison exhausted the last of their supplies, and starvation set in? Better not to think of that.

'Here you are, sir,' the butcher said, wrapping a shoulder steak in a scrap of linen and passing it to Adam. He could hardly ask for more. Under the ruling of the defence council, all meat from slaughtered beasts was supposed to be shared in common. The steak was a rare indulgence, and Adam took it with gratitude.

Cradling the hunk of warm and bloody flesh, he dipped his head and walked through the rain, across the mud of the outer bailey towards the inner ward. At least, he thought, the weather would deter the enemy from launching any incendiaries today.

It was late October, and four months of siege and bombardment had left Kenilworth Castle a shattered ruin. Only the great keep still had its roof intact. After the hot weather broke at the end of August, persistent rain had turned the open areas of the bailey to a muddy waste. The inner ditch was flooded, and the soil thrown down to cover the ordure and rotting carcasses in the summer had turned to repugnant black slime. All across the bailey were the distinctive depressions of shallow graves, each one set with a wooden marker but steadily sinking under the rain. And amid the mud and the rubble, the graves and the refuse, over a thousand people still eked out a life. Even with the rations halved, hunger stalked them all.

As he made his way over the slippery planks of the bridge, repaired many times and sagging in the middle, Adam saw the figures huddled around the archway of the inner bailey. They had been watching him, he knew. Civilians, women and children and a few wounded men among them. He threw back his cloak so they could see his sword as he passed the gateway, and ignored their hungry stares. In his mind he saw again the horse carcass sliced by knives, and imagined all too clearly teeth rending raw and bloody meat.

Through the arch, he entered the oval of the inner courtyard. Directly to his right the massive rusty-brown cliff of the great keep rose from its stepped base. The other buildings were little more than shells now, roofless and partially collapsed. The vaulted stone undercrofts of the residential chambers were still standing, and were now home to several hundred people. The kitchens were still in operation too, among the rubble. Fires spat in the rain, and smoke hung in a grey shroud around the broken walls. Adam smelled hot kitchen grease, and his stomach roiled.

The chapel to the left of the inner bailey gate had surrendered its religious function, as none of the surviving priests or chaplains in the garrison cared to defy the papal legate's holy injunction. Adam knelt quickly beneath the crucifix on the leaning rood screen nonetheless, bowing his head and crossing himself.

Peter of Radnor had his own little curtained alcove, which had once served as the vestry. 'Blessings upon you!' the arch-deacon said as Adam parted the drapes. He had given up shaving as penance during his excommunication, and a grey beard now covered his chin and upper chest. He motioned to one of his servants, who took the bloodstained bundle from Adam.

'It was honestly obtained, I suppose?'

'It was my own horse, if that's what you mean,' Adam replied.

Peter of Radnor appeared satisfied at that. But he raised his hands anyway, beseeching the few remaining roof timbers. 'Now horses, next dogs and rats! May the Lord have mercy upon us!'

His servant was already unwrapping the meat; it would be tenderised, diced and cooked upon a griddle for the archdeacon and his little household to savour privately. Peter gestured to another servant, who knelt and retrieved a smaller bundle, pass-ing it to Adam. 'Baked this very morning, with almost the last of the wastrel flour,' the servant said.

Adam nodded his thanks, and then he waited, giving the arch-deacon a significant look. Peter cleared his throat, made another gesture, and the servant measured a small amount of white pow-der and wrapped it in a rag. Adam stowed it in his belt pouch, then knelt briefly for the archdeacon's benediction.

Back across the courtyard, the precious bundle clasped beneath his cloak, Adam passed through the wide doorway of the forebuilding that covered the entrance to the keep. John de Tarleton was inside, with three men at arms, and he nodded a terse greeting. Enclosed by the forebuilding, a timber stairway climbed in a dogleg. There were more guards on the stairs, crossbowmen with their weapons propped against the wall as they played dice on the wooden landing. Adam stepped over them, and climbed on upwards.

At the head of the stairs was a heavy iron-studded door, recessed deeply into the massive thickness of the wall. Two more men sat at the threshold, and one rose as Adam approached and banged on the studded oak. The portal swung open, hinges shrieking, and Adam entered the keep.

Since the destruction of so many of the castle's buildings, and those of the inner bailey in particular, many of the more prestigious members of Kenilworth's garrison had chosen to move to the keep, along with their wives and families. The gloomy lower chamber, accessible only by the spiral steps within the thickness of the wall, was used by the wives and families of the servants, and of the men at arms and archers of the garrison. The upper chamber, where the meetings of the defence council had once been held, was now home to everyone else.

Beneath its soaring ceiling the room was packed and clamorous. The stench of the cesspit in the latrine tower mingled with the smell of unwashed bodies, damp clothes and wet dogs. Smoke rose from the central hearth and hung in a grey pall beneath the roof beams, and a constant low stir of voices filled the air, cut through with the cries of infants. Adam picked his way from the entrance passage, passing the trestles and mattresses of Master Philip's relocated infirmary. There were far too many sick and wounded now for Porpeis to attend in person; until two days ago, he had been spending most of his time trying to save the life of John de la Warre, struck in the face with a crossbow bolt during an assault on the walls. But the valiant constable had been beyond help, and had died on the infirmary trestle.

The ladies of the castle had established themselves at the far end of the chamber, surrounded by low walls of piled chests and trunks and canvas screens. Adam had found Joane a sleeping place in one of the deep window alcoves, where she could benefit from the little light and fresh air that penetrated the narrow opening. It gave her a small amount of privacy as well. Two women attended her, both skilled midwives.

She was sitting on her mattress when he arrived, reading a book in the beam of scant light. Kneeling beside her, Adam glanced at the open page. 'Your Psalter?' he asked. Surely by now she knew every word of it by heart.

'No, this is a romance,' Joane told him, closing the book. '*The Tale of Jehan and Blonde*. Master Philip found it for me in one of the tower chambers. It's diverting enough, although the lady of the tale is none too vivid. Supposedly she's the Earl of Oxford's daughter, and betrothed to the Earl of Gloucester, and the knight Sir Jehan falls in love with her, but his station is too lowly . . .' She paused, blushing a little as she realised the implication. 'Anyway,' she went on hurriedly, 'it's all very chivalrous, although I suspect the author has never spent time in a real castle under siege.'

'I hope it ends well,' Adam said, then to cover his sudden embarrassment he slipped the bundled loaf from beneath his cloak and passed it to her. 'Save this for the hours of darkness,' he told her quietly.

Joane smiled, breathing in the freshness of new bread. 'Thank you,' she said, and pressed his hand. They could permit themselves no greater signs of affection now.

Her smile widened as Adam took the packet of powder from his belt purse. At once she tugged it open, moistened a finger and put a dab on her tongue. 'Oh, I've been craving this! Where did you find it?'

'Peter of Radnor keeps a small supply,' Adam told her. She offered him the packet and he shook his head. *Blanchepoudre*, precious sugar ground with ginger, was too sweet for his tastes.

Joane shared it instead with her attendant women, who both rolled their eyes at the rich flavour. From somewhere outside came a rending crack and a sigh of falling masonry. Everyone tensed, and then eased their shoulders down. The king's trebuchets still lobbed occasional shots, but the crews seldom wasted their ammunition against the great keep any more. The walls were solid stone and fifteen feet thick. Here, at least, was safety.

Joane set the pouch of powder aside and idly ran her hands over the swell of her belly. She appeared visibly pregnant now, and had done for a month or more. Adam was still both amazed and embarrassed that he had not realised sooner. But he knew so little of what Master Philip had called *the mysteries of nature*; what were the signs he had failed to notice? He had at least calculated the dates; the night they had spent together at Chesterfield, he had decided, was surely the beginning. But Joane had been taken away by Reginald de Grey only the following morning, and had spent a month or more in his keeping. Adam dared ask her nothing more about that; already he had offended her enough. But he wondered, all the same. And tried not to think too much about the implications.

'Do you know what day it is tomorrow?' Joane asked, lying back against her heap of pillows as she savoured the lingering taste of the powder.

Adam considered for a moment. They still heard the bells of the priory ringing the daily hours, but without regular mass on Sundays it was hard for the inhabitants of the castle to keep a grip on the passing days and weeks. He shook his head.

'It's the Feast of All Saints,' Joane told him. 'October has passed – I missed the anniversary of Sir Humphrey's death, on the vigil of Simon and Jude!'

Adam raised his eyebrows, marvelling. Had it really been over a year since that terrible day at Beeston Castle? It had been raining then as well, he remembered. 'Do you still think of him?' he asked.

'Of course,' Joane said, her eyelids fluttering closed for a moment. 'I cannot say that I enjoyed his company. But he was my husband, all the same. If I had such a rare thing as a candle, I would light it in his memory. And at All Souls I shall pray for him.'

They were both speaking quietly. In public, Joane was still the widow of Master Porpeis's brother, her late husband an anonymous victim of the kingdom's ongoing turbulence, the child she so obviously bore conceived in wedlock while he yet lived. Adam did not know how many believed the story, but very few knew the truth, and it was better that way.

But when her eyes opened, he was surprised to see a tear roll down her cheek. 'You mourn him still?' he asked quietly.

'No!' Joane said, with a sudden bitterness in her voice. 'I mourn myself! Isn't that stupid of me? I mourn the woman that I used to be!'

Adam took her hand once more, but she pulled it away. He understood her sorrow. Any ideas they might once have had about slipping away from Kenilworth were gone now. Joane could scarcely present herself before her cousin, Countess Margaret, still less before Earl Humphrey de Bohun, in her current condition. How could she argue for the return of her dower lands, when she was so obviously pregnant? All would know that her child was illegitimate.

Joane sniffed, wiping her face with the back of her hand. She smiled, with some effort at looking apologetic. 'I mourn my cousin, Robert de Dunstanville, as well,' she said. 'I was thinking of him earlier as I read the book . . . I cannot help but think that we would not be in this place, if he had survived.'

'If I knew any way that we might leave,' Adam said, 'I would take it, no matter the danger.'

'I know,' she said. 'I'm sorry, I meant no criticism . . . It seems every day I must relearn how to live in the prison my life has become. The prison it has been, for so long.'

Adam shook his head, wanting to contradict her but knowing the truth of her words. Nothing in what he had learned of this world, in what he had heard in the stories of chivalry or acquired through the hard lessons of knighthood, had taught him how he should behave now. Besides, the two midwives had grown more attentive, and he could risk no further intimacy.

'Sir Adam,' a voice from the chamber behind him said. Turning, he saw a youth of about fifteen standing with his thumbs hooked in his belt. Adam could not remember his name; he was one of the new squires that Henry de Hastings had raised from among the sons of garrison soldiers. 'Sir Henry wants to see you,' the youth said curtly, and glanced at Joane with a look of mild distaste.

'Tell him I'll see him shortly,' Adam said. 'I doubt either of us have pressing engagements elsewhere.'

He was halfway back across the chamber, stepping between the mattresses and the heaped possessions, when one of the ladies stretched her hand from a truckle bed and pulled at the hem of his cloak.

'I know who she is, you know,' the woman said, in a breathy undertone. Alice de Nafford was the widow of a knight lately killed in an assault on the walls. She was young, Joane's age, with a receding chin, pale straw-coloured hair and dark circles beneath her large eyes. 'I know!' she said again. 'I can recognise true nobility when I see it – she's no humble clerk's widow, that's plain to see . . . But only I know that she's . . .' She dropped her voice to the tightest whisper. '*Lady Mary de Ferrers, the Earl of Derby's wife*! Half-blood niece of the king himself . . . Have no fear, I'll tell nobody – but be sure to remember that I kept her secret safe!'

'Certainly, yes,' Adam said in a vague mumble. The woman was grinning and nodding, wide-eyed, as he detached himself from her grip.

*

Henry de Hastings had established himself and his small retinue in the upper chamber of one of the keep's corner turrets. The room was not large, but compared to the cramped quarters that Adam shared with John de Tarleton and a dozen other men, it felt comfortably spacious.

'How is de Bohun's widow?' Sir Henry said, as he passed Adam a cup of wine from his own private supply. He had dismissed his squires and other servants, and they were alone. 'Miraculous, eh, that she should conceive a child even after his death? She must have prayed most fervently for an heir to inherit his estates!'

Adam tensed, and he fought the urge to fling the cup of wine in de Hastings's face. But Henry seemed merely amused by his anger.

'Calm yourself,' he told Adam. 'You think I didn't recognise her, the moment you both got here? You can put a pack-saddle on a palfrey, but it will not become a sumpter horse.'

Adam was speechless a moment, caught between offence and an unexpected pride. A sense of possession too. 'Speak of it to nobody else,' he said.

'Oh, they'll hear nothing from me,' de Hastings replied. 'If the lady wants to hide her true station then I'm sure she has her reasons. Though I did wonder, you know, if you'd intended to use her to further your cause in some way. Earl Humphrey, her old father-in-law, is in the king's camp outside . . . As is Reginald de Grey, who I hear was seeking her hand in marriage. Both would be eager to have her returned to them, despite her current condition.'

'Never!' Adam broke in. 'She is not a hostage, and never will be.'

De Hastings shrugged, a lazy smile crossing his face. 'As you say,' he said. 'Provided you continue to keep faith with me, of course.'

He paced to the embrasure of a slit window in the eastern wall, gesturing for Adam to join him. Adam took a sip of wine, mastered his displeasure, and then crossed the chamber.

Together they gazed into the grey light of late October. The rain had stopped, but clouds still sealed the sky.

Beyond the battered walls of the castle and the trenches and palisades of the siege works, the land stretched bare to the horizon. A plain of undulating mud and pools of water. Months of sun and rain had turned the tents and pavilions of the king's encampment to mottled brown, and faded the bright colours of the banners.

'What are they discussing over there, do you think,' de Hastings said, 'all those great magnates assembled to decide our fate?'

Adam shook his head. The king had summoned all the great earls, barons and bishops of England to his parliament over two months ago, towards the end of August, and they had been in session at the priory ever since.

'They're trying to decide what to do with us,' de Hastings said. 'They can't break us, and they refuse to bow to us. The king won't leave until the castle is his, but winter approaches . . .' His voice trailed off.

'What do you think of the temper of our people here?' he asked abruptly. 'You've been among them. Are their spirits still bold?'

'They're holding out,' Adam told him. 'Most still believe that the rebels in Ely will force the king to break the siege. Or that Lord Simon's son will come from France with an army.'

De Hastings nodded, his lips moving as he ran his tongue over his teeth. 'But still many among them openly speak treason, I know that,' he said quietly. 'Not just de Amundeville and his supporters, pouring milk in everyone's ears. You know the ones I mean – civilians and townsmen. Their cowardice is like poison.'

'Hunger and despair,' Adam told him, 'not cowardice. Would they have held out this long if they lacked courage?'

De Hastings frowned, but gave a nod. Both of them knew that the defence of Kenilworth had been staunch all through the summer and the early autumn. Repeatedly the men of the

garrison had made sallies against their enemies, conducting great
mounted raids even in daylight that wreaked havoc among the
trench lines and the encampments. Often they had brought back
captives, and exchanged them for any of their own that the king
still held. They had brought back trophies too: one wall of de
Hastings's chamber was hung with rich crimson silk, embroidered with three golden lions *passant gardant*. The royal banner
of England. John de Clinton had cut it down from above one of
the king's pavilions during a raid on the royal camp, and brought
it back with him in triumph.

But their attackers had been vigorous too. They had tried
undermining the palisades of the barbican, until their tunnels
flooded. In mid-September the king had sent another siege tower,
greater even than the first, against the eastern defences. *The Bear*,
the garrison had called it. But the tower had proved too heavy
and cumbersome to push over the causeway that spanned the
eastern moat; the king had filled it with archers, crossbowmen
and springalds instead, but the remaining catapults in the castle
had destroyed the tower a few days later. The broken timbers
still remained, jutting up just beyond the moat like a thornbush
bristling with arrows.

Yes, Adam thought, Kenilworth had held out, and would
continue to do so. But the seasons were changing, and once
winter set in there would be a limit to what any of them could
endure.

De Hastings was teasing at his beard as he gazed into the bar
of light through the window slot. 'Still too many fainthearts,' he
muttered. 'Too many rusted blades. Whatever they intend for
us, out there,' he said, nodding towards the distant priory where
the king's parliament was assembled, 'we'll need strong men to
respond to it.'

He stepped closer, clapping Adam on the shoulder. 'You're
like me, you know that?' he said, tightening his grip. 'I didn't see
it before, when we were prisoners together for so many months,

but now I do. De Montfort gave you everything, didn't he? He made you a knight, and he gave you lands to hold . . .'

'The lands my father held,' Adam broke in. 'He restored them to me.'

'Yes, yes,' Sir Henry said, with an irritated gesture. 'But he *made* you. And you owe him everything . . . As do I! Oh, I had lands and estates before I came to support Lord Simon's cause. But he made me a baron — he gave me that honour, and raised me to sit among the greatest men in England. And I loved him for that. *They* don't understand that,' he snarled, stabbing a finger towards the far window slot. 'De Amundeville and de Pateshall . . . They think this is merely a matter of expediency, of negotiation and compromise. But you and I know otherwise, do we not? We know this is a matter of honour, and the debt we owe to Lord Simon!'

And when Adam looked into the pale blue of Sir Henry's eyes, he saw the furious glint of madness.

*

The clouds had parted by the time Adam left the keep, and the wet stone and puddled paving of the inner bailey gleamed in fresh sunlight. He heard the music as he passed through the forebuilding and stepped out into the courtyard. The scrape and whine of a vielle, a drum beating and a human voice raised in song. At one end of the shattered great hall, where the ceiling timbers still provided a scrap of shelter, a crowd had gathered around a smoking fire.

Pacing across the cracked paving, Adam stood in the open arch of the doorway. Lambert FitzThomas was among the gathering. Stephen of Thurlaston too. For a moment Adam recalled the great feast where he had first met them, in this very hall. His stomach groaned at the memory of the food they had eaten, the wine they had drunk without thinking it a blessing. Perhaps the same musicians had played then, when they had all danced with such abandon. It seemed a lifetime ago. Lost in recollection, it was a few moments before he caught the words, and recalled the melody.

> 'Those by his side for justice died,
> So England might be free.
> But by his death, the Earl Montfort,
> Gained the victory!'

That same song he had heard at Leicester, sung by the minstrel Nubbe. It may have been the woodsmoke hanging in the cold air, but Adam's eyes were suddenly watering.

> 'The wicked men, they cut him down,
> And hacked him to the ground.
> But on his corpse, such precious prize
> A hairshirt there they found!'

'It does our people good to hear music!' a voice said, and Adam turned to find Peter of Radnor at his side. There were tears on the clergyman's cheek as well, and glittering in his beard.

The tune came to an end, with a last shriek of the vielle and a battering on the drum. Ragged cheers and scattered applause came from the assembled people.

The archdeacon clapped too, calling out his praises to the musicians. A stir went through the crowd gathered around the fire as they noticed him and Adam standing in the doorway. More laughter, bitter this time and resentful. They had intruded upon this merriment, Adam realised. The people of Kenilworth might still revere Simon de Montfort, but the mood in the castle was shifting, just as Henry de Hastings had suggested.

Adam was just about to escort Peter back to the ruined chapel when a shout came from somewhere outside, then a wild cry. There were men running across the courtyard, more of them spilling in through the gate arch from the outer bailey. 'Heralds!'

one of them cried. 'Heralds from the king – they're crossing the causeway now!'

'There's a treaty,' another man shouted. 'A treaty of peace – the king has pardoned us all!' With a whoop he pulled off his linen coif and tossed it into the air.

'God be praised!' Peter of Radnor declared, lifting his hands to the sun streaming down through the shattered roof beams. 'God and his saints be praised – our sufferings are over at last!'

But his words were drowned by the wild and joyous tumult that burst all around him.

Chapter 24

'**No!**' Henry de Hastings shouted through the storm of voices, and brought his fist down on the table. 'No, never, *no!* We cannot accept this. We cannot surrender on these terms! . . .'

'It is hardly a surrender, Sir Henry,' Richard de Amundeville said forcefully. 'A compromise, a negotiated peace . . .'

'The treaty says,' Simon de Pateshall reminded them, 'that the king will grant a full pardon to any who has borne arms against him since the beginning of the war, and will cease the policy of disinheritance . . .'

'I know what it says!' de Hastings bellowed, his face reddened. He was breathing hard, snarling as he braced his fists on the table. 'And I tell you it is surrender! What else does it say, de Pateshall? The *damnable and treasonous acts* of Lord Simon are to be nullified and destroyed! Everything for which we have fought all these years, cast into oblivion!'

'And all of us compelled to pay a ransom to regain our own lands too,' John de Clinton added. 'A ransom heavier for some than for others.'

'I do not like this at all, friends,' Peter of Radnor said, tapping the document on the table. The council had convened in the ruined shell of the chapel, with the table placed before the altar, and he alone of the leading men had remained seated.

'This article states that Lord Simon shall not be considered just or holy, and all the – what does it call them? – *vain and fatuous miracles* attributed to him shall not be discussed, on pain of flogging . . .'

'They put that in to spite us, nothing more,' Gregory de Caldwell said. 'Because we mocked their legate, I expect.'

'Yes, it is the legate's own doing for sure,' the archdeacon replied. 'The Pope himself refuses to sanction Lord Simon's sainthood.'

'But how can we pay *five times* the value of our lands as a ransom?' de Clinton said, exasperated. 'Where are we to find such sums?'

'Five times is cruel enough,' de Hastings said. 'Why am I alone required to pay *seven* times?'

'You and Earl Robert de Ferrers, it says,' Peter of Radnor confirmed, peering once more at the document. 'And those involved with the mutilation of the king's messenger. But John de la Warre is dead.'

'The rest of you agreed to it too!' de Hastings cried.

'Some of us did not,' Richard de Amundeville said crisply.

'*Many* of us did not,' Simon de Pateshall added, shaking his head.

Adam sat at the back of the chamber, keeping silent. Only now was he beginning to realise the guile of the king's negotiators, the wisdom of those who drafted this document, this *dictum* as it was called. They had given rebellion and redemption, honour and chivalry a fixed price. A price that some would find easier to pay than others. And by setting the terms of the ransom much higher for the rebel leaders, they had driven a wedge between the fiercest of their foes and those they led.

He had done the calculations already, of course. They all had. But Adam possessed nothing besides his horse and his arms, and a handful of silver pennies. Any ransom would be too much for him to pay.

'I agree with Sir Henry,' he said, standing up. 'There's no justice in this treaty. I say we've held out this long, and we should
hold out for better.'

'Yes! Hear him!' de Hastings cried. De Amundeville was shaking his head.

Before anyone else could speak a host of men surged in at the
doorway, calling for admittance as the serjeants and squires held
them back with levelled spears. Adam's hand went to the hilt of
his sword. Lambert FitzThomas was at the head of the intrud-
ers, with William of Thurlaston and another dozen burgesses
and civilians behind him. 'We demand a say in this!' FitzThomas
exclaimed, raising his fist as he forced his way forward into the
chapel. 'We too have endured this siege, and we demand that you
accept the treaty!'

'Accept it!' another man said. 'Let us be absolved, and our
souls saved from hell!' A volley of shouts supported him.

'You speak of surrender,' de Hastings growled back at them.
He threw aside the hem of his mantle to expose the mail he wore
beneath it, and the sword belted at his side. 'Have you forgotten
your oath, FitzThomas?' he yelled, stabbing a finger towards the
doorway. 'You swore to be one with us until the end, and never
to desert or betray the community of this castle!'

As he spoke he vaulted up onto the table and swept out his
blade, men reeling from him in alarm. Two or three others drew
their weapons, and the crowd in the doorway shrank away.

'Any who speaks of surrender, or who seeks to desert, or sub-
vert the community,' de Hastings snarled, brandishing his steel,
'shall be branded a traitor. And *every man's sword shall be turned
against you, and you shall die a traitor's death*!'

FitzThomas had thrown up his hands, but the crowd shoving
at his back prevented his retreat. For a moment, as Henry de
Hastings leaped from the table and strode towards the doorway,
Adam feared that he would cut the man down in cold blood. But
instead de Hastings halted at the threshold and turned, swiping

his sword back into his scabbard. 'Almighty God has spared us from death and defeat,' he announced, his voice echoing in the recesses of the ruined chapel. 'Should we spite him by giving up now? What pitiful worms we shall be, if all we can offer in return for God's protection is our submission!'

He paced a circle on the cracked paving, gazing at each face in turn. Somebody coughed. None could form an answer.

'Before he died,' he went on, dropping his voice, 'John de la Warre, our fallen captain, told me of a letter he had received. A letter from Simon de Montfort the Younger, the son of Earl Simon . . . A letter saying that he and the king of France were mustering an army at Boulogne, ready to cross the sea and march to our aid. By now, that army could be on English soil! Another month, another fortnight, and we might see their banners on the horizon . . .'

'Where is this letter?' Richard de Amundeville spoke up. 'Why have we not seen it before now?'

'Yes, show us!' FitzThomas cried from the doorway.

But Henry de Hastings just raised his palms and smiled. 'I can only give you my word,' he said. 'On my honour as a knight, and as a Christian, I tell you what I know. Just put your trust in God, and victory will be ours before the year is out. And if any of you dare speak of surrender,' he said, his voice rising suddenly to a furious shout, 'then by all the devils in hell I'll *kill you myself*!'

*

'Was there really a letter from France?' Joane asked, days later. She and Adam were walking together across the muddy outer bailey, in bright autumn sunlight that seemed almost unnervingly calm after all they had endured.

'If there was, I never saw it,' Adam told her. 'Although I know that John de la Warre and several of the others sent out

messengers, and received some in return. Who can say? The suggestion was enough.'

'It was,' Joane agreed. She was clasping his arm as they walked,
her other hand on the smooth curve of her belly. 'I would never
have believed it possible.'

Adam would not have believed it either. Many long hours it had
taken to agree. Many threats and much bluster for all to accept.
But the truth was all around him: the sky free of arrows, bolts
and catapult stones, the people of the castle walking upright and
unhurried, without fear. It was, he thought, almost miraculous.

After much negotiation, the king's party had agreed to a truce
of forty days. They would let the castle garrison send messengers
to find Simon de Montfort the Younger, wherever he might be,
and determine if he was really bringing an army to break the
siege. Within the forty days, those messengers must return with
an answer. No doubt, Adam thought, the king and Lord Edward
trusted that the mission would fail. Because if the forty days ran
out and no answer came, surely the castle would have to surrender. What would happen then?

At first, as news of the truce spread, a mood of festivity had
gripped the beleaguered garrison. There had been music and
dancing in the shattered inner bailey, fresh ale brewed with the
last of the grain, the few remaining casks of wine broached at
last. But all too soon the mood had quietened and grown tense.
The king's men were maintaining their blockade, and without
the possibility of sending out plundering raids, the people of the
castle were already feeling the renewed pinch of hunger.

Adam looked around him as they neared the eastern wall. The
encampment of tents and hovels had reappeared now that the
catapult stones had ceased falling. The canvas and wood looked
more ragged than ever, the people huddled around their smoky
cooking fires more grimy. There were plenty of armed men as
well. Henry de Hastings had knighted all of his squires, several
of them only in their mid-teens, girding them with swords taken

from the captives and the slain. The newly made knights swaggered around the gates and ramparts, hard expressions on their youthful faces, watchful for any signs of defeatism or surrender.

'Look at them,' Joane said in a low voice, 'they're just boys with blades. But they wouldn't hesitate to cut us down if we tried to escape this place.'

'They might,' Adam told her. 'Although I don't think it's us they're intended to terrify.' He nodded towards the clustered tents and hovels, and the knots of civilians and servants gathered around them. Even so, he felt the chill run up his spine. Richard de Amundeville and two of his men had gone out to the king's camp to act as hostages until the return of the messengers. Without his influence, Kenilworth was almost totally dominated by de Hastings and his faction.

'But it's a blessing to walk about in the open without fear of attack, at least,' Joane said, and drew a deep breath. 'The company of the great chamber was becoming oppressive.'

'Do the other women still think you're the Earl of Derby's wife?'

'Among other possibilities,' Joane said with a smile, then shuddered. 'Some of them have taken to prostituting themselves for food,' she whispered. 'We hear them every night, as soon as it gets too dark to see, and must pretend we heard nothing when daylight comes! Your friend Hugh of Oystermouth has a regular arrangement with poor Alice de Nafford, it seems – I see him slinking past me at dawn, and I cannot meet his eye . . .'

Adam grimaced. Hugh's position as castle quartermaster had opened many an opportunity for corruption, especially now that supplies had run so short. And his friend had never been the most scrupulously honest of men.

They had reached the eastern curtain wall now, and Adam helped Joane climb the broken steps to the battlement. Breathing hard, she stood on the exposed walkway and gazed out across the stubs of the merlons. She inhaled deeply, and her breath misted as she released it.

'He's out there, isn't he?'

'His name was on the document, yes,' Adam replied. He had seen it himself, and there was no doubt: Earl Humphrey de Bohun, the father of Joane's late husband, was with the king's army. Just a short distance away, as well. From where they were standing they could see, in the clear November air, the spire of the priory church and the gleam of the wet roofs beneath it. The tents and banners of the royal encampment appeared to gleam in the sunlight, and the few remaining trees in the far distance were aflame with autumn colour.

'They'll drag me back into their world soon enough,' Joane said in a low voice, 'to face their punishments.' She cupped her belly, and Adam heard the catch in her voice. There would be no way of hiding her condition now, to anyone who recognised her. 'Oh God, they cannot be allowed to see me like this!'

'Then, if it comes to a surrender,' Adam told her, barely breathing the words, 'we must find another way out of here.'

*

November slipped by, but the messengers did not return. The weather grew steadily colder, a raw breeze whining around the shattered ramparts and desolate baileys of the castle. Frost rimed the rutted mud, and as the end of the month approached the puddles and the water in the moats grew a skin of brittle ice.

Henry de Hastings trained his new-made knights at the wooden pell, his serjeants shouting themselves hoarse. But the people of the garrison were falling sick, and many were so ill they could not eat; Master Philip's infirmary had spilled out from the keep into the old kitchens. Dark rumours seeped and spread: the water supply had been poisoned by royalist sympathisers, the knights and wealthier men were hoarding food, the king was planning a sudden assault to take them all by surprise . . . Day by day suspicion hardened into hatred, and anguish curled into fear.

De Hastings remained in his chamber in the great keep, issuing his orders and demands, and steadily terror took hold.

It was the Eve of St Catherine's, and Adam was over by the stables rubbing down his horse with a fistful of dry rags. Blanchart stood with lowered head, and Adam felt the hard ridges of the horse's ribs through his hide. Sorrowfully he rubbed the destrier under the chin and blew in his nostrils. There was little more he could do for the poor animal now.

'Sir,' a voice said from behind him. Adam turned and saw Gerard, his squire. The boy had grown a downy beard which made him almost unrecognisable. He sounded slightly evasive as he spoke as well. 'Sir, there's somebody outside the gates, asking to speak with you.'

'Who?' Adam asked, throwing down the clout of rags. Blanchart breathed warmly into his palm.

'Sir Henry said you should come, master,' the squire said.

He did not seem inclined to say more. 'Outside the gates, you say?' Adam asked. Gerard nodded. 'Very well – saddle my horse. I'll at least go out there looking like a knight.'

By the time he had dressed and fastened his sword belt, Gerard had fitted the warhorse with bit and bridle, and was tightening the girth straps of a light riding saddle. Adam buckled on his spurs, then slipped his foot into the stirrup and swung up onto the back of the animal.

The squire followed him on foot as he rode towards the great gatehouse that opened onto the causeway. Henry de Hastings was waiting for him, standing on the parapet above the inner gates, just as he had been on the sunlit morning months before when Adam had first arrived at Kenilworth. Now the sky was grey overhead, and the tattered banner whipped and snapped in a cold breeze.

'He asked to speak to you in person,' de Hastings called as Adam drew closer. The gates were open, and at the far end of the gloomy vaulted passage Adam could see the open expanse of the causeway, and the small band of mounted men waiting at the centre of it.

'I thought, when he first appeared,' de Hastings went on, in a surly tone, 'that he'd come from Ely, with a message from D'Eyville and the others. But it seems that he's submitted to the king's mercy!' He spat loudly and violently. 'Just hope he isn't intending to persuade you to the same course.'

'He won't,' Adam called up to him, slowing as he reached the gate.

'Best for you he doesn't,' de Hastings replied, glaring down at him. 'You know we've got two springalds in the gate towers, aimed along the causeway. One bolt could take each of you.'

'As I say, he won't,' Adam said with grim emphasis. He shook the reins and nudged with his heels, urging Blanchart on into the gate passage. For a moment the sound of the hooves echoed under the stone vaults. Then, as he rode out onto the causeway, Adam clearly heard the creak and rhythmic click as the two big bolt-shooters were braced for loading.

It was still early, and the cold grey surface of the water on either side was sheened with mist. In the middle distance a flight of birds crossed the lake. There were three riders waiting for him. One was a serjeant with a white rag tied to his spear. The second was a squire. Only as he drew closer did Adam recognise their leader.

'Lord Baldwin,' he said, and bowed curtly from the saddle as he drew his horse to a stand.

Baldwin Wake was dressed in a heavy cloak trimmed with black fur and secured with a jewelled brooch. He had grown fleshier since Adam had seen him last, but he was still a handsome, assured-looking man, and he smiled wryly as he gave an answering bow.

'You wanted to speak to me in person?' Adam asked. He felt the pressure of the two loaded springalds aimed at his back. For an uncomfortable moment he recalled the men he had seen being struck by one of the machines during the siege tower's attack. The bolts piercing flesh and bone, pinning bodies together.

'I did,' the Lord of Bourne replied. 'Although perhaps not *to* you but *through* you.' He laughed at Adam's frown, then adopted a proud attitude. 'As de Hastings must have told you, I've been fully pardoned of the king's indignation and rancour, for all that happened during the recent disturbances in the realm, and accepted into his peace.'

'Was that before or after you massacred the Jews of Lincoln?' Adam said, unable to conceal his angry disdain.

Baldwin's expression clouded. 'Ah, yes,' he said, with a note of shame in his voice. 'I had no part in that. It was D'Eyville and his men. I would have stopped it, but . . . Anyway, that was what persuaded me that this war had to come to an end. The violence, the lawlessness . . . I'd had enough of it. I'm surprised to find that you have not.'

'Some of us might find surrender easier than others,' Adam said. 'Some of us have nothing to lose but our honour.'

He could see that the barb had caught. Wake shifted in his saddle. 'I'm betrothed to wed Hawise de Quincy,' Lord Baldwin said, changing the subject with an abrupt air. 'You'll remember her, I suppose?'

Adam just inclined his head. His horse stirred beneath him, blowing and pawing at the grit.

'Have you come to invite me to the wedding?'

Wake coughed a sudden laugh. 'No . . . no, although I'm sure that Lady Hawise would be pleased to see you there. She remembers you with fondness, it appears.'

'I still have the pennon she sewed for me,' Adam told him.

'Actually I wondered,' Wake went on, 'if you might have any idea where I could find her sister, Joane. I'm not suggesting she's in the castle with you, of course . . . But if you do happen to meet her, you might tell her that her cousin, the Countess of Derby, has arranged the return of her inheritance.

Lady Joane is to have Ware, and one or two other estates. Over a hundred and thirty pounds income per annum. My betrothed is to have the other half. There's nothing to stop her taking possession at once, of course – except that nobody knows where she might be.'

'I'm sorry I can't help you locate her,' Adam said. He fixed Lord Baldwin with his stare, unblinking, then urged Blanchart forward a few paces.

'Ah well then,' Wake replied, with a thin smile.

They had drawn closer now, barely a sword's length between their two horses. Adam suppressed a smile as he imagined Henry de Hastings back at the gatehouse trying to determine what they were saying.

'We both know I'm going to ask you to follow me out of here,' Baldwin said, leaning over his saddle bow. 'There's nothing to stop you.'

'We both know I'm going to refuse,' Adam replied.

Lord Baldwin snorted a laugh. 'We both know you might think again. I speak seriously now – if you come with me, I can protect you. I've accepted the terms of the dictum. I'll have my lands back soon, and all my household. Come with me, and I will be your lord, and lead you to the king's mercy.'

Adam sat a moment, listening to the distant wing-beat of the birds crossing the water. Then he smiled and shook his head.

Wake smiled too. 'Let it not be said that I didn't try. I hope we can meet again, in happier times.'

He shook his reins, turning his horse to ride back towards the barbican at the other end of the causeway. But Adam held up a hand, halting him. Slipping his feet from the stirrups he dropped lightly from the saddle.

'You gave me this horse, back at Duffield,' he said. 'I return him to you now.'

Tossing the reins to the ground he stepped backwards along the causeway. Blanchart turned his head and gazed at Adam, but did not move. Perhaps, Adam thought, the horse understood. Nobody would be slaughtering him for meat now.

Wake's squire rode forward and took the destrier's bridle. Then Lord Baldwin raised a hand in salute, waved towards the far gatehouse, and led his little retinue back towards the other end of the causeway.

De Hastings was waiting in the arch as Adam paced slowly back towards the gates. A couple of his newly made young knights flanked him, gripping their swords.

'Well?' Sir Henry demanded. 'What did the traitorous dog want from you?'

'As you said, he wanted me to join him,' Adam replied. It seemed preferable to telling him the whole truth. Besides, he knew it reflected well on him. 'I refused.'

'You took some time to consider it, though, eh?' de Hastings said, moving to block Adam's path as he tried to walk onwards.

'It wasn't your threats that stopped me leaving,' Adam told him, refusing to back down. He stood face to face with Sir Henry, both men with hands upon the hilts of their swords. 'I'm not here for you,' Adam said. 'I'm here to fight for justice, for what I love and for what was taken from me. That is all.'

'And for your lady, I suppose?' de Hastings said. He feigned a sigh. 'Chivalry is not dead in England!'

The armed men gathered around him laughed, but Sir Henry appeared more crestfallen than amused. Adam shoved past him and strode on along the gate passage and out into the open bailey. Distant cries reached him, and he squinted towards the great keep.

De Hastings had followed him from the gates, three of his knights at his heels still avid for further confrontation. 'I must say,' he said, 'I've had my doubts about you of late, de Norton.'

Adam laughed. 'I believe you have more to worry about than me,' he said.

Henry de Hastings stared back at him. Adam pointed across the bailey, towards the tower of the great keep. The cries were becoming more insistent now. Yells of outrage, and of defiance.

From the keep's topmost tower, a flash of crimson silk streamed against the grey sky, three golden leopards displayed *passant gardant*, blue tongues flickering. De Hastings let out a shout of outrage and disbelief.

The king's banner flew over the castle of Kenilworth.

Chapter 25

At the first blow of the ram, the door shivered in its mounting, and a drift of masonry dust fell from the stone arch above it. The ram was a heavy timber beam taken from the collapsed roof of the great hall. But the door of the keep's forebuilding was six-inch-thick oak, bound and studded with iron, and secured with a locking bar. Once again the six men charged at the door, running up the three steps to the threshold. Once again the ram struck, and the door shivered but held.

'We should use fire,' somebody said. 'Burn the treacherous bastards out!'

'No!' Adam cried, his shoulders tightening in dread. 'There's too many of our own people in there . . .' A few others growled their agreement.

'Almost funny, one might say,' John de Tarleton commented, with a twisted smile. 'The besieged turn besiegers, eh?'

But Adam could find no mirth in their situation. Joane de Bohun was trapped in the besieged keep. A prisoner, or a hostage, of the men who had seized it in the king's name. Hugh of Oystermouth was in there too, and Master Philip Porpeis. Outside was a mob of vicious and vengeful knights, serjeants and men at arms, prickling with cold sweat and cursing as they planned their vengeance on those who had betrayed them.

'How many of them are there?' Henry de Hastings snarled. 'Do we even know?'

'No more than thirty of fighting age,' John de Clinton told him. 'A few loyal men managed to get out before they barred the doors. Lambert FitzThomas is captain of them all, of course. Him and Stephen of Thurlaston. No doubt it was them that turned the rest of them against us.'

'Verminous traitors, may God pluck out their eyes!' de Hastings swore. His face was red, his eyes burning blue, his rage incandescent. FitzThomas and his faction had taken advantage of one of the few times that de Hastings had left the keep to stage their mutiny. The banner flying from the topmost turret was the trophy captured from the king's camp, that he had displayed on the wall of his chamber.

'Aside from them, there are maybe ten other burgesses and townsmen,' de Clinton went on, 'with a score or so serjeants and crossbowmen they've seduced to support them, and a handful of castle servants and artisans. They may have two or three squires with them as well, though none of any worth or station.'

De Hastings was nodding, chewing his lip as he gazed up at the sheer red-brown cliff of the keep wall. Adam stood nearby. All of them were turning the same thoughts. Every few moments they snatched glances towards the bailey gate, fearing to see the king's army advancing across the causeway towards them.

'Does anyone know how many prisoners they have?' Nicholas de Boys asked.

'A hundred. Perhaps two,' de Clinton told him. His own wife and children were among them. Simon de Pateshall's wife Margery as well, and the widowed Alice de Nafford. Most of the sick and wounded were in there, but nobody could say how many others had found themselves caught within the keep's massive walls when FitzThomas's conspiracy had broken into rebellion.

The men with the ram had paused to rest and swig water. The day was cold, an icy breeze swirling around the ruined buildings of the inner bailey, but they were sweating and breath-ing hard. 'Come on, get back to it!' de Hastings yelled at them.

The door to the forebuilding was the keep's only point of entry. The foundations of the building itself were solid stone, impossible to dig through or to undermine. Above that was the basement floor, with only a few narrow slit windows in the outer walls. On the upper floor was the great chamber; the entrance passage was only accessible by the timber stairway, enclosed by the stone forebuilding. A fortress within a fortress, Adam had thought often enough. Now that impregnable-looking defence had been turned against them.

'I'm sure they'll be expecting a grand reward for turning over the castle to the king,' John de Tarleton said, shaking his head. 'They surely think that gold will fly from his fingers into their purses!'

'Or they think they'll get a full pardon and their lands and property restored, without having to pay the penalty,' Adam said. Put like that, he had to admit, he could almost see the wis-dom of their actions. Perhaps he might even have considered joining them, if FitzThomas and his comrades had tried to draw him into their conspiracy. But no; that would not be his way out of Kenilworth, or Joane's either.

Now men were stepping back and craning upwards, staring at the ramparts of the forebuilding. A voice was calling to them, out of the cold grey sky.

'De Hastings! Do you hear me?'

'We hear you,' de Hastings bellowed. 'And may God tear your flesh with hooks!'

Lambert FitzThomas appeared on the parapet above them, silhouetted against the pale grey sky. Adam noticed crossbow-men all around the bailey taking aim. Peter of Radnor angrily gestured for them to lower their weapons.

'Lambert FitzThomas!' the archdeacon cried. 'This vile rebel-lion will bring you to no good end! You have broken the solemn bond you swore, and turned against your oath! Send out the women and children at least . . .'

'De Hastings, listen to me,' FitzThomas shouted down to them, ignoring the clergyman. 'We hold an impregnable position here. We have the stores, the armoury, and the infirmary. We have fifty men well armed and armoured, and have pledged to defend ourselves against you. You have no choice but to submit to our demands!'

'He's got a big head, that bastard,' John de Tarleton scoffed. 'I'd fancy knocking it off his shoulders!'

A few others hissed at him to stay silent. Gerard, Adam's squire, came running from the gateway, breathing hard. 'No movement from the king's camp, or Lord Edward's,' the young man reported. 'They're all just standing along the shore of the mere, watching what's happening.'

'As long as they stay there, we might have a chance,' Adam replied. De Hastings had been careful to station watchmen all around the perimeter wall and at the gates, but if the king or Lord Edward decided to take advantage of the rebellion within the castle, the defenders would be quickly overwhelmed.

'What are your demands then?' Peter of Radnor shouted up to the man on the rooftop. 'Tell us, and let us reach some compromise!'

Furious yells from the multitude in the bailey. 'Is this what our great struggle has become?' de Caldwell growled. 'Bickering with churls about *compromise*?' He spat furiously. But the archdeacon brushed away the dissent.

'Send a messenger to the king,' FitzThomas shouted over the tumult, his voice growing hoarse. 'Tell him you are surrendering the castle, and beg for his mercy and pardon, on the terms set out in the dictum.'

'Never!' de Hastings yelled back, and an angry chorus echoed his cry.

'Let us return to the sacraments of the church, and save our souls!' FitzThomas went on hurriedly, his voice rising and cracking.

'Kill him now, before his evil words poison my ears!' de Caldwell shouted. 'Crossbows! Shoot the noxious dog down!'

'No, no!' Peter of Radnor yelled back. He was pointing up towards the high rampart of the keep itself. Following his gesture, Adam saw the crenellations lined with other figures, leaning out against the sky. Some were standing up between the merlons. Narrowing his eyes against the wintry glare, his breath caught. Some of the standing figures had their heads in nooses, others gathered behind them ready to shove them over the parapet.

'We do not want to harm anybody!' Lambert FitzThomas declared. 'But if you refuse our terms, or persist in your attacks upon us, there will be consequences!'

'Christ's love protect us,' de Tarleton said in a low voice.

One of the prisoners on the rampart was Philip Porpeis, Adam realised. The others he could not distinguish. All, at least, were men. But he dared not imagine the condition of the women and children within the keep, and the terror they must be feeling.

'We have no other choice!' Gregory de Caldwell told Sir Henry. 'We either drive them out of there, perish from want of food, or wait for the king's men to break the truce. We *must* attack, and let the devil take them if they harm the captives!'

Henry de Hastings gave a stiff nod. 'Bring down that door!' he commanded.

With a grunt of effort the six men picked up the heavy ram once more. Others ran to assist them, adding their muscle to the attack. Someone counted to three, then they surged forward and up the steps to slam the wooden beam against the oak. When Adam glanced up he saw that FitzThomas had vanished from above them.

Again the men ran at the door, and again the ram struck. A scream, a cry of warning, and a great stone block tumbled from

between the merlons over the forebuilding parapet and plummeted downwards to crash into the men with the ram as they
reached the door for the third time.

Adam turned away just as the stone fell. The noise alone was
sickening, a crunch of flesh and breaking bone. When he looked
back, four of the men who had carried the ram were lying
crushed on the steps, and the ram itself was shattered.

Cheers from the defenders on the parapet above. Screams of
hatred and rage from the men in the yard below them.

'Axes,' John de Tarleton said, with a brisk nod. 'Axes and ham-
mers, that's what we need.'

Adam watched the squires and grooms remove the bodies of
the dead and injured from before the door. He lifted his gaze to
the glowering stone wall of the keep, and the line of narrow windows that marked the great chamber on the upper floor. Joane
was in there, he thought. And he had no way of reaching her.

*

Breaking down the door took the rest of that day and the night
that followed. Henry de Hastings ordered the castle carpenters
to build a heavy wooden shelter with a pitched roof, then had
it carried forward to screen the doorway and deflect missiles
dropped from above. Into the hours of darkness men worked
with axes and mallets, hacking and battering at the heavy oak.
All the while the fires burned in the paved oval of the courtyard, lighting the work of destruction and casting huge distorted
shadows over the towering face of the keep. Crossbowmen posi-
tioned all around the inner bailey wall and in the ruins of the
buildings shot their bolts at anyone appearing, firelit, above the
parapet of the forebuilding.

An hour after midnight a cold rain began, damping the fires
and thawing the icy paving of the yard, and as the bells of the
distant priory rang for matins de Hastings called a halt.

'We bring down the door at first light,' he ordered in a low voice, as the men assembled in the dripping gloom of the ruined great hall. 'The storming party goes in immediately, before they can muster their defences.'

'I'll lead it,' Gregory de Caldwell said.

'And I'll go with you,' Adam said at once. Several other knights spoke up at the same time. All of them were weary after a night without sleep. All of them hungry, their bellies pinched and empty. But all burned with the same desire to bring the occupation of the keep to an end as soon as possible.

'If they have any wits, they'll have barricaded the inner doors and have every crossbow they possess aimed at the outer ones,' de Caldwell said.

De Hastings gave a grim smile. 'Only if they have time to prepare themselves,' he said. He gestured behind him, into the darkness of the ruined hall. Sharpening his eyes, Adam could just make out a looming shape, picked out by the glow of a brazier. It was one of the big springald bolt-shooters from the main gate-house; the crew had dismantled it and reassembled it here under cover of darkness. As he watched, he saw men tightening the internal bracing of heavy torsion cables. The machine was aimed out across the open space of the courtyard, towards the battered door of the great keep.

'One shot from that thing should be enough to break the lock-ing bar and give us an entrance,' de Hastings said. 'As soon as it's down, we go in. And with God's blessing, we'll catch those inside off their guard . . . Kill anyone who opposes you,' he added, in a low growl. 'Show them no mercy – they're not knights or nobles, they're commoners, and oathbreakers too!'

Gregory de Caldwell slapped the head of his mace into his mailed palm, his scarred features creasing into a smile. 'Do not trouble yourself on that account,' he said.

The rain slackened as the sky grew pale, and they crossed the slippery paving of the bailey to assemble on either side of the doorway. 'Aim well, you bastards!' John de Tarleton told the springald crew. Pressed against the wall, they waited and tried to remain silent. The spatter and drip of water was all around them.

A movement from the darkness of the ruined buildings; Henry de Hastings raised his hand and brought it chopping down. Then the sudden crack of the springald, and the heavy bolt slammed into the door.

'Now! Now, in the name of God!' de Caldwell cried, throwing himself from the shelter of the wall and dashing up the steps. Adam was right behind him, his shield lifted over his head. John de Tarleton and two other knights flanked him. They reached the door together; the locking bar still held it, pierced through by the springald bolt, but de Caldwell charged it with his shoulder and broke the splintered timbers. The door was open, and they were through.

Solid darkness inside, the noise of their yells and the clashing of their steel echoing in the emptiness of the guard chamber. Adam was wearing his coat of plates over a full mail hauberk, a ventail covering his nose and mouth. De Hastings had offered him John de la Warre's old great helm, but it would have left him almost blind in the darkness; instead he wore the wide-brimmed iron helmet buckled over his coif. Still he felt dangerously exposed as he followed de Caldwell into the darkened building. At any moment he expected the roar of the enemy attack out of the shadows, the punching impact of arrows and bolts, the furious rush of spears.

The assault party crowded against each other as they advanced. They were through the guardroom now and into the hall of the stairs. Early daylight filtered down from the broken roof high overhead, but the hall was a pit of shadow. Nobody in sight. The noise of their shouts died into the hollow silence around them.

'Where are they, by Christ?' de Caldwell swore.

'No matter – get up the stairs, quickly!' Adam told him. John de Tarleton barged against his shoulder, stumbling. Others were piling in behind him.

'Above us!' somebody yelled from the back. 'Guard yourselves!'

A heartbeat later the first crossbow bolts spat down from overhead, slamming into Adam's raised shield and clipping the rim of his helmet. De Caldwell was hit on the shoulder. The first volley was followed swiftly by a second, a pelting rain of sharpened steel hammering down around them with a noise like a hundred maddened cooks beating on kettles. Adam felt the impact on his back, the plate armour and hauberk repelling the bolt. De Caldwell was down on one knee, roaring in pain and fury.

'Forward!' John yelled. 'Up the steps, before they can reload!'

In the swirl of faint light they could all see the heavy barricades around the head of the stairs, trestle tables and timber beams stacked up to make a redoubt for the archers and crossbowmen guarding the inner door to the keep. Still the brutal hail came down at them: stones and lumps of broken masonry between the arrows and bolts.

Adam and John were first to reach the stairs, the injured de Caldwell right behind them. They crabbed their way backwards up the first flight, feeling each step with their heels as they shielded themselves from the attackers above. A crossbow bolt struck the wall behind Adam's head, and sparks jumped from the stone.

Now their own bowmen were rushing into the chamber below, aiming upwards at the defenders behind their barricades. Bolts and shafts flickered in the dimness, clashing and clinking off the walls and thudding into the timbers.

'Just keep moving,' de Tarleton said through his teeth. 'Keep your shield up and *climb*!'

They were past the first landing, and could turn and scale the steps straight towards the barricade. Adam held back a moment. The temptation to storm upwards immediately was powerful, but they would be stronger if they worked together. A falling rock crashed against his shield, staggering him back to a lower step.

Other men were pressing up behind him. The wooden treads groaned beneath their weight. Something spat past his face, and Adam heard a stifled cry of pain. An armoured body fell sprawling, the men below lifting it between them, but they were stamping their way upwards now and Adam could not risk a backward glance.

They had climbed halfway when the men at the top wrestled a heavy wooden bench over the barricade. Adam threw himself against the wall to his left. De Caldwell was not so quick, and the tumbling bench knocked him sprawling. Already other men were clambering over him, unrecognisable in their full mail. A catapult stone rolled and crunched down the wooden steps, and Adam stepped neatly over it and kept climbing. He was in the lead now, first target of the bowmen lining the top of the barricade.

Two bolts struck his shield, and a third banged against the skull of his helmet. He was close enough to make out the faces of the defenders, every time they raised their heads above their improvised rampart. He could hold back no longer.

'After me!' he cried, and the words came out as a muffled bellow. The ventail of his coif was soaked with sweat and spit. 'After me!' he shouted again, and began to charge up the remaining steps towards the barricade. His limbs were heavy with the weight of his armour, and he stumbled with every step. But a violent energy rose through his exhaustion, through his fear, powering him onward. Arrow shafts caught at his ankles and broke beneath his feet. He could only pray that somebody was following him.

A stone cracked off his helmet, and something collided with his shins and almost tripped him. Snatching a glance from behind his arrow-studded shield he saw a crossbowman appear above the barricade, weapon levelled directly at him. Three more running steps, trusting to God and the speed of his charge. He heard the snap as the bolt was loosed, and ducked his head as the bolt whipped past him.

Then he was at the barricade, ramming his shield up against the scarred oak of a tabletop. He stabbed his blade over the top of it, aiming for the crossbowman, but his target had already dropped to reload. An axe came chopping down from behind the barricade, and he caught the blade on his shield and turned it aside.

His sword was not enough here. He let it fall from his hand and reached for the axe in his belt. The man on the far side of the barricade swung wildly at him, the shaft of his weapon banging against the timber. Another man angled a spear over the top and tried to stab at Adam; a mailed fist grabbed the spearshaft and dragged it forward, then Adam delivered an overarm blow and the spearman screamed and fell back.

The men on the other side of the barricade were shoving at it, piling their weight behind the wood and trying to push their attackers back down the stairway. Head lowered, Adam braced his legs and pushed back against them. Gregory de Caldwell had gained the top of the steps now, and joined the press of armoured men jostling around him. For a few long moments there was no sound but heaving breath and creaking timber, curses hissed through clenched teeth, the crunch and rasp of mail.

Adam was struggling to breathe. With a yell he straightened up, swinging his axe back and chopping across the top of the barricade. His felt his blade strike one of the defenders. A loaded crossbow was levelled at him, the stubby steel bolt only inches from his face, and he swung his axe wildly to one side. The bow released, the bolt veering away into shadowed emptiness, then Adam wheeled his arm and hacked at the bowman's head. A scream, then another; de Caldwell had given up pushing at the barricade and seized it instead, hauling it towards him.

'Stand aside!' he yelled. Adam flattened himself against the wall as the timbers gave way, the trestle tables and beams collapsing outward. A man tumbled at his feet. A blow to his neck, and Adam was clambering forward over the sprawling bodies and the tangled ruin of the barricade. The remaining defenders were falling back in terror, scrambling for the passageway that led into the keep. One dropped to his knees, hands raised as he begged for quarter. De Caldwell slammed his mace into his skull and kicked him down.

Adam was almost at the passageway. Already the heavy wooden door was closing, those within forcing it shut against the boiling mass of fugitives. The noise of screaming came from within.

Flinging aside his arrow-battered shield, Adam shoved himself into the gap of the door, one mailed arm reaching out to seize the men within. The heavy oak crashed against his forearm, and he heard the crack of bone. A yell of pain burst against his clenched teeth. The door eased slightly and he snatched his arm back just before the agony flowed through him. Before he could throw his weight against the door again, it slammed closed and he heard the locking bar bang into place. Dragging the last few terrified defenders aside, de Caldwell crashed his mace against the solid oak. But it would not yield.

Slumping back against the wall, Adam felt the fury of battle ebb from him, the tearing pain of his injured arm consuming him instead. He was sickened, weeping tears of bitter anguish. They had gained the forebuilding and the outer stairs, but the keep was still firmly closed against them.

In the stair chamber below, the body of John de Tarleton lay where the other men had dragged him. A crossbow bolt jutted from his chest, another from his shoulder, and his face was bleached white in death.

*

It was the morning of Advent Sunday when they finally broke through the keep's inner door, and the hymns of the king's monastic choir were drifting across from the priory as they stormed down the passage and into the upper chamber with steel and killing fury in their hearts. Adam saw none of it; his left arm was broken and the wound too badly inflamed for him to risk battle. He heard about it all the same.

Henry de Hastings led the attack, followed by John de Clinton and a wedge of serjeants in mail armour, but the resistance of the defenders came to an end as soon as the ram brought down the door. Many of them died even so, hacked to death in the screaming chaos of the great chamber, or pursued up the spiral steps and onto the battlements. Stephen of Thurlaston was speared in the back as he tried to flee. A dozen or so others were shot down by crossbows, or slain as they tried to surrender by de Hastings's infuriated men. It was all over within the time it might take to say the paternoster.

Adam saw the king's banner cut down from the ramparts, the cheers rising as the red silk slid across the crenellations and fell to the muddy ground eighty feet below. He was waiting outside the arched doorway of the forebuilding as the more prestigious prisoners were escorted out: first Margery de Pateshall, and the pale and trembling Alice de Nafford. A file of other women too, clerks and chaplains with them, all crying out thanks to God for their deliverance. Joane was one of the last to emerge, her head covered with a shawl and her two attendant women flanking her. Adam moved towards her, calling her name, but she flinched away and pushed past him.

The triumphant braying of the victors echoed from within the keep. Now they were leading forth their captured enemies. Lambert FitzThomas appeared first, his fine clothes ripped and blood down his tunic. Jeers greeted him as he was hustled into the courtyard. A stream of other men followed him through the doorway, those rebels and oathbreakers who had not been slain during the assault, all with arms bound behind them and a serjeant dragging them at each elbow. Adam watched dispassionately. He felt no hatred for these men now, only contempt for the futility of their actions, and the death and destruction it had caused. Then another figure emerged into the cold daylight, hands bound and head lowered, and Adam's breath caught.

The last of the captured rebels was Hugh of Oystermouth.

Chapter 26

'Can nobody stop this cruel farce?' Joane demanded, her voice tight with rage and disgust.

'Alas, cries of vengeance are often louder than any call for justice,' Philip Porpeis replied, tucking his chin down into the woollen folds of his cloak.

It was the day after the crushing of the insurrection, and the men accused of leading it were on trial in the courtyard of the inner ward. Henry de Hastings presided over the hearings, seated on the steps of the king's chamber with John de Clinton and Gregory de Caldwell flanking him and Peter of Radnor in attendance. The nine accused men stood in the centre of the court, stripped to their shirts and braies, their hands tied and their heads bare. All around the yard, spectators packed the ruined buildings.

The morning was cold, the keep and the castle walls vanishing into white mist. Everyone's breath steamed. Adam was more conscious of the burning pain of his injured forearm; Master Philip had examined the wound, splinting the broken bone and binding it in linen. Adam now wore his left arm in a sling, his hand tight to his chest. Even the slightest movement caused a wave of fiery prickling heat to spread through his body. But he forced himself to direct his full attention to what was happening before him.

'Lambert FitzThomas, John le Fevre, William Crane,' one of de Hastings's squires declared, in a ringing voice, 'Ambrose Harper, Alan Sweetcote, Thomas Palmer, Nigel de Lodbrok, Richard of Wolverton and Hugh of Oystermouth . . . all of you are adjudged to be authors of malicious conspiracy and sedition, traitorous betrayers, and breakers of the holy oaths you swore to this community. Can any good man say why any one of you should not suffer mortal penalty for your crimes?'

'Alan Sweetcote did not swear the oath,' a voice announced. Sir Nicholas de Boys stepped forward and pointed to one of the accused. 'He is a kitchen servant and nothing more.'

'A poisoner!' another voice called from the crowd, and others growled their agreement. 'He poisoned us all on the orders of his masters!' So many of them had fallen sick in recent days, it was all too easy to believe.

Henry de Hastings nodded and held up his hand. 'They're quite right, Sir Nicholas,' he told de Boys. 'The man is as guilty as the rest, and should die with them.'

'There's no poison here!' Master Philip muttered into his cloak. 'Just rotting meat and foul water – the flux, that's what ails them!'

Adam scanned the faces of the prisoners. All appeared pale, blue around the lips and racked with the cold as they stood barefoot, awaiting their sentence. Two were town burgesses, two veteran men at arms. One was a farrier, another a musician and another a cook. Nigel de Lodbrok had been one of John de la Warre's squires; he was only eighteen or nineteen, and sniffed back tears as he stood.

And then there was Hugh. Surely, Adam had told himself, Hugh could not have been involved with the insurrection? For all his mistrust of Henry de Hastings, the Welshman could not have believed that the desperate plan would succeed? More importantly, he surely would not have betrayed Adam himself. Or would he? The uncertainty gnawed in Adam's soul. But he knew that, whatever happened, he could not let his friend die.

Already he had done his best to argue for Hugh's innocence. Joane had tried to plead for him the day before, and even Alice de Nafford too. But the testimony of women – particularly pregnant women and grieving widows – could not be admitted by the court. After all, had they not been captives themselves, and exposed to the wiles of their captors?

At first Joane had been too shocked to speak of her experiences. Adam had assumed that she was simply stunned by what she had seen. He soon discovered that he was only half right. Joane de Bohun was no stranger to bloodshed and atrocity: she had witnessed the carnage in Evesham's abbey church, and had been in the midst of the fighting at Chesterfield. But what she had seen and heard in the last few days had filled her with horror.

'The captivity was bad enough,' she had told Adam, when finally she was ready to speak of it. 'Those men, and the chaotic madness of their scheming – it was terrifying. At least they sent us all to the tower chamber. All of the ladies, and the clergymen too. But then, when de Hastings and the others started breaking through the doors and everyone began to panic . . . then it was far worse. I thank God that I did not have to see what happened when they stormed the chamber.'

She shuddered, pulling her mantle tight. The two women who attended her were nodding in agreement. 'We were kept safe, at least,' Joane went on. 'It was Ambrose, the minstrel, who protected us and made sure we were shielded from the worst of it. But I saw it as we were escorted out. They'd killed anyone who tried to flee from them, whether conspirators or captives. Like they wanted to wash away the shame of their own failings in the blood of others . . .'

'What of Hugh?' Adam asked. 'I need to know – was he truly involved in this?'

Joane shook her head. 'I did not see,' she said. 'I'm sorry. As I say, we were kept apart from the others.'

She had argued with de Hastings and the other trial judges for the innocence of the minstrel Ambrose too, but again it had done no good. Master Philip had already made his case for mercy for all of the accused – they should be sent out of the castle, he had suggested. But he had been shouted down by the assembly; had he not been inside the keep himself during the insurrection? Perhaps he secretly supported it? Was his appearance on the battlements wearing a noose a mere ruse to allay suspicions? Perhaps he too should be standing before the court, shivering in shirt and braies . . .

No, Adam thought. It would take another voice yet if there was to be any justice here. He thought of his friend John de Tarleton, of John de la Warre, and all the others who had given their lives in Kenilworth's defence. He must speak for them now. Before he could think about what he was doing, he shouldered his way forward through the crowd and into the open space of the courtyard.

'Sir Adam,' de Hastings said. 'Have we not heard from you already?'

'Not today,' Adam replied. 'Not here, in public, for all to witness.'

'Let him talk,' de Caldwell grunted. 'He's earned it, with his wounds.'

Adam breathed deeply, feeling the sting in the air. The pain of his bound and splinted arm faded to a dull red pulse. Turning slowly, he stared into the mob that ringed the court. They watched him silently, all of them ragged, pinched by the cold and the emptiness of their bellies. Half looked fevered, or sick. The valiant defenders of Kenilworth resembled a congress of the dead. But a slow milling heat radiated from them as they waited for him to speak.

'I have shed my blood in the defence of this castle,' Adam said, raising his voice so all could hear. 'And for the defence of you all. Just as I did on the battlefield of Lewes, and at Evesham, where Lord Simon de Montfort fell.'

A stir of muttering from the crowd. Adam saw more than a few people crossing themselves reverently. He waited as long as he dared, the blood beating slow and heavy in his throat, then spoke again.

'Several of these men before you are guilty, as they have been accused,' he said, forcing himself to gaze at the prisoners. Hugh kept his head bowed, and did not meet his eye. 'But several are innocent, and most of you here know it.'

Now the crowd began to bristle, a few raising angry voices against him. 'Remember, Sir Adam, you can only speak for *one* of the accused,' Peter of Radnor called from the steps.

Adam looked along the line of prisoners. The young squire, Nigel de Lodbrok, stared tearfully back at him. His lips moved as he shaped a silent plea. Beside him stood the minstrel, Ambrose. Adam remembered him now; he had played the vielle and sung at the Feast of the Apostles, months before when Adam and Joane first arrived at Kenilworth. Later, too, when Adam had heard him playing in the ruined hall. He was a handsome young man and stood with his back straight, facing his accusers directly. Adam dared not glance back towards Joane.

Instead he turned to Hugh. His friend's head was still lowered, his shoulders trembling. *Look up*, Adam willed. *Look at me . . .* He needed suddenly to look Hugh in the eyes and see the truth there.

'This man,' he said, pointing. Hugh started abruptly and lifted his chin, gazing back at Adam. 'This man was with me at Lewes, in de Montfort's army. He rode with me to Evesham too, and would have died beside Lord Simon if I had not ordered him away. How many of you could claim such service?'

Silence now as he paused. Hugh's eyes were wide, his mouth hanging open.

'And here at Kenilworth,' Adam went on, 'he was made quarter-master by John de la Warre, a duty he performed without complaint. Can he be blamed if the food ran short, months later? Would you have wanted a magician in his place, who could produce loaves and hams out of the air, and fill every cask with new ale?'

A smattering of laughter now, hard-edged but genuine. Low voices muttered and rasped. Adam hardly dared to say more. He knew there would be plenty who might find fault with Hugh, and his nocturnal activities in particular. But none could call such things treason.

'On my honour as a knight,' Adam declared, raising his right hand. 'Hugh of Oystermouth is innocent of the crimes laid upon him.'

Gregory de Caldwell was chewing his lip, while John de Clinton scowled. Peter of Radnor was nodding, brows raised. Adam gazed only at Henry de Hastings, a direct challenge in his eyes.

'Oh, very well then,' Sir Henry declared. 'We shall give the prisoner the benefit of the doubt.' His two assistants considered further, then nodded. A few cheers rose from the crowd as the serjeants came forward to untie Hugh and lead him aside. A few angry jeers as well.

The squire Nigel de Lodbrok was weeping openly and loudly now. One of the other prisoners bent at the waist and vomited. Hugh was white-faced and trembling as he walked up to Adam and took his right hand. 'Thank you, my God, thank you,' he said, forcing out the words.

Adam could only nod in acknowledgement. As he turned away he saw Joane, wrapped in her mantle, tears in her eyes.

'I'm sorry,' he said to her. 'I'm sorry I could not do more.'

*

They executed the prisoners on the morning of the following day, the Feast of St Andrew. Adam watched from the roof of the north-west tower. The eight remaining men were brought out into the wintry sunlight and stripped to their braies. One by one they were tied by the ankles and lashed behind one of the few surviving horses, then dragged around the outer bailey, through the mire and the filth, trailed by an abusive mob who pelted them with stones. Then, when each had been hauled in a full circuit of the keep, they were taken to the long wooden gibbet erected beside the ditch of the inner bailey. Each man's neck was placed in a noose of rough hemp, and after a few words from Peter of Radnor and the attendant chaplains they were hoisted up to the crossbar. It took nearly an hour to hang them all.

From the tower Adam could see the spectators watching the proceedings from the king's camp, and from the far side of the mere as well. None made any attempt to halt what was happening. And why would they? This, Adam thought, was the true death of de Montfort's cause. Those cries for liberty, justice and the rights of Englishmen had ended with eight half-naked bodies kicking in the chilly breeze. FitzThomas's insurrection had driven a wedge between the knights – men like de Hastings, like Adam himself – and the common people they had claimed to represent. Now nothing remained but force, and violent retribution.

The bodies were still hanging on the crude gibbet three nights later, when a freezing mist came down to wrap the battered walls of the castle. The paving of the rampart walkway was slippery as Adam emerged from the tower's spiral stairway. The watchmen further along the wall were only vague shapes in the murk.

'One day, you know, I will repay you for this, I swear it,' Hugh said, his voice wavering as he shuddered in the damp chill. 'By the chin of St David . . .'

Adam hushed him, holding up a hand. A figure was pacing towards them. Mail clinked from beneath the muffling cloak. Then another voice from the mist.

'De Norton, that's you?'

'It is.' Adam made out Nicholas de Boys's nod, then the other man turned and retreated. He released his breath. He had hoped that de Boys and his men would be guarding this part of the wall, and would make no move to oppose him. Hugh of Oystermouth had evaded death once, but Adam could not risk him remaining in the castle. Whether his friend was truly innocent or not, he knew that Henry de Hastings would turn on Hugh again before long, and this time would not be cheated of his prey.

Gerard had the rope, and Adam helped with his one good arm as the squire lashed it around Hugh's waist and made sure it was firm. Then they helped the Welshman scramble between the broken spurs of the merlons. Silence was impossible, and Adam was glad of the mist that deadened the sound of scraping stone and heaving breath. Finally Hugh was over the wall, suspended by the rope with his head jutting up above the parapet. 'I'll find you,' he said in a taut whisper. 'I don't know how, but . . .'

Adam reached across the parapet and squeezed his shoulder, silencing him. Then he and Gerard fed out the rope between them, lowering Hugh down into the darkness. Very soon it went slack, and a moment later they drew it back up again. Adam stared into the wet gloom but saw nothing. He heard only the faintest splash, a muffled curse, as Hugh waded across the morass of the moat and vanished into the night.

*

'And so another rat has slipped away!' Henry de Hastings declared the next morning. 'And you, I believe, helped him.'

No point attempting to deny it. Adam had not expected Hugh's escape to remain a secret for long. 'You yourself declared him innocent,' he said. 'Was he supposed to wait until you changed your mind?'

'Well, he's proved his treachery now! No doubt he's already told the king of our weakness, and informed him of the best ways to attack us . . . I should order you chained, de Norton.'

Adam fought down his anger. Everything now depended on a cool head and calm words. His bound arm prickled maddeningly. 'But you will not, of course,' he said.

De Hastings snorted a laugh. He too had fallen sick now, with the same malaise that afflicted so many in the garrison. Like the others, he too suspected poisoning as the cause. He had taken up his quarters once more in the corner tower of the keep, the same chamber where Joane and the other ladies had been confined during FitzThomas's brief insurrection. Now the small room was dark, the shutters closed. The air was thick, dirty, and stank of fever and fear. Philip Porpeis sat on a folding stool beside the curtained bed, mixing herbs for a hot compress.

'How bold you've become, de Norton,' Sir Henry said, grinning sourly as he sat propped up on bolsters. 'And now you come to me with requests. Bold indeed!'

'There's nothing bold about it,' Adam replied. 'Merely merciful and humane. Lady Joane did not swear any oath to remain here, so you must allow her to leave.'

'Oh, must I?' de Hastings said angrily. Master Philip leaned closer, restraining him as he struggled to sit upright. 'And you with her, I suppose? And then no doubt de Pateshall will request that his wife leaves, and he accompanies her. And then de Boys, and then . . .' He broke off with a choke of disgust. Master Philip was kneeling beside the bed now, trying to press a wad of cloth over his forehead. De Hastings batted him away.

'Our only strength here is in unity,' he went on. 'That is why we swore as we did, to stand together. No, no, I cannot allow anyone else to leave, and spread tales of our debility – I will not!'

Adam had hardly dared hope for anything different. But he needed at least to try this course, before attempting another.

Days before, he had told Joane of Baldwin Wake's visit, and of what he had said about her inheritance. Now, more than ever, it was vital that she leave Kenilworth without being seen by anyone in the king's army. If she could just return to her manor at Ware, and hide herself from view until the birth of her child, then . . . Beyond that point she and Adam had discussed nothing. Accomplishing that alone seemed a near impossibility. At seven months pregnant, Joane could not shin down walls or traverse moats as Hugh had done. And all the gates were guarded by Sir Henry's loyal knights and squires.

'How many days remain of the truce?' Adam asked. 'Do you truly expect de Montfort's son to arrive with an army before that time elapses?'

'Yes!' de Hastings exclaimed. His eyes were wide open, glaring in the light of the brazier. 'Daily I await news. Already he could be on the march . . . I expect it, yes. I pray for it. And God will deliver it!'

Adam drew a breath through clenched teeth, determined on one last attempt. 'A pregnant woman can be of no help to us here,' he said, keeping his voice steady. 'Give me leave to accompany her back to her estates, and I will return again before the forty days of truce come to an end – I give you my word.'

'Impossible!' de Hastings said, with a rasping laugh. 'If I let you out of here you'd never return. We both know it.' He struggled again to sit up, and this time Master Philip did not restrain him. 'The king,' Sir Henry said, 'is preparing new siege engines, so we hear. He aims to deploy them as soon as the truce expires. I'm not so sure that Lady Joane is useless to us here. Indeed, day by day she appears more valuable. If Earl Humphrey de Bohun, for example, knew of her presence . . .'

'Never, by Christ!' Adam swore, abandoning his attempt at calm. 'Give me leave, or I will take it.'

'By the death of God, if you try then I will have you hanging from that gibbet feeding the crows with those other traitorous dogs!' de Hastings shouted, his face dark with fury. 'You and the Lady Joane too, pregnant or not!'

'You threaten me?' Adam's sword had been taken from him when he entered, but his right hand went to the knife on his belt.

De Hastings stared back at him, and for a moment Adam held his fierce gaze. 'Oh, such bold warriors we are!' Sir Henry said through his teeth. 'A one-armed man, and another sick with fever. But I have others I can call upon, and you do not! I have young men committed to me, men I knighted myself, devoted to my cause. And they will not hesitate to do what I order. If I tell them to sling you and your lady love in a mangonel and hurl you over the walls, they'll do it. Do you doubt me?'

'No, I believe you,' Adam said, feeling his blood grow chill with the certainty. Everything was very clear to him now. With a last curt bow, he turned and left the chamber, collecting his sword and pushing his way past a couple of de Hastings's squires who loitered on the stairs.

'He's getting worse, as you see,' Philip Porpeis said, when he found Adam warming his hands by the fitful glow of the hearth in the great chamber. He sat down beside Adam, shivering. There were plenty of other men in the chamber, and they kept their voices low.

'Let me see your injury,' the surgeon said, and unwrapped the bindings. The swelling had gone down now, and the broken bone appeared to be straight. With luck, and with rest, Master Philip pronounced, it should heal cleanly.

'I've been dosing Sir Henry with dwale,' the surgeon said, barely moving his lips, as he bandaged Adam's arm once more. 'Hemlock and poppy. Dangerous, but it keeps him relatively placid. If you need to go, you should do so tonight.'

'How?' Adam whispered. 'All the gates and ramparts are guarded by his men.'

Master Philip tied off the bandage and fastened the sling around Adam's neck.

'There might be another way,' he said.

*

They assembled an hour after midnight. The cold mist had come down once more, hiding the light of the waxing half-moon, and outside the feeble glow of the watch-fires the castle was drowned in darkness. Wrapped in mantles and cloaks, they made their way slowly from the inner ward, across the creaking timbers of the bridge and past the gibbet with its dangling corpses. Stepping carefully in the thick mud and slime of the outer bailey they traced a path through the sleeping encampment, between the hunched tents and hovels and through the wraith-trails of smoke from the fires. Only as they approached the western rampart did Adam halt and turn to address them.

'We must go alone from here,' he said quietly. He could hear the two women sniffing back tears as they bade their silent farewells to Joane. From the shadows Gerard approached him, and he embraced the young squire.

'Take good care of them for me,' he said, nodding towards Joane's former attendants. 'I'm also giving you care of my armour and shield, and the rest of my possessions too. I'll be needing them back, one day.'

Gerard too was weeping, snivelling in the darkness as he tried to argue with the decision. 'I should come with you,' he said. 'Your arm . . . you can't fend for yourself and for Lady Joane too . . .'

Adam shook his head, and clapped the young man on the shoulder. 'I'm sorry,' he said. His words were truer than Gerard knew. 'You wanted chivalry and bold deeds of arms,' he said. 'But I've shown you only squalor and despair, and the worst of humanity. One day, I promise, I will strive to do better.'

No time remained for fine words. Adam bade a silent farewell to Gerard, then led Joane from the company of her women.

Together they crossed the last distance to the postern gate. As Master Philip had promised, it was unguarded. A boy appeared from the shadows of the wall: one of the boatmen's lads, paid with silver for his night's work.

Adam was just lifting the locking bar from the gate when he heard Joane's indrawn breath behind him. He eased the heavy timber to the ground with his good arm, then turned with his back to the gate.

It was one of Henry de Hastings's new-made knights. Had he learned of Adam's plan, or was this just an unlucky chance? He strode heavily from the darkness, a thin smile on his face, his hand on the hilt of his sword.

'Fine time for a fishing expedition,' the knight said. He was young, Adam noticed. Barely twenty. He looked like a vicious child, dressed and armed as a man.

'Keep walking,' Adam managed to say, his throat tight. 'Go, and let us leave.'

The young knight laughed. 'Oh?' he said. 'And why would I do that?' He drew the sword silently from his scabbard, lifted the blade and tapped it against his shoulder. Then he took a long stride towards Joane. She flinched and gasped, but the tip of the sword was at her throat.

Adam had drawn his sword as well, but terror quickened his blood. If he attacked now, the other man would have to move his sword to parry the blow. But it was too much to risk. He could hear Joane breathing quickly. He could almost feel the heat of her fear.

'There will be no violence,' another voice said from the misty darkness.

A figure appeared, pacing slowly. Adam turned, keeping his sword raised. Another man moved in from his left, wrapped in a heavy cloak. Then a third, and a fourth. He was surrounded, his back to the gate.

But the young knight appeared dismayed. He swung his sword towards the newcomers, and Joane stepped away from him. As the mist swirled the newcomers moved closer, emerging from the murk.

'Sir Adam,' Nicholas de Boys said. 'This young knight will give you no further trouble.'

'He will not,' said John de Pateshall, stepping in from the other side. They had others with them, men at arms and a few crossbowmen, some who looked like camp servants. In the mist and darkness, they could almost have been ghosts.

With a rattling breath, the young knight slipped his sword back into his scabbard. Then he turned his back on Adam and walked stiffly away, veering between the surrounding figures. De Boys gave a nod to Adam, then he too turned and retreated. One by one his companions dissolved into the darkness, until only Adam and Joane and the boatman's lad remained.

'We don't have long,' Joane said, shuddering out of the lock of fear.

Beyond the gate they found the boat easily enough; it was the only one remaining, tied up at the end of the wooden jetty. A narrow punt, with barely space for the two of them and the boy who was to pole it across the shallow waters of the mere. Adam helped Joane into the prow, then seated himself behind her. The boy untied the rope and clambered into the stern, shoving off with one foot. Skilfully he steered them between the remaining stakes and nets, the only sound the lap of the freezing water against the hull, the plash as the boy raised and lowered his pole.

Within moments they were away from the shore, the silvery mere spreading before them in the night's dark. It was much colder here, out on the open water. The marshy ground at the far western end of the mere lay outside the limits of the king's siege works. The boy would leave them there, and then take the boat back to the castle. Adam and Joane had a cold night ahead, and a wet one.

'What have we gained?' Adam asked bleakly. Despair dragged at him. 'In all those months of struggle, what have we gained?'

'We tried,' Joane said, so quietly he could barely hear it. 'Now we must try a different path, that's all.'

She stretched and gazed over his shoulder. Turning, Adam saw the crenellations of the castle's rampart vanishing into the mist. For a moment he could make out the bulk of the great keep, before it too was swallowed by the darkness. Then they were alone, the boy poling them silently out across the stillness of the water.

Fog rolled in their wake, consuming the castle utterly.

Chapter 27

'Do you even know where we're going?' Joane asked, as the light faded towards evening.

The track they were following meandered between the hills, dwindling to a strip of trampled mud in places. Adam had lost all sense of direction long ago, and the rain was soaking through his mantle and dripping down his neck.

'We keep straight on,' he said. 'That's what the ferryman back at Shipston said. Straight on, and we reach Banbury.'

'And yet I see no Banbury,' Joane said from the back of her plodding horse. 'I see . . . *nothing.*'

Grimly, Adam considered that Joane's haughty attitude had survived Kenilworth. He could almost laugh. But it was true, he thought as he gazed around him. There was no habitation in sight, no trace of smoke against the sky. A few bare trees scratched at the low black clouds, but aside from the bedraggled crows there were no living things in sight. The strip fields appeared unkempt, untended by man.

This was their sixth day since leaving Kenilworth. They had slipped past the king's sentries easily enough in the wet darkness, but after a night under a thornbush wrapped in their cloaks, they had found the river south of Warwick in spate and the ford impassable. At a straggling village on the riverbank Adam had managed to buy a horse, one of the few not taken by the king's requisitioners. It was a shaggy-looking old sumpter beast with a twitching head, barely waist-high at the saddle, and it cost Adam most of the remaining silver in his purse.

'What did you do to your arm?' the man who sold it had asked, as Adam struggled to help Joane into the saddle.

'Fell off a horse,' Adam said without thinking.

The man laughed. 'You'll be fine with this one then,' he said, with a toothy grin. 'Not so far to fall!'

They had journeyed on through that day, on a path that fol- lowed the high ground above the coils of the river. Joane sat perched across the horse's back, with their few sacks and bags slung around her, and Adam walked ahead leading the animal. Barely a word passed between them before evening. There was a bridge at Stratford, they had learned, where they should cross the river and head east. But at Stratford, almost without discussion, they had continued downriver instead. Evesham lay in that direction, and both of them felt the pull of the place, the compulsion to close the loop of all that had happened since last they were there.

In the bleak gloom of winter the surrounding land had appeared quite different, stark brown and bare grey where all had been green under the stormy summer skies. But still the memory of the battle had returned to Adam, so intensely that he almost expected to see the sodden turf still puddled with blood.

At the abbey they found beds in the guesthouse, and after evensong they had entered the abbey church, breathless and silent. Both were excommunicate, polluted with sin, but that secret they had kept to themselves. The altar and choir had been scrubbed and cleansed, the stones and cloths and sacred vessels scoured, and the church reconsecrated after its violation, by the papal legate himself. As they knelt before the choir screen Adam raised his eyes to the carved and painted figures, but saw no trace of the gore that had spattered them that day.

'Just there at the far end of the choir, before the steps of the presbytery,' an attendant had whispered to them, 'are buried the mortal remains of Sir Hugh Despenser, and of Sir Henry de Montfort, son of the earl.'

Glancing up, Adam caught the man's wink of complicity. 'Lord Simon himself was buried there too,' the attendant said, 'until his remains were removed by the king's order, as he died excommunicate and a traitor, supposedly. Perhaps, for a consideration, you might like to know where they lie now?'

But Adam had shaken his head. He had no wish to revere the remains of Lord Simon, though no doubt plenty coming here did so. *For a consideration*. He thought of the scrap of bloodied cloth that Lambert FitzThomas had so prized. The monks of Evesham must have driven quite a trade in relics.

'Where are the other bodies buried?' Joane had asked. 'All of those slain in the battle?'

'Ah, yes,' the attendant said, straightening. 'There were so many, you know – we could only lay them in a common pit. You'll find it on the far side of the burying ground, marked with a cross. On the morrow you might visit it, perhaps?'

And on the morrow they did, when the rain briefly eased. They found the place easily enough, and stood before the low mound with bowed heads, in silent prayer for the soul of Robert de Dunstanville, and all the countless unknown others who shared his grave.

They had remained in Evesham another two days, unwilling to leave the guesthouse and venture out once more across the wet bleak country. The guestmaster had found it incredible that they should do so at all, with Joane so heavily pregnant and without even a servant to accompany them. The surrounding lands were still in ferment, he told them, and had been for the year and a half since the battle.

But the rain had eased by the following day, and as one of the abbey servants was journeying to Shipston, the guestmaster

suggested that he guide Adam and Joane there. A long day
brought them to the Abbot of Worcester's manor, where they
slept in the common hall, and the next morning took the road
towards Banbury.

And now it was raining again, the sodden clay underfoot alter-
nately dragging and slipping beneath Adam's shoes. His wet feet
itched, and his injured arm flared hotly under his cloak.

'Which way do we go?' Joane said.

Ahead of them several roads converged in a spreading smear
of mud. The ruts of a cart went in one direction. Hoofmarks
showed the tracks of animals going in another. But there were
three or four other routes as well, none more obviously leading
to any habitation.

'That way,' Adam said, and set off in what seemed a straight
line.

They had only travelled another bowshot or two before the
horse gave up. Hooves planted in the mud, it lowered its head
and refused to move until Joane dismounted. The rain was still
falling, night was coming on, and Adam heard Joane's breathing
growing ragged. He was shivering himself. If they did not find
shelter before darkness fell, they might not survive the night.
Reaching beneath his sodden cloak he brushed the medallion
of St Christopher with his fingertips. Had the saint's protection
deserted him now?

Up ahead, between the thin trees, he made out the hump of a
thatched roof.

'There,' he said, narrowing his eyes. Joane was stumbling after
him as Adam broke into a run. The building was a barn, and he
threw the bar from the doors, dragging the creaking wooden
leaves wide. Near empty inside, but the thatch had kept the place
dry, and at the far end was a damp heap of straw. Joane staggered in through the doorway, pulling the horse after her. By the
time Adam had closed the doors and wedged them shut, she had
dropped to sit on the straw, hugging her knees and shivering.

'We need a fire,' he said, already kicking around in the gloom for dry tinder. The roof above them was soaked, no danger of a blaze spreading. He gathered scraps of dry straw and dusty wood into a pile, then took the flint and striking steel from his belt pouch. It was difficult with one hand, but by trapping the steel beneath his toe and striking at it with the flint, he managed to raise a spark. The horse stood in the shadows, nibbling at the thatch.

Adam was still kneeling over his heap of tinder, trying to coax a flame, when he heard Joane's voice from the darkness behind him. 'You should leave me here,' she said.

'Never,' he told her, cupping his palm around the heap of tinder and blowing on it. A wisp of smoke rose.

'You should leave me. Go back to your own lands. Your . . . *betrothed*. To Isabel de St John,' Joane said. Her voice sounded slurred, as if she spoke from a dream.

Adam said nothing. He fanned gently at the dry straw until the tinder caught.

'You're only helping me because you think the child I'm carrying is yours.'

He felt the word like a blow on his spine. But still he said nothing.

'It might be, I suppose,' Joane went on. 'Or it might not. I lied to you, Adam, I confess it now. I lay with Sir Reginald, freely and willingly, and more than once. I did it to protect myself, you see. Just as I lay with you, that night beside the river, so you might think the child was yours when I began to show. I knew by then, of course.'

I don't believe you, Adam thought. But still he did not speak. He did not trust his own voice. He was still kneeling, hunched over the fire as the flame twisted upwards.

'You do not know what a vicious sinner I have been!' Joane said, her voice cracking. 'I have prayed – *prayed* – to the Blessed Virgin and all the saints to take this burden from me. So many times I have dreamed of throwing myself down stairs, or from the castle wall. I hoped, when I was injured, that the pain or the medicines would kill the child inside me – Adam, I *wanted* that! But not even the devil himself could aid me.'

'Stop!' Adam cried, the word a kick in his throat. He eased himself up from his crouch, forcing himself to turn and face her. 'Tell me no more,' he said in a harsh whisper.

By the fitful light of the fire he saw her sitting hunched against the far wall, the glow of the flames in her unseeing eyes. She rolled over onto her side and lay in the straw, and when he knelt beside her he could feel her body shaking with fever. Her breath caught, and she let out a racking cough. 'You're unwell,' he said. 'I'll move you closer to the fire.'

He laid their wet mantles and cloaks around the tiny blaze, hoping they might dry a little before morning, and sat feeding straw and sticks to the flames until weariness dulled his mind. Then he lay down with Joane, shaping his body to the curve of her back, holding her with his one good arm as she shivered in her sleep.

When he woke he thought it was full daylight already. But as he blinked and raised his head he knew that the sun had not yet risen. Something had woken him even so. The horse too was stirring, stretching its neck and blowing. Silently Adam rolled upright, tied his shoes as best he could with one hand, then picked up his scabbarded sword and went to the door.

There were four of them, advancing from the blue-grey wintry gloom. All wore hooded cowls and mantles, working-men's clothes. One carried a sword, another an axe. The other two had hunting spears. Adam watched them as they approached. Their faces were gaunt, rawboned and bearded. But these were poor men, and they did not handle their weapons like fighters. Even the weakest of Reynard's gang could have routed them with ease. But alone, one arm in a sling, in the cold of a winter's dawn, Adam could not underestimate their threat.

'God's peace to you,' he said curtly. Clasping the scabbard under his injured arm, he drew the sword with his right hand. The four men exchanged glances. As the first spark of sun cracked the horizon, Adam lifted the blade to his shoulder. 'Come any closer, and at least one of you will die,' he told them.

He saw their resolution ebb, their stances ease. They were not killers, these men. They were local villagers, field labourers. No doubt they had seen the glow of the fire in the hours of darkness. Perhaps they thought him as much a threat as he considered them.

Then he heard the rasp of a breath behind him, and glanced back. Joane stood in the open doorway of the barn, her hair loose and her chemise tight over her swollen belly. She was holding Adam's battle-axe in her hand.

She did not have to say a word. When Adam flicked his gaze to the four men they were already backing away, lowering their weapons. He stuck the point of his sword in the ground and reached into his belt pouch. Silver winked in the dawn light.

'Point us the way to Banbury and this is yours,' he said to them. 'We'll be on our way soon enough.'

One of the men raised his spear, the tip extended towards the rising sun.

*

At Banbury Adam found them lodgings in the upper chamber in the Bishop of Lincoln's inn, which looked out onto the broad marketplace, opposite the castle. He used coin from Joane's purse to pay for it, and for their food and the stabling of the horse. But it was worth the price; Joane was exhausted and feverish, coughing fitfully, and needed rest and comfort. The innkeeper's wife made her broth, sending a servant up to feed her, and for the next four days Adam could only sit on a stool beside the bed, watching over her. At night he slept on the floor, the sword by his side.

On the third night Joane's fever broke, and by the following day she was well enough to sit up in bed, clear-eyed and weary. 'Those things I told you, back in the barn,' she said. 'They were cruel. I ask your forgiveness.'

'Were they untrue?' Adam asked.

'Some of them,' she replied, unable to meet his eye. 'I have sinned greatly, I cannot deny. At times I have wanted an end to this.' She ran her hands over the swell of her belly. 'At other times . . . I do not know what to think or feel.'

'But the child is mine?' he said, insistent. She nodded, and gave him a pale smile which he found did not reassure him as much as he wanted. Strangely, he discovered that he did not care as much as he had believed he might.

'Whatever happens,' he said, 'I will stay with you now. I will take you to Ware, and to your own people. After that . . .'

'After that God alone knows what will happen to us,' she said.

The next morning Adam left her resting and went out to buy provisions for the journey ahead. Banbury was a thriving market town, but that morning there were more than the usual numbers of people in the muddy streets. Men and horses thronged the road that led to the castle gates, and the alehouses were packed to the doors.

'Goodsir,' the innkeeper said when Adam returned. 'I'm afraid I must ask you and your lady to move from the upper chamber tonight. I can find you beds in the common hall if you desire, but there are several great retinues passing through our town tomorrow and the day after, and I need to accommodate them together.'

'Whose retinues are these?' Adam asked him.

The man widened his eyes. 'Oh, you haven't heard? The king himself is coming to Banbury, on his road to Oxford. Many great men travel with him — his son Lord Edmund, and the earls of

Pembroke and Hereford, and the legate of His Holiness the Pope too! Most will be lodging in the castle, of course, but their harbingers have already been here demanding beds—'

'The king is coming *here*?' Adam asked, cutting him off. 'He's no longer at Kenilworth?'

'Why no, sir,' the innkeeper said, with the smile of one who bears good tidings. 'We heard the news yesterday – the siege ended on St Lucy's day! The rebels surrendered the castle, and the king and his great council gave them leave to depart freely, with life and limb and horse and harness and whatever they could carry with them, and safe conduct to go wherever they would. They say,' the man went on, leaning closer, 'that when the king's men entered the castle the stench was so great that many were sickened almost to death as soon as they passed the gates. Like dogs living in their shit, those rebels were! And now the king has decreed that he will keep his Christmas Court at Oxford. No doubt many are praising Blessed St Lucy that these troubles are ended at last!'

*

'You're sure he said the Earl of Hereford was coming?' Joane asked him later that day, as she rode. She appeared to have recovered completely, although Adam knew that such things could be deceptive. He felt almost feverish himself, his mind churning with anguished despair.

'Very sure,' he said as he walked ahead of the plodding horse. 'Earl Humphrey, the king and his son, and the papal legate too. Ill fortune has crossed our path with theirs.'

'Do you think Reginald de Grey might be with them?' Joane asked anxiously. Both of them glanced back along the road, fearing the sight of riders galloping in their wake. But they had long since branched off the road to Oxford, and the land behind was empty under a colourless sky.

By evensong they were at Bicester Priory, and the following day they moved on. At Aylesbury they slept in the straw of a hayloft, and then joined a party of pilgrims and other way-farers along the lower flanks of the Chiltern Hills, beneath Ivinghoe Beacon and all the way to Dunstable. Further stories reached them at the guesthouse fire that evening, of rebellion in the fens of Ely and fresh discord between the king's support-ers. As the winter tightened its grip, there seemed no end to England's woes.

Ice sealed the water butts the next morning, and frost hard-ened the mud of the road. Adam felt it through the thin soles of his shoes. As he walked he tried to calculate the days that had passed since they fled Kenilworth. Thirteen, was it, or more? He felt every one of them in his aching limbs, in the steady itch of his bound arm, the pinch of his frozen toes. But with every step the end of the road grew closer, and soon Adam's spirits rose above his weariness. The sky was bright, the hills blazed cold blue in the sun, and by the end of that day they were safe in the abbey lodgings at St Albans.

The following day was a Sunday, and they remained in the lodgings resting before the last leg of their journey. At dawn, as the pony stamped and blew in the cold cobbled yard, Adam forced down a few mouthfuls of barley porridge and a cupful of sour ale. Joane stood apart, wrapped in her mantle with a shawl pulled over her head. Their breath steamed.

'Let's go,' she said, and held out her hand for him to help her into the saddle. Her mood had ebbed, and only her will and her pride were keeping her from sinking back into illness.

The road took them along the south bank of the River Lea, and as the light began to fade into a grey winter dusk they glimpsed the town of Ware on the far side of the bridge. Ice glittered below the stone arches as they crossed. By the time they arrived at the house it was fully dark. They heard the barking of the dogs first, then the voices of challenge. Joane rode forward in silence, as if

in a daze, and it was left to Adam to announce them, calling out
from the yard and then hammering on the door.

The porter was not inclined to believe the name he gave. But
soon enough his cries were heard by those within. Lights flared
in the gloom of the passage, voices pierced the winter hush, and
then the door was flung wide. 'Is it really you, my lady? You sent
no word of your arrival! . . . We were unprepared!'

Joane entered the house without a word, and Adam followed.
In the hall, she walked into the wave of heat from the flaming
central hearth, and everyone was gathered to meet her. Petronilla was there, plumper than before, and Joane's old chaplain,
and many new faces besides, all of them calling out greetings
and blessings. Lingering in the dark passageway Adam felt for
a moment the urge to turn away into the night once more. He
shrugged off the thought. This, after all, was a glorious occasion.
Only five days until the Feast of the Nativity, and Lady Joane de
Bohun had returned home at last.

*

'Big with child, seven or eight months gone, and none to say
who the father might be! Not her late husband, that's for sure.
Mayhap the young knight that brought her in, but few would be
bold enough to swear to it openly . . .'

Adam listened to the voices of the women in the yard outside
the window. The shutters were closed above the bed where he
lay, and he did not know the people of the manor well enough
to identify the speakers. It did not matter. He heard the stamp of
their feet in the cold of morning, the splash of water into a pail.

'God's mercy on her, I say,' the other woman said as they
walked off, 'and all of us too!'

His bed was a straw mattress in the old storeroom beneath the
solar chamber. A week had passed since his arrival at Ware, and
he had still to find a place here. Joane had fallen ill once again

only days after their arrival, the same malaise that had gripped her during the journey, and had taken to her bed. Sir Adam was officially her household steward now. He had overseen the restrained celebrations of the Nativity, sitting alone at the high table in the hall. But he knew how they talked of him, even Petronilla the Flemish maidservant, who had known him for years. Joane's bailiff and her other officers had maintained Ware quite adequately in her absence. Adam was neither required nor trusted. Suspicions massed around him.

It was on the Vigil of Epiphany, over two weeks after their return, that Adam heard the cries from the solar and knew that something was wrong. Petronilla blocked his way as he mounted the stairs; other maidservants crowded the door above. 'Her water's have broken!' the Flemish woman hissed, in a tone of accusation. 'The baby is coming, a month and more too soon! This is dangerous, you understand? Go, quickly – be useful. Find the *sage-femme*, you know – the birthing maid!'

Adam found the midwife himself in the town of Ware and brought her back on a pony. She was a broad red woman with a knowing squint, but seemed capable. Unsurprised, too, to be summoned so abruptly, for all their care in concealing Joane's presence at the manor. Once again the women of the household closed around the bed and the bedchamber, leaving Adam alone in the cold of the hall, beside the flickering hearth. Still he heard the frightened words, the agonised cries, the fear in every breath. He knew the danger, but he could do nothing but wait.

Instead he went out to the chapel and knelt on the hard stone floor before the altar as the evening faded into night. He was trying to pray, his right hand pressed to his chest, but the words would not come, the sense of purity in his heart and clarity in his soul. He was excommunicate, he told himself. Joane too. Both of them walled off from God's love and mercy. But surely the legate's sentence could not have included the new life in her womb? Not even the Pope's own representative could consign an unborn soul to perdition. With horrible clarity he remembered Joane's pained words. *'I have prayed to the Blessed Virgin and all the saints to take this burden from me'*. . .

No, he told himself as his injured arm ached fiercely; no, he could not allow such ideas to take him in their grip. And yet, when he tried again to direct his mind to prayer, all he heard was the mocking voice of Gaspard de Rancon, the man he had murdered at Beeston a year ago. *'Not even God Himself cares anything for you now!'*

As the night of his vigil wore on, the cold and the anguish worked steadily through him, breaking down his pride. His mind opened to strange and dangerous thoughts. He began to recall the stories he had heard on the road. The rumours and the relics. The last hopes of desperate men.

For so long, Adam had resisted the notion that Simon de Montfort, the man he had seen killed and hacked to pieces at Evesham, was a saint or a miracle worker. In truth, he no longer knew if his cause had been just, or his rebellion honourable. Could a man so stained with violence in life possibly be so exalted in death? But if Christ and his saints had deserted him, Adam thought. If he had nowhere else to seek mercy . . .

In the darkest hour, he raised his head and closed his eyes. Barely breathing the words, he shaped his plea. 'Lord Simon de Montfort . . . whether you are saint or sinner . . . Whether you abide in heaven or in hell, hear my prayer. If you have any power on this earth, then use it now. For the blood I have shed in your name, protect her. Protect Joane. *Do not let her die* . . .'

When the first grey light of dawn came he rose, stiff in every limb and saturated with the cold, and made his way back to the house. It was quiet, and fear clamped his heart as he walked. In the hall he found Joane's chaplain sitting at the common table with a cup of hot wine before him. The man looked up as Adam entered, and his expression confirmed the assumption.

'The child came too soon for this world,' the chaplain said. 'I am sorry. It was a boy.'

'And Joane?' Adam said, bracing himself on the table.

The chaplain nodded, eyes closed. 'She lives, although she has suffered greatly and is very weak. You had best leave her to rest . . .'

Adam was already moving for the stairs. This time nobody tried to bar his way. He found Joane in bed, the curtains drawn around her, three maids slumbering on the floor and the midwife snoring on a bench. From the corner of his eye he saw the basin and the bloodied rags beneath the bed. He parted the drapes; Joane was deathly pale, all life and colour washed from her, only her hair vividly red as it spread loose across the bolster. At first he thought she too was sleeping. Then her eyes opened, grey-green in the morning daylight, and she looked at him. He dropped to his knees beside the bed, and took her hand.

'You survived. Thank God.'

'One of us did,' she said, her voice a bitter husk. 'And you may thank God if you please. But I do not.'

Chapter 28

Hugh of Oystermouth arrived at Ware one morning in the middle of January, tramping along the frozen lane with nothing but the staff in his hand and the sack over his shoulder. Adam heard the barking of the dogs in the yard, and went outside to find the stablemen trying to turn the newcomer away from the gates. He was certainly ragged and disreputable, more like a wandering pedlar than a clerk or a herald.

'Blessings upon you!' Hugh cried as Adam approached, and threw his arms around him. 'I prayed to St David that I would find you here.'

In the empty hall they sat beside the fire drinking spiced winter ale. 'I've been scuttling about the country like a three-legged dog this past month,' Hugh said. 'And this is a harsh season to be doing it too. Welcoming hearths are few in these times, by Christ.'

He warmed his hands over the embers as Adam told him all that had happened since last they parted: of the escape from Kenilworth, the journey back to Ware, and the loss of Joane's child.

Hugh exhaled, shaking his head as he listened. 'I confess, I knew some grievous tragedy had befallen you,' he said gravely.

'Your face tells as much. But the lady is recovering from her ordeal?'

Adam dropped his head, hiding his expression. For a moment his throat was too thick to force out the words. 'She's barely left her chamber these last ten days. She nearly died, so they told me afterwards. And she may never be able to endure another birth . . .'

He broke off, closing his eyes until he could speak again. He took a mouthful of ale. 'I am to blame for it,' he told Hugh firmly. 'It was my sin that almost killed her.'

'No, no,' Hugh said, reaching out and clasping him by the hand. 'These things are sent by God, not wrought by men. Besides,' he went on, raising his eyebrows, 'were it not for you she would still be in Nottingham, and doubtless the wife of Reginald de Grey by now! You preserved her from that, and brought her back home, didn't you?'

Adam nodded. That at least was true, and Joane had told him as much, though he was loath to accept it. And the threat of Reginald de Grey was far from abated. Not a day passed that Adam did not expect to hear the hooves of his horses on the road, and the shouts of his men from the yard. For now he and Joane were living in the quietness of obscurity, but that could not last for long. Sooner or later they would both have to step out into the daylight, and the glaring scrutiny of the world. And the world, it seemed, remained a dangerous place.

'But whatever you choose to do now,' Hugh went on, 'I am bound to assist you, if you'll accept my service. I owe my life to you, after all! If you remain here then so shall I. If some madness takes you, and you decide to go and join the rebels once more in the fens of Ely then so shall I, if it costs me my skin. And if you cross the sea to France, the Empire, Italy . . . well, then I shall be your follower there too.'

'Thank you,' Adam told him, and felt unexpectedly reassured. 'I accept gladly.'

'But now,' Hugh said, draining his cup and setting it down, 'if you have any sway over the people of this house, might I beg for a bath? God alone knows how long it has been since I've immersed myself in hot water!'

*

Six days later, on the Feast of St Agnes, Adam saw the riders approaching the manor. He had been out on horseback himself, exercising the chaplain's palfrey, and noticed them as he came over the hill. A nobleman's retinue, he knew at once, with sergeants in double file ahead and behind and packhorses in the middle. None wore armour or carried lances that Adam could see, but he made out the figure of the leader, swathed in a dark mantle and carrying a hawk upon his glove. A lady rode behind him on a jennet. Something familiar about them both. Something threatening too. Adam shortened his reins and kicked with the spurs, urging the palfrey down the slope to reach the house before they did.

Eight weeks since his injury, and his arm had almost entirely healed. Still he felt the twinging memory of pain if he moved too quickly or put stress upon the bone. He wondered how he would fare in a fight, with a shield strapped over the old wound. But as he reined to a halt in the muddy yard before the house and looked back at the approaching riders, he realised that there would be no fighting today. He dismounted, and the leading household servants assembled behind him to greet the newcomers.

'De Norton!' the nobleman said, passing the hawk to one of his followers. 'I was not sure I would find you here.' Baldwin Wake swung down from the saddle, strode over to Adam and enfolded him in an embrace. 'But I'm glad I did. I have something to return to you,' he said.

Adam recognised the silver-grey destrier as soon as the groom led him forward, and his heart swelled. Blanchart appeared to recognise him as well, dipping his head for Adam to rub his neck and jaw. 'He looks much finer than he did when last I saw him,' he told Wake as the horse nuzzled at his palms.

'Indeed,' Baldwin said, standing with fists on hips. He was smiling broadly, pleased to have had the opportunity to show largesse, as a great lord should. But his eyes held a glint of steel. 'My new sister Joane is within, I hope?'

Adam was bemused for only a moment. Then the young woman on the jennet threw back the hood of her riding cloak and smiled, with all the easy assurance of a married woman, and a magnate's wife. She dismounted, and Adam bowed before her.

'Lady Hawise Wake,' he said.

'Sir Adam. God has preserved you, I see. We feared the worst when we heard that you were not among those that left Kenilworth at the surrender.'

Around them now the yard was filling with horses and men, Lord Baldwin's household knights, his squires and valets, grooms and sergeants. The household steward and the chaplain with their clerks were coming forth to present themselves, the grooms and stablemen rushing to attend to the animals, while the cook, the butler and the pantler yelled orders to the other servants; dinner that day would be a far grander affair than usual. Joane appeared last of all, stepping from the porch with a fur-trimmed mantle pulled up to her throat. She still looked pale, almost unearthly; this was the first time in days that Adam had seen her cross the threshold. But she smiled, and Hawise ran to her at once and embraced her warmly.

At the high table, Joane took the central place between her sister and her new brother-in-law. Smoke from the hearth hazed the room, churning in the beams of winter sun from the high windows.

'One would have thought,' Lord Baldwin said as they ate, 'that Kenilworth's surrender would have put an end to England's pains. But still the kingdom bleeds! Our old friend Henry de

Hastings has already broken the terms of his amnesty, and joined D'Eyville on the Isle of Ely. They say, you know, that he only agreed to give up the castle because his physician told him he would die without proper medicines!' He paused to laugh, then became grave once more. 'But they've been raiding out of the fens, all across the lands of Cambridge and Huntingdon – they ravaged some of my own estates too, the devil take them!'

For a moment, as Wake spoke Adam felt a surge of sympathy for Henry de Hastings, still resolutely refusing to submit after all this time. But then he remembered the trial in the frozen courtyard at Kenilworth, the bodies kicking beneath the gibbet, and the feeling died inside him. He had no love now for men like Henry de Hastings, or John D'Eyville. They no longer fought beneath Simon de Montfort's threadbare banner. Now they fought only for themselves, to scrabble back what they had lost, and to avenge the insults they had suffered.

'Last month,' Baldwin went on, 'they even attacked Norwich – plundered and burned half the town, murdered the leading Jews and dragged the rest off as hostages.'

You did similar things once, Adam thought. Across the hall, he caught Hugh's eye and then looked away.

'Can the king do nothing to stop them?' Joane asked.

'The king,' Wake said, raising an eyebrow, 'is *considering* a response. He's summoned another parliament, at Bury St Edmunds, to debate action against the rebels of Ely. But there's fresh trouble in the northern counties as well, so we hear. Reginald de Grey failed to quell it effectively, and Roger de Leyburne's replaced him as Constable of Nottingham—'

'Where is de Grey now?' Joane interrupted, and Adam heard the abrupt stiffness in her voice.

'Well, he could be anywhere,' Wake replied, in a sly tone. 'I hear he is still trying to locate you, though. And I managed to find you easily enough, so I don't doubt his bloodhounds will do the same. I can protect you to an extent, now we are related.

But I am not as powerful as the Earl of Hereford, and he will not easily repay what de Grey gave him for your marriage.'

'There is another,' Joane said quietly, 'more powerful than either de Grey or the Earl of Hereford.'

'The king? Well, yes – you should pay your homage to him, now you hold lands in your own name. But even the king might not wish to interfere in this matter with de Grey.'

'I was thinking of one more powerful still.'

Listening from Baldwin's left, Adam could not make out the brief conversation that followed. The surrounding noise of the hall rose around him instead: mingled voices from the lower tables, and the plangent sounds of music from the harpist in the corner. Hawise's laughter came from the far end of the dais as she spoke with the chaplain. Her happiness on returning to her childhood home had been obvious, and Adam had seen that Joane's heart was warmed by it too. He could begrudge her none of her joy and contentment. Could he ever, he wondered, have given Joane what Lord Baldwin had given Hawise? Would she even have wanted it?

'And what will you do now?' Wake asked, startling Adam from his thoughts. 'You have safe conduct, you know, until Candlemas – all those who were in Kenilworth were granted it at the surrender. After that date, you will be considered a king's enemy once more. Any loyal man should take you or slay you, in the name of justice.'

'Would you do that?'

Wake raised an eyebrow, considering. His smile was broad and easy, but his eyes remained hard. He raised a finger, as if a thought had struck him.

'The king is travelling to Bury St Edmunds from Westminster soon, for the parliament,' he said. 'He will break his journey at Waltham, at the Abbey of the Holy Cross. Come in with me, under my protection, and I will swear security for you.'

'To surrender, you mean?'

'To accept the king's mercy, yes.'

Either that or live in hiding, as a hunted rebel, Adam thought. Or travel overseas, as once he had considered. But still the idea left an ashen taste in his mouth.

'This war must *end*, Adam,' Wake said, leaning closer. 'God knows, the land must heal, if it is to be renewed. The king and his ministers know they cannot continue to punish people indefinitely. They know they must reform the government, or face further revolts. That cause has been won, don't you see?' He dropped his voice. 'Lord Edward understands that, at least. Already he holds the reins of government. And one day soon, he will be king! And a great king too – *then* we will see the realm for which we have fought and prayed.'

He spoke in a whisper, as it was treason to discuss the death of the monarch. But Adam was dubious. Could the man who brought de Montfort down and ordered his death and mutilation really be the one to bring his dream of England into being?

'It will happen, when we have peace,' Baldwin went on. 'But until men like you – and Henry de Hastings – lay down your swords then the violence will continue.'

He waited a moment, watching Adam as he considered. Then the broad smile lit his face. 'Turn it in your mind,' he said lightly. 'My wife and I are travelling on to her manor at Colne tomorrow. I've yet to pay the fine demanded by the king's dictum – I shall have to go to the Jews for that, no doubt! – so the only lands I currently hold are those my marriage brought me. But I shall return here before the month's end, and you can give me your answer then.'

It was the following morning, Lord Wake and Hawise and their retinue already departed on the long road to Colne, when Joane found Adam in the stables. He was grooming the horse that Baldwin had returned to him, working over Blanchart's silver-grey hide with a currying comb, and at first he did not notice that she was standing just outside the stall.

'This was where we first spoke, you and I,' she said with a smile.

'I remember,' he replied. 'You asked me to pray with you, and I thought you meant us to kneel right here on the stable floor.' He laughed.

'Five years ago, that was. Almost to the day. A bitter season it was then too.'

Five years, Adam thought — surely it must have been longer? So much had passed, so much changed in that time. They had been little more than children then.

He tossed the currying comb aside and joined her. Together they walked into the spill of wintry sunlight through the open doors. 'Do you still long to go on pilgrimages, and adventure in foreign lands?' he asked, remembering those words she had spoken long ago.

She laughed quietly. 'Perhaps,' she said. 'And perhaps I'll do so yet. But for now I have lived enough to relish what I have, and not to long for romances.'

They walked from the stables along the path that led to the riverbank. Joane shivered, pulling her fur-lined mantle closer, then took Adam's arm. There was a sense of truce between them now, he thought. A sense that they had passed through struggle and found peace.

'This is a great gift, you know,' she told him, gesturing at the house and the river and the surrounding country. 'To hold all this in my own name at last, in freedom. Not to be under the power of my uncle or my cousins. Or of a husband either. It was joyous to see what Hawise has gained, but I would not want that for myself. I feel no need to play at being the great lady, the noble wife. I did that, and now I'm free of it. Do you understand?'

'I believe so,' Adam said. He had been expecting this moment for a long time. He had expected it to be more painful. The pain would come, he knew, but for now all he felt was a deep sense of acceptance.

'Sometimes, to find the thread of your life you have to follow it back to where you began,' Joane said, gazing around her. 'And yet, all of this could be taken from me in a breath. Earl Humphrey still withholds my dower lands. And the right to my remarriage belongs to Reginald de Grey . . .'

'He cannot marry you against your will,' Adam said fervently. 'If he comes here, I'll fight for you . . .'

'No,' Joane said, tightening her hold on his arm. 'This cannot be solved by trial of combat, or by valour alone. Even if Reginald de Grey gives up his claim, another man will step in to try to take it. I cannot be truly free until that threat is gone. So . . . I have decided.'

'What will you do?' Adam asked her. He could barely breathe.

'When I told Baldwin Wake that there was a power greater than the king,' Joane said, 'it was no jest. Oh, I am not immune to doubt – perhaps Master Philip was right, and there is no divine will directing the world. Perhaps we have no immortal souls, and no heaven to reward our piety . . . Perhaps the bread and the wine are just plain bread and wine. But such notions have force in this world, and that's what concerns me. I have decided that I will take a vow. You know what that means?'

Adam nodded. Now the pain struck him. For a moment he could not speak.

'I will devote myself to God, and to perpetual widowhood. To chastity, of course, although I will retain my home and lands and not join a convent. Reginald de Grey will be compelled to give up all right to my marriage. He will have no hold over me, and nor will Earl Humphrey or any man. I will be free, Adam.'

And alone, Adam thought. But he understood. He had known knights who renounced the flesh and took holy orders. He knew of ladies who did so too. By taking her vow, Joane would set herself apart from the world and its demands. There was security in it, to be sure, and honour as well. But he would be sundered from her.

'If the child had lived, would you have decided differently?'

Joane's breath caught, and he saw her throat tighten as she averted her face from him and gazed at the cold grey waters of the river. 'I cannot answer that,' she told him, exhaling. 'The child did not live, and that was my message. But now I have decided, and you must decide too. You swore an oath to me.'

'To serve you, and to be your knight, yes.'

'I absolve you from it,' Joane said. She turned to him now, taking his hands. 'I cannot give you what you want, Adam. Or what you deserve. But you can take it yourself. Go with Lord Baldwin to the king. Seek his mercy. Then reclaim what is yours.'

Adam looked away sharply, anguish choking him. How could he reclaim his lands when he had nothing? For a baron like Baldwin Wake, raising the sum needed to pay his ransom was a heavy burden, but one he could bear. For Adam, though, even the redemption of a single manor was beyond him.

Joane pressed his hands. 'Listen to me – Baldwin was right. Master Elias would lend you what you need to ransom your lands, or some of it at least, I'm sure.'

The Jewish moneylender Elias was Robert de Dunstanville's old friend, and Belia's brother. Adam had considered approaching him before. To pay so much – five times the value of his estates, close to one hundred and fifty pounds in silver – to a man like Hugh de Brayboef or his son would be bitter indeed. But the thought that he and Joane would soon be separated was more bitter still. She was not his lover, would never be his wife, but she had become a closer companion to him than any he had known.

'Let there be no blame between us,' Joane said. She was becoming tearful as she spoke, but he recognised her determination. 'It was not us that poisoned the cup that we must drink – that was done long ago, before we even met. You have led me through peril to safety, Adam de Norton, and I will never forget that. You have guided me in darkness. But my road ends here, in this place, and yours does not.'

He embraced her, and they stood locked together on the riverbank. She was freeing him too, he realised, even if that freedom
burned in his soul.

*

They passed beneath the abbey gateway, the hooves of their horses
ringing on the frozen paving. It was St Bride's Eve, the last day of
January, and the royal retinue had only arrived at Waltham that
morning. The icy grey courtyard outside the hall and chambers
still thronged with grooms and valets, squires tending horses,
and knights waiting attendance on the king.

'Stay close to me,' Baldwin Wake said, his breath steaming as
they reined in and dismounted. 'Remember, I am your pledge
here. I speak for you. Remain silent until you are before his
majesty.'

'I understand,' Adam said, almost under his breath. Wake's
habitual smiling good humour had dropped from him like a discarded cloak. The Lord of Bourne was an altogether sterner and
more dependable man, Adam was discovering, than he had once
believed. A more trustworthy one too.

Baldwin placed his hand on Adam's shoulder, walking beside
him as they crossed the courtyard. Hugh of Oystermouth followed, as Adam's sole valet, and a pair of squires brought up
the rear. For all of his apparent calm and assurance, Adam could
sense Baldwin's nervous tension. He felt it himself too. Even
with the safe conduct that granted him freedom to approach the
king unmolested, he knew that threat massed all around him.
Until he had his pardon secured, every man he saw here was his
enemy.

The mob of knights and serjeants around the doors of the hall
parted as Adam and Baldwin approached. Adam tried to keep his
head straight, his eyes locked on the path before him, but could
not resist a darting glance, and then another. He recognised some

of the faces that surrounded them now. Some smiled coldly, others remained grave, hostile. These were men he had fought. Men he had faced across the ramparts of Kenilworth, or in the streets of Chesterfield. Men who had exalted over the field of slaughter at Evesham, or tasted the ashes of defeat at Lewes. No sign of Lord Edward among them, or of Earl Humphrey de Bohun. No Geoffrey de Brayboef, or Reginald de Grey either. Adam was glad of that; it was easier to face unknown adversaries. Easier to endure their sneering disdain, and fight down their silent reproach. The doors opened before him, and Lord Baldwin conducted him inside.

They surrendered their weapons to the guards at the threshold, Adam removing his belt and sword. Then they were led into a broad antechamber. Incense flavoured the chill air, and from the depths of the building came the sound of chanting voices. The king was attending his second mass of the day in the abbot's private chapel, an usher informed them.

Adam stood, trapping a shiver between his shoulder blades as the cold draughts swooped across the stone floor. Behind him he could hear the tapping of Hugh of Oystermouth's teeth. Others came and went around them, directing glances more curious than unwelcoming. A squat, jowly clergyman with a beaky nose came and stared at Adam, appraising, but moved on without a word.

Then a trumpet sounded from an adjacent room, and the doors at the end of the hall swung open. The king was at last receiving his guests. Adam and Baldwin were far from the first to be called; the hall had filled steadily around them. Every time a new group was summoned forward and the doors opened, Adam caught a glimpse of the chamber beyond. The waxed floor tiles shone a deep blood-red in the light of banked candles, dispelling the gloom of midwinter. To either side were tables where clerks in long black gowns worked at the royal correspondence. And at the far end sat the king, upon a dais with the red-robed figure of

Cardinal Ottobuono, the papal legate, seated to his right. Adam had not seen King Henry since the day of Evesham, when he was led through the streets after the battle by his son's victorious troops. He had looked old then, dazed and wounded. Now, Adam saw as he peered between the opening doors, the king looked far older still. Sitting on his gilded chair, he could have been a figure carved from ivory, or bone.

One of the clerks sidled up to Baldwin Wake, muttering to him.

'They need more than one man to give mainprise for you,' Wake told Adam, his voice tight with annoyance. 'It seems that I am insufficient security to pledge for your good behaviour!'

'I will give it, gladly,' another voice declared. 'As I am glad to see you here, Adam de Norton, and to repay the debt I owe you.'

Adam had last spoken to Ralph de Grendon in the forest of Sherwood, when he freed him from captivity, and had seen him later only from a distance from the walls of Kenilworth. But as the man clasped him by the hand and gave him the kiss of greeting Adam recognised him immediately.

'I too will pledge, if you need it,' another man said, striding from the crowd around the far doors. He was older than de Grendon or Wake, well dressed in a fur-trimmed surcoat, and this time it took Adam a few moments to recall the name: Sir Martin des Roches had attended William de St John's winter hunt at Basing, on the day that Adam had first met Isabel.

'And I know,' des Roches went on, raising his eyebrows, 'that William will be pleased to hear of this. He has been cruelly unwell for a month and more, but I'm sure he will have no hesitation in returning your lands, once the redemption is paid . . .'

'Lord William, you mean?' Adam said, ignoring Baldwin's injunction to keep quiet. 'Lord William de St John holds my lands? Not de Brayboef?'

Sir Martin's face creased as he grinned. 'Oh yes, Geoffrey de Brayboef seized your manor at Selborne as soon as the news of Evesham reached us,' he said. 'But Lord William petitioned against it, and the king found in his favour and granted all your estates to his keeping.'

For a moment Adam felt unsteady on his feet, and only the hands of the other men clasping his shoulders supported him.

'And William will not be alone in welcoming you back, I think,' Martin des Roches went on, with a knowing nod. 'Although I should speak no more of such things . . .'

But then the doors creaked open, and one of the royal serjeants-at-arms stepped forth and called Adam's name. Drawing themselves upright, the party assembled around him and walked forward, over the threshold and into the warm candlelight of the hall. The king barely moved as Adam drew closer. The cardinal leaned across the arm of his chair and whispered a few words, and the thin carved bone of the king's face twitched slightly.

Adam dropped to kneel on the hard tiled floor, and heard the king's secretary speak his name.

'You may approach his majesty,' the voice said.

Chapter 29

Snow had fallen in the night, not deep enough to block the road along the valley but sufficient to turn the bare winter woodland into a strange and alien place. Adam rode slowly, letting his palfrey find its own path in the whiteness. He was leading Blanchart on a long rein, and behind him came two other riders and three packhorses, the breath of both animals and men steaming in the frigid morning air. High overhead, birds flickered across a gash of blue sky between the petrified treetops.

Adam knew this road well enough. Behind him was Waverley Abbey, where he had spent the preceding day, and up ahead was the village of Alton, where a road branched northward towards Basing. He had come this way the autumn after the Battle of Lewes, as he went to reclaim his manor from de Brayboef's men. And now, he thought, he was engaged in a similar task. But how different he felt about it now, and how gravely his situation had changed in the intervening months.

In his saddlebag, safely wrapped in leather and sheepskin, was a copy of the document attesting Adam's surrender and pardon. The royal clerks had drafted it, back at Waltham, and it was sealed by the king, by Baldwin Wake, de Grendon and des Roches, and by Adam himself.

'*Remission to Adam de Norton,*' the document read, '*of the king's indignation and rancour against him by occasion of his trespasses in the time of the late disturbance in the realm . . .*'

Before the pardon was issued, Adam had knelt before the papal legate and made his full confession, so the sentence of excommunication could be lifted from him. Absolved, restored to the holy sacraments of the mother church, he had made his submission to the king.

'*. . . so that he shall be granted the king's grace and his firm peace, without peril of life and limb, as he has sworn on the Holy Gospels that he will never again bear arms against the king or his heirs . . .*'

And the following day he had attended the ceremony of Candlemas at the abbey, and Joane too had come from Ware to seek absolution from the cardinal, to pronounce her vow to him, and to give homage to the king for the lands she now held in her own name. Adam had felt proud for her, even as his heart ached. She was the Lady of Ware now, immune from the demands of prospective suitors. Immune from the world entirely. As was Adam himself.

'*. . . provided he will stand to the Dictum of Kenilworth as to the lands given by the king to another by reason of his late trespasses. And if he offends again his body shall be at the king's will, and his lands forfeit.*'

In London, Adam had visited Elias. He had told the money-lender of everything that had happened in Nottingham – another sort of confession – and of his sister Belia and her life there. Elias had been happy to agree the loan, and a much larger one than he would usually have offered a poor knight with only a remote possibility of future repayment. He did it for Belia's sake, of course, and for the memory of his friend Robert de Dunstanville. But now Adam had coin at least, a weight of silver filling the panniers of his pack animals – insufficient to pay the whole ransom, but enough to buy back a small portion of his former estates. Quite possibly William de St John would have returned his lands without the fee, but such was the law, and the terms of his redemption.

After all this time, all this blood and struggle, it all came down to land and coin. The great rebellion that Simon de Montfort had begun, England's fury for liberty and reform, had died away finally in a welter of parchment documents and wax seals, of loans and promises, of life and honour measured out in silver. A business of clerks and legal men, of moneylenders and bailiffs.

It was enough, Adam thought. Even to return to something like the life he had once known, his own lands with his own house, his own people, would be some recompense for what he had lost, and what he had been unable to salvage from the ruins of his ambition. But there was more than that, of course. There was Isabel, and the promise that she held of a different future altogether.

A year and eight months had passed since last he saw her. She would surely have changed. It amazed Adam even to learn that she was still unmarried. But Martin des Roches had confirmed it, before he left Waltham.

Adam had no idea what he might find when he reached Basing. He had sent Hugh of Oystermouth on ahead of him, two days beforehand, to give notice of his impending arrival. No more than that – he must explain the rest of it himself. Explain his long absence, his disgrace and partial redemption. And he must present himself to Isabel, as the man he had become in that long absence, and let her choose. Let her forgive him, if she so wished.

He would not blame her if she did not.

So he rode slowly, his head lowered into the folds of his thick woollen cloak. He was thinking about Isabel, and about the woman he had left behind him. His parting with Joane had been muted, both of them guarding their feelings. He had expected a howling grief to consume him, the death of love. Only now did he feel torn inside, flung wildly between extremes of feeling. At one moment a sorrow so intense it was close to pleasure, at the next a hope so desperate it was almost painful. With one breath his heart soared, and he wanted to shout and to spur his horse forward through the snow, rushing on to Basing. Then, a breath later, he was plunged into sickening anxiety and black woe, and feared that shame would engulf him.

He had betrothed himself to Isabel while still holding his love for Joane a secret in his heart. Now that love was banished from him, could he declare himself to her truly? He did not know. He would have to stand before her, look her in the eyes and speak the words to her.

I will not lie to her, he told himself. *Never again.*

But it was hard, all the same, to be returning with so little. He had his warhorse, his belted sword and the coin in his saddlebags, but little else besides. His travelling retinue consisted only of a single groom to manage the packhorses and a mounted serjeant he had engaged in London. The serjeant was a stout man with silver bristles on his chin, who rode slumped in the saddle and wheezed with every breath.

Martin des Roches had warned Adam that the roads around Basing and Alton were infested with brigands, lawless men who robbed travellers and ravaged isolated settlements. He had also warned that William de St John was even more gravely ill than he had implied, and was not expected to live another month. The need to see the man, to make his peace with him, before the end came drove Adam onward, through the depths of winter, with only the scant protection he could afford.

Up ahead the road narrowed, thornbushes and bare beech trees pressing close on either side. Those lords who held the neighbouring estates were supposed to clear the woods from the verges of the highway, but all too often they did not. With the kingdom in so disturbed a state these last years, most had attended to other priorities.

'Sir,' the groom called, his voice a constricted gasp.

The lad had reined to a halt, the packhorses halting in a line behind him. The animals stood, breathing steam, as the riders turned in the saddle and stared at the trees around them.

'Merciful saints protect us!' the serjeant said.

Adam reached beneath the fold of his cloak and freed the hilt of his sword. His axe was hanging on the back of his saddle, and he readied that as well. He could hear the serjeant spanning his crossbow, the bolt tapping against the stock as the man loaded it with trembling hands.

All around them, the trees were hung with corpses.

Mastering his nerves, shortening his reins, Adam forced himself to look carefully at them. Impossible to tell how long they had hung there, eerily motionless beneath the bare branches. Some were spotted with snow. Others had been pecked and gouged by crows. There were eight, nine, maybe more.

'It's just the remains of some brigand band,' he said, trying to keep a steady voice, 'caught on the highway and hanged as a warning. Dead men can't hurt anyone. Come on!'

He jogged his horse forward, dragging at Blanchart's leading rein. The animals were nervous, stamping and blowing as they walked. When he glanced back he saw the groom hurrying after him with the packhorses, and the serjeant kicking with his spurs. All seemed eager enough to escape that frozen grove of death. Adam felt the tight lock of fear between his shoulders, and tried to ease his head up. He needed to stay alert now. If the hanging bodies had been a warning of a different kind, he should heed it.

Around a bend in the road, the bushes and trees opened out. The ground rose ahead, the grey trees stacked tall in their white mantles. It was still too early for the sunlight to reach down here into the valley depths, but Adam could see it lighting the sky overhead. As soon as they had passed through the woodland, he thought, their way would be clear and they could ride in the sun all the way to Alton.

Then a pair of figures stepped from the thornbushes onto the road ahead.

At once Adam saw motion all around him. Other men were in the trees, appearing from between the beech trunks and the tangled scrub. They were grey as the winter woodland, dressed in drab woollens, here and there a gambeson or a leather jack. These were not labouring men, like the ones he had encountered on the road to Banbury. Turning in the saddle, his hand on the hilt of his sword, Adam saw the curves of bows, the glint of an arrowhead.

'They're all around us!' the groom cried, his voice breaking.

Adam had his sword in his hand, the blade low against his right leg. He could kick with the spurs now and try to ride clear through the cordon, dragging Blanchart after him. But that would mean abandoning his baggage, and the precious bags of coin on the pack-horses. Besides, he did not doubt that an arrow would hit either him or his horse before he cleared the next bend.

One of the figures blocking the road ahead walked forward. Adam saw his close-set eyes, the spreading black beard that covered his lower face. His blood chilled. It was a face from his worst nightmares.

Their gazes locked, and the man's beard split to show his clenched teeth.

'Adam de Norton, just as I thought,' Fulk Ticeburn said.

He appeared pleased, relishing the moment. Almost as if he had expected to meet Adam here. *Almost as if he had known.* Of course, Adam realised; the brigands would have spies all along the road, giving them information of approaching travellers. Perhaps one of the monks of Waverley had told them of his identity? Ticeburn had been de Brayboef's man once, and had tried to kill him several times before, most recently during the murderous slaughter in Evesham Abbey. Now, here on an isolated road in the dead of winter, he had his chance.

The serjeant threw down his crossbow and raised his open hands. 'Mercy, goodsirs,' he cried. 'I'm just a hired man!'

From all around them now came the crisp crackling of the undergrowth as the other figures approached through the trees. Some wore cloths tied across their faces. But Fulk Ticeburn needed no disguise. He carried a broad-bladed axe in both hands, and wore a sword belted at his side. His black beard was even denser now, but frosted with grey.

'That's him?' one of his men called, gesturing at Adam. Six of them had bows drawn, arrows nocked and aimed. 'Let's shoot him down now.'

'Oh yes, that's him,' Ticeburn replied, a rolling swagger in his step as he came closer. Adam had forgotten how big the man was, how massive his shoulders. He slapped the blade of the axe against his palm as he spoke. 'Sir Adam de Norton. The same man who killed my brother Warin, and helped his friend to kill my brother Eudo. The same man who drove us off our land, and made outlaws of us.'

'You made a vow,' Adam managed to say. 'You swore you would not return here. Your master, Hugh de Brayboef, swore too.'

'That cringing worm de Brayboef's not *my* master any more,' Ticeburn said. 'I'm my own master now! And a master of men . . .' He gestured at the surrounding archers. 'As for swearing vows . . .'

He spat thickly into the frozen dirt.

'Why should I abide by anything I swore to the likes of you?' he demanded. 'You've broken every oath yourself, haven't you? Or is it different for *knights*, do you think? Are oaths and honesty only for common men like me, eh? The ones who fight and bleed in your wars!'

Some of the men surrounding the clearing laughed, while others growled in agreement. They had lowered their bows now, and were leaning on their spears. Two of them dragged the serjeant from his horse and made him kneel; two more shoved the groom down beside him. One slapped the lad across the face to stop his frightened gibbering.

'Seems to me you're an outlaw yourself nowadays, de Norton,' Ticeburn said, swinging his axe to warm his muscles. 'Any honest man can kill you like vermin, and think it a good deed.'

'Not any more,' Adam said, his back teeth clenched. 'I've been granted the king's mercy. I have a document to prove it.'

'Parchment and wax!' Ticeburn said, and looked like he would spit again. 'That don't make a man loyal. You're a *traitor*, de Norton.' He snarled the word. 'To men, to your king, to God . . . No, killing you would please even Christ Himself!'

He was close now. Almost close enough for Adam to reach him with his sword, if he spurred his horse forward. Was that what he wanted? Grinning, Ticeburn slung his axe across his shoulders.

'But we know how it is with you knights,' he said. 'Very concerned about your honour, and your *word*. So I challenge you! A trial by combat . . . and let God be the witness to the vengeance I serve upon you.'

Adam stared at him, disbelieving for a moment. 'If I beat you . . . your men will let us leave in peace?'

Ticeburn laughed. 'Oh, you won't beat me. This fight is to the death, boy. I'm going to hack you to pieces!' He swung his arm, the axe blade slashing the air. 'Just step down off that horse, and we'll set to it.'

Hardly daring to draw a breath, Adam slipped the sword back into his scabbard and swung himself from the saddle with a heavy creak of leather. Fear bloomed inside him, and he felt the sweat break in prickling waves all across his body. He had not expected this fight, not against a man like Ticeburn. He had not wanted it. But now, just when he had imagined that all danger was past, he could not escape it.

Trying to keep his hands from shaking, he unpinned the brooch at his neck and threw his cloak over the saddle of his horse. He unbuckled his waistbelt, dropping his pouch and his sheathed eating knife to the ground, then settled the sword belt more securely over his hips. He wore no armour, not even a padded aketon. Three layered woollen tunics were his only protection.

'At least grant me a shield,' he said, forcing the words through a tight throat.

Ticeburn glowered, considering, then motioned to one of his men. The brigand slipped a plain wooden shield from his shoulder and dropped it on the ground, then kicked it towards Adam.

'Maybe when I've killed you I'll cut up your corpse, like they did to your master, the traitor de Montfort!' Ticeburn said. He had started swinging the axe again, cutting great steel arcs in the cold air. 'I'll cut off your arms and legs,' he snarled. 'Then I'll cut off your cock, and stick it in your mouth! Then I'll cut off your head! And maybe I'll send it to Lady Isabel de St John, heh?'

The axe whistled as it cut the air. Adam felt a spike of raw terror as he heard the name Ticeburn had uttered. But of course the man would know. Anger sharpened his nerves. With one smooth motion he drew his sword.

'Would she like my gift, do you think?' Ticeburn went on. 'Would she dandle it on her pretty knees? Would she weep over it?'

Lunging to one side, Adam snatched up the shield. Ticeburn let out a bellowing roar, swinging the axe above his head and bringing it whirling downwards. Adam dodged aside just in time, slamming his left arm through the shield straps. He felt the ache of his old injury, burning through the cold. Sidestepping, his sword raised in a high guard, he circled around to Ticeburn's right.

But Ticeburn was on him again at once, the axe whirring. For such a big man he was terrifyingly fast and agile. Adam brought the shield up and managed to turn the axe blow, feeling the shock of it deep in the bone of his forearm. He swung a cut with his sword, but Ticeburn slammed it aside with the haft of his axe.

Both of them were breathing fast and deep now, their feet shuffling and kicking at the frozen turf. Around them the watchers were silent, motionless as the fighters circled and struck.

Adam tried to watch the man's face, guess his movements, but the gleaming axe blade was moving in great snakelike curves and his eye was drawn to it instinctively. *I've forgotten everything*, he told himself. All the lessons that Robert de Dunstanville had worked into him, all that he had gained in years of conflict. He was no better than a green youth, facing imminent death. He sucked in a breath, then stamped forward as the axe passed him and lunged with his sword.

'Bastard!' Ticeburn yelled as the blade bit. He roared again, jerking his axe back and then driving it at Adam like a spear. The tip of the hooked blade stabbed beneath Adam's arm, and he felt the bright pulsing wash of pain.

He was cut, bleeding from the wound, but the blow had broken no bones. Ticeburn was injured too – Adam saw him drop a hand to his hip and glance down at the blood on his palm.

For three heartbeats they circled, weapons raised. Suddenly Adam felt his mind clear, the pain focussing his movements. He dropped back a step, waited for Ticeburn to swing another great reaping cut, then stepped forward into the attack. His angled shield caught the axe blade and deflected it, but he followed with a lunging shove that sent his attacker stumbling backwards. Before Ticeburn could regain his footing Adam swung down with his sword, whipping the blade into the back of the other man's knee and slicing through his hamstring.

Ticeburn bellowed, his fury driven by pain. He slashed again with his axe, but he was down on one knee now and Adam easily evaded the clumsy blow. Circling, Adam lifted his shield and pressed the inside of his right wrist against the wound in his side. A jolt of hot agony, and when he looked down his wrist was bright red. He could feel the blood soaking through his tunic, and pooling above his belt. He needed to end the fight quickly, or he was done.

His adversary was crippled now, crouching on his bent knee, but he could still swing his axe whenever Adam got close enough.

Wait for the moment, Adam told himself. He let his mind still, glazing over the pulse of pain and the furious kicks of fear. Raising his shield again he edged inside Ticeburn's reach. The man grinned, then swung an overarm blow.

The axe blade cracked into the wooden shield facing, splitting the boards. Before Adam could press his attack, Ticeburn wrenched the weapon aside. The shield slipped from Adam's arm, and Ticeburn hurled both it and the axe away from him. Heaving himself forward, he seized Adam's sword arm as it descended, and with his other hand he grabbed Adam's throat.

Staggering backwards, Adam toppled with the man's weight on top of him. He had dropped his sword now, and his left arm felt numb. Ticeburn was screaming as he grappled Adam, releasing the grip on his wrist to swing a punch at his face. The blow cracked against Adam's cheekbone, bursting white pain through his skull. All the while Ticeburn's thick fingers were squeezing his throat, steadily crushing his windpipe.

'*Die*, bastard!' Ticeburn was hissing through spit-flecked teeth. There was bloody froth in his beard. '*Die*, and may your soul be damned!'

Adam's right hand was free now, scrabbling in the dirt for his fallen sword. But he felt only the brittleness of frozen leaves, and twigs that broke beneath his fingers. Distantly he seemed to hear voices calling his name, and when he forced his eyes open a bright light was glaring all around him. For a moment he thought that angels were dancing above him, a great door in the sky swinging open and the heavenly host issuing forth to avenge his death. He could hear the blast of their horns, their cries as they descended . . .

Then his reaching fingers found the end of the belt he had dropped earlier. He tugged it towards him, and his hand closed around the hilt of his eating knife. With one motion he pulled it from the sheath and reversed it in his hand. Then he swung his arm up, driving the short blade into the side of Ticeburn's neck with all his strength.

A jolt went through the man's body, Adam saw the leering face above him tighten in a rictus of pain. He twisted his hand, and hot blood gushed over his fingers. Then, as the grip on his throat slacked, he shoved himself upwards and threw Ticeburn's heavy carcass off him. The body rolled and lay on its back, the hilt of the knife still jutting from the black beard.

He had not imagined the sound of the horns. Again he heard them, and the drumming of horses' hooves on the frozen earth. When he turned his head he saw motion all around him. One running figure with a cloth across his face was shot down by an arrow. Another threw aside his spear and bolted for the trees. A horse galloped after him, the rider aiming a spear. For several long moments, as the shock of his survival poured through him, Adam could make no sense of it at all.

'You're alive, God be praised!' a voice cried. A man was kneeling beside him. It was Hugh of Oystermouth, Adam realised as his friend pressed a wadded linen bandage to the wound in his side and called for assistance. How had he come to be there? Then he tasted the wine that Hugh was pouring into his mouth, choked once, swallowed and was awake to the world once more.

When he turned his head again, Isabel de St John was sitting beside him. Her blue eyes were wide as she studied the injuries on his body. 'By the blessing, nothing looks fatal,' she said to Hugh.

The sun had risen above the trees, and the light was spilling down into the frozen glade, turning the grey and dun to a torrent of glittering light. Isabel had laid Adam's head in her lap as another man – a squire, it seemed – attended to his wounds. There was blood smeared on her dress, and on her hands, but she appeared not to notice. Her loosened hair hung in blonde curls around her face as she bent over him.

'Thank the holy angels your herald told us you would be on the road today,' Isabel said. 'I hoped I would reach you before you left Waverley . . .'

'You brought an armed escort?' Adam asked her.

'Of course! Father is too sick to travel, and both my brothers are at Portchester Castle, so I came myself. Though it appears you won your fight!'

Adam felt the ache in his throat as he smiled. He remembered now how decisive Isabel could be, how strong-willed. There was so much he had forgotten about who she was. So much he had to remember. He winced suddenly as pain lanced through him.

'Apologies, sir,' the squire muttered, tying off a bandage. 'It's a little tight.'

'I didn't win,' Adam said, as the pain subsided. When he glanced to his left he could just make out Ticeburn's corpse, sprawled in the dirt, neglected now.

'I didn't win,' he said again. 'I've been away so long . . . forgive me . . .' There were tears in his eyes, sudden grief in his heart, and he grasped Isabel's hand. 'I've betrayed everything, and everyone. I've failed at every test. I've lost every battle I fought . . . I've lost *everything*.'

'No . . . no,' Isabel was saying, bending to kiss his brow. 'You haven't lost at all. You've *found* everything,' she said.

Her grip on his hand was fierce.

'Come home, Adam.'

Chapter 30

The first trumpet sent the birds scattering across the dawn sky. Adam peered upwards into the blue and watched their wings beating over the scrub copses, the reed beds and the pools of marshwater. It was mid-July, and would be another hot day. Already the air above the wetlands was hazed with tiny insects.

Summer's heat had aided the cause of war. Months of burning sun had dried out the meres and the marshes, narrowed the rivers to rivulets and baked the mud to dry dust. The Isle of Ely, once an inaccessible fastness amid the black waters of the fens, was now open to attack. It was the Hand of God, or so the king's priests had declared.

And throughout those months Lord Edward, the king's son and heir, had been sending his labourers forward to fill the drying swamps with bundles of reeds and fallen trees, staked and lashed together to make causeways. Now, at daybreak, he had led his main army forward over the improvised road, first pouring in waves of archers and crossbowmen to surround the last refuge of the rebellion, then following up with his mounted knights and serjeants.

'Why do we not charge against them at once?' John de St John asked, standing beside his caparisoned destrier with his great helm under his arm. 'We're sounding trumpets and giving them time to muster, when we could storm over there before they know we're here . . .'

'And slaughter them in their beds?' Baldwin Wake replied. 'Lord Edward doesn't want to bathe in blood today. Nor should we. England has seen enough of needless killing.'

John sniffed, but accepted the rebuke. Lord Wake was the older man, and the more experienced in war. Standing between them, Adam said nothing. De St John was his brother-in-law now, and Lord of Basing since his father's death; old Lord William had lived just long enough to renew his blessing on Adam's marriage to Isabel. Currently Adam was serving in the retinue that John de St John had brought to answer Lord Edward's military summons, although he would have preferred to fight alongside the veteran Baldwin Wake, who had brought his own powerful array from his lands in Lincolnshire and Cumberland.

Adam had spent the earlier summer at Basing and on his estates. He had missed the dramatic events of that time, when Earl Gilbert de Clare had suddenly thrown his support behind the Disinherited, and marched an army down from Wales to seize London. By the time Adam heard of what had happened, everything was over. The king had agreed to relax the terms of the Dictum of Kenilworth, and return the seized lands of the rebels before they paid the redemption fines. For all Adam's intense dislike of the Red Earl, he had to thank him for that. Now he had his lands back at last, with time enough to pay off what he owed.

Many of the rebels from Ely had come to London to support Earl Gilbert, and most had made their peace when he did. Nicholas de Segrave, even John D'Eyville, had sought the king's mercy and laid down their arms. Only a small band still remained in the fens of the Isle of Ely, with Henry de Hastings as their leader. And now, Lord Edward had determined to crush the last flickering sparks of rebellion that remained in England.

'Messires!' a voice shouted from away to the right. 'To horse!'

Another trumpet blast, as sixty knights and as many squires and serjeants swung up into the saddle. Ahead of them, across the tall thickets of reeds, the marsh was full of noise and motion. Lord Edward's infantry had moved up to the margins of the rebel encampment, and already the opposing archers were lofting their arrows against them. The air flickered, and here and there a voice rose in pain.

Adam set his mailed foot in the stirrup and pulled himself up onto Blanchart's back, settling into the high war saddle. Behind him, Gerard was already mounted. The squire had rejoined Adam shortly after his return to Basing, bringing with him the armour and equipment he had left at Kenilworth. Now Adam was fully dressed for war, in mail hauberk and coat of plates, coif and broad-brimmed helmet. By his side was a shield faced with leather and painted with a golden lion rampant on a field of green. His surcoat was green silk, and his saddle was red leather studded with gilded nail-heads. On the lance that Gerard carried was his green pennon, the yellow lion with flickering red tongue dancing on the breeze.

'My wife sewed that for you, I think,' Baldwin Wake said to Adam, pointing at the pennon. 'She'll be glad to know you still have it.'

Adam merely inclined his head in acknowledgement.

'Did I tell you she's with child?' Wake went on. 'A boy, I believe. I have a sense for these things.'

I'm sure you do, Adam thought. It was strange to be talking of new life on the brink of battle. Isabel too was already expecting her first child, though she had shared the news with none but Adam and her maids.

To Adam's other side, John de St John rode beneath a banner of spotless white, a red band at the top set with two gold stars. His white surcoat and the caparison of his horse were liberally spattered with the black mud and slime of the fenlands. All around them were other lords and other retinues, their banners bold and

fierce in the summer sun. Some had been allies before: Nicholas de Segrave, who had fought for de Montfort at Lewes and
Evesham, and the Yorkshire knight Osbert de Cornburgh, who
had survived his captivity after Chesterfield. But many more had
been enemies: Henry of Almain and John Balliol, Warin de Bassingborne and Roger de Clifford. Adam's gut tightened as he saw
the familiar banner of Reginald de Grey across the reeds to his
left. But all served a united cause now, their conflicts forgotten
and hatreds forgiven. So, at least, they claimed. If England was to
have peace, they must at least pretend friendship.

A man rode up beside Adam on a pony. He was dressed all in
scarlet, gold rings on his fingers. Adam recognised him as the
beaky-nosed clergyman he had seen at Waltham Abbey months
before.

'It is true,' the man asked in strangely accented French,
'that you were one of those rebels who held the *castello* of
Kenullewurz?'

Adam was about to answer, when another voice cried loudly
from behind him. 'Yes, it's true enough, Teobaldo!'

Adam and those around them all turned in the saddle, alert
to the familiar royal lisp. Lord Edward rode forward to join
them. He was mounted on a powerfully muscled grey destrier,
and dressed in glittering mail and a surcoat of deep red embroidered with the hissing golden leopards of England. Behind the
king's son rode a wedge of squires, banner-bearers and household knights.

'Then it is good that this young man has repented, and turned
from his treason,' the clergyman said. He was Italian, Adam realised. One of the legate Ottobuono's archdeacons.

'Not at all!' Lord Edward went on, reins tight as he held his
spirited horse to a walk. 'Sir Adam de Norton has no cause for
shame. It was a gallant defence, and a noble one – such men
are England's strength, and not to be despised! Do you know,'
he called back, turning in the saddle, 'that they dressed their

surgeon as the papal legate and had him give a mock excommunication from the ramparts?' He laughed loudly.

'Blasphemy!' muttered the Italian, rolling his eyes to the burning sky.

'Whatever happened to that surgeon?' Edward asked, flinging the question vaguely at Adam. But without waiting for an answer he rode forward and drew his horse around in front of his assembled knights. His squires and banner-bearers massed behind him.

'Barons! Messires!' the king's son yelled, standing in his stirrups to address them all. 'We have before us the last redoubt of rebellion!' He jutted a mailed arm towards the tangled scrub woodland across the reed beds. 'Almighty God has decreed our victory this day, leading us with his guiding hand through these trackless marshes and bringing us to our enemy. Now the final blow will fall!'

Growls of assent from the assembled horsemen. Across the reeds came the sounds of arrows and crossbow bolts hitting home, the cries of the wounded. But there were banners showing among the distant trees as well. The Disinherited were mustering for battle.

'We must keep in mind, friends, that our foes are Englishmen,' Edward went on, his one drooping eyelid giving him an imperious glare as he scanned the ranks of his knights. 'Many among them are noble and proud, though sunk deep in error. We have known enough bloodshed in this realm. I would have no more valiant men slain! So I have decreed an edict, offering a full and immediate pardon to any that lay down their arms at once. But to those who resist I offer only blood and war! If any of my own men are harmed, or if my way is hindered, then those responsible will die the deaths of traitors, and their necks shall feel either the noose or the blade!'

Roars of approval from the assembled men, many drawing their swords and raising them to the sky. Trumpets were

sounding; already Edward's heralds were crossing the last causeway towards the enemy lines, calling out their terms of surrender.

Watching Edward as he circled his horse, Adam recalled their
first exchange of words, in the tournament pavilion at Senlis.
He thought of how dismissively the man had spared his life after
Evesham. Of all the months he had spent as his prisoner at Beeston. But he recalled too Baldwin Wake's favourable words about
him. Could Edward one day become the great king that Wake
had described? Perhaps, Adam thought, if his pride and his fury
allowed it. He certainly looked impressive enough, mounted on
his champing grey and dressed in the full panoply of war. A man
to follow, perhaps. Or a man to fear.

'Look!' John de St John cried, stretching in the saddle. 'It's
happening – the cowards are giving up!'

Across the reeds the opposing banners were wavering. Adam
saw a white flag emblazoned with a red sun lowered. Another,
quartered green and yellow, went the same way.

Baldwin Wake hissed loudly between his teeth. 'No, they see
the path of wisdom,' he said. '*Now* we press them!'

The brass cry of the trumpets, and at once the knights drew
on and laced their helmets, the squires passing the lances for-
ward as the great armoured mass of horsemen began to move.
Adam took his lance from Gerard and fell in behind John de St
John. One touch of the spurs and Blanchart broke into a trot.
Lord Edward remained beneath his banners, his horse tossing
its head as he gripped the reins. 'Get me Henry de Hastings!'
Edward cried as the riders streamed past him. 'Take him alive.
I'll grant him mercy this day if I have to shove it down his throat
with my fist!'

Churned black mud lay ahead, a path through the trampled
reeds. Crossbowmen and light troops pulled back to either
side as the armoured wedge of knights ploughed on towards
the causeways. Arrows spat from the air, but the volleys were
slackening now. Very few of the enemy banners still remained

defiant. The advance slowed as the leading riders crossed the last causeway, the bundled reeds crushed into the mire under the weight of their horses. Ahead of him Adam saw the black banner of Nicholas de Segrave, the reformed rebel who had led Edward's men through the outer defences of the Isle. Baldwin Wake's red and yellow were right behind him, and then came John de St John's retinue. Horns were crying wildly, the armoured riders bellowing from inside their great helms as they drove their sweating horses onto the rising ground of the island.

After holding Blanchart to a trot as he crossed the causeway, Adam let out the reins. The horse leaped forward at once, plunging through a crackling screen of reeds. Black water opened suddenly ahead. A concealed pool, the murk swirling up to the saddle girths. Men on the far side rose from concealment in the further reed bed. Adam held his lance raised clear of the water as his warhorse surged up out of the pool. His opponents fled before him, throwing aside spears and crossbows.

Onward, through the reeds and the last expanse of muddy bushes. '*King's men! King's men!*' the attacking riders were yelling. Off to the left, a column of horsemen crossed a second causeway, Henry of Almain and John de Balliol in the lead.

Open ground before him now, fugitives scattering in terror on all sides. Adam saw more banners falling. Men were dropping to their knees, hands clasped in surrender. Gregory de Caldwell's red silk lay trampled in the mud. Turning his head, sweat running down his face, Adam scanned the thorn thickets and the grassy clearings for one banner in particular. Already he could hear John de St John's men cheering a bloodless victory.

Then he saw it, over to his right through the denser scrub woodland. A red *maunch* on gold. Screwing at the reins, he turned Blanchart's canter and kicked with the spurs again. Leaping, the horse cleared a thick brake of fallen trees, and Adam saw the fleeing riders ahead of him. The woods opened into a long tongue-shaped sward of grassland. Water glinted at the far end.

For a moment Adam saw only the distant figure of a mounted squire holding the banner, and thought his quarry had escaped him. Then he caught the flash of movement from the corner of his eye, the thud of galloping hooves on turf. He managed to turn Blanchart just in time as Henry de Hastings charged in from his right with his lance couched. The other rider blazed past him, yellow silk and steel burning in the sunlight.

At the far side of the sward de Hastings slowed, dragging his horse around in a tight turn. 'De Norton!' he roared through the dull iron of his great helm. 'I always knew you would turn traitor!'

'Surrender, in the king's name!' Adam shouted back, his voice cracking.

'Never!' De Hastings brought his lance down again, digging savagely with his spurs. His mount was back on its haunches, whinnying, but at once erupted forward.

Adam kept his lance raised, turning Blanchart to confront his opponent's charge. The silver-grey destrier was hot-blooded, already primed for battle, and needed barely a touch of the spurs. Hooves kicking up the dirt, the two horses closed at speed.

Head lowered behind his shield, lance wavering, Adam watched the distance shrink between them. No time now for any of the fancy jousting tricks that Robert de Dunstanville had taught him. All useless if the other rider intended to kill – and Henry de Hastings had his lance directed at Adam's face, unprotected beneath the rim of his open helmet.

Three heartbeats, then four, the sun flashing between the converging riders. Then Adam brought his lance down and couched it, the honed steel tip like a plunging hawk aimed at the red blazon on the other man's shield. In the moment before impact he raised his own shield, lifting it to protect his head as he bunched his whole body behind the weapon.

He felt Henry's lance slam against his shield, deflect upwards and clip his helmet bowl. Then, almost at the same moment, his own weapon struck hard and true. The shaft of the lance shattered in his hand, then he was past and riding clear, already hauling at the reins to slow the destrier and turn for the next attack.

Sweat was in his eyes, blinding him in the dazzle of low sun as he reached down and seized the battle-axe from his saddle bow. Blanchart had managed to turn on his hind legs, rearing, and now Adam spurred forward again.

No sign of his adversary at first. A horse with a yellow caparison was running free at the far end of the sward, the saddle empty. Then Adam saw the body sprawled on the turf. De Hastings had dropped his shield as Adam's lance blasted him from the saddle. As Adam rode closer he saw the man struggling to rise, drawing his sword to defend himself.

The horse slowed, circling the fallen man. Kicking his feet from the stirrups, Adam slid from the saddle in one smooth motion. With quaking legs he strode across the trampled grass. Henry de Hastings dragged off his helmet and threw it aside. His leg was injured and he could not stand. Grimacing, his face a red mask of sweat and fury, he watched Adam approach and stand over him.

With one foot Adam shoved him back onto the turf. Then he stood on Henry's right wrist, trapping his sword hand. 'Yield,' he said, raising the axe against the sun.

Henry de Hastings laughed grimly, jogging his left hand from his mail glove and raising an open palm. 'You'll get no good ransom from me,' he said. 'All I have in the world is my horse and armour.'

Adam seized his hand, claiming his victory.

'There's only one thing I want from you.'

*

Sometimes, to find the thread of your life you have to follow it back to where you began. True enough, Adam thought as he approached the castle gates. Returning here now was like returning to the time of his youth. Five years and more had passed, and he was a different man altogether now.

As he rode across the drawbridge and beneath the timber gatehouse, he saw the familiar bailey opening before him. He had thought Pleshey Castle a formidable stronghold once, with its moats and wooden palisades, but compared to Kenilworth, Nottingham or Rochester it was a poor-looking place. The only person that he recognised was Natural John, the earl's fool, who ran to him as he dismounted, grinning and nodding. Adam embraced him as a friend; it was good to see him again, although he would not be staying long.

Grooms led his horse to the stables, and a household squire – a boy like Adam had once been himself – escorted him to the hall and brought food and wine. An hour passed before another man came to show him into the presence of the earl.

Humphrey de Bohun the Elder, Earl of Hereford and Essex, Constable of England, sat in his chamber with the shutters closed against the summer sun. Even in the gloom Adam could see how old he appeared now, how hollow his features had become. But there was still power in the set of his jaw, and the sharpness of his gaze. He said nothing as Adam reached into his belt purse and withdrew the gold swan ring he had taken from Henry de Hastings.

Stepping closer, Adam placed the ring on the table beside Lord Humphrey. The old man glanced at it a moment, and let out a rattling breath. With one knotted hand he took the ring, slipped it on his finger and turned it to the light.

'It is no easy thing,' he said, his voice low and rough, 'to lose an eldest son. To lose *two* sons – yes, I acknowledge Robert as well. To have them turn against you . . . even fight against you.

And then to hear of their deaths, and not to be able to grieve as a father should, as they had died traitors.'

He drew a breath, his eyes hazing. Adam stood in silence before him.

'But I thank you for returning this to me,' the earl said, a catch in his voice. 'I shall give it to my grandson, my son's heir. A link, with what we have lost. With family, and heritage. Such things are important, and worthy of love, you know.'

Still Adam remained silent. His only link with heritage was the land he held, which his father had held before him. Land he had regained so recently, and at such cost. His only family, his only love, was Isabel. Her, and the children they would have together.

'You'll want a reward, I suppose, for restoring this to me at last?' Humphrey said, his jaw tightening into something like a smile.

'I ask only that you return the dower lands of Joane, Lady of Ware,' Adam said.

'Do you indeed?' the earl said quietly, and his smile appeared more genuine now, if no warmer. 'Well. It cost me a fair penny reimbursing that fool Reginald de Grey for her marriage rights, you know. But . . . yes. Very well.'

Adam nodded, then took a step back.

'But there's another matter, isn't there?' Humphrey said. 'My son . . . he never paid the balance of what he owed you for my ransom after you captured me at Lewes.'

Adam inclined his head. Strange, he thought, to hear the man talk so candidly.

'I recall the day well,' the earl went on, smiling to himself as he reminisced. 'Odd, isn't it . . . I didn't even know your name when you captured me! Well, I know it now. You've gained quite a reputation for yourself, Adam de Norton.'

Stretching forward again, he opened the lid of a carved wooden box on the table. Rolled parchment uncoiled from within. Taking one roll, Earl Humphrey studied it for a moment in the scant light. 'My treasurer,' he said, 'estimates that the amount my son owed you at his death, minus the loan from Aaron the Jew of Hereford that he repaid with interest on your behalf, totals one hundred and sixty-six pounds, thirteen shillings and sixpence. Does that seem correct to you?'

Adam could only nod. He had never expected as much.

'Good,' the earl said briskly. 'I do not care to have unpaid debts lingering. As I get older, I feel them weighing on my soul. My clerk will write you a note for the full amount, and you can present it at the treasury of the Templars in London and draw it from my funds.'

Abruptly he stood up, tall in the faint light. With one hand on the table to steady himself he took a step towards Adam.

'I do not expect we shall meet again, de Norton,' the earl said. 'So heed my last words to you. Peace is the greatest blessing a man can have. Better than honour, or any chivalric nonsense. Peace . . . and family. Protect the ones you love, you hear me? As for all the rest . . . Let them go to the devil!'

*

The sun was low as Adam rode towards the house. To his right, strip fields of ripe wheat and barley stretched to the horizon, gold under the cloudless summer sky. Next month's harvest would be bountiful, after so many years of want. Adam's own lands would be flourishing too, and he thought of them as he rode. He thought of the people of his estates, of John Ilbert the reeve and his son, and all the others he had come to know once more. Most of all he thought of his wife, of Isabel. Soon enough he would be seeing her again. Adam recalled Lord Humphrey's parting words. Yes, he thought: if God willed it, England had seen the last of civil strife and bloodshed. He would not have to fight these wars again, and nor would his children. All of them could live securely, in the king's peace.

As he entered the yard the grooms came out to take his palfrey. He was waiting in the sun, brushing the dust from his tunic, when she emerged from the house and came to greet him.

'You don't intend on staying long, I suppose?' she asked.

Adam shook his head. 'Hugh of Oystermouth and my squire are at Waltham,' he told her. 'I'll join them before evening. Tomorrow we ride for London.'

He would visit the treasury at the New Temple, and present the note that the earl's clerk had given him. Then he would go to Elias and repay the loan. Even when he had settled his redemption fee in full he would still have funds left over. Such good fortune was almost dizzying. But it was not his alone.

'You gained justice for us both then,' Joane said, when he told her of the earl's promise to restore her dower lands. 'I thank you.'

Joane de Bohun was not much changed since they had last parted, but she appeared much happier now. She was plainly dressed, but her gown was of the finest worsted and the single brooch at the neck was of gold. When she returned his smile he saw the light in her eyes. But her glance was appraising too.

'A married man then,' she said. 'It sits well upon you. Although you resemble Robert less nowadays.'

'Perhaps I should be glad of that,' Adam said. 'How do you find the life of a vowess?'

Joane took a long breath. 'I live as I please,' she said. 'I ride, I hunt with the hawk. I require little luxury, but know no hardship. I think I'll tenant the house here and take up residence in the chambers in the priory grounds. They may prove more comfortable. I plan to travel too, on pilgrimage. The shrine of the Virgin at Walsingham first, and maybe next year to Pontigny.'

'Lord Edward wants me to go with him to the Holy Land,' Adam told her. 'He believes we might liberate Jerusalem together.'

'And will you?'

'I suspect not,' Adam said.

He smiled again, and there was an ease between them that hinted for a moment at a greater possibility. But both of them knew better now.

'Since you are to be the traveller,' Adam said, 'I'd best return this.' He reached up and untied the medallion of St Christopher from around his neck. Joane had given it to him many years before, when they parted after their first meeting.

'You wore it all this time?' she asked as he placed it in her cupped palm.

'Of course.'

The sun was almost at the rooftop now, the shadows stretching long across the yard, and there were still many miles before him. The grooms had watered his horse and brushed the dust from its hide. Now they stood waiting.

Adam set his foot in the stirrup and swung up into the saddle. Joane stood and looked at him, and he could see the cord of the medallion twisted in her hands. For three long heartbeats their eyes met, their last unspoken words hanging in the evening sunlight. The palfrey blew and shook at the bridle, eager for the journey's end.

Joane raised her hand in parting, then Adam jogged his horse forward. When he reached the lane to the bridge he glanced back and saw her still standing there, watching him as he rode away. For a fleeting moment his fingers tightened on the reins, ready to turn the horse. Instead he urged it on to a trot, and when he looked again Joane was gone.

As he crossed the bridge the bell of the priory church was ringing for compline. The last few labourers were returning from the fields. He rode on, and behind him the sound of the bell faded into silence.

Historical Note

Most histories of the conflict known today as the Second Barons' War reach their conclusion in 1265, with the grisly death of Simon de Montfort on the battlefield of Evesham. In reality the war went on for two more years, as King Henry struggled to force his will upon a kingdom battered by strife and bloodshed. A darker and more complex ending in many ways, but one no less dramatic.

Sources for the period are short on detail and unclear about exactly what happened. Dates are often contradictory, and the numbers of men involved are seldom mentioned. While there were no full-scale pitched battles, there were plenty of bloody clashes; surviving documents make it clear that the kingdom was in a state of considerable ferment, and in many districts came close to anarchy.

The siege of Kenilworth is often called the longest in English history, and was certainly the greatest. Records of royal expenditure attest to the massive efforts made by the king's army to take the castle. Contemporary writers provide a wealth of anecdotes too: the verse chronicler Robert of Gloucester describes the mass excommunication of the defenders by the papal legate, and the surgeon Philip Porpeis's mocking response from the castle ramparts, while the Hailes Abbey Annals preserve the story of the disaffected faction seizing the keep and raising the royal banner over it, and their subsequent executions. Other sources detail the attacks on the siege camps by the defenders, the exchanges of hostages, and the honourable treatment of a prisoner who died in captivity.

Kenilworth's surrender did not end the war. But with de Montfort dead and his remaining supporters brought to heel, the king could finally show leniency; the Statute of Marlborough, issued in November 1267, addressed many of the original demands of the baronial rebels. It was a compromise born of great struggle, but it was sufficient to win peace in England for decades to come.

Even so, there were many for whom peace held little appeal. The royal hunting forests of Sherwood and the High Peak – only partially woodland – had been the haunt of outlaws and brigands for generations by the mid 13th century. Some of the stories told about these men are vivid and dramatic, and show that people of the Middle Ages appreciated a tale of adventure just as much as we do today.

The most famous outlaw associated with Sherwood, of course, is Robin Hood, and a few later chroniclers suggest that he lived during the period of the Barons' War. But even if Robin was a real man and not a composite character born of popular myth, his name carries the weight of too much legend, and too much historical uncertainty, to fit neatly into the background of this tale. However, a bandit called Reynard (probably a *nom-de-guerre*) supposedly preyed upon travellers in the Peak District around this same period; a cave in Dovedale still bears his name, and an archaeological survey there turned up a coin of Henry III.

Legends and stories of Simon de Montfort continued to circulate long after his death, in many cases spread by wandering friars and itinerant minstrels. In 1323 King Henry's grandson, then reigning as Edward II, paid two women in Yorkshire to entertain him with 'songs of Simon de Montfort'; presumably by then the threat to royal authority posed by de Montfort had receded, and in any case the young king had recently dealt with rebellious noblemen of his own. Maybe he simply wanted reassurance that the crown always wins in the end?

Acknowledgements

In putting together this novel, and the two that preceded it, I have received invaluable help from many people, including several leading historians. I am most grateful to the staff at Manchester University Library for sending me some copied pages from the sole transcript of the Hailes Abbey Annals. Professor Emilia Jamroziak at the University of Leeds very helpfully answered my questions on burial customs in Cistercian monasteries, while Dr Sophie Therese Ambler was kind enough to share some of her latest research into Simon de Montfort and his legacy.

My sincere thanks go to everyone who has supported and encouraged me as I have worked on these books: to my agent Will Francis, to Morgan Springett, and to Nick Sayers at Hodder; to Jason, Sam and Emma for persuading me to keep the bear; and to Narmi for the poem that unlocked the closing chapters.

Most of all I would like to thank you, the reader, for continuing to appreciate these stories. Writing them has given me great satisfaction, and I can only hope that you have enjoyed them too.